Books by Andrea Penrose

Murder on Black Swan Lane

Murder at Half Moon Gate

Murder at Kensington Palace

Murder at Queen's Landing

Murder at the Royal Botanic Gardens

Murder at the Serpentine Bridge

Murder at the Merton Library

MURDER
at the
SERPENTINE BRIDGE

ANDREA PENROSE

❦ *A Wrexford & Sloane Historical Mystery* ❦

KENSINGTON
PUBLISHING CORP.

www.kensingtonbooks.com

KENSINGTON BOOKS are published by

Kensington Publishing Corp.
119 West 40th Street
New York, NY 10018

All Kensington titles, imprints, and distributed lines are available at special quantity discounts for bulk purchases for sales promotion, premiums, fund-raising, educational, or institutional use. Special book excerpts or customized printings can also be created to fit specific needs. For details, write or phone the office of the Kensington Special Sales Manager: Attn. Special Sales Department. Kensington Publishing Corp, 119 West 40th Street, New York, NY 10018. Phone: 1-800-221-2647.

The K with book logo Reg. US Pat & TM Off.

ISBN: 978-1-4967-3254-5
First Kensington Hardcover Edition: October 2022
First Kensington Trade Edition: September 2023

ISBN: 978-1-4967-3255-2 (ebook)

10 9 8 7 6 5 4 3 2 1

Printed in the United States of America

For Lawrie Mifflin, Keri Keating Ricci, Margy Wiener
and Rachel Hockett

Best friends since the freshman days of our
Bright College Years.
And the bond has only grown more special
over the long and winding road.

Love you guys beyond words!

MURDER
at the
SERPENTINE BRIDGE

PROLOGUE

Darkness had settled over the city, and yet the night was quite pleasant, the first hints of summer warmth softening the breeze. The lone figure stood on the front steps of the elegant townhouse, taking a moment to savor the stillness and the play of moonlight on the ornamental plantings before turning his steps for the street.

The hour was late, and no clatter of carriage wheels echoed off the surrounding stone and brick.

"Peace and quiet," murmured Jeremiah Willis, after looking up and down the north side of Montpelier Square. "Thank God." Not that the evening hadn't been enjoyable. The conversation had been interesting—how could it not have been, given the subject—and the meal superb. Still, the cacophony of voices clashing with the clink of crystal and silver had begun to make his skull throb.

"Though maybe," reflected Willis, with a wry smile, "the headache had more to do with the very fine brandy poured after supper than anything else." He drew in a deep breath.

Only to regret it. After all these years, he still hadn't reconciled himself to London's foul-scented air. Oh, how he longed for . . .

But Willis quickly pushed the thought from his mind and began walking. He had made choices in life that required sacrifices. He didn't regret them.

The sound of his steps on the cobblestones seemed unnaturally loud as he turned up Charles Street and came to Knightsbridge, the main road skirting along the south edge of Hyde Park. Feeling a little muzzy from all the wine and spirits, he looked around for a hackney.

But oddly enough, there wasn't a vehicle to be seen. Even the area around the Life Guards barracks was deserted.

It must be even later than I thought.

As he halted, undecided on what to do, the scent of fresh meadow grass and spring leaves wafted over from the shadows across the road. Cocking an ear, Willis thought he could hear the breeze stirring a whisper of waves upon the nearby Serpentine. It was, he conceded, likely just his imagination. But the walk to Cumberland Gate, at the northeast corner of the park, wasn't all that long, and a glimpse of starlight rippling over the dark water of the forty-acre man-made lake within the sylvan grounds would be a very pleasant sight.

On impulse, Willis crossed the street and found the footpath leading into the trees. Yes, brigands and footpads were known to hunt for prey within the park.

"But as I don't look like a rich toff," he murmured, "there's no reason to think I'll attract any trouble."

His boots sank into the soft sand as he walked along Rotten Row, the popular bridle path that was once part of the King's Old Road connecting St. James's Palace to Kensington Palace, and followed it until he heard the lapping of water. Smiling, Willis made his way through an opening in the bushes and approached the stone embankment marking the eastern end of the massive lake.

Fed by the River Westbourne, the Serpentine had been built at Queen Caroline's demand in 1730, and formed the boundary between Hyde Park and Kensington Gardens. This part of the lake, known as the Long Water, was a broad swath that ran in a straight line to the distant stone bridge, where the lake then narrowed and took a sinuous turn to the north. The night was clear and stars scattered a winking of diamond-bright points of light over its rippling surface. Willis stood very still, mesmerized by the view as he spotted a lone swan ghosting along through a swirl of silvery mist.

Lakes, rivers, oceans—he had always found something magical about a body of water. Closing his eyes, he recalled the enchanting sound of the surf from his youth. *Ebb and flow. The elemental rhythm of Life, constantly in motion.* Perhaps that had appealed to him because he had always been a nomad.

But perhaps it was time to return to his place of birth and put down roots. He had begun to question—

The sudden crunch of steps on the graveled path behind him broke through his reveries.

Turning, Willis saw two men approaching. Surprised, he stumbled back a few steps. His first instinct was to flee, but then reason reasserted itself. He had nothing of value to offer, and thieves, however ruthless, didn't risk themselves for naught.

Moving into a blade of moonlight, he faced the strangers and held up his arms. They would see a man beginning to bend with age, clothed in an old-fashioned tricorn hat and a well-worn coat. "My good fellows, I'm not worth the effort of an attack," he called. "I've no fat purse." Waggling his bare fingers, he added, "No fancy rings or gold pocket watch. I'm just a laborer who works with his hands to make a living."

As they came closer, Willis found himself relaxing. They weren't ruffians. Indeed, to his eye, they had the unmistakable aura of gentlemen. Perhaps they were foxed . . . or perhaps they had an assignation. Ladies of the night were known to offer their favors in the Italian garden by the bridge—

"You're far too modest, Mr. Willis." The voice, though soft, cut like a knife through the still air. "In truth, you're a very valuable man."

How the devil did they know his name? "I—I fear you've made some mistake," he replied.

A nasty laugh, made even uglier by the deep-throated, cackling sound. "Are you suggesting that you're not easy to recognize?"

Willis retreated another few steps, only to feel the stone retaining wall at the very edge of the lake beneath his boots.

Damnation. Fear was beginning to rise in his gorge.

"No, I'm suggesting that whatever you want, you've come to the wrong man."

"I think not." It was Knife Voice again, the click of a pistol being cocked punctuating his words. "Come with us."

Willis slid a step to his left.

"It wasn't a request!" snarled Cackle Laugh. He, too, brandished a weapon and started forward.

Whirling around, Willis leaped to his left. His knee buckled as he hit the uneven ground, but he regained his balance and set off at a run. Low-hanging branches slapped at his face, knocking off his hat.

Faster, faster! But his body had gone soft from so many hours crouched over his workbench. Already his lungs were burning, his muscles screaming in agony . . .

Slipping and sliding over the loose stone, Willis veered back toward the edge of the lake, where a narrow walkway atop the stone embankment along this section of the Long Water would provide better footing. He dared not look back, and his heart was pounding too hard for him to hear whether the strangers were giving chase.

With luck—

A hand grabbed at the tail of his coat, but summoning a frantic burst of speed, he managed to break free.

However, he knew he hadn't a prayer of escape. His strength was ebbing . . . How strange that at such a moment, his one thought was how beautiful the moonlight looked shimmering over the dark water.

The water.

It was, Willis decided, his only hope. An excellent swimmer, he hesitated for only an instant, then dove toward the darkness. But at the very same moment, his pursuer grabbed out again, catching just enough of his coat to slow his momentum and send him into a spinning fall.

Pain exploded through his consciousness as his skull smacked against the stone retaining wall, and then everything went black . . .

He was far beyond any further mortal feelings as his body plummeted into the depth of the lake.

CHAPTER 1

The Earl of Wrexford paused to survey the surroundings. It was just past midnight, and the mild evening was beginning to show some teeth. A gust swirled, nipping through the darkness and rustling the leaves of the nearby trees. The air had turned chilly and was heavy with the threat of impending rain.

Wrexford sighed and turned up the collar of his coat. Much as he would have preferred to be sitting comfortably in his workroom with a book and brandy in hand, he and his three companions had just entered Hyde Park through the Stanhope Gate and were now making their way along the footpath leading toward the Serpentine—

"Wrex! Wrex!" The shout rose from somewhere close by.

A moment later, Hawk, the younger of the two boys accompanying him, broke free of the mist, nearly tripping as he tried to keep pace with an iron-grey hound, whose large size and fearsome jaws caused many people to mistake him for a wolf. "May I let Harper off his leash now?"

Squinting against the gloom, Wrexford took a last look around the vast swath of meadowland and wooded groves. "Aye, lad," he answered. "But remember what I said—I expect you and your brother to keep the beast from wreaking any havoc, or else there will be no further nocturnal forays."

In truth, given the hour, there was little danger of running into any difficulties. However, he had sensed that the boys wanted to feel they were having a slightly risky adventure. They were used to having unfettered freedom to roam the city as they pleased. However, their lives had recently undergone a momentous change.

As has mine . . .

A happy *woof* drew him back to the moment as Hawk unfastened the length of leather from Harper's collar. The hound danced a few circles around the boy and then loped off into the nearby grove of elms.

"After him, lads!" called the earl. Few people ventured into the park after dusk—and those who did usually preferred to remain unseen. Still, he didn't wish to take any chances.

Raven, Hawk's older brother, appeared from out of nowhere and let out a snicker as he fell in step beside the earl. "Ha! As if there's any reason for alarm."

"With you two Weasels, there's *always* reason to expect mayhem," replied Wrexford. During his first encounter with the brothers, Raven had stuck a knife in his leg and Hawk had hit him with a broken bottle . . . *All with good cause*, he conceded, as they thought he was threatening Charlotte Sloane.

The earl made a wry face as the footpath led into the trees. Life's journey was full of strange twists and turns. Much to everyone's surprise, that initial angry confrontation had softened into friendship. And then . . .

A smile touched his lips. The unexpected alliance had deepened in ways that defied words. He and Charlotte had recently married, and Raven and Hawk, the two wild urchin orphans she had taken under her wing, had become his legal wards.

They were all now a family—an unconventional one, to be sure. But perhaps that made the bonds even stronger.

"I've already checked the area," continued Raven. "There's nobody around." A pause. "And you know as well as we do that Harper wouldn't hurt a flea."

"That's because the beast has grown as spoiled and lazy as a dowager's lapdog," retorted the earl. "However, I'd rather he didn't frighten someone to death."

"You know"—the boy fixed him with a cheeky grin—"you should show a little more respect for Harper. After all, he recently saved your life."

"And *you* should show a little more respect for *me*," said Wrexford. "I'm considered a very dangerous man to annoy."

The boy made a rude sound. "Like Harper, your bark is worse than your bite."

"Don't be insolent, Weasel," he growled.

Which only drew a laugh from Raven. The earl had called the boys "Weasels" during that first attack, and the moniker had stuck, much to their hilarity.

Wrexford scowled, though the corners of his mouth betrayed a twitch of amusement.

A bark sounded from beyond the trees.

"You had better go keep your brother and Harper from getting into any real mischief," he said. "The Serpentine is quite deep at this end of the park, and I don't fancy having to fish either of them out of the water."

The boy nodded and darted off, a fast-moving blur that was quickly swallowed in the shadows.

Leaves rustled as the breeze swirled again. From somewhere in the trees came the twitter of a nightingale. Wrexford continued on at a leisurely pace, his thoughts straying once again to family. As a man ruled by the principles of reason and scientific logic, he had always thought himself immune to the vagaries of love. And yet, Charlotte Sloane had taken hold of his heart in ways he couldn't begin to define.

A chuckle rumbled deep in his throat. *So much for logic.*

He couldn't imagine life without her.

Indeed, their recent marriage had proven—

"Harper!" Hawk's cry shattered the stillness. "Nooooo!"

Damnation. Wrexford quickened his steps . . .

At the sound of a loud splash, he broke into a run. To his knowledge, the boys didn't know how to swim.

As he burst free of the trees, he caught a glimpse of the moon-dappled Serpentine up ahead, but the flitting shadows around the lake's edge made it impossible to discern what was going on.

Where were they?

"Raven!" he shouted, feeling as if his heart was about to leap into his throat. "Hawk!"

"Here, sir!" A muffled answer floated up from the terraced stone embankment edging the end of the lake.

As the earl scrambled over the rough terrain to join the boys, he spotted the big hound swimming through the murky water, dark ripples trailing in his wake.

"What the devil—"

"S-Something spooked Harper," explained Hawk. "His hackles rose, and then, before I could grab him, he let out a bark and leaped into the lake. I—"

"Holy hell—there's something floating out there," said Raven in a tight voice. "It looks like . . ."

Wrexford saw it, too. "Get back, lads," he ordered. "I want you both well away from the water's edge."

The edge of alarm in his voice must have warned them not to argue. Raven took his brother's hand and quickly led him off to the grassy verge.

Looking back to Harper, Wrexford saw the hound had taken hold of the dark shape with his teeth and was laboring to tow it back to shore. The earl glanced around. To his left, the stone embankment ended, giving way to a bank of earth, rocks, and grass.

"Harper, Harper!" Waving his arms, he picked his way to a gently sloping patch of ground.

As the hound paddled closer, Wrexford's worst fears were confirmed.

A body. And by the look of the injuries to the poor soul's head, there was little chance of him being alive.

"Well done, Harper." He ruffled his fingers through the panting hound's sodden fur before grasping the body by the shoulders and pulling it up to the footpath bordering the Long Water.

Crouching down, Wrexford turned the man over—and let out a grunt of surprise . . .

One didn't often encounter a person of African descent in the exclusive environs of Mayfair.

His brow creased in thought as he fingered the fine linen of the man's shirt and cravat. Especially one dressed as a gentleman. But he quickly pushed aside his initial shock. Whatever reason had brought the poor fellow to the park at this hour, it had cost him his life.

There was no need to check for a pulse. The head injury was too ghastly. Wrexford guessed that the man had been dead before he hit the water. Perhaps, he mused, that was a mercy.

And yet . . .

The earl sat back on his haunches, gazing first at the lake and then moving his eyes to the stone embankment. The top flagging was narrow, but not overly so. Looking down at the lifeless face, he frowned.

"How the devil you contrived to fall off is a mystery." So was where he landed. Basic laws of physics seemed to indicate the dead man had been running at full tilt . . .

"Yes, a mystery," he repeated softly. But one for the authorities to solve. His only duty was to fetch one of the night watch-men patrolling the park and inform him of the accident.

"Weasels!" he called, suddenly aware that they were no-where to be seen. Harper, who had stretched out beside the body, lifted his shaggy head and pricked up his ears.

No response.

A chill teased against the back of the earl's neck, as if the Grim Reaper had touched an icy finger to his flesh. Wrexford rose abruptly and called again.

The hound shot up as well, a growl rumbling in his throat.

"Oiy, oiy!" Raven's reply was muffled by the thick shadows twined within the trees. Holding his breath, the earl stared into the darkness, unsure of why he was so on edge. Granted, death was always unsettling, an unwelcome reminder that existence was finite. The clockwork universe ticked through the same el-emental cycle for all living creatures, great and small. And yet, this seemed to stir an uneasiness . . .

The boys materialized from the darkness, a flutter of moon-light revealing that Raven was cradling something in his arms.

"I found this near the stone wall," announced the boy, rush-ing to hand over an old-fashioned tricorn hat.

It was well-worn, but like the dead man's shirt and evening coat, it was made of quality material. Closer inspection re-vealed a maker's mark on the inside band. Wrexford didn't rec-ognize the name.

"There were footsteps, too," offered Hawk. "One set of tracks came from the direction of Knightsbridge, while two other sets came from the same footpath we used. They met up right at the end of the Long Water. And then—"

"And then, it looked like they had a confrontation," inter-jected Raven. Having spent most of their early years in the London stews, both Weasels were far more savvy and obser-vant than other boys their age. Their skills had also been sharpened by having played a part in previous murder investiga-tions—much to Charlotte's dismay.

"Judging by the length of the stride," continued Raven, "the Knightsbridge tracks took off at a run."

"An attempted robbery, perhaps," mused Wrexford. Though footpads were usually smart enough to choose a wealthy-looking victim. After crouching down again, he felt inside the dead man's overcoat pockets and found a purse. "They would have been greatly disappointed," he added after giving it a jingle.

"Perhaps they were partners in crime, and had a quarrel," of-fered Raven.

"A good surmise," replied Wrexford. "But it's pointless to speculate." In his opinion, the exact reason for the death—be it an unfortunate accident or some more nefarious cause—would likely never be known.

He shifted. "There's nothing more for us to do. We need to fetch a watchman and be done with this sorry affair. You two stay here . . ." However, as his hand brushed up against a bulge inside the dead man's evening coat, the earl hesitated. If the dead man had been chased for something on his person, then a pair of dangerous ruffians might well be lurking nearby, hoping to get their hands on the body.

"On second thought," said Wrexford, "I want the two of you to run to the powder magazine by the stone bridge." A watchman would be on guard there. "Explain that we've fished a body from the Serpentine and bring him back here."

"Shall we take Harper with us?" asked Hawk.

The hound wagged his tail.

"I think it unwise, lad," he replied. "The sight of Harper might be intimidating and discourage the watchman from obey-ing the summons." To Raven, he added, "Move quickly and stay alert."

"You expect trouble, sir?"

"No." But alas, trouble seemed to take a pernicious delight in appearing in their lives when least expected. "I simply wish to err on the side of caution." Wrexford waved them away. "Off you go."

Harper huffed a canine sigh and lay down with his head between his paws.

"Don't look at me like that," muttered Wrexford. "There are times when your ferocious face doesn't work to our advantage."

The hound's response was to roll over on his side and sink into a gusty slumber.

Turning his attention back to the corpse, Wrexford probed at the bulge beneath the wet wool. It felt like a rectangular case made of metal. *Perhaps a silver box for cheroots—though it feels a little large,* he thought, working the object free of the inner pocket and holding it up to what little moonlight was dribbling through the overhanging leaves.

A glimmer of gold winked from the brass corners of the case. Other than that, it was crafted out of a fine-grained dark wood. *Ebony or rosewood,* he guessed as he turned it over in his fingers, admiring the workmanship. There was a decorative inset at the center of the lid, which appeared to be ornate initials made of ivory.

Wrexford clicked open the latch and looked inside.

Set on a bed of black velvet lay a set of precision drafting instruments. *Compass, protractor, dividers, and tiny ruler . . .* Somehow, they gave the dead man an individuality—he was no longer just a nameless victim of circumstance, but a person with flesh-and-blood interests . . .

Angling the lid higher, Wrexford looked for a name, but the inside of the lid was also covered in velvet—

A sliver of white silhouetted against blackness caught his eye. There was, he realized, a pocket sewn into the fabric. Taking careful hold of the folded paper, he eased it out. The exquisite craftsmanship of the box had sealed out most of the lake's water—it was damp but still intact, and as Wrexford smoothed the sheet open, he saw the pencil lines hadn't blurred beyond recognition.

It was a sketch . . .

"Bloody hell." Drawing a deep breath, he looked down at the dead man's shadow-dark face with a searching stare.

"Who *are* you?"

CHAPTER 2

Charlotte watched in dismay as a pair of footmen wrestled yet another two traveling trunks into the baggage carriage. "Ye heavens, one would think we were transporting a regiment of hussars to the battlefields of America," she muttered under her breath. In the not-too-distant past, a few battered bandboxes and canvas valises would have carried all her worldly possessions.

But life has changed. She was now the Countess of Wrexford—which held a certain irony, as in her rebellious youth, she had eloped to Italy in order to escape from living life within the English aristocracy's gilded cage.

But then, she had met Wrexford . . .

An irascible, sarcastic earl, who possessed one of the leading scientific minds in all of Britain. Her lips twitched. As a brilliant chemist, he would no doubt have a rational explanation as to why the volatile combination hadn't blown up in their faces.

However, against all logic . . .

Charlotte hurried down the grand marble entranceway of their magnificent townhouse on Berkeley Square and joined her husband amidst the commotion of preparing for their visit to Kent.

"Wrex, do stop growling at Tyler," she murmured after flashing the earl's valet an apologetic smile. "The fault is all mine for accepting my brother's invitation to attend a gala birthday celebration given by his wife's side of the family." Wrexford disliked frivolous social engagements just as much as she did. "But Hartley was so eager to have us meet his sister-in-law and her family that I didn't have the heart to say no. However, I promise that I won't make a habit of saying yes to such distractions."

A sigh. In truth, she was already reconsidering her decision. Much as she valued her recent reconciliation with her long-estranged brother—the current Earl of Wolcott, now that her father and oldest brother had shuffled off their mortal coil—she had never before allowed personal concerns to cause her to put aside her principles. It took only one small—and innocent—step to start the slide down a slope that could all too quickly turn devilishly slippery. "Like you, I have far more interesting things to do with my time."

Despite his troubled expression, Wrexford allowed a gruff chuckle. "Like poking fun at Prinny?"

Tyler choked back a snort.

Among Charlotte's many secrets was the fact that under the guise of her nom de plume, she was the infamous A. J. Quill, one of London's most famous satirical artists. She used her pen to expose corruption and scandal within the highest circles of Society and government, as well as to puncture the vanity of pompous prigs.

"But of course." Charlotte made a face, reminding herself that she would only be absent from the city for two days. "Given the grand Peace Celebrations about to take place in London to honor the Allied victory over Napoleon—not to speak of the coming festival in August marking the centennial of the Hanover family ruling Britain—I fear there will be more than enough fodder for ridicule over the coming weeks."

Napoleon's recent defeat by the Allied Coalition, led by Britain, Russia, Austria, and Prussia, and his exile to the island of Elba, had finally brought peace to Europe. And to celebrate the momentous occasion, the Prince Regent had invited the other Allied heads of state to a month-long series of lavish balls, concerts, entertainments, and fireworks. *The Tsar of Russia, the King of Prussia, the King of Austria, along with the leading Allied generals and a host of important international dignitaries . . .* It promised to be a spectacle unmatched in the city's history. Already a number of minor royals had arrived in the city and the partying had begun.

"The Allied leaders ought not celebrate too hard, and the Duke of Wellington would be wise to keep his saber sharpened," muttered Wrexford. "I think they've made a grave mistake in putting Napoleon on a tiny island just a stone's throw from the coast of France."

"Don't be so pessimistic," chided Charlotte. "After over a decade of war, surely the world is tired of conflict and carnage. Surely you don't think that the French would welcome him back to the throne."

"As you know, I tend to think the worst of people," replied the earl. "That way, I'm rarely disappointed."

Charlotte chose to ignore the remark and returned to the subject of the upcoming festivities. "Prinny is in a fit of pique over the fact that Tsar Alexander is more popular with Londoners than he is."

"Alexander is said to possess a boyish charm to balance his many faults," said Wrexford dryly. "Though I daresay we'll have a chance to experience that for ourselves."

They had, of course, received an invitation to each of the most sought-after events, she reflected. Which would no doubt provide ample opportunity to observe the peccadilloes of the high and mighty.

"Yes," replied Charlotte, "and I expect that, along with all the grand displays of fireworks planned for the celebrations along the Serpentine, we're also likely to see a great many pyrotechnics in the ballrooms."

Again Wrexford smiled, but shadows remained pooled in the depth of his gaze.

"Tyler, might you oversee loading the rest of the baggage while I have a private word with His Lordship?"

"But of course, milady."

Taking Wrexford's arm, Charlotte drew him to the graveled path leading around to the back gardens. "Are you still troubled by the events of last night?" Neither of them was a stranger to unnatural death, but she sensed that something about the discovery of the body was bothering him.

He didn't answer right away.

"You instructed the watchman to take the sketch and drafting instruments to Griffin . . ." The Bow Street Runner had worked with them on solving a number of previous crimes. And while some people took his plodding movements and taciturn manner to mean that he was slow-witted, she and Wrexford knew otherwise. "If there's any reason to suspect foul play, he'll find it."

A hint of humor sparked beneath his lashes. "Perhaps that's what I'm afraid of. I was hoping that we might have an interlude of peace and quiet in which to begin our married life."

"Peace and quiet?" She raised her brows. "Admit it, Wrexford—then you would be grumbling about being bored to flinders!"

"Speaking about grumbling," he muttered.

"I know, I know." Charlotte flashed an apologetic smile. "I, too, expect this upcoming visit will be exceedingly tedious. But thankfully, it will also be short and—"

"And cursedly *boring*."

"Bring along your books on Priestley's experiments with oxygen," she soothed while trying to fend off exactly the same thought. "I shall make sure you have ample time for reading."

A shout rang out before he could respond.

"M'lady, m'lady!" An instant later, Hawk skidded around the corner of the townhouse, followed by his brother. Their relationship had changed immeasurably since the boys had first taken to calling her by that name, but they all felt comfortable with it.

The two boys were another of her secrets. Wrexford had procured official documents—she had never inquired as to how—stating their lineage, along with all the necessary paperwork making her their legal guardian. But, in truth, they were orphan guttersnipes that she and her late first husband had found sheltering outside their house and had taken under their wing.

Her heart swelled as Hawk gave a gap-toothed grin. *Love came in many guises . . .* She glanced at Wrexford and then back at the boys. Perhaps the ones that were unexpected made them even more precious.

"We were just wondering . . . may Harper come with us to the country?" asked Hawk, a hopeful note shading his voice.

"I fear not, sweeting," answered Charlotte. "It would be impolite of us to bring along a dog." Indeed, it was rare that a country house party invitation included children, but their hosts had insisted that tomorrow's picnic was to be a festive affair for family and friends of all ages. "In any case, our hosts have a boy around your age, and there will be other child—er, that is, young people—at the picnic tomorrow with whom to play."

A pinch of disappointment spasmed over his face.

"And don't forget, your uncle Hartley mentioned that the gardens at the Belmont estate are very grand," she quickly added. Hawk was a budding artist, with an interest in botany. "There will be much for you to explore and to draw, so be sure to bring along your sketchbook and paints."

"Be quick about it, lad," counseled Wrexford. "If we are to arrive at the appointed hour, we must leave shortly."

Raven lingered as his brother raced away. "It doesn't sound like a very interesting excursion," he said, not quite meeting her gaze. "I'd rather not go. Lady Cordelia said that she and Lord Woodbridge would be delighted to have me stay with them while you are gone."

Lady Cordelia and her brother were part of her and Wrexford's inner circle of close friends. They had all met during a previous murder investigation—one in which Cordelia had, for a short time, been the prime suspect—and had proven valuable allies in solving more recent conundrums. A brilliant mathematician, Cordelia also tutored Raven in the subject.

Be that as it may, the request took Charlotte by surprise. "I would have thought you'd enjoy meeting another boy of our extended family, and attending a party with his friends."

"I've seen the fancy little aristocrats who come to Gunter's Tea Shop for ice cream," muttered Raven, "and they strike me as puffed-up popinjays. Why would I want to spend any time with them? We have nothing in common."

It hadn't occurred to her that he might worry about fitting in. Granted, the other boys and girls attending the party had grown up within a world of privilege and plenty, but that didn't mean that they all would be featherbrained widgeons. "It's unfair to make such a sweeping assumption," said Charlotte.

"Even though it's likely true?" challenged Raven.

"You know very well that the world is rarely painted in aught but black and white," chided Charlotte. She then tried another tack, hoping to lighten the boy's scowl. "It's only for two nights."

Wrexford was far blunter in his response. "Being part of a

family requires us to do things we might not want to. M'lady wishes to make her brother happy, and is asking us for our support." His dark brows arched up to accentuate his stare. "Surely, you wouldn't be so churlish as to refuse?"

"I . . ." Raven bit his lip. "Might I borrow your book by Leonhard Euler on his method for finding curved lines, sir?" The boy had a special gift for mathematics, and was taking advanced lessons in the subject from Lady Cordelia. "I should like to take it with me on the trip."

"Let us go fetch it," answered the earl. "And as I, too, wish to take along reading material, you can help me collect it . . ."

Charlotte gave him a grateful look as the two of them moved away. Despite his reputation for snaps and snarls, Wrexford was very good at dealing with the Weasels. Raven, who had always possessed a stubborn streak of independence, was reaching that difficult age when boys felt compelled to challenge authority. She was still trying to feel out how to handle such confrontations, but the earl seemed to have an intuitive understanding of when to loosen the reins and when to tighten them.

But even more worrisome was the fact that as Raven grew older, he might feel out of place in the beau monde . . .

"M'lady?" McClellan, the redoubtable Scotswoman who had served as jack-of-all-trades in Charlotte's previous household, cleared her throat with a cough. "According to our schedule, the carriages need to depart in a quarter hour." Though her current official title was lady's maid to the Countess of Wrexford, everyone in the Berkeley Square town house knew that she and the earl's longtime butler were co-commanders of the establishment. "So we had better hurry upstairs and collect your shawl and reticule."

"Sorry," apologized Charlotte. "I was woolgathering."

"Hmmph. By the look on your face, they must have been *very* mangy sheep."

She sighed. "Raven just made an unexpected request to cry

off from the sojourn. Of late, he's had so many changes in his life that I was loath to press him, even though my brother would have been disappointed if he didn't come. But, thankfully, Wrexford handled the situation with greater skill than I could have managed."

"That's because he's aware that boys will be boys, and naturally seek to press the boundaries of behavior." McClellan waggled her brows. "If they're not told no, they know they haven't pushed hard enough."

Suddenly all the complexities and challenges of her new life felt a little overwhelming.

"Don't be apprehensive about the future, m'lady." McClellan's flinty features softened for a moment. "I've never met anyone as strong and sensible as you are. Whatever challenges lie ahead, you'll chart a safe course through them."

"Let us begin by navigating the next few days without mishap," murmured Charlotte.

"Speaking of which, your shawl and reticule are waiting," reminded McClellan.

"You go on." She felt the need for a moment of solitude in which to settle her thoughts before the journey started. "I'll be up in a trice."

The maid's steps receded, leaving her with only the rustling of the ivy as company.

Was Raven's small rebellion a sign that he was growing unhappy with his new life? It was true that Polite Society bristled with small-minded superficiality. And yet, there were also kindred souls who defied conventional thinking. One simply had to—

"Your pardon, milady," called the earl's butler, pulling her back to the present as he hurried down the back terrace stairs. "Forgive me for disturbing you, but a note just arrived from Madame Franchot, and I thought you would wish to see it right away."

Madame Franchot was London's most exclusive modiste.

She was also part of Charlotte's network of eyes and ears within every circle of Society—an army from which no secret or scandal was safe.

"Thank you, Riche." Repressing a sigh, Charlotte accepted the missive, hoping against hope that it was merely a message about new fashion or fabric. But the smooth stationery stirred a prickling of foreboding as she unfolded it. And sure enough . . .

"Wrex—" Christopher Sheffield, the earl's closest friend since their days at Oxford, stopped short in the doorway of Wrexford's workroom and frowned in consternation. "What the devil is going on?" he demanded, eyeing the stack of books on the desk and the half-filled traveling satchel beside it. "Why are the carriages being loaded?"

"We are taking a journey," answered Raven, with a martyred sigh. "To Kent," he added as he tucked the remaining books into the bag.

"It's not as if you're being transported to the penal colonies in the Antipodes, lad," called Wrexford from the depths of the storage alcove. He finished searching through one of the cluttered cabinets and moved on to the next one. "Blast it all." The mutter was meant for himself. "Where did Tyler put the old issues of the Royal Society's journal?"

"To Kent?" repeated Sheffield. "But whatever for?"

"To do our *duty*," intoned Raven.

Wrexford bit back a reproach. Despite dropping his plea to cry off from the trip, the boy clearly hadn't shaken off his unhappiness about it. But while the situation was exasperating, the earl reminded himself that at Raven's age, he had often butted heads with his father . . .

And likely driven the late earl to distraction.

Spotting an as-yet unopened package from Hatchard's book emporium lying among the other recent deliveries waiting to be sorted, Wrexford removed the wrapping paper. "Ah, I see the new mathematics book by Rochambert has just arrived," he announced, hoping to coax the boy into a better mood. "Would you like to take it along with Euler's book?"

"Oh yes!" came Raven's enthusiastic reply. "Thank you, sir! I've heard a great deal about his work." To Sheffield, he added, "Lady Cordelia is very excited that Rochambert is coming to Peace Celebrations as part of the French king's delegation."

Wrexford emerged from the alcove and handed the volume to Raven, who ran a reverential hand over the gilt-stamped leather binding.

"He's a brilliant mathematician," continued the boy, "and is famous for creating—"

"Yes," interrupted Sheffield. "I know who he is."

Wrexford was surprised by his friend's sharp tone. Cordelia and Sheffield were not only partners in a very profitable shipping-and-manufacturing company, but recently their friendship had seemed to be taking a more serious turn.

However, romance—if romance it was—rarely followed a straight path. Of late, he sensed that there had been several bumps in the road . . .

But he quickly pushed such musings aside. "Alas, lad, we've no time for chinwagging. Put the book in the satchel and take it out to Tyler," said Wrexford. "We are expected to arrive in Kent for a family supper, so we can't afford any further delay."

Heaving a grunt, Raven hoisted the heavy bag into his arms.

"And do be sure to leave the sulky face behind," counseled the earl.

Sheffield stepped aside to let the boy pass.

The earl moved to his desk and began sorting through the piles of paper. "Damnation," he grumbled, pausing to peruse an invitation from the Royal Institution, one of Britain's leading scientific societies. "I had forgotten that von Wageren's lecture on nitrates is tonight."

"I still don't understand. What sort of duty could possibly be dragging you to Kent?" pressed Sheffield.

Wrexford didn't answer, hoping to discourage his friend from any further probing.

"It seems so very unlike Charlotte," observed Sheffield. "With all the high-and-mighty dignitaries beginning to arrive in London for the Peace Celebrations, I'd have thought that she would be all afire to keep an eye on them and make sure that no scandal or clandestine intrigue goes unnoticed—and unreported to the public."

Friendship demanded that he respond. "In this case, she decided a family obligation must take precedence over all else."

Sheffield's expression betrayed his surprise. "But I thought . . ."

As did I.

Wrexford was a little worried that Charlotte had allowed guilt over her youthful rebellion and elopement to influence her decision to accept Hartley's invitation—and that her conscience was now troubling her about it.

"Never mind Charlotte and our upcoming peregrination to Kent," he replied. "What brings you here at this hour?" A pause. "Other than the hope that my cook is still serving breakfast."

"It has been some time since I've trespassed on your generosity," said his friend a little stiffly.

Wrexford let out a grunt of satisfaction on finally finding the journals for which he had been searching. "True. The bill from my wine merchant no longer sends me into a swoon."

He looked up and instantly regretted his sarcasm. Sheffield looked away, but not quite quickly enough. The forced smile didn't dispel the shadows hovering beneath his friend's lashes.

"I'm sorry, Kit. Our whole household seems to be at sixes and sevens this morning." He ran a hand through his hair. "I suppose it didn't help that last night in the park the lads and I stumbled over a dead body—metaphorically speaking, that is. The poor fellow was actually floating in the Serpentine."

"How—"

"It was Harper who fished him out."

"*Murder*?" asked Sheffield.

"There's no question that the man fell and hit his head on the rocks, so it's most likely an unfortunate mishap," he answered. "However, certain evidence around the scene raised enough questions that I instructed the night watchman to summon Griffin to inspect the scene."

"What evidence?" Sheffield had become more and more involved in their sleuthing efforts during their last murder investigation—and was proving to be good at it.

"That's not important. As I said, I doubt the incident will prove to be anything nefarious." Wrexford studied his friend's face for a moment and saw he had missed other subtle signs of distress. "What's troubling you?"

"I . . . I was simply hoping to . . ." His friend hesitated.

"Milord!" McClellan's stentorian shout echoed down the corridor. "The carriages are all loaded!"

"Blast," muttered the earl, regretting the interruption. "Go on, Kit. It will do no harm for the coachmen to hold the horses for another few minutes."

"Never mind." Sheffield's gaze turned shuttered. "It can wait until you return."

Friendship, decided Wrexford, was just as important as family. "No, it can't." He moved to shut the door—

Only to find himself face-to-face with Charlotte as she hurried into the room.

"Read this," she said without preamble. "It just arrived from Madame Franchot. She overheard the wife of the foreign secretary gossiping to a friend about the body found in the Serpentine. The dead man has been identified by the authorities. His name is Jeremiah Willis."

Wrexford unfolded the paper, and as he skimmed its contents, his brows pinched together in puzzlement. "Why does that name sound familiar?"

"Because," answered Charlotte, "our experience with Professor Sudler spurred me to do a series of prints on mechanical innovations six months ago and I made mention of him. Willis is an engineering wizard, who is much admired for his imagination in envisioning and creating new technology."

She paused. "Apparently it runs in the family, for his father made a fortune by designing a revolutionary machine for processing sugarcane."

"Ah, yes. Now I recall. The fact that he was of African descent stirred some nasty gossip within the Royal Institution." The earl frowned. "My sense is he must have been extraordinarily talented to overcome the prejudice against Blacks and garner the respect he deserved."

"Actually, I believe Willis is mulatto," said Sheffield, "as his father married a White Englishwoman."

"Correct," confirmed Charlotte. "The elder Mr. Willis was an enslaved plantation worker from Virginia who ran away to serve a British officer during the American Revolution. If you recall, our government offered freedom for all Blacks who threw off their chains and sided with us."

"Much good it did the poor souls who took us at our word," replied Wrexford. "We left most of them to their fate when we conceded defeat and sailed home."

"Be that as it may, Willis the elder was one of the lucky ones. The officer was impressed with his new servant's skills in repairing mechanical objects," continued Charlotte. "He saw to it that Willis came with him back to Britain, and arranged an apprenticeship with Watt and Boulton's steam engine company. After that, Willis moved to Scotland for further study and then returned to the New World and settled in Barbados."

"Which, I assume, is where he sold his machinery designs to all the planters in the Caribbean who grew sugarcane and then became very rich," mused the earl.

"Yes."

The clatter of hurried steps in the corridor rose above the momentary silence.

"So, if Willis the younger inherited his father's genius for engineering, what exactly was he working on?" asked Wrexford.

"That's just it." Charlotte drew in a troubled breath. "I never learned the answer."

"But why—" began Sheffield.

"Because I was told it was a government secret."

CHAPTER 3

"Bloody hell," uttered Sheffield.

Wrexford's response was far more practical. "Can you hazard a guess as to what it was?"

Charlotte shook her head. "Not really. Willis's name came up when I was gathering information on the rising stars of technology and engineering. I drew him as part of a group portrait of innovators, but as the thrust of my commentary was on industrial machines, I didn't do any further research on him."

"M'lady! Milord! If you wish to arrive for the family gathering on time, we *must*—" McClellan stopped short in the doorway, the rest of the rebuke dying on her lips.

"My apologies, Mac," said Charlotte. "The delay is my fault."

"Are we having a council of war?" demanded the maid.

Sheffield looked to Wrexford. "Are we?"

The earl reflected on the question before answering. "I'm assuming that if Madame Franchot learned the news from the wife of the foreign secretary, then by now Griffin has been informed of the dead man's identity."

"A logical surmise," agreed Charlotte.

"Then, no, we are merely having a discussion," answered Wrexford. "Knowing Willis's identity doesn't change the fact that investigation is being handled—and rightly so—by Bow Street."

He met Charlotte's gaze. "You have no connection to Willis or his work, so I can see no reason for us to get involved."

"Nor can I," conceded Charlotte. Which was a great relief, she thought rather guiltily. She really didn't wish to disappoint her brother.

"Does that mean we will *finally* be departing for Kent?" demanded McClellan.

"Yes. I'll hurry and fetch my shawl and reticule."

"Thank you so much for coming, Charley." Charlotte's brother, Hartley, the Earl of Wolcott, gave her an affectionate hug before turning to introduce her and Wrexford to their hostess, Louisa Belmont, who was his wife's older sister. "Louisa, allow me to present my sister, Charlotte, and her husband, Lord Wrexford."

"How kind of you to come, Lady Wrexford," replied Louisa.

"Please call me Charlotte, since we're all now family."

"Yes, of course! And you must call me Louisa," responded their hostess. "Let us not stand on ceremony."

And yet, Charlotte sensed a certain rigidity beneath the gracious manners. However, she quickly dismissed the thought as uncharitable. Meeting new members of an extended family wasn't always easy. Louisa was likely nervous that everything would go smoothly.

"Indeed," Wolcott chimed in as Wrexford bowed over Louisa's hand and replied to her greeting with the requisite pleasantries. "I assure you, we all favor informality."

"I must apologize for my husband's absence," said Louisa,

after Wolcott's wife, Elizabeth, had added her welcome. "Belmont is very sorry to have missed this evening's intimate family gathering. But, alas, he sent word earlier today that a pressing matter at the ministry demanded that he remain in Town tonight."

"Belmont is a senior attaché at the Foreign Office, and is helping to oversee all the arrangements for the Peace Celebrations," explained Wolcott.

"With the imminent arrival of so many foreign rulers and dignitaries, I imagine there are a great many challenges facing your husband," murmured Wrexford.

"Yes, I fear that his duties are very . . . demanding." A look of distress flitted over Louisa's face. "But he will, of course, join us tomorrow for the main festivities."

"Politics is always a fraught subject," said Wolcott. "Let us move on to more pleasant things." He smiled and gestured to Raven and Hawk, who had been hovering by the drawing room entrance, waiting to be summoned. "Step forward, lads!"

To Louisa, he added, "Allow me to introduce Charlotte and Wrexford's delightful wards—my nephews, Thomas Ravenwood Sloane and Alexander Hawksley Sloane."

From the start, her brother had enthusiastically embraced the boys as family, a kindness that had warmed Charlotte's heart.

"But they prefer to be called Raven and Hawk," added Wolcott. He winked at them. "Or the Weasels."

"It's a pleasure to meet you both," murmured Louisa, after the boys went through the required ritual with a flawless show of manners. "Belmont and I are also guardians to an orphaned family member." She quickly picked up a bell from one of the side tables and rang for a maid. "It will be a treat for Peregrine to have some playmates his own age during this visit."

Charlotte hoped Louisa didn't catch Raven's pained grimace at the word "playmate". Recalling his comment about well-born boys, she hoped that Peregrine wasn't too much of a stick-in-the-mud.

"Keating, please fetch Peregrine from his room," said Louisa as a maid entered the room and bobbed a curtsey, "and bring him down to meet his relatives."

"Has Aunt Alison arrived?" asked Charlotte as Wolcott moved to the sideboard and popped the cork on a bottle of champagne.

"Yes—forgive me for neglecting to mention it." Louisa looked a little flustered. "The dowager is taking a nap to recover from the journey. I expect her down shortly."

"The nap was my idea, not hers," added Wolcott, a glint of amusement lighting his eyes. "I only convinced her to do so by pointing out if she wasn't tired, she would be able to imbibe *two* glasses of brandy after supper instead of just one."

Charlotte laughed. Her great-aunt, the dowager Countess of Peake, was known throughout the beau monde as The Dragon for her feisty spirit and sharp tongue. She had proven an invaluable ally in several murder investigations—a fact that had pleased her to no end. "I daresay that even if Alison does drink two brandies, she won't get into any mischief."

"With the dowager, I wouldn't make any such assumptions," said Wrexford, which earned a chortling from the Weasels. "She—"

The family banter was interrupted by the return of the maid. "I'm terribly sorry, Mrs. Belmont, but Lord Lampson isn't in his room. I've checked the schoolroom, as well as the library . . . Shall I send the footmen out to search the gardens?"

Lord Lampson? Charlotte took care to mask her surprise. She hadn't heard any mention of the boy having inherited a title. But then, family trees could branch out and become complicated, and she knew nothing of the Belmonts and their relations.

"N-No, that won't be necessary." Louisa waited until the

maid withdrew and shut the door. "Peregrine often takes a walk outdoors after his supper. It . . . it must have slipped his mind that we had visitors arriving this evening." She forced a smile. "Perhaps it's best if we wait until morning for introductions. I'm sure Raven and Hawk are hungry and would like to have supper brought up to their rooms."

"An excellent suggestion," agreed Charlotte.

"If you'll excuse me for a moment, I'll go make arrangements for them to be taken—"

"Please don't trouble yourself. If you'll send one of your servants to fetch my lady's maid, she'll take charge of them."

Louisa looked uncertain. "Are you sure . . ."

"Quite sure," answered Charlotte. "McClellan and the boys get on very well together. She'll have them settled in a trice."

The arrangements were quickly made, and with her usual brusque efficiency, McClellan quickly escorted Raven and Hawk out of the drawing room.

"Thank you," murmured Louisa as Wolcott handed her a glass of sparkling wine and then served the others. "I realize you're unfamiliar with this side of the family. I had intended to explain our relationship to Peregrine when I introduced him to you. But since he has wandered off, I shall do so now."

Wrexford took a seat on the sofa beside Charlotte.

"Peregrine . . ." Louisa heaved a sigh. "Forgive us, but Belmont and I find it hard to suddenly have to call our twelve-year-old nephew Lord Lampson, so to us he is Peregrine. At least until he gets older."

"The boy has told me he prefers the informality," murmured Wolcott.

"Yes, he's said the same to us," agreed Louisa. "He's the son of my husband's older brother, Declan, who perished along with his wife when the ship on which they were traveling foundered off the coast of Scotland a little over a year ago. I confess, Belmont and I were quite surprised when we learned Declan had named us as guardians for the child. Our two sons are grown and we hadn't . . . We hadn't expected to raise another."

From the stiffness of Louisa's voice, Charlotte guessed that the tension ran far deeper than that.

After taking a sip of champagne, Louisa continued. "But, of course, it made great sense. Belmont had grown up here and was intimately familiar with all the workings of the estate. Indeed, he had managed it for his brother for a number of years after Declan inherited the barony, but then chose to live abroad."

Ah, yet more reason that there is no love lost between the young baron and his relatives, thought Charlotte. For years, Belmont likely thought that he, and his sons after him, would inherit the title and lands.

And then the older brother produced an heir later in life.

"We, of course, are happy to do our duty and serve as caretakers of both the lands and our nephew," finished Louisa with a smile that wouldn't melt ice.

"How very kind of you." As Wrexford rose and fetched the bottle from the sideboard, Charlotte forced herself to murmur the sort of polite platitudes that she abhorred. Much as she valued her reconnection with Wolcott, she vowed to avoid future gatherings such as these, where everyone simply performed as pasteboard cutouts, rather than reveal any individuality.

Indeed, Charlotte now regretted not letting Raven cry off from the trip. The last thing she wanted was for the boys to become comfortable in a world of gilded artifice and lies.

"Cheers!" said Wolcott after the earl had refilled their glasses. Candlelight winked off the faceted crystal as he swirled his champagne, setting off a shower of pale gold sparks. "Let us raise a toast to . . ."

He paused to cock an ear.

Charlotte heard it, too—the thump of the dowager's cane was coming closer and closer.

"Ah, I see we're finally all here." Alison eyed the bottle in

Wrexford's hand as she entered the drawing room. "Well, don't just stand there, Wrex. Pour me a glass!"

"To our extended family!" said Wolcott, once the dowager had been served.

"To family," echoed Charlotte, though she couldn't help adding a silent thought . . .

However tangled in secrets and subterfuge.

The champagne seemed to dispel any lingering awkwardness, and supper segued into a pleasant interlude, filled with cheerful conversation and shared family memories.

Wrexford was happy to see Charlotte's earlier tension melt away as her brother told several amusing stories about their youth. Wolcott's wife, Elizabeth, he noted, seconded her husband's efforts to keep the mood convivial, and managed to coax her sister into joining in the genial laughter.

However, his gaze lingered for an instant on Louisa Belmont. She played the role of gracious hostess well, but there was a brittleness about her, as if an errant nudge might cause her to crack.

He wondered why.

Wrexford swirled the ruby-red claret in his wineglass and took a sip. Her ward's failure to appear had seemed to put her further on edge. Perhaps, he mused, there was something not quite right about the boy.

"Well, this has been a very enjoyable evening," announced Alison, after finishing a slice of fruit tart topped with cream. "However, I think I shall forego postprandial libations. Encroaching old age compels me to retire in order to be ready for tomorrow's festivities."

The earlier look of tension returned to Louisa's face "Again, I apologize for Belmont's absence."

"No need for apologies. We all understand he has other demands weighing on him right now." The dowager looked to Charlotte. "Shall we go up and check that the Weasels are settled into their quarters? I should like to give them each a good-night hug."

"A splendid idea," responded Charlotte.

"I, too, shall take my leave and look in on Peregrine," said Louisa. She rose. "To make sure he's not feeling unwell."

"I'll come with you," offered Elizabeth. "And leave Wolcott and Wrexford to enjoy their brandy."

Led by Louisa, the ladies took their leave.

"Thank you for coming, Wrexford," murmured Wolcott, once the door was closed. "I have a feeling that this sort of gathering isn't your . . . cup of tea." He made a wry face. "Nor is it Charlotte's. But it was kind of her—and you—to humor me. Elizabeth was very eager to have all of you meet her side of the family."

"Charlotte was delighted with the invitation. Her reconnection with you has been a source of great joy." Charlotte's elopement had caused her late father and mother to disown her, but the dowager had arranged a reconciliation between brother and sister.

"However," added Wrexford, "don't count on us appearing frequently in the future. As you've probably heard, I'm not terribly sociable."

Wolcott laughed. "You and Charlotte have better things to do with your time than flitter through the superficialities of Polite Society." A pause. "Like helping the authorities unravel dastardly mysteries and bring miscreants to justice."

"Be assured, we don't make a habit of that—"

A hurried knock cut off the rest of his words.

"Forgive me for interrupting, milord." Tyler cracked open the door and held up a folded square of paper. "But this missive just arrived—it was forwarded from Berkeley Square."

A frisson of alarm prickled down Wrexford's spine as he quickly rose to take it. His butler wouldn't have passed it on unless he deemed it important.

The crack of the wax seal sounded unnaturally loud in the silence that had taken hold of the room. It took only a moment to read the short message . . . though the Bow Street Runner's handwriting was so untidy that the earl made himself read it again.

"I do hope it's not bad news," murmured Wolcott in concern.

"No, it's merely a question."

Tyler's gaze sharpened as Wrexford refolded the note and put it in his pocket.

"However, you'll have to excuse me for the rest of the evening. In order to decide how to answer it, I really must go and confer with Charlotte."

CHAPTER 4

The breakfast room was empty, though the sideboard was filled with covered chafing dishes ready for those who chose to rise early. Charlotte rang for a pot of coffee, but rather than fill a plate, she moved to gaze out the mullioned windows at the gardens sloping down from the back terrace.

Wrexford had gone for an early-morning ride with Tyler . . .

To plot strategy? she wondered.

A good question. She wasn't sure whether to feel alarmed by the note that their London butler had forwarded from Griffin last night. The message had seemed innocuous enough. It simply requested an interview with Wrexford about the discovery of Willis's body when the earl returned to London.

"But perhaps I'm not reading what lies between the lines," Charlotte whispered.

Or perhaps Wrexford hadn't told her everything about the state of the engineer's injuries, or the other clues found around the Serpentine.

The thought provoked a frown. She hoped that marriage hadn't made him feel compelled to protect her from the sordid crimes that often intruded on their lives. If anything, she was more aware than he was of the depravities that men and women were capable of inflicting on each other.

"Might I bring you eggs and toast, milady?" inquired the footman who brought out the coffee.

"Thank you, but not at the moment." Charlotte poured herself a cup. "I think I shall stroll on the terrace for a bit and enjoy the morning sun."

The subtle scent of the early-blooming summer flowers perfumed the breeze as she opened the French doors and crossed the stone flaggings to a set of stairs leading down to the graveled walkways. She chose one at random and was quickly lost in thought.

Whether by mishap or by murder, people died every night in London. There was no mystery to that fact. And for most of the violent deaths, the motives were very personal. *Greed, jealousy, lust*—the fight between good and evil was an elemental part of human nature.

It was only on rare occasions that a probing deeper into murder uncovered a nefarious web of intrigue and deception. The more she thought about Willis . . .

Up ahead, Charlotte heard the bustle of workmen setting up the tent and trestle tables for the gala picnic party on the main lawns. Spotting a side footpath that wound through a high hedge and led around to the rear wing of the manor house, she quickened her steps and darted through the opening.

Shadows from the prickly branches flickered over the gravel as her thoughts returned to the dead man. Charlotte thought about the rumors she had heard regarding his work for the government. Should she and Wrexford allow vague whispers to stir up suspicions?

Willis was a talented mechanical engineer. That he was carrying a pocket case of drawing instruments was hardly a reason to assume the man's fall hadn't been an accident. As for the sketch found inside the case . . .

"Good heavens, let us not make a mere scribble into a specter of evil. Artists let their imaginations run wild all the time," muttered Charlotte. "I've seen fanciful renderings of grotesque monsters. That doesn't mean they are real."

The holly leaves crackled in the breeze as she followed the hedge to a walled garden area butting up to the back of the rear wing . . . and suddenly her musings were once again distracted. Half the perennial plantings were dead and the surviving ones scraggly and unpruned. Broken terra-cotta pots and shards of glass littered the beds, and a few rusted rakes were propped in the corner. Looking up, Charlotte saw that several of the window openings were boarded over.

The run-down appearance seemed to signal that the Belmonts were having difficulty in maintaining the house and grounds. She looked around more carefully and spotted other more subtle signs of neglect.

Is the estate in financial trouble?

How else to explain letting the place slip into such decline? Yet another troubling question.

But Charlotte quickly reminded herself that this particular one wasn't her concern. Turning her back on the ramshackle scene, she cut across to a different path, intent on circling back to the terrace.

After passing by a cluster of high holly bushes, the way led through a grassy allée bordered on both sides by beds of flowering greenery. The plantings here were well tended, with the dead blooms trimmed away and the weeds removed. As she paused to admire a group of lush peonies, Charlotte made a note to bring Hawk here to do some sketching. There were a number of lovely specimens—

Out of the corner of her eye, Charlotte suddenly caught a flutter of movement just up ahead. Shifting her stance, she saw one of the garden boys lying on his belly, his head hidden in the lacy fronds of a large fern.

She moved closer and saw that rather than performing any

pruning, the boy was studying one of the fronds with some sort of magnifying glass.

"What unusual leaves," she remarked.

The grass must have muffled her approach, for her voice caused him to flinch and drop the glass.

"Forgive me for startling you."

The boy scrabbled in the dirt to retrieve the brass-handled instrument and then slowly looked up.

His face had a softly chiseled beauty, and on seeing the shape of his features, the tight curls of his dark hair, and the café au lait color of his skin, Charlotte immediately recognized him as being of mixed race.

"That's quite a complicated-looking device." Her work as A. J. Quill had taught her all too well how cruel people could be to those they considered different from themselves, so Charlotte was careful to make no comment on his looks as she crouched down beside him.

Instead, she focused on the scientific-looking instrument in his hands. She had never seen anything like it. There were a number of intricate dials and two adjustable lenses. Curious, Charlotte asked, "Are you inspecting the fern for some sort of mold or harmful insects?" It seemed a logical reason, and yet it struck her as odd that the head gardener would entrust such an expensive instrument to a young underling.

"No," he answered, averting his eyes to avoid meeting her gaze. "I'm testing the different degrees of magnification that can be created by moving the lenses up and down."

"How very fascinating." Just as unexpected as his looks was the fact that he spoke in the cultured tones of a well-educated boy. It was yet another puzzling piece to the Belmont family. Perhaps it was only because her own emotions had been on edge lately, but Charlotte couldn't help feeling that a tangle of hidden troubles lurked beneath the veneer of wealth and privilege.

"And how very clever," she added, forcing her thoughts back to the mysterious boy.

Was that a shy smile? He looked down too quickly for Charlotte to be certain.

Hoping to put him at ease, she decided to introduce herself. "I'm Lady Wrexford, a guest of the family staying here at the manor house."

He looked up again with a start, his eyes flaring wide in alarm.

"Please don't be frightened." Charlotte flashed an encouraging smile. "You won't get into any trouble for speaking with me." Seeing that he still looked apprehensive, she added, "What's your name?"

"I—I . . ." He bit at his lower lip, and then blurted out, "Aunt Louisa says I owe you an apology for my rudeness in not being there to greet you last evening, milady. I'm very sorry." He lowered his lashes. "I . . . I forgot."

Good heavens—this is Lord Lampson?

Not wishing to just sit there gawking, Charlotte quickly gathered her wits. "I don't blame you. I don't much like meeting strangers either, Lord Lampson."

His gaze turned uncertain. "Y-You don't?"

"No," she replied. "That's because one can never be sure of whether they'll be nice or whether they'll be unpleasant."

He looked away. "Some people aren't very nice. They stare at you and look as if they've just been sucking on lemons."

"That must be very uncomfortable, milord," said Charlotte.

"I prefer to be called Peregrine," responded the boy in a small voice.

"It's very nice to meet you, Peregrine," she replied. "I assure you, my two wards aren't the sort of boys who suck on lemons." A pause. "That is, not unless they need the peels as an ingredient for making stink bombs."

That sparked a twitch of a grin at the corners of Peregrine's mouth.

"You shall meet them at the picnic," added Charlotte.

At the mention of the party, Peregrine scrambled to his feet and inclined a hurried bow. "Please excuse me, Lady Wrexford. I had better hurry back to the house before Aunt Louisa dispatches the footmen to find me." A guilty look ghosted over his face. "I'm supposed to be dressing for the party, not spending time with my magnifying lenses."

"Your secret is safe with me," she assured him.

He gave her a grateful look, then turned and raced away.

"Lud, what a coil," murmured Charlotte as she watched him disappear into the greenery. She now had an inkling as to one of the undercurrents of tension at the estate. An orphan heir living with resentful relatives . . .

However, his last words reminded her that she, too, had better return to the house and begin preparations for the gala picnic.

Charlotte made her way through the allée and turned down the path leading back to the breakfast room. But as she reached the opening in the hedge, the sound of steps on the main walkway rose above the rustling of the breeze. Loath to be spotted coming from a part of the estate that the family might wish to remain unseen, she stopped short.

Edging closer to the hedge, Charlotte ventured a peek through the tangled branches.

A gentleman in riding clothes was approaching, an air of authority to his purposeful stride. Wind-snarled hair, mud-spattered boots, lines of fatigue etched on his face—by the look of him, he had traveled a good distance and at a demanding pace.

It must be Thurston Belmont, she thought. Louisa had said that her husband would be arriving from London sometime this morning.

Charlotte held herself very still, willing him to pass by her hiding place without a second glance. But to her dismay, the gentleman came to halt at the fork in the path and let out a harried oath.

After an instant of panic, she quickly mustered a smile. Now that she had been spotted, there was nothing to do but act like nothing was amiss. He had no way of knowing for certain what she had seen—

But the oath, she quickly realized, wasn't because of her, and so she remained hidden.

He had pulled a piece of paper from his coat pocket, and through the leaves, she could see the look of agitation that came over his face as he read it.

"Damnation." Removing his hat, the gentleman blotted the sheen of sweat from his brow before jamming it back over his auburn curls. "Damn. Damn. Damn." Beneath the flush of exertion, it appeared that his cheeks had gone pale.

Though perhaps it was merely a trick of the light.

However, there was no mistaking his shaking hands as he thrust the note back into his pocket and pulled out a silver snuffbox. It took several tries for him to work the latch open and take up a pinch of tobacco.

A ragged inhale, followed by a second pinch, and then an explosive sneeze. Which appeared to do nothing to purge his unsettled mood. Swearing again, he shifted and stared at the manor house. The look on his face—

"Halloo!" In the next instant, Wrexford and Tyler appeared on horseback, heading up the bridle path leading to the stables.

The gentleman hurriedly snapped the snuffbox shut and fumbled to put it away.

"Mr. Belmont?" added the earl.

A gruff nod. "And you must be Lord Wrexford."

"Yes, and as you see, I'm already taking advantage of your generous hospitality, sir," replied Wrexford pleasantly. "You have some very fine horseflesh in your stables."

"My apologies for not being here to show you the most scenic ride through the estate lands," replied their host. "As well as for my absence from the festivities of last evening."

"None are necessary." The earl dismounted and handed the reins of his stallion to Tyler, then signaled for the valet to continue on to the stables. "Given your responsibilities at the Foreign Office, I imagine you've far more important things to do than play host to a gaggle of strangers."

"Family is family," answered Belmont.

"Whether we want them or not," said Wrexford dryly.

Their host didn't smile.

A moment of awkward silence followed. Belmont appeared distracted, and Charlotte noted that he shot another look at the house.

The earl made another attempt at polite conversation. "You must have left Town before first light to arrive here at this hour."

"One does what one must," came the terse reply. "I couldn't very well take the chance of missing my wife's birthday celebration."

"Indeed not," agreed Wrexford. "I hope it wasn't too pressing a problem that kept you in Town last night."

"I'm not at liberty to discuss what goes on within the Foreign Office. Our dealings are highly confidential," said Belmont. "I trust you understand that."

A priggish answer, if ever there was one, thought Charlotte. Belmont struck her as a martinet, and she found it hard to summon any sympathy for whatever pressures he was under—especially having just met his ward.

"Quite," responded the earl. He was saved from having to make any further response by the appearance of a harried-looking man striding toward them from the front lawn. In his hands was a sheaf of untidy papers.

"If you'll excuse me, milord, that is the wine merchant in

charge of libations for the party," said Belmont, shifting a half step as he spoke. "I had better go and see that everything is in order. Louisa is a gracious hostess, but she has no head for numbers."

Charlotte waited until their host met up with the merchant, and the two of them had entered the manor house, before she called softly to Wrexford.

"How cowardly of you to remain hidden in the bushes, leaving me to do the pretty with Belmont," he replied. "I'm surprised you trusted me to keep a civil tongue."

"There was a reason, which I shall explain." She slipped through the leafy opening. "As for your restraint, it was quite admirable."

The earl's lips twitched. "I thought so."

"For a diplomat, Mr. Belmont is sadly lacking in—" Charlotte stopped short as she spotted a flutter of paper crushed in among the small stones of the walkway. Bending down, she quickly picked it up and fisted her hand around it.

Wrexford raised a brow.

"Come, let us stroll toward the stables," she said, hooking her arm in his before he could respond.

They walked on for several steps before a sound—something between a snort and laugh—rumbled in his throat. "How is it that even at a country picnic in bucolic Kent we manage to stumble upon intrigue?"

"Surely, there's some principle in chemistry to explain the elemental attraction."

"Actually, I would say it's the laws of physics, not chemistry, that are at play here with us. We seem to be like magnets, inexorably drawing the iron filings of trouble."

"Hmmm, that's a wonderful visual metaphor—I must keep it in mind for a future drawing," she said.

"You're skirting the subject."

"That's because I'm not sure there *is* any intrigue." A pause. "Though I did discover several things that stir some questions."

"We're not here to ask questions," he muttered. "We're here merely to attend a party in which neither of us has any interest—"

"Let us stop here," she interrupted. A stand of young oaks screened them from the manor house, affording a measure of privacy. "I'd like to read this before I recount all that I've discovered." As she had mulled over what she had seen, an unsettling idea had been taking shape . . .

A papery crackle sounded as the crumpled note unfolded. "Hmmph."

Wrexford waited for Charlotte to say more.

"Hmmph," she repeated, and looked up. "I was curious as to whether the message might confirm my suspicions. But it's hard to say if it does."

"To have suspicions," murmured the earl, "would indicate that you *do* think intrigue was afoot."

" 'Intrigue' is too harsh a word. I have simply seen some things that strike me as odd."

She handed him the note.

It took only a moment for the earl to read it. "As you say, it could mean a great many things. As for being odd, why—"

"Please, just hear me out, Wrex."

Receiving a gruff nod in answer, she continued, "Purely by chance, I stumbled upon a reason to believe that Belmont is having financial difficulties. The estate looks prosperous, and yet . . ." Charlotte explained what she had seen during her earlier walk.

"I don't question your eye for detail, my dear," he said when she had finished. "But there are any number of explanations as to why a section of the house might be in disrepair." Wrexford thought for a moment. "Beginning with the fact that Belmont's older brother, the late baron, may have stripped the family coffers bare." A shrug. "Belmont can hardly be expected to pay the upkeep on the place out of his own pocket."

"You have a point," she conceded. "But let me finish."

He nodded.

"I decided to remain hidden behind the hedge when I spotted Belmont," continued Charlotte, "because I feared it might embarrass the family if I was seen coming from the run-down part of the manor house. However, as Belmont chose to pause by my hiding place, I couldn't help but notice his distress. He took a letter from his pocket—I assume it was the one you're holding—and his expression turned even more agitated."

"Go on."

"Belmont then took some snuff to calm his nerves, which must have been when the letter fell out. Your hail—"

"Flustered him further?" suggested Wrexford. "Charlotte, the Foreign Office is helping to orchestrate a visit to London by some of the most powerful rulers in the world. It's not unreasonable for him to be on edge."

She blew out her breath.

Wrexford wasn't sure why she seemed so intent on seeing specters lurking in every shadow.

"When I add his reaction to the note with what I saw earlier, my intuition tells me the family is in financial straits," responded Charlotte. "So why throw an extravagant party?"

"Oh, come, my dear." He huffed in frustration. It wasn't like her to overreact, but he feared she was allowing the complications of family to cloud her judgment. "You're intimately acquainted with the follies of the aristocracy. Heaven forfend that practicality or prudence override pride. Louisa Belmont mentioned last night that this party has become a June tradition in the area. Apparently, it's been held every year since the couple married."

Charlotte didn't argue with Wrexford's sarcasm. And yet, she couldn't quite let go of the subject. "I wonder if Hartley is aware of the family's financial troubles."

"Belmont strikes me as a gentleman who would keep any

weakness a secret from others," replied the earl. "So even if it does exist, he wouldn't thank you for revealing it to your brother." A pause. "And in all honesty, I think doing so could put your brother in an awkward position with his wife. Louisa is her sister."

Another sigh. "You're right, Wrexford. Meddling in family affairs is always fraught with peril. However, you haven't heard—"

He cut her off with a cough. "I, too, have something to tell you. And as I see Tyler coming, I need to do so now."

Her eyes narrowed. "I thought we agreed that there was no need for you to return to London today. Griffin's note said there was no urgency."

"Yes, but it occurred to me that I can do both. The picnic begins at noon. I can celebrate for several hours and then be back in London by late evening."

"Milord," called the valet as he approached. "The stablemaster has agreed to lend me a horse so that I may accompany you back to Town."

"I'm planning to take the horse that our groom rode here last night," he explained to Charlotte, "and he can ride back with the baggage carriage."

"Ye heavens, if Raven gets wind of your plans, he, too, may mutiny," grumbled Charlotte. "I can't help but wonder . . ." She looked up and held his gaze. "Is there some detail about the death you haven't told me?"

"Were I to dare hold anything back from A. J. Quill," he replied lightly, "I'm well aware that my liver would be chopped into mincemeat."

"That's not an answer, Wrexford."

"I've told you everything I saw. But in the light of day, Griffin might have spotted other clues, and I may be of use in helping him piece them together."

"I can't deny you work together well," she admitted.

Her stubbornness was perplexing. The party meant nothing

to her, and the real family duty had been done the previous evening. "Then it's settled?" he pressed.

"But I haven't yet told you the third thing I saw . . ."

The notes of a violin rose from the main lawn as a musician began to tune his instrument.

"Charlotte, Tyler and I really must make a quick visit to the stables and make arrangements now, otherwise I will be late in dressing for the festivities—as will you." He shifted his stance. "Can't whatever you wish to tell me wait until later?"

"Very well." Fisting her hands in her skirts, she turned for the house, adding under her breath, "You'll find out soon enough."

CHAPTER 5

The terrace overlooking the back lawns was festooned with a tasteful array of flowers, their fragrances perfuming the sun-warmed air. But despite the cheery colors and the lilting notes of the violin quartet playing beneath a pergola twined with climbing roses, there seemed to be an undertone of tension to the gaiety.

Or maybe it's simply my imagination, thought Charlotte as she and Wrexford joined Wolcott and his wife, Elizabeth, by a table sparkling with freshly-poured flutes of champagne.

"What a lovely party," she murmured, swallowing her dislike for mouthing such odious hypocrisies. Having agreed to come, she felt it her duty to be pleasant.

A quick—and guilty—glance at Wrexford showed that he was already bored to perdition.

"Louisa is always such a splendid hostess," responded her brother, though he, too, sounded a little tense. "Do have some champagne—it's a superb vintage."

Charlotte accepted a glass and turned her attention to making polite conversation with Elizabeth and several other local ladies, while Wolcott led the earl away to introduce him to a group of gentlemen smoking at the far end of the terrace. She hoped he would temper his tongue—his scathing sense of humor often caused offense.

Not that she wouldn't secretly enjoy seeing Belmont's feathers ruffled. An uncharitable thought, perhaps. But all pompous prigs deserved no less.

The dowager drifted over and drew Charlotte away from the other ladies.

"Thank you," she said under her breath.

"Your smile," said Alison, "looked in imminent danger of coming unglued."

"Speaking of which, we had better go rescue Wrexford."

"Let's not." The dowager flashed an evil grin. "A show of pyrotechnics would likely be the most entertaining event of the afternoon."

"What are you two chortling about?" Wolcott appeared with a plate of lobster patties.

"The weather," replied the dowager airily. "Despite the sunshine, Charlotte and I were wondering whether a thunderstorm might be in the offing."

Wolcott darted a look at the horizon and raised his brows in puzzlement. "I doubt—"

"Those look delicious," interrupted Alison, eyeing the patties. "I do hope you've brought them to share."

He handed her a fork, and then offered one to Charlotte.

"Thank you, but I've already had far too much rich food and drink and feel in need of a stroll through the gardens to clear my head. I think I shall ask Wrexford to accompany me."

"I imagine he would be delighted to do so," said Wolcott, a twitch of humor pulling at his mouth. His expression then turned serious. "I apologize that this visit hasn't been as festive as I had hoped. Belmont appears . . . on edge, and I think that's affected everyone's mood."

"Understandably so," replied Charlotte. "The upcoming gathering of sovereigns from all of Europe is no doubt a very demanding event to organize. There are so many things that might go wrong."

"Indeed," agreed her brother. "I must say, nothing could tempt me to visit London during the next few weeks."

"You don't enjoy pomp and pageantry?" asked the dowager.

"I would much rather savor all the follies of the royals by perusing A. J. Quill's satirical drawings from the peace and quiet of the country," he replied.

"No doubt there will be much fodder for Quill's pen," remarked Charlotte. "Now if you will excuse me . . ."

With good-mannered smiles, the gentlemen allowed her to draw Wrexford away from the group. The earl waited until they had turned down the graveled path leading to the ornamental lake before releasing a sigh—along with a few words that were inappropriate for polite company.

"Please say no more," she murmured. "At least you will be free to leave this unhappy place in an hour. While I must maintain a facade of politeness until tomorrow morning."

"Hmmph. Better you than me."

Charlotte didn't disagree. "I do hope the boys aren't getting into any mischief. Louisa sent them down to the lake to . . . er . . . play with the other children." A sigh. "Which I confess, given their normal activities, isn't an edifying thought."

That made Wrexford chuckle. "Weasels running wild among a flock of little lambs? Ha, ha—what could possibly go wrong?"

"That is *not* amusing, Wrexford."

"I beg to disagree," he said.

The path led through a small glade of oaks, the fluttering canopy of leaves providing a welcome respite from the bright sun. Charlotte felt herself relax. She wasn't quite sure why her nerves were on edge, but something about the situation—

Wrexford came to an abrupt halt. The glade had given way to a lawn that sloped down to the lake, and while they were in the shadows of the trees, they had a clear view of the scene below.

While a gaggle of younger children huddled silently by the water's edge, a big burly boy, who looked to be a year or two older than Raven, gave a nasty shove to Peregrine.

Three other boys, who appeared to be the bully's friends, laughed. "Looks like the little lord is a coward," they jeered. "Do it again, Randall. Throw him in the lake and see if he can swim!"

The bully grinned and shoved Peregrine closer to the water.

Moving with deceptive quickness, Peregrine sidestepped the next attack and retreated away from the lake.

But the bully refused to be robbed of his fun. He followed and lashed out a punch that knocked Peregrine to the ground, drawing more hoots and taunts from his gang of friends.

Nose bloodied, Peregrine rose, and though far shorter than his assailant, he balled a fist and tried to hit back. Randall easily blocked the blow and unleashed a flurry of punches and kicks, which once again knocked Peregrine to the ground.

Charlotte started forward, but Wrexford held her back.

"Oiy!"

The sudden cry drew her gaze to the stone folly by the side of the lake. She saw a movement within its archway, and then an instant later, Raven appeared, followed by Hawk.

"Oiy, there," called Raven again as the bully paused to look around with a scowl. "Leave him alone. Only a lily-livered varlet picks a fight with someone half his size."

"You calling me a varlet, you skinny little runt?" Randall, once again egged on by his friends, stripped off his jacket and put up his fists. "I dare you to come closer and say that."

Raven, too, removed his jacket and calmly handed it to Hawk.

"Wrexford, let go of me!" hissed Charlotte. "We have to stop this."

His grip tightened. "Absolutely not."

She watched in dismay as Raven rolled up his shirtsleeves and approached the bully. She knew he and his brother both possessed the skills to defend themselves. And yet his opponent was so much bigger and brawnier . . .

"But it's primitive—"

"Yes, the law of the jungle," agreed the earl. "That's exactly why in this case we mustn't interfere. I know how you feel about violence, but Raven won't thank you for stopping him. And if he thrashes the leader, the gang's power is over. The younger children watching—and the boy they are bullying—will see their weaknesses."

Charlotte bit her lip. Much as she hated to admit it, she knew too much about life in the slums to deny that he was right. "The boy they are bullying is Lord Lampson, the lord of the manor," she said.

Wrexford raised his brows. She had not yet had a chance to tell him about Peregrine. "Interesting. I hadn't realized—" But before he could go on, Raven sauntered up to the bully and the fight began.

"Bloody his beak!" cried his friends as Randall cocked a fist and threw a vicious punch.

Raven ducked it with ease, and lashed out a kick that buckled his assailant's knee, dropping him to the ground.

With a roar of rage, Randall scrambled to his feet. "For that, I'll thrash you to a pulp."

"You can try," retorted Raven. "But seeing as you're a slow-footed oaf, you ought to quit while you're still standing."

Fists flailing, Randall rushed again at Raven. And once again was knocked flat on his arse. He rose more slowly, his nose bleeding from a lightning-quick blow from Raven's elbow, and began to circle his opponent a little more warily.

"Get him, Randall!" The shouts from his friends took on a note of urgency. "You're bigger and stronger!"

Raven suddenly darted forward, taking his opponent by surprise. He landed a hard gut punch and several kicks to the bully's shins before dancing back out of reach.

One of the younger children let out a cheer.

Now hopping mad, Randall charged in a bull-like rush. Several of his flailing punches connected, drawing hoots from his friends. But Raven's fists were striking fast and furious—chin, cheeks, stomach—and the bully's strength looked to be flagging. In desperation, Randall flung himself forward and seized Raven in a bear hug.

A sound rumbled in Charlotte's throat.

"Don't worry," counseled Wrexford, and an instant later, the bully let out a bloodcurdling scream and crumpled to the ground. "Raven is smart enough to exploit an opponent's weakness when it presents itself," he added with a satisfied smile.

"*Men.*" Charlotte blew out an exasperated sigh.

"We are savage creatures," admitted the earl. "But as you well know, the world is a savage place." He gave a nod at the lake. "That gang of bullies won't be bothering the other local children again. Power is closely tied to perception. When word spreads of their humiliation, they'll be reduced to a mere shadow of their former swagger."

"I know, I know—my work as A. J. Quill is based on that very principle." Charlotte allowed a wry grimace. "That doesn't mean I have to like it."

Smiling, he shifted his stance. "Come, let us leave the lads to sort things out by themselves. I need to prepare for my departure to Town."

"Leaving me to face Belmont," she murmured, "and explain why, thanks to Raven's fists, a child of one of his guests is black and blue."

"You're very skilled in the art of distraction and deception," said Wrexford.

"Yes, almost as good as you are."

He laughed. "Yet another reason we are so well matched."

Raven pulled a none-too-pristine handkerchief from his pocket, and after dipping it into the lake, he handed it to Peregrine. "Lean your head back and press this hard against your beak. It will help stop the bleeding."

Wincing, Peregrine wordlessly accepted the damp cloth and did as he was instructed.

"You must get thwacked often," observed Hawk. "You're not very good at fisticuffs."

Peregrine shifted the handkerchief. "My uncle—Uncle Jeremiah, *not* my guardian—has always stressed to me that cerebral skills are even more important than brute force," he mumbled with some dignity, despite his swollen lower lip.

"Well, if you ask me, it isn't very smart to let a bully use your head as a target for his fists," replied Raven. "You're very quick and agile, but you don't seem to know how to use those assets to your advantage."

"Oiy," chimed in Hawk. "When you're small and skinny like me, you've got to know how to use your opponent's strength against him."

Peregrine blinked. "H-How?"

"It's all about mechanics and the laws of physical motion," quipped Raven. "Levers, fulcrums—"

"Y-You mean . . . like engineering?" stammered Peregrine.

"Oiy, you could say that."

"If you like, we could show you a few tricks for defending yourself," added Hawk.

Peregrine's expression turned wary. "Why are you being nice to me?"

Raven shrugged. "Because you looked like you could use a friend." A pause. "But maybe we were wrong."

The breeze freshened, its whisper stirring the leaves of the nearby trees. A crow cackled within the greenery.

"C'mon, Hawk," he added. "Let's return to the house. I want to finish the chapter I'm reading in Euler's book on mathematics."

"W-Wait!"

Raven looked around.

"I—I haven't thanked you yet," stammered Peregrine.

"We don't need thanks for doing the right thing," said Hawk. "Wrexford says a gentleman should never let a bully go unchallenged."

"Not," added Raven, with a snigger, "that we're gentlemen."

The remark drew a gap-toothed grin from Hawk.

"I wish *I* weren't a gentleman," confessed Peregrine, with a shuddering sigh. "And so does Uncle Belmont. He thinks that I'm a . . . a stain on the family."

"What about your parents?" asked Raven.

"Drowned," answered Peregrine tersely. The boy looked away to the lake, where the breeze was raising ripples across water. "I—I miss them. Papa never minded that I was . . . different."

"There's nothing wrong with being different," said Raven.

Peregrine chuffed a mirthless laugh. "As if you two would know about being different."

"You might be surprised," shot back Raven. He held out his hand. "By the by, I'm Raven, and this is my brother, Hawk."

After a small hesitation, Peregrine accepted the offer. "I'm Peregrine."

The announcement made Raven laugh. "Well, fancy that! It appears we really are birds of a feather."

"Oiy," agreed Hawk. "Welcome to the flock, Falcon."

"F-Falcon?" A smile slowly lit Peregrine's face at the tacit offer of friendship.

"You have to have an informal moniker if you want to fly with us," said Raven. "What do you say?"

"I . . . I'd like that very much!"

"Then come along and let us show you how to beat a bully at his own game." Raven indicated a secluded clearing within the trees bordering the lake. "If we're going to be friends, you can't embarrass us by getting yourself thumped black and blue by a nitwit."

"D-Do you really read books about mathematics?" ventured Peregrine as the three of them started walking.

"I know, I know—it's horribly boring. But Raven happens to be a wizard with numbers," piped up Hawk. "I prefer botany."

"Talk about boring," retorted Raven, though he said it with a smile. "What about you, Falcon? Any special interests?"

"I like making things," answered Peregrine. "Useful devices, like a magnifying glass with dual lenses." A shy grin. "And actually, I find mathematics really interesting . . ."

After seeing Wrexford and Tyler to the stables, Charlotte reluctantly returned to the birthday celebration. The afternoon had turned wiltingly warm, and many of the ladies had sought shelter within the shade of the lawn tent, where chairs had been set up—with servants wielding large Oriental fans of woven bamboo to stir a cooling breeze.

The gentlemen, however, seemed happy to stave off the heat with iced champagne. As a result, the mood of the party had turned mellow, the earlier undercurrent of tension giving way to convivial good cheer.

Perhaps I was merely imagining a note of discord because of my dislike of our host, conceded Charlotte as she joined her brother and several of the local squires, who were discussing the merits of the various horses entered in the county's annual steeplechase.

The afternoon passed more pleasantly than she expected, helped along, no doubt, by the effervescence of the sparkling wine.

At this time of year, the sun would linger until long into the evening, but as the clock in the drawing room struck five, the guests began to take their leave in order to return to their homes before dark.

"The party went well," murmured Wolcott as he offered Charlotte his arm. "I do hope Louisa will be pleased."

"I'm sure she's delighted," replied Charlotte. "There wasn't so much as a blade of grass out of place."

Wolcott chuckled. "Damned with faint praise." A pause. "Not that I blame you. Had I realized that the upcoming Peace Celebrations would put so much strain on Belmont and Louisa, I wouldn't have pressed you and Wrexford to come here."

He paused. "I think part of the reason Belmont is on edge is because he has some very unfortunate news to tell his young ward."

"Peregrine?"

"Yes. Belmont told me earlier today that the poor boy's uncle on his mother's side met with a fatal accident in London several nights ago."

Charlotte felt a sudden chill slither down her spine.

"Apparently Peregrine was very fond of the fellow, so it won't be a very pleasant task."

"Are you perchance referring to Jeremiah Willis?"

"Why, yes." Wolcott looked surprised. "How did you know?"

She chose to evade the question. There was no reason to reveal their involvement in discovering Willis's corpse. "Wrexford and I heard about the death before leaving Town. Willis is known in the scientific community as an inventor. And as there aren't many individuals of African descent who move within the higher circles of Society, it seemed a logical guess."

"I didn't realize Willis was an inventor," mused Wolcott.

"There's no reason you would. It's my understanding that his work is quite specialized," said Charlotte.

"Ah." Her brother released a mournful sigh. "The poor lad. To lose yet another member of his family . . . how very painful."

Especially as his guardians seem to resent his existence, thought Charlotte as she gave a wordless nod.

They passed through the open French doors of the music room and made their way to the central foyer of the manor house.

"I think I shall retire to my rooms for a nap before we regather for a late supper," announced Wolcott. "And you, Charley?"

"An excellent idea. But first I shall look in on Raven and Hawk to make sure they're not engaged in some mischief."

"They seem far too well-behaved to get into any mischief," he replied with a genial chuckle. "Don't be hard on them. Boys that age shouldn't be *too* perfect."

"Perfection is not the word that comes to mind when discussing the Weasels," she said dryly, and turned for the guest wing, where she and the boys were lodged.

A grand staircase rose in stately splendor to the third floor. Raven and Hawk's bedchamber connected to a nursery filled with books and games for visiting children. Charlotte heard chortling—along with a loud clanking and whirring—as soon as she reached the top landing.

Quickening her steps, she hurried down the corridor and pushed open the nursery door . . .

Only to collide with a three-foot-tall wood and metal dragon, whose spiked tail was slapping up and down against the floor, much to the delight of the Weasels.

She jumped back in surprise, nearly falling on her derriere.

Which provoked another round of mirth from Raven and Hawk.

However, Peregrine, who was crouched between the Weasels, turned ashen.

"I—I'm so, so sorry, milady," he stammered. "I—I know I shouldn't be showing my oddities to others. It's u-unnatural and u-unbecoming of a well-born boy to enjoy engaging in manual labor to build such things."

Charlotte crouched down for a closer look at the dragon. "On the contrary, it's quite marvelous!" she said, admiring the precision of the brass joints and scales of shiny tin. "And quite ingenious."

Raven grinned at Peregrine. "I told you that m'lady wouldn't mind us playing with it." To Charlotte, he added, "Falcon built this."

"Did you?" She fixed the boy with an encouraging smile. How very clever of you.".

"My uncle made the parts in his workshop—he's very skilled at engineering and invents things—and we assembled the moving parts together when I visited him in London over the Christmas holidays."

It appeared that Belmont hadn't yet informed his ward of Willis's death, and Charlotte couldn't help but think it cruel of him to risk having Peregrine hear it from a servant or neighbor. Or . . .

She darted a swift glance at Raven, who flicked a brow up in question. A tiny shake of her head indicated that he should say nothing. Thank heaven he and his brother had been wise enough to keep their lips locked.

"I finished the decorative details on my own," explained Peregrine. "Aunt Louisa and Uncle Belmont think it a shameful waste of time, but I am permitted to do so after all my lessons are done for the day."

"Falcon is also interested in botany," piped up Hawk. "He's

going to take me to the gardens shortly so we can examine some of the planting with his special magnifying glass!"

That the Weasels had given Peregrine an avian moniker indicated that they had accepted him as a friend. Seeing the boy's face light up as he and Hawk chattered about the most interesting specimens to choose, Charlotte realized what a lonely life the young baron must live.

Not to speak of an unhappy life, for clearly his guardians treated him with cold disdain. And the poor boy was about to learn he had lost the last flicker of warmth and love in his little world.

"Well," said Charlotte, rising and shaking out her skirts. "I shall leave the three of you to your adventures, as I must dress for the evening."

But instead of heading to her own bedchambers, Charlotte retraced her steps to the main wing of the house, hoping to find Louisa free for a private chat.

As she turned down the main corridor, she heard voices coming from the side parlor.

"What the devil are we going to do?" It was Belmont, his voice rough with irritation. "I refuse to have the brat underfoot in London. We'll be hosting a number of gatherings for the visiting dignitaries, and I'll not allow myself to be embarrassed by my brother's foolish choices in life."

"I—I don't see how we have any alternative," replied Louisa, sounding equally upset. "We haven't enough staff to leave him here in the country. Given the entertainments we must host, all the servants must come to London with us."

"We can place him with one of the tenant farmers," muttered Belmont.

"Do you really think that wise?"

A grunt.

Charlotte quickly retreated, her steps silenced by the thick

Turkish runner, and approached again, taking care to make more noise as she stopped in front of the door.

"Louisa?" she called tentatively.

"Yes, yes, do come in, Charlotte." Louisa turned away from Belmont and greeted her with a brittle smile as she entered the room.

"What a splendid party," said Charlotte. "The setting, the refreshments, the weather—everything was absolutely lovely." That, at least, was all true.

Belmont acknowledged the compliment with a gruff nod. "We're delighted that you and Wrexford were able to attend."

Louisa echoed the sentiment.

"An idea has just occurred to me . . ." Charlotte feigned a light laugh. "A silly one perhaps, but I stopped up in the nursery to check on Thomas and Alexander . . ." Heaven forfend that she call them Raven and Hawk in front of the stiff-rumped Belmonts. "And found them conversing with Peregrine . . ."

Stretching her smile, she went on. "It seems the boys have formed a friendship, and, well, I suddenly thought that having a new playmate might help keep our wards distracted during the next few weeks." A sigh. "Wrexford and I will be swept up in the social swirl of the Peace Celebrations—as, of course, will you. If we were to have Peregrine stay with us in London, it might, well, kill two birds with one stone, so to speak." A pause. "I just learned from Hartley that the boy's maternal uncle perished in an unfortunate accident."

Louisa seemed to hold her breath as she flicked a look at Belmont—and then released it as a smile slowly curled the corners of his mouth.

"What an excellent idea," he said. "I confess, I've been concerned about Peregrine and how our official duties will keep us from entertaining him in Town."

"Then it's settled!" exclaimed Charlotte. "He shall stay with us for the duration of the Peace Celebrations." She cleared her throat. "We plan to depart in the morning, and Hartley seems to think that Peregrine isn't yet aware of his uncle's death . . ."

"I shall make sure to inform him of it this evening," said Belmont.

"Thank you," replied Charlotte. "How fortuitous that it suits all of us."

"Y-You are sure it's no trouble?" murmured Louisa.

"Oh, no trouble at all," assured Charlotte. "After all, it's not as if three young boys can get into any real mischief."

CHAPTER 6

The carriage clattered to a halt over the uneven cobbles. Wrexford descended, happy to be back in London, even though the scents perfuming this part of Town were far less pleasant than the ones of a fancy country estate.

"Thank you for coming, milord." Griffin stepped out of the shadows that shrouded the narrow side street.

"How could I resist the pleasure of emptying my purse while you stuff yourself with supper," he responded.

"Ah, but this time you're not the one paying for the refreshments," said the Runner.

"Who's the new pigeon?" asked Wrexford. "And why aren't you already seated at the table enjoying a platter of fresh oysters?"

"Actually, we're not eating here. There's a hackney waiting for us around the corner."

"Why all the skullduggery?" asked the earl as they climbed into the vehicle.

"Patience, milord—"

"I have none—as you well know."

Griffin gave a half smile, but then his expression turned serious. "Still, milord, I can say nothing more. You must wait until we arrive at the appointed rendezvous place for answers to your questions."

They traveled in silence for another quarter hour, threading through streets that turned increasingly shabby.

"You have better taste in your choice of taverns than your mysterious friend," groused Wrexford as they stopped in front of a ramshackle building that sagged in a jut of drunken angles.

"This way, milord."

The interior was dimly lit, the smoke from the oily lanterns adding a haze to the tangled shadows. None of the hardscrabble patrons looked up at their entrance.

This was, observed the earl, the sort of place where nothing was seen or heard.

Griffin led the way to a table set in a recessed alcove, where a lone man sat waiting.

"Who the devil are you?" demanded Wrexford, without preamble, after taking a seat.

"Oh, I'm naught but the dogsbody," answered the man. "My name isn't important."

"If you're only the dogsbody, then who holds your leash?" Wrexford pondered his own question. "My guess is it's Grentham."

The shadowy Lord Grentham, whose rather innocuous title of Under Minister of State Security belied the fact that he was reputed to be the most feared man in London, was said to be an iron-willed, iron-fisted master of espionage and any other underhanded means needed to keep Britain safe from its enemies. Rumors swirled about his ruthlessness in crushing any perceived threat to king and country.

"It's not important who sent me, milord," replied Dogsbody. "We've far more pressing questions to discuss."

"Like what?" retorted Wrexford, though he suspected that he knew why he was there.

Dogsbody leaned back and raised three fingers to the barman tending the tap before answering. "Like whether you're willing to use your considerable sleuthing abilities to help the government resolve a very delicate situation."

"Yet again," snapped the earl.

"Yet again," agreed Dogsbody. "You've saved the Crown considerable damage, not to speak of embarrassment, through your previous investigations. We are hoping you'll agree to help solve a very dangerous conundrum."

A barmaid appeared from the sooty gloom and thumped down three tankards of ale.

Judging by the smell wafting up from the dented pewter, the earl decided the main ingredient was horse piss.

"What conundrum?" he demanded, pushing his tankard aside.

"You fished the body of a man named Jeremiah Willis out of the Serpentine." Dogsbody took a sip of his ale. "He was working on a project—a very secret one—for the government." Another sip. "You're a clever fellow. I imagine you can guess what it is."

Wrexford didn't bother answering.

"So the answer to your question is twofold. You see, the technical information and prototype to Mr. Willis's invention have gone missing. So firstly, we need to discover who stole them. And secondly, we need to get them back."

"Why come to me?" pressed the earl.

"Because you seem inordinately adept at moving within both the highest and lowest circles of London society." A pause. "Because you're foul-tempered and sardonic enough that nobody will suspect you're working for us."

Dogsbody flicked a bit of foam off the rim of his mug. "And because you're clever enough to match wits with diabolically cunning adversaries and beat them at their own game."

"Be that as it may," answered Wrexford. "I'm a newly married man, and for the time being, my wife and I wish to settle into a peaceful and quiet life of connubial bliss."

Griffin made a rude sound. "I can't quite picture Lady Wrexford devoting her days to embroidering samplers or dabbling in watercolors."

Wrexford fixed the Runner with an imperious stare. "Actually, my wife is a *very* talented artist."

"I beg your pardon, milord." A flicker of the sooty light accentuated Griffin's apologetic grimace. "I—I meant no disrespect to Her Ladyship. It's just that she seems . . ." The Runner hesitated and then appeared to decide it was unwise to continue.

Silence shivered through the cramped space.

"We have no interest in your wife's hobbies, Lord Wrexford." Dogsbody ran his finger around the rim of his tankard. "Or should we?"

Wrexford schooled his face to betray nothing, but he felt his innards turn to ice. If anyone had the tentacles to dig out the deepest, darkest secrets in London, it was Lord Grentham. He and Charlotte had been oh-so-careful, and only a small number of trusted friends knew the truth about her activities . . .

However, as she had so often said herself, no secret was ever truly safe.

"I can't imagine why." He, too, allowed a small pause. "Unless, of course, you or your master would like to have your portrait painted. She's quite gifted in the art of capturing an accurate likeness."

Dogsbody appeared genuinely amused. "I wouldn't dream of wasting your wife's talents on a face as unremarkable as mine." A smile played on his lips. "As for my master, he's not the sort of fellow who cares about fripperies."

"A pity," said the earl, with unflinching calm. "She would do an excellent job."

Their gazes met for a moment.

"Be that as it may . . ." Dogsbody cracked his knuckles. "It's *your* skills that I wish to discuss, milord."

Wrexford remained on guard. He might only have imagined the veiled reference to Charlotte's secret. But with men such as Dogsbody and his master, one couldn't be too careful. "You'll have to be more forthcoming about the situation, and what you expect of me," he replied.

"I shall trust in your discretion—"

"I think I've given you and your master no reason to think otherwise," interjected Wrexford.

Dogsbody ignored the comment. "As you saw, Mr. Willis was working on a revolutionary technical innovation for our government, one that would give the country that possesses it a very powerful advantage over its peers."

The earl nodded for him to go on.

"After learning of his death, we, of course, immediately dispatched people to retrieve his drawings and all his notes on the engineering specifications," continued Dogsbody. "However, we couldn't find them in either his workshop or his residence."

A wraithlike curl of tobacco smoke floated past his face. "So we must assume they've been stolen."

"And you have no idea by whom?" asked Wrexford, unable to keep an edge of sarcasm out of his voice. "Surely it was a very closely-guarded secret."

Dogsbody maintained his air of unruffled calm. "However well guarded, no secret is ever entirely safe."

Willing his expression to remain unchanged, he replied, "From what I've heard, Grentham is very good at what he does, so you must have some suspect in mind?" He thought for a moment. "The obvious answer to me is a traitor within our own government. Someone with access to knowledge of the project."

"That is one possibility," agreed Dogsbody. "But there are several foreign military attachés who have been stationed in

London for the last year to coordinate the Allied war efforts against Bonaparte who might have gotten access to information and arranged the theft."

"Russia, Prussia, or Austria," mused Wrexford.

"Those three are certainly the ones that come to mind," agreed Dogsbody.

"In which case," the earl said, "it's likely long gone from Britain."

"Actually, it's not that simple." Dogsbody took a moment to contemplate a greasy stain on his coat cuff. "You see, we've reason to believe that whoever possesses the information has decided that the opportunity to profit personally from the invention is too tempting to pass up. We've just received word that it's going to be offered for sale."

Dogsbody looked up. "Given the nature of the invention, the gathering of European rulers for the Peace Celebrations here in London makes it the perfect opportunity to create an auction. With the plans and prototype being sold to the highest bidder."

"I imagine it will command . . . a great deal of money," responded the earl dryly.

"Yes." Dogsbody glanced at Griffin, whose face looked leached of color in the skittery light. "As I said, whichever country possesses it will have a priceless advantage over all the others, so one must assume that the seller will make a bloody fortune."

"And how do you see me fitting into this international chessboard?" asked Wrexford.

"As the knight-errant," replied Dogsbody. "Very few people are aware of your involvement in solving the previous crimes. And those who do know can be counted on to keep their mouths shut. So your public reputation as a loose cannon who has little respect for the powers that be will allow you to move freely within the highest circles of Society. Circles that are closed to our usual espionage agents."

Wrexford shifted, wondering just what sort of bargain he was being offered. "Which implies that if the traitor is someone from our own government, he's someone of high rank."

"That's a logical assumption." Dogsbody didn't elaborate.

Wrexford thought about it for a moment. In other words, he was being asked to step into an unholy nest of vipers.

"As you pointed out earlier," he said slowly, "I'm not known for being altruistic. So why should I put myself—and quite possibly my family—in danger?"

"Because of your love and loyalty to king and country?"

A low laugh. "You'll have to do better than that."

Dogsbody pursed his lips. "Let's just say the country would be very, very grateful."

A bribe for keeping Charlotte's secret?

Deciding he had heard enough, Wrexford scraped back his chair. "I'll think about your request."

"Very well," came the answer. "But do so quickly, milord."

Charlotte untied her bonnet and placed it on the entrance table with an audible sigh.

"Welcome home, milady," murmured the butler as he closed the front portal.

Home. She was still getting used to thinking of the earl's elegant townhouse as her home. "Thank you, Riche."

"I trust the trip went smoothly."

"The weather was good and there were no delays on the road," answered Charlotte absently, her mind on more pressing things. Peregrine appeared to be taking the death of his favorite uncle well. But she had a feeling that the boy had learned how to keep his true feelings well hidden.

"Is Wrexford in his workroom?" she asked.

"He is. And Mr. Sheffield is with him."

Repressing another sigh, she smiled. Sheffield was a dear friend and always a welcome visitor, but she had been hoping to find Wrexford alone. "Thank you."

Shrugging off her shawl, Charlotte placed it next to her bonnet and headed for the rear of the house.

The door to the workroom was half-open. "Wrexford . . ." she began, and then stopped upon catching sight of Sheffield's face.

"Good heavens, Kit—what's wrong?"

Sheffield forced a smile. "Oh, it's really nothing at all. Wrex and Tyler were simply being kind enough to listen to me vent a little steam over a trifling matter."

"A trifling matter?" Charlotte glanced at Wrexford and his valet, their faces confirming her suspicion. "What fiddle-faddle! You're a very bad liar, Kit."

He flushed.

"I would hope that we're good enough friends that you would confide in me, too," she added.

"I—I didn't . . . That is, I—"

"Cut wind, Kit, and confess," counseled the earl. "The truth is, Charlotte's advice on your dilemma will be far more valuable than ours."

She raised her brows in question, her own concerns put aside for the moment. "Oh?"

Sheffield sank into one of the leather armchairs by the hearth and ran a hand through his hair. "It's Cordelia."

The announcement wasn't unexpected. Indeed, Charlotte had been wondering about the relationship, which was rather . . . complicated. However, she waited for him to go on.

"She . . . She . . ."

The earl took pity on their friend. "According to Kit, Lady Cordelia is smitten with Monsieur Rochambert, a brilliant mathematician, who's here as part of the Peace Celebrations."

"He's French," said Sheffield darkly.

"The Royal Institution is hosting a scientific conference with the French Academy of Science," explained Wrexford. "To celebrate the beginning of a new era of cooperation and collaboration."

Charlotte felt a stab of sympathy. Sheffield had a reputation as a charming rakehell, and his good looks and sunny sense of humor made him a great favorite with the ladies. But she and their circle of friends knew that his devil-may-care insouciance hid a very sharp mind and a heart of gold. He had reformed his wild ways some time ago in order to form a business partnership with Lady Cordelia and several of her female friends. And he was proving quite skillful at it . . .

The trouble was, he was used to thinking of himself as a shallow fribble.

There are those of us who tend to see our weaknesses rather than our strengths.

"Kit, it is understandable that Cordelia may express an admiration for Rochambert's mathematical abilities. It's a field that interests her," she said slowly. "But, ye gods, it was *your* steadfast loyalty and friendship that saved her from ruin—"

"I don't want her to feel beholden to me out of guilt," muttered Sheffield.

"That's not at all what I was implying," said Charlotte. "My sense is, she cares very deeply for you."

"Ha!" Sheffield made a face. "She doesn't show it."

Charlotte cleared her throat with a cough. "A lady is not encouraged to show her feelings, especially if she's uncertain about the gentleman-in-question's sentiments. Have you given her any indication as to how *you* feel?"

A rush of red colored his cheekbones. "S-Surely she knows."

Ah, the vagaries of the heart. It rarely listens to the head.

"And, besides," he muttered, "if she cares for me, why was she shamelessly flirting with that damn jackanapes at Lady Aldershaw's musicale?"

"Perhaps you misunderstood—"

"I did not! In fact, I took her aside for a private chat and told her she was making a bloody fool of herself." Sheffield expelled a harried breath. "In reply, she told me to go to the devil!"

"Actually, I'm surprised she didn't knock your teeth down your gullet," observed Wrexford.

"I . . ." Sheffield made a face. "I—I suppose I could have been a trifle more diplomatic."

Tyler sniggered.

"We will all have a chance to hone our diplomacy over the next few weeks," said Wrexford. He cleared his throat. "Speaking of which—"

"Forgive me, Charlotte. What an arse I am!" exclaimed Sheffield. "Here I've been whinging on about my romantic prospects—or lack of them—when Wrex was just explaining to Tyler and me that we needed to have a council of war as soon as you returned."

"A council of war," repeated Charlotte slowly as she fixed the earl with a searching look. "Why on earth would we need to have a council of war? Are you saying that your meeting with Griffin—"

"Griffin was merely the go-between," interrupted Wrexford. "The real tête-à-tête was with a man who simply identified himself as the dogsbody of someone higher up in the government. Given the nature of Willis's work, I suspect that person is Lord Grentham."

Tyler let out a low whistle. "A man with whom one doesn't trifle."

Charlotte's face betrayed the fact that she didn't disagree.

"So his reputation says," replied the earl.

"Deservedly so," replied the valet. His brow furrowed in thought. "What did the dogsbody look like?"

"Thoroughly unremarkable," replied Wrexford. "Average height, average build, his hair an average shade of brown." He thought for a moment, trying to remember the sort of details that Charlotte would have noticed. "The only bit of individuality about him was a long patrician nose ending with an elegant little hook."

"Pierson," said Tyler decisively. "It had to have been George Pierson." His mouth thinned to a grim line. "Which isn't good news. He's Grentham's top operative—hard as granite and ruthless as sharpened steel. Meaning the government must see a grave threat to its security."

"What sort of threat?" asked Sheffield.

The earl hesitated. "Damnation, Kit. It might be better for you if I didn't say."

"Right." Sarcasm dripped off the single word like sun-warmed honey. "Because I'm the sort of lily-livered coward who'll snatch the first chance to stay snugly safe, while his friends rush off to battle a dangerous enemy."

"I haven't agreed to fight anyone—at least, not yet," said Wrexford. "But if that changes, and you're really so bloody afire to jump into yet another hellhole of trouble with us . . ."

Tyler made a rude sound.

"Then we shall, of course, welcome your help."

"You're saying that the government arranged a clandestine meeting with you to request your help in investigating Willis's death?" asked Charlotte.

"In a manner of speaking," answered Wrexford, keeping his words deliberately vague.

Charlotte had been watching him intently throughout the exchange. "Why?" she said softly. Her gaze sharpened. "Why is there any hesitation about saying yes? Especially as we have an inkling of what the inventor was working on at the time of his death."

Damnation. Leave it to Charlotte to cut unerringly to the heart of the question.

"It seems to me," he responded, "that government has a cadre of experienced operatives to handle threats such as this."

Her gaze turned even more searching.

Wrexford shifted just enough that he didn't need to meet her eyes. "It also occurred to me that a bit of peace and quiet might be welcome. You and the Weasels are settling into a new residence and a new life, which will bring inevitable changes. I wish for you to have a chance to get . . . comfortable."

"Comfortable?"

An unwise choice of words. He gave himself a mental kick. Unlike most highborn ladies of leisure, Charlotte didn't give a fig for comfort.

"The search for justice is rarely comfortable, Wrexford." Charlotte allowed a moment of silence before adding, "Which is all the more reason not to shy away from it."

"We can't solve all the wrongs in the world, so we must choose our battles carefully," he countered. "In our previous investigations, we had a personal connection to the crime—"

"As we do now," said Charlotte.

The statement took him by surprise. Clearly something had happened since his departure from the country house party. He knew Charlotte too well not to recognize that her passions had been aroused.

"May I ask how?"

"Actually, I was just coming to explain that . . ." She shot an apologetic look at Tyler and Sheffield. "Might I have a private word with my husband?"

CHAPTER 7

"That was certainly a dramatic announcement. One worthy of the great Sarah Siddons," drawled the earl, once the door had clicked shut. "Tyler and Sheffield are likely tussling for the right to glue an ear to the keyhole."

"A waste of effort, as they would be sadly disappointed," she replied. "It's simply a mundane domestic matter and has nothing to do with international intrigue."

She smoothed at a crease in her skirts. "I made a spur of the moment decision regarding our household, and felt you should hear about it without an audience."

He lifted a brow. "In case I disapprove?"

"I hope you won't." Charlotte took a moment to study his face. She was still getting used to the fact that he was more than just an occasional presence in her life. *The shape of his jaw, the texture of his skin, the contours of his muscled body*—all had become intimately familiar to her. And the joy of it still took her breath away.

"But yes," she said, her voice a little shaky, "if you wish to ring a peal over my head, I feel that is best done in private."

"Should I be quaking in my boots?"

"You never quake." A smile teased at her lips. "Roar, perhaps, and hurl invectives . . ."

Wrexford heaved a sigh. "Go on."

"I've invited Peregrine to stay here with us during the upcoming Peace Celebrations." She quickly explained about the three boys having formed a friendship, and the unsettling comments she had overheard from the Belmonts. "I know what it is to feel alone and cut off from the love of one's family, so perhaps I'm overreacting. But I couldn't bear to abandon the boy when he's just lost the only person who showed him any affection—"

"Ye heavens," he interrupted. "You thought that I might object?"

"You've already had an unruly pair of urchins invade the peace and quiet of your townhouse—"

Two swift strides brought the earl close enough to sweep her into his arms before she could finish.

"*Our* townhouse," he corrected after brushing a kiss to her brow. "And given the mayhem caused by the Weasels, I doubt that we'll even notice Peregrine is here. He's such a quiet and reserved little lad, I fear he'll never get a word in edgewise."

"You haven't yet seen—or heard—his mechanical dragon," said Charlotte dryly, stepping back from his hold.

"I doubt it can hold a candle to a stink bomb in causing mayhem." Amusement flickered in his eyes a moment longer before fading to a more serious mien.

She didn't miss the subtle change. "Let us put aside Peregrine for the moment. What is it you're not telling me about the meeting with Grentham's man?"

His hesitation stirred a frisson of alarm.

"I thought we had agreed that keeping secrets from each other can be dangerous," pressed Charlotte.

Wrexford drew in a measured breath, and then surrendered it in a sigh. "You're right. There *is* something else."

"Don't keep me in suspense."

He looked away, shadows pooling beneath his dark lashes. "Skilled intelligence operatives like Pierson are not only privy to a wealth of highly sensitive information that may prove useful in their work for the government's intrigues." His gaze came back to lock with hers. "But they are also experts at the art of innuendo and manipulation."

Charlotte felt her muscles tense.

"I may have misinterpreted a casual comment," he continued. "But however unsettling, it would be unwise to dismiss the idea that Grentham knows about your secret."

She had always told herself that this moment might come. But strangely enough, though it hit like a punch to the gut, the blow didn't hurt as much as she had expected.

"Secrets are like smoke," murmured Charlotte. "No matter how tightly you seal them away, no container is perfect, and the tiniest fissure will allow them to slip free."

Wrexford was watching her, his gaze rippling with emotions she couldn't quite name.

"Did Pierson say it as a veiled threat, to compel you to agree to help the government?" she asked softly.

"We must assume that was the intent," he answered carefully. "But as I said, it was done so obliquely that I might be seeing trouble where, in fact, there is none."

Charlotte allowed a small smile. "Trouble seems to take particular delight in dogging our steps."

He didn't respond.

"I take it you considered not telling me because you feared that I would, out of principle, refuse to help the government."

That drew a twitch of his lips. "The thought did occur to me," confessed Wrexford. He then quickly explained about Pierson's comment concerning Charlotte's hobbies.

"Hmmm." She frowned in thought. "As you say, it could simply have been a cleverly cryptic comment deliberately designed to throw you off balance. To plant a seed of fear in your mind that the government knows some deep, dark secret about your wife."

A pause. "After all, most everyone has dirty little secrets that they wish to keep hidden. It's no surprise that someone like Pierson knows how to exploit such fears."

"We can spin round and round, making ourselves dizzy trying to parse his motives," muttered Wrexford. "However, it seems to me that a far more logical reaction is to simply accept the uncertainty and decide how we wish to deal with it."

"In this case, your logic and my intuition agree. As for the decision, it's an easy one," replied Charlotte. "You're right. On principle, I won't let myself be bullied into doing something simply as a matter of self-preservation. But there are higher principles at stake here—like justice and right versus wrong—that take precedence over any personal concerns."

She fell silent for a moment, before adding, "I like to think I'm not so self-important that I'd sacrifice seeking justice for a good man who was foully murdered just to make an intellectual statement."

"As if I've ever doubted your dedication to noble principles for an instant," said Wrexford. "However, I feel beholden to point out one last thing to consider before you make a final decision."

His expression turned grim. "Once a blackmailer feels he's forced a victim to do his bidding a first time, he won't hesitate to ask again." A pause. "And again."

The lamplight flickered, sending a sudden skittering of shadows across the far wall.

"A possibility," conceded Charlotte. "But the next time we're dealt a fresh hand of cards, we'll be playing a new game."

That drew a grudging smile from him. "The idea of having to gamble with the devil more than once ought to terrify you."

"Oh, fie, Wrex. I've been gambling with the devil ever since I plucked A. J. Quill's pen from my late husband's lifeless fingers. I respect him. But I'm not terrified—because I know that the devil can, on occasion, be beaten."

"As do I." He met her gaze and held it, a look of concern flickering beneath his lashes. "But I also know from experience at the gaming table that a run of success can make one feel invincible."

"And I know from experience on the streets of the slums that no one is invincible."

His expression turned inscrutable. "Then let us both temper confidence with caution," he murmured. "Our responsibilities are now—"

"Far more complicated than in the past," she finished for him. "Be assured that knowledge is lodged in the very depth of my heart."

The shadows around them flickered, and suddenly she was in his arms. "As it is in mine," he said. "It's not the risks that frighten me. It's that we may allow hubris to make us believe they aren't really a threat to us. And that, my dear, would be dangerous."

Charlotte nodded. *He's right—we mortals need constant reminders that hubris is punished by the gods.*

"I think that neither of us will fall prey to that danger," she answered. "We are each capable of wielding a very sharp pin if the other's hubris becomes too inflated."

A sound—was it a chuckle?—stirred in Wrexford's throat. It was, she knew, not a surrender of his worries, merely an acceptance of them. "It seems we've settled that. So now I had better tell you exactly what we're up against." He went on to explain what Pierson had told him about the possible suspects. "I imagine he might be more forthcoming once I agree to get involved.

But my sense is, they are counting on us to do the real dirty work."

Charlotte pondered the statement for a long moment. "Speaking of wielding a sharp object, I need to compose my next drawing," she said. "Perhaps I can use my pen to start probing . . . and see what serpents start slithering out of the shadows."

CHAPTER 8

Tyler looked up nervously as Wrexford entered the workroom late the following evening, knowing that the earl had been to a second rendezvous with Grentham's dogsbody. "How did the meeting with Pierson go?"

"Swiftly," answered the earl. After shrugging off his coat and loosening his cravat, he moved to the sideboard and poured himself a whisky.

"Did he . . ." The valet hesitated. Wrexford had confided Pierson's enigmatic comment to the valet, though he still hadn't told him what Willis's invention was. "Did he give any hint as to whether . . . as to whether he truly knows milady's secret?"

Shards of light reflected off the cut-crystal glass as Wrexford lifted it to his lips.

"Sorry. A foolish question," muttered Tyler in response to the silence. "Of course he'll keep the knifepoint at your throat—and enjoy pricking it against your flesh to make you march to his wishes."

"Never mind about Pierson and his intentions right now," growled the earl. "Our mission is to recover the technical drawings for Willis's innovation—along with the prototype."

He took another swallow of whisky. "And, though it's not the government's priority, we also need to bring his killers to justice. Charlotte won't hear of anything less than that. Once that's accomplished, I'll deal with how to dull Pierson's blade."

Tyler nodded. "So, how do you and milady intend to begin?"

"By attending a gala reception in honor of the Russian tsar's arrival in London tomorrow evening." Wrexford drew two folded sheets of paper from his coat pocket and dropped it on his desk. "I asked Pierson to return the prototype sketch that I found in Willis's instrument case, as I may need it in doing some scientific sleuthing—"

"Are you going to tell me what it is?" asked the valet.

"Not at the moment," said Wrexford. "There is a reason, but I prefer not to voice it right now."

Tyler's eyes narrowed, but he didn't argue.

"He also gave me a list of possible suspects within our government," continued Wrexford, "as well as several foreign attachés whose work with the military staff at Horse Guards might have put them in a position to learn of Willis's research."

"What about a private consortium of criminals who might have stolen the plans?" suggested Tyler.

"If one exists, even the grand spider Grentham—whose web of intrigue stretches into every dark nook and cranny of Europe and the New World—has no idea of who they might be." He allowed a sour smile. "Though I suppose it should be of some consolation that the dratted fellow doesn't know every secret."

Tyler picked up the decanter and came over to refill the earl's glass.

The paper gave a whispery crackle as Wrexford unfolded the list that Pierson had given him and passed it to Tyler. Five names—three of them were foreigners—were written in elegant script, along with each of their government positions.

Tyler studied the names before handing the list back to the earl. "What can I do to help?"

Something about the list was bothering Wrexford, though until he had a clearer idea as to why, he decided to keep such thoughts to himself.

"You can start by visiting your usual cesspool haunts and see what rumors regarding an auction of some very valuable stolen information are wafting through the malodorous air."

"Are you implying that I'm at home rubbing shoulders with the dregs of society?" Tyler tried to sound affronted . . .

Which only drew a rude sound from Wrexford. "Yes." He refolded the note. "Your familiarity with London's underbelly is even more useful than your secret formula for boot polish."

"Hmmph! I'll have you know that the Duke of Devonshire would hire me at twice my current salary to possess my polish."

"Devonshire is a tedious arse. You would go out of your mind with boredom within a fortnight."

"But I'd be a lot richer."

"Money isn't everything," retorted Wrexford. He waved him away. "Off you go. We haven't any time to lose."

"We should have Sheffield make the rounds of his gambling dens and dockyard hellholes," said Tyler as he moved to fetch his hat and coat. "As we both have reason to know, criminals and cutthroats seem to have a sixth sense for knowing when some sordid mischief is afoot."

"An excellent idea. Perhaps you might stop by his residence and ask him to do some sleuthing," replied the earl. "Having something useful to do might keep him from bolloxing his romantic hopes with Lady Cordelia."

"You really shouldn't have been eavesdropping on Wrex and Tyler," chided Hawk.

Raven eased the door of the laboratory's library room shut.

"Tyler gave us permission to come in here and fetch some books. Ergo, it wasn't technically eavesdropping."

A scowl twisted Hawk's features. "Dressing it up in Latin doesn't make it right."

"Would you rather be in the dark about what's going on?" demanded his brother. "And not be able to help?"

Hawk's eyes widened. "Are Wrex and m'lady in trouble?"

"Not yet," said Raven ominously. "But . . ." He stopped abruptly, and glanced at Peregrine, who was watching them with solemn interest. "We'll talk about it later—"

"S'all right, I'll leave," interrupted Peregrine. He hesitated, but held Raven's gaze. "But just so you know, I'm good at keeping secrets."

"I'm not saying you aren't," replied Raven. "However, with us, trust is something you have to earn—"

A low *woof*, and the heavy thump of a paw against the closed door, cut him off.

"Shhhh!" Raven hissed a warning to the hound through the thick oak. "Quiet, Harper!" he added in a hurried whisper. "Go away!"

Too late.

The door eased open and Harper bounded in, his tail wagging fiercely. "*Woof!*"

Behind the flurry of fur, Wrexford stood framed in the open doorway, his hand still on the latch. "What are you Weasels doing in here?"

"Nuffink!" replied Hawk, whose pronunciation tended to lapse when he was nervous.

His brother maintained a stoic silence.

The earl's brows winged up in skepticism. "Nuffink?" he repeated softly.

Raven still didn't flinch. "Tyler gave us permission to fetch some books to take up to the schoolroom." He indicated a stack of leather-bound volumes sitting on the carpet.

"I'm sorry, milord," interjected Peregrine. "Raven mentioned you had some books on automata, and I asked if I might see them. If anyone is to be birched for the transgression, it's me."

"In this household, reading is always encouraged, lad," answered the earl. "As for punishments, the rod is never wielded here. It is my opinion that only bullies and tyrants resort to physical force as a means of discipline."

Peregrine's expression betrayed wary surprise.

"If any transgressions take place, we discuss them rationally," added Wrexford. "Along with what would be a fair punishment, if one is deemed necessary."

He disappeared for a moment, then returned with a parcel wrapped in brown paper. "Speaking of automata, Peregrine, given the dragon that you and your late uncle built, I ordered several books from Hatchards that I thought you might enjoy. They just arrived this afternoon."

The earl removed the wrapping. "There's an illustrated volume by Professor Winchester of Oxford on the mechanics of making devices with moving parts. And a book of colored engravings of famous automata, including 'Tipu's Tiger.'"

"T-Thank you, sir," stammered Peregrine, looking awestruck as Wrexford offered him the books. "Uncle Jeremiah told me the tiger is a magnificent mechanical creation." The boy hesitated. "But Uncle Belmont says it's the work of savage heathens, and ought to be destroyed for showing the beast attacking a British soldier."

"I think," growled Wrexford, "that your uncle Belmont is—"

"Is entitled to his own opinion," said Charlotte smoothly as she slipped out of shadows of the main workroom and entered the library. She smiled at Peregrine. "But that doesn't mean you have to agree with him."

The earl looked about to add something, but on catching her warning look he remained silent.

"Oiy." Raven hastily gathered up the books on the carpet

and shot to his feet. "Come along, Falcon, let's fly up to our eyrie and start exploring the pages of your gifts."

Peregrine bobbed a shy bow to Wrexford and Charlotte before Hawk grabbed his sleeve and, following his brother's lead, quickly hustled their new friend out of the room.

Charlotte waited until the patter of footsteps died away before asking, "Were the boys up to some mischief?"

Wrexford hesitated just a fraction before replying. "A good question."

"That," she murmured, "isn't a very reassuring answer."

A wry smile. "It wasn't meant to be." He then chuffed a sigh. "Apparently, Tyler gave them permission to poke around among the books in here, but that fact seemed to have slipped his mind when I returned from the meeting with Pierson. Which means the boys might have overheard several things that I would rather they hadn't."

"Have you any grounds for your suspicion?" asked Charlotte.

"Aside from the fact that Raven has batlike hearing?" quipped Wrexford.

She waited.

"When I queried them on what they were doing in the room," he added, "Hawk's reply was nuffink."

"Oh, dear. That's not a good sign." Charlotte frowned. "What might they have overheard?"

"That we've accepted a mission to recover the missing technical specifications and prototype for Willis's invention," he answered. "And that we intend to bring his killers to justice."

"Drat—"

"That's not quite all," he interjected. "Tyler asked a few questions that indicated that the government might know your secret."

Charlotte felt her face go pale.

"But again, I'm not at all certain they heard anything." He made a face. "They could very well have been poking around in my collection of rare medieval books—which they've been asked not to touch—in search of chemical recipes for making more potent stink bombs."

She mulled over his explanation for a long moment before releasing a sigh. "At this point, speculation is pointless, and only serves as a distraction, which we can ill afford. So I suggest we put aside any worries about the boys and concentrate on finding Willis's missing technical specifications and proto-type—along with his killers."

A pause. "Did Pierson perchance pass over any useful infor-mation on where to begin our hunt?" Her voice took on a steely edge. "Or are we merely being thrown to the wolves and expected to fend for ourselves?"

"He gave me a list of possible suspects . . ." Wrexford took her arm and led her back into the main workroom, where they sat themselves in the two armchairs by the hearth. "And an in-vitation to the gala reception tomorrow evening welcoming Tsar Alexander to London."

Charlotte took her time in studying the names that Pierson had written down. "Hmmph. Why is it I smell a rat?" She re-folded the note. "Or at least a moldering mouse."

His lips pinched to a grim smile. "I, too, sensed an odor teas-ing at my nostrils."

"Given Grentham's reputation for having the most ruth-lessly effective spy network in all of Europe, this list of suspects is unimaginative. More than that, it's obvious." She stopped to think. "*Too* obvious."

"On rare occasions," he murmured, "the obvious answer is actually the correct one."

"True. But then, that begs the key question," she responded.

"Which is," said Wrexford as he tapped his fingertips to-gether, "why do they need us to investigate?"

She nodded. "Speaking of obvious answers, getting rid of a gadfly like A. J. Quill would likely please a great many people in the government. Including the Prince Regent."

A gruff laugh. "Heaven forfend that we make Prinny happy." His humor giving way to a grimace, he then added, "Pierson wasn't very happy with the fact that A. J. Quill's latest drawing brought the name of Jeremiah Willis to the public's attention."

Tap-tap.

"So let us watch our steps as we dance our way through the glittering lies and silken innuendoes during the coming few weeks."

"And try not to fall into the traps that will open up beneath our feet," mused Charlotte.

Wrexford rose and took up a poker to stir the banked coals. Flames licked up from the orange-gold sparks, and for an instant they seemed to be wagging at her in silent laughter amidst the hiss and crackling.

"It will be a challenge." He straightened. "The trouble is, you *like* challenges. Even when they're damnably dangerous."

"That is akin to the pot calling the kettle black," she said lightly. However, as the word 'black' echoed in her head, her expression quickly sobered. "I don't deliberately seek out danger. But when truth and justice are at stake, I won't turn away."

She watched the fire die down to a hide-and-seek glow. "Especially as the villains—whoever they may be—likely assume that Mr. Willis's death won't be investigated very carefully because of the color of his skin."

Wrexford, too, was gazing into the light and shadows flickering within the fireplace. "*We* won't turn away." He approached Charlotte's chair and surprised her by crouching down and taking her hand in his.

The feel of his fingers, warm and strong as they touched her flesh, sent a shiver of awareness through her.

"Of all the many things I love and admire about you"—his voice was low and oddly husky—"your courage, your conviction, and your compassion for others truly take my breath away."

Charlotte felt a flutter deep in her chest. Wrexford rarely gave voice to such naked emotion. Freeing her hand, she pressed her palm to his cheek. "I think from the first moment you stormed into my little house and demanded that I help you learn the truth—"

"In order to save my neck," he murmured.

"Bollocks! You would have gone to the gallows without complaint, had you been guilty of the crime," she replied. "It's your unflinching respect for the truth—in science and in life— that captured my heart during our first meeting."

"I was yelling at you."

"Yes—perhaps that's why the moment was hard to forget." Her mouth twitched. "You have a very loud and very deep voice."

"Then I'll stop talking." Wrexford leaned closer and kissed her.

Silence, save for the whispery sighs of the still-warm coals, reigned for a lengthy interlude.

"Is that better?" he asked after slowly releasing her lips.

"Much," said Charlotte, matching his smile. Still a bit breathless, she tucked a loosened lock of hair behind her ear. The intensity of the intimate physical chemistry between them had been both unexpected and elating. The pleasures of the marriage bed with her late husband had been pleasant, but with Wrexford . . .

Her flesh began to tingle.

"Now we had best turn our attention to sleuthing," she said hastily, forcing her thoughts back to the problem at hand. "Fetch a pencil and paper, then let us get to work on making our own list of possible suspects."

Her eyes narrowed in thought. "I'm sure that Russia, Prussia, and Austria have very formidable espionage services. However, if a foreign country has stolen the invention, it's long gone from Britain. So given that it's up for sale, it seems to me that the most logical suspect for the theft of such a well-guarded secret is someone within the highest echelon of our own government."

"As I mentioned, Pierson suggested that one of the resident foreign attachés may have learned about the invention and decided to profit from selling it to the highest bidder." Wrexford took up a penknife and began sharpening a pencil. "We can't rule that out. But I agree with you that the ringleader is likely someone from within the beau monde."

"The very worst sort of betrayal," mused Charlotte. "But then, greed is one of the elemental weaknesses of our Good-versus-Evil human nature."

He nodded. "So we should be thinking of which departments within our government have access to military secrets, and which foreign attachés liaison with the top officers at Horse Guards."

"Which means," she murmured, "that when we begin our hunt tomorrow evening at the Prince Regent's reception, there will be more than enough suspects to go around."

CHAPTER 9

The sonorous sounds of a string quartet floated out through the open doors of Carlton House, the Mozart melody echoing off the magnificent marble columns of the entrance portico to the Prince Regent's London residence, where the gala diplomatic reception for the Tsar of Russia was taking place.

"Kit has received an invitation, too," murmured Wrexford as he and Charlotte joined the crowd of guests making their way into the Octagonal Vestibule. "Perhaps he'll have learned something from his sleuthing in the stews last night."

He noted that Charlotte's gaze was focused on a group of gentlemen conversing in the archway as they waited to proceed to the Crimson Drawing Room. Making a mental note, he decided with an inward smile, of their peacock finery and gaudy medals for A. J. Quill's next satire.

"Cordelia is also coming, along with her brother," she answered.

"Let us hope that won't be a distraction for Kit."

Her lips twitched. "You're not usually so optimistic about human nature."

He covered his chuckle with a brusque cough. "What puzzles me is that Kit has a great deal of experience in charming the ladies. And yet, he seems to be intent on deliberately provoking her."

"Love often addles the brain."

"Are you saying that emotion and reason can't come to a mutual understanding with each other?"

Charlotte smiled and gave a mock flutter of her lashes. "There are rare exceptions." The flash of humor quickly faded as her gaze angled back to the gentlemen, who had begun moving. "Do you know who the big bearlike fellow is? The one who is wearing more diamonds than the dowager Duchess of Roxhaven."

The dowager was notorious for her fondness of glittery baubles.

"I believe that's Prince Rubalov," answered Wrexford. "The Russian military attaché who serves as the tsar's liaison with the senior officers at Horse Guards." He didn't need to add that the prince was one of the names on Pierson's list.

"I doubt he's ever seen a battlefield," she quipped. "But then again, the ballrooms and drawing rooms of London can be far more dangerous."

"A fact we would do well to remember," he said softly.

On that note, they reached the West Ante Room, where a contingent from the Foreign Office was greeting the guests before they entered the main reception room.

Belmont was one of the British diplomats handling the logistics. He greeted Wrexford and Charlotte with cool politeness—making no inquiry, noted the earl, to Peregrine's well-being.

Charlotte didn't miss the omission, either. "Let us hope he takes his government responsibilities more to heart than those of his family." Her tone had an ominous edge. She had taken an immediate dislike to the man. As had Wrexford. But that was good reason to make sure it didn't color their judgment.

"His career offers the possibility of advancement," replied

the earl. "While I imagine he sees no profit for himself in caring for his ward."

She took a moment to study the array of magnificent gilt-framed paintings that hung on the walls. "An interesting observation." She waited until a trio of Austrian officers, resplendent in dark blue-and-canary yellow uniforms dripping with gold braid, passed by them before adding, "Perhaps we should consider adding him to our list." Belmont wasn't one of Pierson's suspects.

"Being an arse is not the same as being a traitor," he said dryly.

"True. But the two aren't mutually exclusive."

"Ah, Wrexford!" Lord Bethany, the secretary of the Royal Society, approached and made a courtly bow to Charlotte. "And Lady Wrexford. Allow me to offer my felicitations on your recent nuptials."

"Thank you, milord," said Charlotte. The two of them had met during an unfortunate incident at the Royal Botanic Gardens, though Bethany was gentlemanly enough not to refer to it. "I understand that a delegation of French scholars and men of science are visiting London as part of the Peace Celebrations."

"Indeed, milady! We are hosting a number of joint lectures at Somerset House and the Royal Institution during the coming months to share our scientific and mathematical knowledge with the public."

"I look forward to attending a number of them," said Wrexford. "Monsieur La Chaze has done some very interesting work in the field of chemistry."

"High praise from you, sir," said Bethany, and then made a face as a group of gentlemen just inside the archway of the Crimson Drawing Room called for him to join them. "If you will excuse me," he said apologetically, "I ought to go keep my French colleagues company."

"But of course," said Charlotte. Her gaze went back to the paintings, which included some very fine works by Rembrandt and Titian. "I've heard that the Prince Regent possesses a remarkable art collection. I see that the gossip isn't mere exaggeration."

She sighed. "No wonder the government is concerned about his profligate spending habits. They worry that when he becomes king, he may beggar the country."

"I hope you're not suggesting we put Prinny on our list," drawled Wrexford.

"He's a selfish narcissist, who lacks any moral scruples," she replied, though in a low whisper that only he could hear.

"He's also too lazy and self-absorbed to be a ringleader of a dangerous conspiracy." He offered his arm. "Shall we join the festivities?"

The room, which had taken its name from the sumptuous blood-red velvet draperies that festooned the window casements and wall niches, was already growing uncomfortably warm from the press of bodies.

Wrexford plucked two glasses of chilled champagne from the tray of a passing footman and passed one to Charlotte. "I see my friend Sir Henry Phelps, a senior administrator in the prime minister's office, chatting with Prince Rubalov and his staff. Let us go join them."

The tiny muscles of Charlotte's jaw were beginning to ache with the effort of keeping a polite smile pasted on her face, while Wrexford discussed politics with the gentlemen. She was leaving the verbal probing to him. Rather than risk ruffling the feathers of the pompous diplomats—something she ordinarily would enjoy—she had decided that watching their subtle facial reactions would be more valuable.

One of the Russians in particular had caught her eye. He had been introduced as the private secretary to Prince Rubalov, and was an ordinary-looking fellow—mouse-brown hair, unremarkable features, slender build, not a glimmer of decorative baubles adorning his dark evening clothes. It was his razor-like gaze, sharp with intelligence, that drew her attention. That, and the fact that he seemed to be watching the people around them with the same veiled intensity as she was.

"Are you interested in art, Mr. Kurlansky?" asked Charlotte, pretending to think he was studying one of the nearby paintings rather than the senior British diplomat who had just joined the conversation.

"I admire creativity," he replied. "But I don't claim to have the expertise to appreciate the fine points of a painting."

"Perhaps one doesn't have to be an expert to enjoy looking at one," she said lightly.

Her words drew a tiny smile. "A very astute observation, milady. You're quite right to point out that it can be a mistake to overanalyze a subject." Kurlansky turned slightly for a better view of the striking full-length portrait of a Georgian lady by Gainsborough.

"The Honorable Mrs. Grant," he read from the tiny brass plaque affixed to the frame. "I would have thought that a lovely lady would want to be depicted as happy and carefree. And yet, she appears . . . pensive."

"You think ladies aren't capable of serious thoughts?"

This time, his smile was more pronounced. "I don't presume to claim to have a clue as to how the female mind works."

"Quite right, Kurlansky," bellowed one of the other Russians. "Females are flighty creatures. No point in trying to make sense of them, ha, ha, ha."

Sir Henry glanced at Charlotte and gave a pointed cough.

"Ah—forgive me, milady," added the Russian hastily. "I—I meant no offense."

"None taken," replied Charlotte.

The awkward silence that settled over the gentlemen was

quickly broken by Alison's arrival in a swirl of sea-blue silk. "If you gentlemen will excuse us, I wish to steal away my niece and introduce her to the Chevalier de Fontaine."

"But of course," murmured Sir Henry, a sentiment dutifully echoed by the others.

The dowager slowed her steps as soon as they were out of earshot and drew Charlotte behind a large plinth holding a massive vase of flowers. "Are you and Wrexford up to some new intrigue?"

"Why do you ask?" replied Charlotte.

"Because the Weasels mentioned that they and Wrexford had fished a body out of the Serpentine. And the victim—Mr. Jeremiah Willis—once appeared in a drawing by A. J. Quill on technical innovators."

Damnation. Her great-aunt was too sharp by half.

Charlotte wanted to prevaricate. That the government might be privy to her secret could threaten her loved ones if they became involved in any clandestine activities. But she knew that half-truths could also lead to trouble.

Consoling herself with the thought that Alison's connections within the highest circles of Society might prove very useful to their investigation, Charlotte sighed and then glanced around before replying.

"Yes," she said softly, "we're investigating Mr. Willis's death. But as it involves some highly sensitive information, it could put us all in grave danger if we're not very careful."

Alison nodded in understanding. "What can I do to help?"

"First of all, you must promise me you won't try to ferret out information on your own."

Alison had evinced an alarming enthusiasm for helping to solve crimes in several of their earlier investigations. That she was rather good at it was even more frightening.

"I'm deadly serious," stressed Charlotte. "The enemy might be a rogue element of a foreign power"—*Or our own govern-*

ment—"who won't hesitate to eliminate anyone who stands in their way."

The dowager's eyes took on a martial gleam. "Then we shall have to outwit them."

Charlotte smiled in spite of her fears. "While Wrexford is chatting with the Russians, I'm interested in meeting two gentlemen in particular . . ." She gave Alison the names of a Prussian military attaché and a senior adjutant who served on the staff of Prince Metternich, the Austrian foreign minister.

"What about the French?" asked Alison.

"We have reason to believe the missing information will be put up for auction while all the Allied sovereigns are gathered here in England. France's finances are precarious. I don't think the country is in a position to participate."

"Don't underestimate the support that Napoleon still has among radical thinkers throughout Europe," said Alison softly. "There are many people who wish to see all monarchies replaced by republics, and understand how such a fundamental change would open up a number of new financial opportunities."

"You think Napoleon has a plan to retake the throne . . ." Charlotte caught herself. "We'll discuss that later." It was best they didn't draw attention to themselves by lingering any longer in the shadows. "For now, let us—"

"Let us go meet the Chevalier de Fontaine, who happens to be a cousin by marriage to the Austrian attaché you wish to meet."

Alison's encyclopedic knowledge of aristocratic bloodlines provided the perfect excuse for approaching the foreigners and inquiring about the well-being of various relatives. The gentlemen were delighted to engage in pleasantries rather than politics—along with a little harmless flirting—and Charlotte was well pleased with the acquaintances she had made. Diplomats, especially the French and the Russians, had a reputation for enjoying both wine and women. Which, she decided, could be made to work in her favor. A man in his cups was likely to allow indiscretions to slip out during conversation . . .

Seeing Alison pat back a discreet yawn after they had circulated through several clusters of gentlemen, she quickly insisted they seek out a seat in one of the side rooms.

"Thank you, my dear," said the dowager as she settled into one of the plush armchairs. "I shall just sit for a bit." She gave a little wave. "You go and join Wrexford."

"First let me fetch you a glass of ratafia—"

"I would rather you allow me to do so," said a voice from just behind her.

"Sir Robert!" exclaimed Alison, her face wreathing in a smile.

Charlotte turned to add her greetings to the baronet, who was one of the dowager's oldest and dearest friends.

"And that way I can join you for a comfortable coze," he continued as he inclined a courtly bow, "rather than endure any more of the uncomfortable crush in the drawing room."

Looking up, he waggled his brows. "Prinny is in a devil of a temper. Tsar Alexander is late in arriving, and he's certain it's meant as an insult."

"Prinny is probably right," remarked Charlotte. The Prince Regent had taken a sulky dislike to the handsome, charismatic Russian emperor—who was far more popular with the English public than he was—and so had made a point of inflicting petty little snubs. Alexander enjoyed returning the favor, which piqued the prince's vanity.

"One would hope that such powerful world leaders might behave with a modicum of maturity," said Alison.

Sir Robert gave a cynical chuckle. "Hope may spring eternal, my dear Lady Peake. But human nature is all too predictable."

"True," agreed Alison. "Do go join Wrexford," she repeated to Charlotte. "Sir Robert will keep me company."

Leaving the dowager and her friend, Charlotte returned to

the Crimson Drawing Room. It was even more crowded, and the cacophony of all the various languages twining with the heat and the overperfumed air was making her head ache.

Wrexford was nowhere to be seen, but she spotted Cordelia conversing with several gentlemen by one of the arched windows. Squeezing her way to the perimeter of the room, Charlotte started to make her way over to the group.

"Lady Wrexford?"

Charlotte hesitated for just a fraction before turning to see who had greeted her. She was still getting used to her new title.

She found herself facing a military officer. His face wasn't familiar, but she recognized his uniform as that of an American naval captain. "Yes?" she said politely.

His smile transformed his rather homely features. One wouldn't ever call him handsome, but the spark that suddenly came to light in his sea-blue eyes was arresting.

"Forgive me for breaching the rules of etiquette, but I heard your name mentioned just now and wanted to be sure to pass on felicitations regarding your recent marriage from my fellow officer, Captain Samuel Daggett."

"You're friends with Captain Daggett?" At his nod, her smile widened. Daggett had recently played a critical role in helping her and Wrexford stop a nefarious plot that would have hurt a great many people. "How delightful. I trust he is well?"

"He is, madam," replied the American, who then quickly bowed. "Please allow me to introduce myself—I am Captain Tobias Hockett."

"It's a pleasure to meet you, sir," responded Charlotte. "I must say, I'm very glad that our two countries have agreed to begin negotiating a peace treaty. As we've seen here in Europe, war wreaks immeasurable pain and suffering. Let us hope we can all learn to live in harmony."

"A noble sentiment, milady," replied Hockett. "As our two countries plan to meet in August to start our peace talks—and as the European diplomats convene in Vienna this autumn to draft treaties and various economic and social agreements—let us indeed hope that the pen can prove mightier than the sword."

However, Charlotte noted that he didn't sound very sanguine.

"Are you part of the American delegation that was recently sent here to work with the British Foreign Office on preventing any further naval clashes between our two countries, now that we're both looking to avoid further hostilities?"

"I am engaged in some of those discussions. But for the most part, I'm merely here as part of my country's show of respect for Britain and the Allied nations who defeated Napoleon."

Another modest answer. Perhaps *too* modest.

"And now, please don't let me detain you any longer. You appeared on your way to join friends," said Hockett smoothly. "However, I look forward to furthering our acquaintance over the coming weeks."

Charlotte watched him move away into one of the side salons, wondering how much Daggett had told him about her and Wrexford . . . and their involvement with the Crown and its clandestine activities. She had a feeling that she hadn't seen the last of him.

Turning her attention back to Cordelia, she saw that her friend was still engaged in an animated discussion with several men and resumed making her way to join the group.

"So, if you take the hypotenuse of the triangle and square it, then divide it by X plus . . ."

As she approached, she heard that the talk was about mathematics, which likely meant—

"Charlotte!" Cordelia's face lit up. "Come, allow me to introduce you to Monsieur Rochambert, a brilliant mathematician who is visiting London as part of the scientific delegation accompanying the French king."

Ah, yes—Sheffield's nemesis, thought Charlotte as she smiled politely at the Frenchman. The fellow, she noted, had beauty to go along with his brains. Tall and slender, with a crown of gilded curls, he had the fine-boned features of a Botticelli angel . . .

And the devil's own smile.

"*Enchanté*, Lady Wrexford," said Rochambert, bending over her hand after Cordelia had performed the formalities. "Though Lady Cordelia greatly exaggerates the scope of my knowledge."

"Lady Cordelia is not prone to exaggerating, especially about a subject as serious as mathematics," said Charlotte dryly.

"Monsieur Rochambert is doing fascinating work in the field of measuring the speed and trajectory of moving objects."

"He's exploring ways to refine the equations of Newton's calculus," piped up one of the Frenchman's companions.

Charlotte shrugged in apology. "Alas, I fear that such genius is entirely wasted on me. I'm fortunate that I can get simple numbers—like four and eight—to add up correctly."

The Frenchman chuckled.

"Raven will be over the moon to meet Monsieur Rochambert!" said Cordelia. To Rochambert, she explained, "Lady Wrexford's ward Thomas—we all call him Raven—is quite gifted in mathematics."

"Lady Cordelia is tutoring him in the subject," added Charlotte.

"Then he's a very fortunate young man," replied Rochambert, a spark of admiration flashing in his eyes as he looked at Cordelia.

Who blushed like a schoolgirl.

Oh, dear, thought Charlotte. Though to her, his Gallic charm seemed a little too effusive.

The other gentleman with Cordelia was Charles White, an acquaintance of Wrexford's, and a fellow member of the Royal Institution who taught mathematics at Oxford.

"Quite right, monsieur," he said. "It's a pity our leading scientific institutions don't allow women to be members. Lady Cordelia can think rings around many of my male colleagues."

"A radical idea," Rochambert observed with a smile.

"Not as radical as some of France's upheavals of the Old Order," replied White. "Though I must admit, Bonaparte's knowledge of mathematics is very impressive. I can't think of any other head of state who has a mathematical theorem named after him."

"Yes, Napoleon's Theorem," replied Rochambert. "Science was lucky in France, perhaps because the emperor respected its rational approach to solving practical problems, as well as seeking answers to the mysteries of the universe. Despite the constant wars, those of us in scientific fields were allowed to work in relative peace."

Rochambert hesitated. "I'm grateful that France was enlightened enough not to allow politics to interfere with science."

"And yet," said White, "France sent Antoine Lavoisier, one of the greatest men of science in the history of your country, to the guillotine."

A flush of color darkened Rochambert's cheekbones. "There were tragic excesses during the early years of the Revolution."

Charlotte noted that he didn't condemn them.

"Indeed," murmured White, and didn't press the point.

A glance at Cordelia showed that she was looking . . . uncertain. And then, as a flutter of movement drew her gaze to the shadows cast by the folds of the velvet draperies, Charlotte gave an inward oath.

Sheffield was standing there, still as a statue. Judging by his expression, she surmised that he had overheard everything.

A hail from nearby drew Rochambert's attention. "If you will excuse me," he murmured, "it appears that the head of my delegation wishes to introduce me to the group from Vienna."

"Ah—I've been wanting to meet von Holtz," said White. "I'll come with you."

The two of them bowed and moved off, leaving Charlotte and Cordelia alone . . . but only for a moment.

Charlotte allowed another silent oath as Sheffield stepped forward. There was a wobble to his step—she suspected he had imbibed a few-too-many glasses of champagne—and a dangerous glint to his smile.

"I wonder," he said, "how many hours it takes for Froggy to tie his cravat in such a perfectly precise Mathematical?" The Mathematical was the name of a style currently in vogue among the gentlemen of the beau monde. "One to arrange all the folds, plus two to admire his own reflection in the looking glass?"

Cordelia drew in a shaky breath . . .

And then stalked away without uttering a word.

"Oh, dear. Did I say something wrong?" inquired Sheffield, though an undertone of remorse belied his sarcasm.

"Not at all," said Wrexford, who had come up behind Charlotte. "You couldn't have been more articulate about the fact that you're a donkey's arse."

Sheffield bristled . . . and then, as if stuck with a pin, his bravado deflated. "How can she admire such a prancing popinjay?"

Charlotte felt her heart clench in sympathy. "I think perhaps you're adding up two and two—and getting five. It's not that simple. Yes, she admires his achievements in mathematics, but as for anything else—"

"He's very handsome," said Sheffield softly.

"I think . . ." The subject was damnable complicated. And he was clearly in no frame of mind to deal with nuances. "I think Cordelia has proven to all of us that she's not some flighty peagoose in danger of being seduced by a wink and a smile."

Sheffield hung his head.

"Come," said Wrexford, taking him firmly by the arm. "You've had enough of Prinny's champagne, and I've had enough of wolf-eat-wolf politics for one evening. Let us return to Berkeley Square, where we can all clear our heads with a pot of strong coffee."

The short carriage ride quickly brought them home. Charlotte breathed in deeply as she descended to the pavement. The evening breeze, redolent with the floral scents of summer, was a blessed relief after the stale air of Carlton House. The night's stillness was also welcome. The only sound, save for the rustling leaves, was the gentle twittering of birdsong within the fenced garden in the center of the square.

Moonlight dappled the flagged walkway leading to the town house's imposing entrance . . .

The door opened before Wrexford could lift the brass knocker.

"Good evening, milord." Riche's calm voice gave nothing away, but Charlotte knew the butler well enough to see the tautness of his shoulders. He waited for the three of them to step into the entrance hall, and then quietly shut the door.

"This arrived for you an hour ago." Riche handed the earl a note. "I hope I didn't err in not sending it on directly to Carlton House, but the messenger . . ." A cough. "There was no messenger. When I came to answer the knock, I found it had been slipped under the door."

Wrexford cracked the seal—which was, noted Charlotte, a simple circle of cheap black wax, with no distinguishing markings—and unfolded the paper.

"Hmmph."

"What the devil is that supposed to mean?" asked Sheffield.

"It means that the first move has just been made on the chessboard," said the earl as he handed it to Charlotte. "Signaling that the real game has now begun."

CHAPTER 10

"Shhhh," hissed Raven as Hawk pulled out a pair of shabby, muck-encrusted boots from a wooden storage box and shut the lid with an audible click. He crawled over and helped his brother maneuver it back under the bed. "I'd rather not wake Falcon and have him see us in our *other* plumage."

Hawk grinned as he tugged on a threadbare jacket and settled a tattered cap low on his brow. "Oiy, we'd have to explain why we ain't looking like little peacocks of the ton."

"Keep your voice down," cautioned Raven, darting a look at the door to the adjoining room. He and his brother were currently sharing one of the two connected bedchambers on the floor of the townhouse occupied by the schoolroom. Peregrine had been given the other one for the duration of his London visit.

The warning, however, was too late. A tiny rustling caught his ear. In a flash, he grabbed the door latch and yanked it open.

Peregrine sat back on his haunches and stared at them in stoic silence, his expression unreadable.

"Hell's bells, you must have awfully good hearing," muttered Hawk. "We hardly made a sound."

"I *wasn't* spying, if that's what you think," replied Peregrine in a whisper. "I—I heard a noise and was curious." He eyed their grimy clothing. "You don't have to worry that I'm going to tell tales to His Lordship and Her Ladyship. I—I can keep a secret."

"We've nothing to hide from them—" began Hawk, before his brother silenced him with a nudge.

Despite the glint of interest that lit his eyes, Peregrine refrained from asking any questions. Instead, he merely shrugged. "S'all right. I understand that you don't feel you can trust me." He looked away, throwing his face completely in shadow. "The boys at Eton all jeer at me, saying that dark skin means a dark—and savage—heart."

Hawk looked at Raven, who hesitated, and then let out a reluctant snort. "Be damned with the little popinjays of Eton. My guess is they're too dull-witted to appreciate anyone who's different."

"Oiy," chirped Hawk. "Wrex and m'lady are of the opinion that unconventional people are the most interesting."

Peregrine considered the statement for a moment before replying. "I'm more than unconventional. I'm Black—"

"Actually, m'lady would say you're the color of café au lait," drawled Raven.

"That's because the French put a lot of milk in their coffee," explained Hawk helpfully.

"Yes, well, I have a lot of milk running through my veins," replied Peregrine. "I'm a quadroon—my mother was mulatto and my father was White. But that doesn't stop people from calling me an evil Blackamoor." He paused, his chin angling up in challenge. "I'll wager a guinea you've never met anyone like me."

Raven and Hawk exchanged grins.

"You've just lost a pile of pretty pennies, Falcon," crowed Hawk. "Several of our best friends are Blackamoors."

"Y-You're bamming me."

"Nay, I'm not!" assured Hawk. "In fact, we were just about to fly off and visit Smoke, who spends his nights in an area near the docklands that's known for its gambling dens."

"We would invite you to come along," said Raven slowly, "but I don't suppose you know how to make your way down a high wall without a ladder, or move swiftly and silently through the night."

"Would you care to wager a guinea on that?" shot back Peregrine. "I've spent a great many nights climbing down from my window at Belmont Manor so I could explore the surrounding woods and feel . . ."

He drew in a breath. "And feel like I could, for a short while, escape from my uncle's disdain."

A gust of wind rattled against the windowglass. The sound died quickly, leaving the room shrouded in silence.

Raven turned away.

"Very well." He crouched down and began to rummage beneath his bed. "We'll give you a chance to win back your loss. But be forewarned—if you're not up to snuff in climbing down from here, you'll have to wait until we can sharpen your skills before venturing out with us. The stews of London aren't forgiving if you make a mistake."

"That's fair," agreed Peregrine.

"Put these on." Raven tossed him a bundle of filthy clothes.

"*Fawwgh!*" Peregrine crinkled his nose. "They stink."

"That's the point," said Hawk. "You have to blend in with the surroundings."

"One last thing. There are two ironclad rules you have to follow if you're going to come along. The first is, you have to do *exactly* as we order without hesitation. And secondly, you have to promise to keep mum when we get to the docklands," counseled Raven. "It's a different world down there, and one fancy word out of your mouth could put us all in danger."

"Oiy." Hawk quickly lapsed into the local slang of the Wapping Street area. "Ye twaddle yer gob and sound like a niffy-piffy toff, and the local cullies will yank yer liver out through yer gullet."

Peregrine's eyes widened. "How did you learn to speak like that?"

"Never mind that now," said Raven. "Hurry and get dressed. We need to fly now in order to be back here before dawn."

"What are we going to be doing in the docklands?"

Raven worked open the heavy brass latch of the casement windows and pushed them open. "Actually, there's a third rule. Don't ask any questions."

"What does it say?" demanded Sheffield as Wrexford drew the door to the workroom shut.

"It's a note from Pierson, indicating that our government has received an invitation to be part of the auction for Willis's invention," he replied. "As a condition of entering the competition, every invitee must agree to the minimum bid of . . ."

Wrexford looked up and named a figure that made everyone blink.

"And furthermore," he went on, "they must all deposit the actual money in an account at Hoares Bank designated by the villains. The bank administrators have been instructed that only one of the deposits—the original deposit of the eventual winner of the auction, plus the additional amount needed to make up their winning offer—will eventually be transferred to another account designated by the villains in a bank outside England."

"And from there, it will quickly become untraceable," mused Sheffield.

The earl nodded. "Every other deposit is simply to be returned to the bidder who originally made it." He paused. "However, in order to play in this heinous game, the parties must make their deposit by the time of the Prince Regent's party at the Royal Ascot horse races, which take place the day after to-morrow, and hand over the deposit slip as proof."

"But—" began Tyler.

"Before you suggest it," said Wrexford, "the Hoares bankers appear to have no reason to believe that this is other than a legitimate commercial competition, and our government has been warned that an attempt to exert any sort of pressure on the bankers would result in Willis's invention being offered directly to our most despised rival."

"Merciful heavens," whispered Charlotte, "these criminals are exceedingly cunning."

"Their plan is even more clever than you think." Wrexford made a face. "All the countries who might be candidates to play this game doubtlessly have large bank balances at various institutions in the London market, so the transfers can be made to Hoares on the tight time schedule. Moreover, nearly each of the most important heads of state and finance ministers are now all gathered here in London for the Peace Celebrations, allowing the villains to run their dastardly auction with a lightning speed that would otherwise be impossible if they were in their own countries."

"And speed makes it even harder for us to try to stop them," said Charlotte.

Wrexford's expression turned even grimmer. "Precisely."

"But when and where will all the parties gather to hold the auction itself?" asked Tyler. "Won't that make them vulnerable—"

"Ah, there's the rub," said Wrexford "You're thinking of the traditional auction format—which, by the by, is called an English auction—where the bidders all gather together with a presiding auctioneer and shout out their competing offers until one bidder finally offers a price that all the others decline to match." He paused. "In other words, the way Sotheby's might auction off a painting by one of the Old Masters."

"But isn't that the way an auction always works?" protested Tyler.

"In this case, the villains can hardly announce a time and place for such a gathering of the bidders," Wrexford pointed out. "Every intelligence service in Europe would be there to swoop up whoever was running the process. Not to mention that none of the bidders would care to show their faces and be caught red-handed trafficking in a state secret stolen from Britain."

Sheffield suddenly sat up straighter. "I'll wager that I know what they have in mind! In the course of running a business, I've come to learn there are other ways of structuring an auction."

The earl was impressed that Sheffield was aware of other, more sophisticated procedures for running an auction that would meet the needs of the villains to keep the process private. "Go on, Kit."

"Our company occasionally participates in auctions for raw materials—all quite legal and honorable, I should note. But sometimes it's not practical to assemble bidders who are spread out throughout the country. So instead, each participant submits a sealed bid for the goods being sold."

Sheffield frowned as he continued to think. "But having participated in this type of sealed-bid auction, I'm aware there are drawbacks. Since you don't know what the other parties are prepared to pay, as you do in an English auction, you're always concerned that you might end up overpaying, based on what others are willing to bid, so you tend to hold back from your true maximum bid."

"That makes some sense," murmured Tyler.

"But the sellers are aware of this and so they will often reveal the highest price offered in the first round of sealed bids and allow the leading bidders to submit another round of sealed offers. This helps to simulate the competition of an open auction, and can go on for several rounds."

Sheffield paused again. "But in this case, the villains need this to happen quickly, so they can avoid detection and be gone with their ill-gotten gains before they can be stopped. And it needs to be wrapped up before the Peace Celebrations are over and the world leaders return home. So they want one round of bidding that somehow secures everyone's absolute best offer." A pause. "One and done, so to speak."

"One and done—a neat turn of phrase, Kit. I shall remember that." Wrexford then felt his smile slip away. "Unfortunately, our adversaries have come up with a fiendishly brilliant solution to the conundrum."

The flickering lamplight showed that Charlotte's face had gone deathly pale.

"According to Pierson's note," Wrexford explained, "once the slips confirming the required deposit are collected at the Royal Ascot races, all the bidders who paid up will be given the information for how to submit their final bid—"

"I imagine they will take the added precaution of having it delivered by an agent who won't know who is behind the plan," said Sheffield. "Or what's at stake."

Wrexford nodded in agreement. "Now, as Kit pointed out, their challenge is to get the best possible price when they can't run a traditional bidding war. And here's how they've solved it."

A hiss and crackling sounded from the hearth as a chunk of the coals crumbled to embers.

"The auction will be won by the party who presents the highest bid in the one—and only one—round of bidding." A pause. "But that winner will only be required to pay the price offered by the second-highest bidder."

"Wait—that doesn't seem so clever!" exclaimed Tyler. "By taking only the second-highest bid, won't the villains risk losing significant quid?"

"Actually, it's damnably clever," replied Wrexford.

"I don't see why," retorted Tyler. "It makes no logical sense—"

"I think I'm beginning to see what Wrex means." Sheffield rose abruptly and began to pace. "Let's look again at the English auction. The format allows you to compare your own idea of what the goods are truly worth against the offers of the other competitors. You'll keep bidding until you reach the maximum of what you're willing to pay—then you either prevail or drop out if others top your bid."

The others all nodded in understanding.

"The dilemma in a sealed-bid auction where you only have one chance to make an offer is how to come up with the maximum amount you're willing to pay," continued Sheffield. "You want to win, but you don't want to overpay."

"Bloody hell," muttered Tyler. "Stop talking in circles! My head is beginning to spin."

"Very well," said Wrexford. "I find it fascinating to work through every step in the thought process, but let us skip over all the details and simply explain why the villains have come up with such an ingenious solution."

The room went silent. Even the lamp flames seemed to hold themselves very still.

"The bottom line is," continued the earl, "the villains have created an auction in which the optimum bidding strategy for all the competitors is to offer the absolute full amount of what they feel the goods are worth in their first and only bid. A lesser bid puts them in danger of losing out, even though they were willing to pay more. And these auction rules ensure that they aren't at risk of paying more than is necessary to best the competition because they are only required to pay the amount of the second-highest bid."

Sheffield expelled a pent-up breath. "Moreover, no bidder would risk bidding more than their own highest estimate of the actual value, because if someone else also did the same thing, then the second-highest bid might also be above what the goods are actually worth. So everyone should just offer their own highest estimate—no more, no less—without trying to guess what the others might bid."

Tyler let out a low whistle. "I've never heard of anything quite like it."

"Actually, I have." Charlotte, who had remained unnaturally silent throughout the discussion, finally spoke up. "And it comes from my world of the arts. A number of years ago, Johann Wolfgang von Goethe—arguably the greatest figure in the history of German literature—was trying to sell a long epic poem he had just written. I've heard that he used some auction process that involved this element of paying only the second-highest price offered."

"Yes," said Wrexford. "I, too, thought of the same incident with Goethe—though that's a story for another day and involved some other factors. In the case of our immediate problem, however, whoever was smart enough to craft this auction arrangement had the genius to meet all the needs of our villains for a quick and hard-to-detect process producing the maximum potential profit."

"Genius of an evil sort," murmured Charlotte.

"Damnation," said Sheffield. He eyed Wrexford with a troubled look. "This is challenging enough—and you are making it more difficult. If I knew exactly what the stolen invention is, I could perhaps be more helpful in thinking about who the villains are."

Wrexford considered the oblique request. He hadn't yet told Tyler the exact nature of Willis's invention, either. Not because he didn't trust them. On the contrary, he knew they would keep any confidences a secret, no matter what was done to pry it out of them.

"Kit, at the risk of repeating myself and having you ring a peal—"

"The less you tell me, the better," interjected Sheffield. "Fine. I shall accept that—with good grace, I might add—if you can honestly tell me that you would do the same if our positions were reversed."

Damnation. The earl tried to come up with some quirk of logic to swing the needle of his moral compass in the desired direction.

"I thought not," murmured their friend when Wrexford remained silent.

"Sheffield has a point, milord," added Tyler. "Given the complexities of the situation"—he glanced at Charlotte—"we need to know exactly what we're dealing with. Otherwise, we may miss a critical clue." A pause. "Or make an inadvertent misstep that could put one of us in danger."

Charlotte caught Wrexford's eye. She said nothing . . .

But words weren't necessary.

"Very well," he conceded. "In a nutshell, the situation is this—the government has asked me to ferret out who stole the technical plans for Willis's invention, and to get it back before it's sold to another country, which may very well change the balance of power in Europe—"

"Yes, we know all that. But what the devil is it?" demanded Sheffield.

He held up his hand. "I'll answer that in a moment. But an even more important bit of information to know is the fact that our own government may be setting a trap for us, too."

His gaze strayed for a moment to the flicking flame of his desk lamp. "So that they may kill two birds with one stone."

"Ye gods, why would they wish . . ." Sheffield stopped abruptly as the answer dawned on him. "Y-You mean A. J. Quill."

"You have to admit," said Charlotte, "that I've been a thorn in the government's arse for a long time."

Sheffield had gone ghostly pale. "But how did they . . ." He blinked. "Did one of us inadvertently—"

"As I've always said, no secret, however carefully hidden, is ever truly safe," answered Charlotte.

"Actually, we're not certain the government knows," explained Wrexford. "But it's best to assume the worst."

"And you worry that we may be hurt in any ensuing scandal?" asked Sheffield.

"Both of you have secrets." Wrexford had never pressed Tyler for the intimate details of his life. But he sensed there was some darkness that was best left buried. As for Sheffield . . .

"And if they came to light," he said slowly, "each of you would find your reputation ruined."

"Seeing as mine was never very good to begin with, I've little to lose," quipped Sheffield.

"Yes, you do," said Charlotte softly. The beau monde would be horrified to learn that a gentleman was sullying his hands by working in trade. Sheffield would find himself shunned. "Being ostracized from Society is more terrible than you can imagine."

She closed her eyes for an instant. "But even more terrible is betraying your own principles because it's expedient." Sheffield knew of her complicated past, and the years she had spent as an outcast. "Life is full of risks, and I'm willing to take this one. To back away from challenges because of fear is worse than any defeat that one might suffer in the fray."

"Right," added Tyler dryly. "What's the fun of cowering in safety when thumbing your nose at authority is so much more exhilarating?"

"But I don't want either of you to have your lives ruined by my choice—"

"With all due respect, Charlotte, that's insufferably insulting," interrupted Sheffield. "The choice about what we do isn't yours. It's for us to decide. And I don't need to think twice about where my loyalties lie."

"Nor do I," said Tyler.

"The two of you are idiots," muttered the earl, though a telltale twitch of his mouth belied the insult.

"Of course we are idiots—we're friends with you, aren't we?" Sheffield moved to the sideboard. After pouring out four measures of Scottish malt and passing them around, he smiled and voiced a toast. "To friendship, no matter where it leads."

Candlelight winked off the raised glasses, flickers of whisky-gold light illuminating their faces.

"And now," added Sheffield, after polishing off his drink in one quick swallow, "I think it's bloody well time you tell us exactly what Willis's revolutionary invention is."

"Hawk and I will go first," said Raven, after slithering out to the narrow ledge. "Watch carefully as to how we make our way over to the ivy vines, and where we put our feet as we climb down."

Hawk quickly joined him.

"You really don't want to make a mistake. One small slip and your head could end up cracked open like an egg."

Peregrine leaned out and stared down at the back garden. A silvery mist floated through the plantings, blurring the contours and making the ground look soft as spun sugar.

"Don't be fooled by how unthreatening it looks," counseled Raven. He tapped his brother on the shoulder. "Follow me."

"Why were you deliberately trying to frighten him?" asked Hawk, once they had shimmied across to the thick vines of ivy growing up the decorative limestone corner facing of the town house.

"Because if he's prone to wetting himself at the first sign of danger, he'll only be a liability down at the docks," answered Raven. "I didn't want to hurt his feelings, but I wouldn't be unhappy if he chooses discretion over valor."

"Are we expecting trouble?"

The sound of boot leather scrabbling over stone rose above the rustling of the leaves.

"Hard to say." Raven squinted through the thickening vapor.

"Nothing rattles Wrex, and yet he appears unsettled by this investigation."

"You think—" Hawk suddenly winced as Peregrine materialized from the mist and nearly lost his footing. He shot out a hand and caught the other boy's sleeve.

"Steady," he said. "Take a deep breath and get your balance."

"Oiy, we've no time for lollygagging!" Raven was already moving with agile grace down through the twisted vines. A moment later his feet hit the earth with a soft thud. He looked up to see Hawk release his handhold and drop to the ground with practiced ease.

Peregrine was right behind him and showing no sign of fear. Without hesitation, he swung his legs out to clear one of the ornamental bushes and let go of the ivy.

"The climb down from Belmont Manor is more complicated," he said after landing with nary a stumble. "There are no vines, so you have to work your way down by using the decorative stone as handholds."

Raven gave a small nod. "You've got quickness and balance. You better have stamina as well. We may need to do some fast running." He crouched down and scooped up some dirt to rub on his face.

After fixing Peregrine with a critical squint, he added, "Your skin's pretty light, so you had better do the same."

Hawk removed his hat and worked some muck into his hair. "Right. The more disgusting we look, the better."

"I—I imagine we would get in big trouble if Lord or Lady Wrexford knew of this," said Peregrine as he dutifully smeared himself with mud.

"Never mind that now," replied Raven. "I'll remind you again of the rules—keep your mouth shut, and stick to us like a cocklebur. If you get lost in the stews, we can't answer for your safety."

A nod acknowledged the orders.

"From now on, you're not a lordly aristocrat," said Hawk. "You've got to shake off all your stiff-rumped formality. Think of yourself as a lowly little rabbit moving through a forest full of predators. Stay alert, and be ready to react at the first glimmer of danger."

"We won't think any less of you if you'd rather not come," counseled Raven. "We can teach you a few basic things before you—"

"I won't slow you down," said Peregrine. "I promise."

Raven's brows gave a skeptical twitch. "You shouldn't make promises unless you're sure you can keep them. And when you venture into the stews, you never know what's going to happen." With that, he turned, and with a quick wave motioned for them to follow.

Wrexford swirled the remaining whisky in his glass, and let the amber liquid slowly settle into a placid calm before answering Sheffield's question. "Willis's invention appears to be some sort of technical innovation that allows firearms to fire multiple shots without reloading," he began.

"Are you implying that you don't know for sure?" interjected Sheffield, a note of skepticism shading his question.

"Yes," he answered. "I only know what I saw on the rough sketch I found on Willis's body."

"But surely Pierson explained—"

"The government has been awfully secretive about the project from the start," said Charlotte. She explained about trying to learn more about Willis's work when doing her series of prints on technical innovators, who were changing the old ways of doing things. "None of my sources were able to discover any details."

"I can understand why the government would wish to enforce such strict secrecy," mused Tyler. "Imagine an army equipped with long guns that could fire multiple shots in the time it takes to load one single shot in a traditional musket or rifle." His expression turned grave. "Such an innovation would all but guarantee dominance over Europe—"

"And perhaps the world," pointed out Wrexford. "What country could stand up to an assault by such weapons?"

The four of them sat in silence. To Charlotte, it felt as if the temperature in the room had turned several degrees colder.

"The answer is none," she said, more to herself than to the others.

Wrexford released a sharp breath. "While I applaud genius and the creative mind in theory," he said, "perhaps there are some cerebral challenges that are best left untouched." A pause. "I cannot say that I trust our government any more than I would trust others not to misuse such a potent power."

Their eyes met.

"Nor can I," agreed Charlotte.

"W-What are we going to do about the situation?" Sheffield pinched at the bridge of his nose. "It feels as if we're damned if we do as the government asks, and damned if we don't."

"For now, I think best that we just concentrate on getting our hands on the missing material," said Wrexford.

"But *how*?" asked Tyler.

"By improvising," said Charlotte, trying to sound more confident than she felt. There were at least four—and likely more—clever and ruthless countries, all scheming on how to get their hands on Willis's invention. It would be the height of hubris to think it would be easy to outmaneuver operatives whose whole world lay within the reptilian shadows of intrigue and betrayal.

"We're very good at improvising," murmured Wrexford, which drew a chuckle from Tyler.

"At times, we don't make it look pretty," said Sheffield, "but we get the job done."

Because we've been damnably lucky, she thought.

But Luck is notoriously fickle.

She shook off the mordant thought and quickly continued. "As Wrexford just told us, the game begins in earnest on the afternoon of horse racing and picnicking at Royal Ascot."

"In the meantime, I'll make some inquiries into auctions and the various ways of running them," said Sheffield. "That may give us a thread to follow."

Charlotte thought it unlikely, but having a mission might distract him from fretting about Cordelia—and doing something stupid that might irrevocably harm his friendship with her.

"And I'll continue my search through the underbelly of the city, rubbing shoulders with the type of men who offer themselves as cutthroats for hire," said Tyler. "I heard no rumors as of yet. But evil has a way of scenting evil."

Power and privilege. A frisson of fear tickled down Charlotte's spine.

"As we move through pomp and pageantry, we must not be blinded by the swirl of glittering lies and gilded deceit," she cautioned. "The clues to the truth will be there—we just have to see them." She hesitated. "And not be afraid to follow them, wherever they lead."

CHAPTER 11

The mist turned to fog as they got closer to the river. "This way," whispered Raven, after pausing to get his bearings. The three of them slipped down a side street that looked lined with windowless brick warehouses—dark, forbidding shapes jammed cheek to jowl in stolid slumber . . .

Until they crept through a crooked turn and a few flickers of lamplight revealed several fancy carriages waiting outside one of the buildings.

"Wait here." Raven made his way a little closer to the carriages and let out a low, feral-cat sound twice in succession. A shape—the silhouette of a boy slightly smaller than Raven— materialized from the gloom several moments later. Their heads came together briefly and then the two of them retreated to rejoin Hawk and Peregrine.

"In here," whispered Raven, indicating a narrow passageway between two of the warehouses.

"Ain't seen ye in a rat's age." A dribble of moonlight showed that the face of Raven's companion was black as coal. "Wot's ye been doing?"

"We've been busy, Smoke," replied Raven.

"Who's the new cully?" Smoke darted a curious look at Peregrine.

"His name's Falcon," said Hawk. "We've taken him under our wing—"

"Never mind Falcon." Raven pulled a small pouch from his pocket and held it out. A whiff of spiced tobacco twined with the less salubrious scents of piss and horse droppings. "We're looking for some information."

"Oiy!" Smoke quickly snatched the offering and tucked it away. "Wot's ye need?"

"Heard any jabbering about the body found in the Serpentine?" Smoke had recently drifted from doing odd jobs around the East India wharves to working at the exclusive gaming hell located in the nearby building. It had a reputation for attracting a clientele of dangerous criminals.

Which, in turn, attracted a certain type of aristocrat—those who also thought the rules of Society didn't apply to them.

"Sounds like yer working fer Magpie on this?" That was Charlotte's street persona when she ventured out dressed as a ragged urchin. It was known in the stews that she paid well for information. But only if it was accurate.

Raven ignored the half question. "If ye know anything, yer palm will be well greased."

Smoke hesitated, shifting his scrawny body just enough to glance nervously over his shoulder at the gloom-shrouded street.

"Ye know ye'll be paid generously," urged Raven.

"Oiy, but . . ." He dropped his whisper so that it was barely more than a breath of air. "The cove ain't someone ye diddle with. They say he's the sort that'll slice yer throat wivout batting an eyelash."

Raven leaned in and named a price.

Smoke wet his lips. "Hell's teeth. Why—"

"Just tell us wot ye know, and don't arsk any questions," countered Raven.

The sum he had named was a fortune for a street urchin. Smoke hesitated again, his face betraying the war between self-interest and self-preservation. The money, however, was too alluring to give up.

He pulled Raven even closer. "I wuz emptying the pisspots in one o' the private chambers when I overheard . . ." He quickly recounted the exchange.

"And ye know who it wuz?"

Smoke nodded and whispered a name.

Raven unbuttoned a hidden pocket inside his jacket and pulled out another pouch. The mellow *chink* of gold against gold sounded as it exchanged hands.

"Iffen ye value yer life, be careful about flashing it around," cautioned Raven as he handed it over.

Smoke gave a solemn nod. "I ain't a green gully." He slithered to the opening of the passageway and looked up and down the fog-shrouded street. "I better scarper. Stay here fer a tick before leaving."

"Oiy," agreed Raven, inching along the filthy brick wall just enough to be able to watch the weak flickers of lamplight from the carriages waiting outside the gambling hell. He waited, watching intently. One carriage pulled away and disappeared in the fog as it turned for the river. Another took its place, passing close to their hiding place.

Satisfied that all was quiet, Raven led them back out to Cable Street, but instead of cutting back in the direction of Mayfair, he continued straight ahead to Rosemary Lane.

"I want to make one more stop before we head home," he explained to the others. "I've a hunch that I wish to confirm."

Peregrine looked about to ask a question, but a warning glance from Hawk speared him to silence.

They walked on for several minutes before Raven led them

into an even narrower lane. The stench of sweet decay from the exposed muck of low tide grew more pronounced.

"I take it we're going to the Red Dragon," murmured Hawk. When his brother nodded, he caught hold of Peregrine's sleeve. "Stay close, Falcon, and be ready to fly like the wind the instant we give the word."

The Red Dragon—known to the London underworld as the Bloody Lizard—was a gambling club notorious for the dangerous carousing of its patrons. It attracted a sinister crowd.

"Sheffield comes here on occasion, and I heard him tell Wrex that whenever there's trouble brewing in London, the denizens of the Bloody Lizard know about it," said Raven, pausing to peer around a corner. "I want to ask Dilly if the gentleman that Smoke mentioned frequents the place."

Hawk turned to Peregrine. "Dilly's one of the barmaids. She's a friend of Alice the Eel Girl, who . . ." He shook his head. "Never mind. We'll explain all that later."

"We'll go that way," said Raven, indicating a narrow cart path leading to the rear of the building. "The privies are located on the other side, so there shouldn't be anyone around."

He cocked an ear, listening for any carriage sounds that might indicate a patron was about to arrive. Satisfied that the street was deserted, he darted across the cobblestones and ducked into the narrow gap, the others following close behind in single file.

"Wait there," said Raven in a low voice, pointing to the muddled shadows cast by several high stacks of empty wine crates and litter waiting to be carted away. "The kitchen and scullery are around—"

Whack! A gleam of brass winked for an instant as the blow from a gentleman's walking stick struck the back of Hawk's head.

"Thieving little vermin." The gentleman, the fall of his breeches still half unbuttoned from taking a piss, raised his stick again.

Raven reacted in a flash, darting in to shove their assailant off balance and drag his brother back toward the street. Softened by the thick wool hat, the strike from the lethal-looking metal ball atop the ebony stick had only stunned Hawk, and he quickly scrambled to his feet.

"*Merde,*" whispered Raven as he looked back, fear flaring in his eyes. The assailant—a big, muscled gentleman with a brutish sneer on his sharp-featured face—now stood between Peregrine and the path of escape.

A menacing *swoosh-swoosh* cut through the night as Sharp Face recovered his footing and swung the stick back and forth. "Looking to pick a pocket?" A nasty laugh. "I think not."

He took a step closer to Peregrine. "Instead, I'll rid the city of a filthy gutter rat."

Raven quickly pushed Hawk closer to the street. "Stay here," he ordered. "And be ready to run like the dev—" The rest of the word stuck in his throat as he turned and saw Peregrine snatch up a broken broom handle from the pile of litter and raise it just in time to parry the assailant's blow.

He froze in place, afraid of distracting Peregrine.

Sharp Face laughed again as Peregrine danced back and assumed a fencer's *en garde* stance. "A duel is for gentlemen." He tightened his grip on his stick, which was clearly designed for combat. "And why is it that I think you're not a gentleman?"

The glow of light seeping through the drawn draperies of the side window illuminated Peregrine's faint smile.

Goaded by the boy's show of calm, Sharp Face launched a flurry of blows—

Which Peregrine deftly parried.

Sharp Face stepped back, and then attacked again with even more fury. And again the boy met the offensive with a series of deft defensive maneuvers. Spinning away, he ducked under a vicious swipe and slashed out with a hard blow that buckled Sharp Face's knee.

"Holy hell," breathed Raven, his gaze narrowing in surprise.

With a grunt of pain, the assailant retreated, his face now black with rage. He feinted one way, and then the other, looking for an opening. But the boy matched his moves. A sudden lunge seemed to catch Peregrine off guard, but at the last instant, he sidestepped the attack, and countered with a swift stab with the broken end of the broom handle, which caught the gentleman flush on his groin.

An unholy howl rattled through the yard as Sharp Face crumpled to the ground.

"Fly, Falcon!" cried Raven, waving his arms frantically. Already there were sounds of alarm rumbling from inside the club.

Peregrine flung aside his makeshift weapon and raced for the street.

"Faster, faster!" urged Raven as he and Hawk started to run with him.

A porter burst out from the main entrance, armed with an iron cudgel, but the boys had already reached the maze of alleyways that spread out like a drunken spider's web from the adjoining street. Knowing the area like the back of his hand, Raven threaded through the zigzagging twists and turns at a dead run, checking frequently that Peregrine was keeping pace. It wasn't until they broke free of the fetid passageways and approached the main thoroughfare of Fenchurch Street that Raven slowed to a halt.

"Lud," he wheezed, when at last he managed to catch his breath. "Where in the name of Lucifer did you learn to fence like that?"

"Oiy—I thought the dastard was going to bash your brains out," said Hawk, wincing as he rubbed at the lump on his own head. And then he began to laugh. "If he doesn't have an heir already, he might never have another chance. That stick looked hellishly sharp."

Raven chortled, but Peregrine turned a little green around the gills. "A-Am I going to be in big trouble for what I did to him?"

"No," assured Raven. "To anyone who saw us, we were just a few of the countless faceless urchins who scavenge through the city."

"But His Lordship and Her Lady—"

"Don't fret about them," said Hawk.

"But—"

"Where did you learn to fence like that?" repeated Raven, before Peregrine could press the matter of Wrexford and Charlotte.

"From Uncle Jeremiah—that is, my uncle Willis," he replied. "A cousin of his was one of the finest swordsmen in all of Europe, and taught him the art of swordplay, which he passed on to me." A look of sadness pinched at his features. "I will greatly miss our practice sessions."

Seeing Raven's brows wing up, he added a little defensively, "I swear, I'm not telling you a faradiddle. My uncle's cousin was the Chevalier de St. Georges, who fenced for the Prince Regent at Carlton House during his visit to England. He was also great friends with Henry Angelo, whose—"

"Whose fencing academy is the most prestigious one in London," finished Raven.

"Yes," said Peregrine. "Uncle Jeremiah told me that a portrait of his cousin hangs in the main room." His mouth thinned. "Though Uncle Belmont birched me when I said so, insisting that no half-breed Blackamoor would have a place of honor in a place frequented by gentlemen."

"Your uncle Belmont," responded Raven, "is a despicable arse."

"He didn't even say he was sorry when he told me of Uncle Jeremiah's death," said Peregrine in a small voice.

"We're sorry," said Hawk solemnly, as he put a hand on Peregrine's shoulder. "And not only that, we're going to help

Wrexford and m'lady find your uncle's killers and bring them to justice."

"W-Why do they care about—" Peregrine bit off the rest of his query. "Sorry. I forgot that I'm not allowed to ask any questions."

"I think you may have earned the right to ask one . . . or perhaps two," drawled Raven.

"But first I have a query," said Hawk. "Did you and your uncle fight with actual *swords*?"

"Yes, we did. The blades were dulled and they had buttons on their tips in order to prevent any injury," replied Peregrine. "However, they were made of steel."

Hawk let out a fluttery sigh. "Wrexford gave us a set of swords when he and m'lady first became friends. But they were ancient broadswords, and awfully heavy. I wonder . . ."

His face scrunched in thought. "If Wrex would allow us to have some real fencing swords, would you teach us how to use them?"

"Aye!" Peregrine answered. "That is, if you'll keep teaching me how to use my fists."

Holding his breath, Hawk cast a sidelong look at his brother, waiting for him to answer.

Raven stepped back into the shadows of a slatted gate and motioned for the others to join him. Kneeling down, he drew out a stag-handled pocketknife from the hidden sheath in his boot.

Peregrine's eyes widened as Raven pressed the hidden catch, releasing a wicked-looking blade.

"If we're going to be friends," said Raven, "that means we'll have to trust you with some of our secrets."

"I give you my word of honor as . . . as a gentleman," said Peregrine, "that you can count on my loyalty and discretion."

Hawk grinned. "We ain't gentlemen."

"Of course you are," said Peregrine in confusion.

"No, we ain't—"

"But our word is just as binding," said Raven. "So, shall we swear a blood oath of friendship?" He pricked his finger with the knife and then handed it to his brother, who did the same. "But think carefully and don't do it lightly. The oath comes with responsibilities." A pause. "Ones that may call on you to put yourself in danger. For friends never leave friends in the lurch."

In answer, Peregrine took the knife from Hawk and pressed it against his thumb. A dark bead welled up, nearly black against his dusky skin.

"I swear," he whispered, "that I'll never betray your trust in me."

Raven nodded and brought their three fingers together, letting blood mingle with blood.

"We're now brothers, in every way that matters."

From the darkened eaves of a nearby building, an owl hooted, breaking the solemnity of the moment.

"Our feathered friend is telling us that we better get moving," announced Raven, after a glance up at the scudding clouds. "It's still a long way back to Berkeley Square."

"Excellent," said Peregrine, falling in step with the others. "That gives plenty of time for you to tell me how we're going to solve my uncle's murder and bring the miscreants to justice."

CHAPTER 12

"You know, your duties don't include making breakfast anymore," commented Charlotte as she entered the kitchen to find McClellan grinding beans for a fresh pot of coffee.

"Just as your place for dining is no longer at the worktable by the stove," pointed out the maid, "but rather in the formal breakfast room."

"Thank heavens that Wrexford's townhouse isn't run according to the normal rules of the aristocracy," replied Charlotte as she took a seat on one of the stools.

McClellan chuckled. "We are an exceedingly eccentric household." Taking the kettle from the stove, she filled the coffeepot with boiling water. "Thank God."

"Indeed." Charlotte inhaled the spicy fragrance and let out an appreciative sigh as she helped herself to a fresh-baked muffin. Life had certainly become more luxurious . . . but she was acutely aware of not letting it make her go soft.

"Might I ask you to accompany me to the park this morning?" she asked. "Wrexford is taking the boys with him to the Royal Institution this morning, so I wish to stroll along the Serpentine and see the place where Mr. Willis met his demise. And then, I thought we might have a look at the new constructions the government has made in Green Park and St. James's Park for the Peace Celebrations and the Hanoverian Centennial."

A number of grand events were planned for the coming weeks, including several displays of fireworks and the reenactment of a famous naval battle on the placid waters of the Serpentine.

"A countess need not ask her maid, m'lady—she merely commands," drawled McClellan.

Charlotte replied with a very un-countess-like word. "If I ever put on such high-and-mighty airs, I devoutly hope you'll dump a pot of scalding hot coffee over my head."

The maid carried two steaming mugs to the table and handed one to Charlotte. "Are we looking for something particular in the parks?"

"I simply wish to get the lay of the land," she replied. "Though, of course, if we happen to encounter some of the foreign dignitaries exploring London, it would only be polite if we engage them in conversation."

"But of course." McClellan took a sip of her brew. "Naturally, their servants would be grateful for a local's advice on what to see and do in the city."

"Naturally." Charlotte smiled through the plume of steam that wafted up from her mug.

"Speaking of exploring . . ." McClellan's voice took on a warning note. "I daresay the Weasels and Peregrine won't be down early."

"Oh, dear." Her smile faded. "They went out last night?"

"I heard them creep up the east wing stairs just before dawn," answered McClellan. "As you know, I'm a light sleeper."

"And they took Peregrine with them?" Charlotte frowned. "I'm very happy that the three of them have become friends. But I think it's unwise for them to take our guest into the stews. It's too dangerous."

"Which is the only reason I mentioned the nocturnal foray. I think you and Wrexford were right not to seek to clip Raven's and Hawk's wings when we all moved here to Berkeley Square. But as you say, Lord Lampson is inexperienced in the ways of the wolf-eat-wolf wilds outside his aristocratic world. One small mistake . . ."

"I shall have a word with the Weasels when we return." Charlotte sighed, thinking not for the first time that the challenges lying ahead as they began to grow out of boyhood were looking more and more daunting.

McClellan refilled her cup. "Let us deal with one task at a time, m'lady," she murmured, as if reading Charlotte's mind. "As soon as you've finished your muffin, shall we go up and dress for our promenade in the park?"

"Weasels!" Wrexford poked his head into the schoolroom. "Would you—" He stopped short on seeing Hawk sprawled facedown on the rug, snoring softly.

There were, noted the earl, still a few clots of mud embedded in the boy's curling hair.

Stepping closer, he gave Hawk a gentle nudge with the toe of his boot. "Dare I ask what mischief you were making last night?"

Hawk's eyes fluttered open—and then widened in alarm. "N-Nuff . . ."

"Nuffink?" suggested Wrexford.

A scarlet flush spread over the boy's cheeks.

"Hell's bells." Hastily tucking his shirt into his breeches, Raven came out of the bedchamber he shared with his brother and expelled a sigh. "You have to learn to be a better liar."

"Just out of curiosity, why would Hawk have to lie to me?" he asked.

"Because," answered Raven, "you wouldn't like the truth."

How to respond? Wrexford made himself think about it for a moment before replying.

"I appreciate your honesty, lad. However, in this case, that answer won't fadge." He looked at the closed door to Peregrine's room. "It's one thing for the two of you to visit your usual haunts. But it's quite another if you took Lord Lampson with you."

Raven averted his gaze.

"I take that to be a yes," said Wrexford.

"Falcon isn't a defenseless chick," piped up Hawk. "He knows how to fence!"

The assertion only stirred a tickle of foreboding at the back of his neck. "And how would you know that?"

Raven speared his brother with an exasperated look.

"Oh . . . sorry," said Hawk in a small voice.

"I do hope that His Lordship didn't slice off someone's ear," quipped the earl.

"No, no. He just bruised the dastard's bollocks," admitted Raven, surrendering any hope of hiding the truth. "Falcon is *very* skilled in the art of swordplay—though he was wielding a broken broomstick and not an actual rapier."

Thank God, thought Wrexford. He didn't relish the thought of having to tell Belmont that his ward had been hauled off to the Bow Street magistrate.

"Can we have some fencing foils?" asked Hawk in a rush. "Falcon says he'll teach us the basics. That is, of course, assuming you give us your permission."

Wrexford tried to maintain a stern expression, but on thinking of how gleefully happy the boys had been when he had given them a pair of clunky old medieval swords, he couldn't hold back a smile. "I shall consider it. *But* first we must address—"

"I'm very sorry if I did something wrong."

Wrexford looked up to see Peregrine standing in the doorway of his bedchamber.

"But the man hit Hawk with a brass-knobbed walking stick," continued the boy. "And—"

"And then the dastard went after Falcon," interjected Raven, "who only wielded his broomstick in self-defense."

"You crossed sticks with a man and beat him?" A note of skepticism must have shaded his voice because Hawk immediately offered an explanation.

"His uncle's cousin was a very famous fencer. The Chev . . . um . . ."

"The Chevalier de St. Georges," said Peregrine softly.

Wrexford blinked in surprise. The late chevalier had indeed been famous throughout Europe, not only for his fencing skill, but also for his graceful dancing, hell-for-leather riding, and virtuoso talent with the violin. And if his memory served him right, the fellow also composed music, which was much admired by Mozart.

"Falcon says a portrait of the chevalier hangs in Angelo's Fencing Academy," said Hawk.

"That's what Uncle Jeremiah told me," Peregrine hastily added. "Though Uncle Belmont says it's a lie."

"Wrex fences with Mr. Angelo," said Raven. "So he would know . . ."

All three boys looked at him expectantly.

Damnation. Was there a portrait on the walls? Charlotte would have noticed such a detail.

"I'm afraid that my focus is not on art when I enter the academy," admitted the earl. But on seeing Peregrine's shoulders slump, he quickly added, "However, I came here to see if the three of you wish to accompany me on a visit to Mr. Hedley's workshop to see some of his latest mechanical creations. And as the academy is only a short walk from the Royal Institution, we could go see for ourselves on the way home."

"Hooray!" cried Hawk.

"That would, of course, mean that you all need to dress as proper little gentlemen."

The statement sent Hawk scurrying into his bedchamber. Peregrine, too, quickly closed the door to his bedchamber. Raven, however, remained where he was.

"If you mean to argue, save your breath," warned Wrexford. "You can either put on proper attire for an outing, or you can stay here and help Harper dig up one of the moldy bones he's buried in the garden."

"To see the inside of Angelo's academy is worth dressing up to resemble a street fiddler's monkey," replied Raven. "I'm aware that some rules can't be broken."

"Excellent. Because—"

"Because you mean to ring a peal over my head for allowing Falcon to accompany us into the stews. But—"

"Actually, I don't," interrupted Wrexford. Discipline was a subject fraught with complications. He remembered his own clashes with his father. The bruises had lingered far too long. "I think you know it wasn't a good choice, and so I won't belabor the point."

"Yes. But—"

Ignoring the attempt to interrupt, Wrexford continued. "However, what I do mean to do is make clear that it's not to happen again."

"Yes. But—"

"Allow me to finish."

Raven's face flushed in frustration.

"You may think of Falcon as your friend, just as you do Skinny, and Pudge, and Alice the Eel Girl," he said. "But Peregrine, Lord Lampson, is a member of the aristocracy, with responsibilities to both the past and the future of his family. He has a guardian who has the authority to set a code of conduct for his behavior. And we have no right to encourage him to transgress those rules."

Raven lifted his chin. "Even if his life is in danger?"

"Ye gods, let us not wax melodramatic," responded the earl a little testily. Granted, from what little he had seen of Peregrine's guardian, he could well imagine Belmont having nefarious thoughts. However, he didn't wish to say so aloud. "And now, I think we've said enough on the subject."

"But . . ."

Wrexford heaved an inward sigh. "But what?"

"But now that we're alone," said Raven in a rush, "may I finally tell you what we discovered last night?"

Diamond-bright sunlight sparkled over the water. Not a breath of breeze stirred the air, giving its surface a mirror-like stillness.

"It's hard to imagine a violent crime taking place in such a sylvan setting," murmured Charlotte as she glanced around at the trees and their newly unfurled leaves.

But, of course, she knew all too well how deceiving appearances could be—especially here, within the environs of the royal palaces and aristocratic townhouses of Polite Society. In the stews of London, the ugliness was there for everyone to see. But in Mayfair, a veneer of wealth and privilege could often hide a core of rot.

"Raven said Willis fell in not far from this end of the Long Water," said McClellan. "Shall we walk down to the stone retaining wall?"

It wasn't that Charlotte was looking for any actual clues. She simply wanted to get a visual sense of the setting. It was strange how the smallest detail—a flash of color, the shape of a stone— could stir an intuitive thought, one that defied conscious reason.

Early on in their acquaintance, Wrexford had dismissed her intuition as nothing but habble-gabble nonsense. But he had come to respect that looking at a problem from a different perspective could sometimes be the key to solving it.

She and McClellan moved from the graveled path and passed through a grove of trees before cutting up to the water's edge. The stone embankment was steep here, and then gave way to a more gently sloping grassy verge toward the middle of the Long Water.

Despite the sun, Charlotte felt a sudden chill as a shadow of sadness seemed to hang for an instant over her heart. It made her even more determined to see that justice prevailed.

"Shall we go on to Green Park?" she suggested after one last look at the lake. "The recently constructed Temple of Concord will likely draw many of the diplomatic visitors eager to see what spectacles have been created for their enjoyment."

"Are you looking to become better acquainted with anyone in particular?" asked McClellan as they started toward Rotten Row, the stretch of bridle path that was a popular promenade spot for the beau monde.

"We have the list of five names from Pierson, but Wrexford and I have not yet come up with any suspects of our own," Charlotte admitted. "Though I don't dismiss Belmont as easily as he does."

"I know that Tyler is making some inquiries among his less-than-virtuous acquaintances to see what they might know of the crime. If Willis was indeed murdered, someone was likely hired to do the deed." The maid thought for a moment. "If your observations are right, and Belmont is under financial pressures, that might make him vulnerable to bribery or black-mail. And I imagine Lady Peake will also have an idea who else among the aristocratic members of the government might have a skeleton in their cupboards."

"Alison does seem to possess a frighteningly accurate knowl-edge of the foibles of the Polite Society," she agreed. "Though I worry . . ."

"Of course you worry about your loved ones," murmured the maid. "Just as your friends all worry about you."

Charlotte assumed Tyler had told McClellan about the possibility that the government knew her secret. "Merciful heavens—don't worry about me," she said forcefully.

McClellan fixed her with a troubled look. "If your identity as A. J. Quill becomes public knowledge because of this investigation, it might strip the power from your pen."

"A good man lost his life, so I consider it a risk worth taking." Recalling the rocks and the water she had just been viewing, she added, "I will gladly sacrifice my pen if it means that the people who are responsible for his death don't get away with murder."

They walked on in an uneasy silence, the small stones crunching underfoot.

Spotting a faint footpath leading through the trees bordering Rotten Row that would shorten their walk to Green Park, Charlotte stepped off the graveled walkway. The leafy shadows were welcome after the bright sunshine, and the coolness seemed to calm the heat of her passions. Pausing for a moment, she exhaled and waited for McClellan to catch up.

She was just about to apologize for her testy mood, when she heard the sound of horses fast approaching. Two riders rounded the bend and suddenly reined to a halt at the edge of the bridle path.

On instinct, Charlotte took shelter behind a thick oak. McClellan quickly joined her.

"Whatever you have to say, make it quick."

Charlotte recognized Belmont's voice. He sounded nervous.

"I would rather that we aren't seen conversing together. It could put me in danger."

"I don't give a rat's arse for what you would or would not prefer," said his companion. "You're up to your neck in this. So allow me to remind you that you don't have any way out except to do exactly as I say."

One of the horses snorted and shifted, kicking up clots of the soft bridle path.

"What do you want?" muttered Belmont. "I already told you that the bank receipts of the invitees who agree to participate in the auction will be collected during the races at Royal Ascot tomorrow. It will be done by the parade ring, during the royal viewing of the horses running in the Gold Cup race."

Charlotte shifted slightly, straining to hear them through the rustling of the leaves.

"Don't play the fool with me," snarled Belmont's companion. "You know damnably well what I want—the name of the man who is behind the auction."

Do I dare try and get a peek at him? she asked herself. His voice had the cultured drawl of a London aristocrat, but with the rustling of the leaves, she wasn't sure she would recognize it if she heard it again—

As if reading her thoughts, McClellan pressed a warning palm to her shoulder. Knowing the maid was right, she held still.

"I told you—I don't know that yet! Whoever he is, he's being very clever in keeping his identity a secret," exclaimed Belmont. "I swear, I'm doing my best to find out!"

"It appears that your best isn't good enough," said his companion in a silky voice. "Which makes you useless to us."

"Someone—I don't know who yet—will circulate through the crowd at Royal Ascot and collect the responses," answered Belmont, a note of fear adding a shrillness to his voice. "I'll receive a message telling me where to meet him, and then I'm to take the packet and hand it over to a more senior messenger. T-That may give me a clue."

"You had better hope so."

"B-But—"

"There are no 'buts' about it. Fail us at your own peril."

Hooves thudded as Belmont's companion turned his horse. Charlotte ventured a quick peek through the greenery. But as a breeze kicked up, all she could see through the fluttering leaves were the burgundy-colored leather tassels swinging from the top of the gentleman's riding boot as he spurred the bay stallion into a canter.

She shifted.

Too late. He was already too far away for her to see more than the back of a dark coat and high crown hat.

As for Belmont . . .

Peregrine's guardian appeared visibly shaken. Reins fisted in one hand, he drew a handkerchief from his pocket and wiped at his brow.

"God help me." The plea hung for a moment in the air before being carried away by the breeze.

Charlotte found she couldn't muster any sympathy for him. Not only was he a cruel guardian to his late brother's son, but her suspicions had proven correct—he was also a traitor to his country.

Expelling an unsteady breath, Belmont stared up at the cloudless sky—a last appeal to the heavens?—then gathered himself and rode off.

"Dastard," muttered Charlotte, trying to swallow the spurt of fury rising in her gorge. The picture of Peregrine's face, eyes clouded with sadness over the death of his dear uncle, flashed in her mind's eye. "But I now know your damnable secret. And I promise you'll pay for your perfidy."

She took a moment longer to compose her emotions before turning to McClellan. "You were right to keep me from being seen. It's imperative that the conspirators don't know we're onto their scent." A sigh. "But I wish that we had been able to identify Belmont's companion."

"Patience," counseled the maid. "We've discovered a vital part of the puzzle. And that always makes it easier to find the other missing pieces and fit them together."

"You're right." Much as Charlotte was impatient to tell Wrexford of Belmont's guilt—she knew he thought that she allowed her personal dislike of the man to cloud her judgment—

there was no reason to rush back home. "My sense is that Belmont is only an underling in this wicked conspiracy—and one who is double-crossing his original master. And as we've also seen, we're not the only ones looking to get our hands on Willis's invention before it goes up for sale."

"Yet another danger to navigate," muttered McClellan.

Charlotte nodded. "Wrexford won't be back at Berkeley Square for some time, so let us go on to Green Park. And pray that we can find more clues that will lead us to the villain before anyone else gets there first."

CHAPTER 13

After hearing Raven's account of what he had learned during the previous night's foray into the stews, Wrexford dispatched Tyler to do some sleuthing regarding the gentleman mentioned by the boy's urchin friend. It was, he conceded, a potentially vital clue. And yet he was conflicted about how to deal with Raven's decision to allow Peregrine to accompany him and his brother on such a dangerous foray.

Independence and initiative was to be encouraged, Wrexford told himself, and given his unusual upbringing, Raven was far more mature than most boys his age.

But he was still a child. And Wrexford worried that the boy's resourcefulness was straying perilously close to recklessness. Yes, Raven knew enough about death to comprehend it was real. But at his age, one always believed that the Grim Reaper's blade would never cut short one's own life.

And so the conversation between the two of them had ended with a warning that a serious discussion about rights and responsibilities would take place this evening. A cowardly decision, conceded Wrexford, as it was a talk he wasn't relishing.

However, there were pressing matters concerning the investigation—which affected Charlotte's fragile secret—to pursue . . .

Putting aside his fretting over Raven, Wrexford hurried through the imposing entrance of the Royal Institution and led the three boys up the stairs to a noisy corridor at the back of the building.

"Hedley?" Doubting that the inventor had heard his knocking over the metallic clattering going on inside, Wrexford opened the door to the laboratory and peered through the scrim of steam. *"Hedley!"*

"Over here!" called a disembodied voice.

Batting at the plumes of ghostly vapor, the earl entered the space and cautiously moved toward one of the side alcoves. "Have a care not to bump into anything," he warned the boys, who followed him in wide-eyed wonder.

Despite the haze, a number of large and complicated steam-powered devices were visible, their belching and snorting adding to the cacophony of grinding gears and clacking levers.

"Ah, Wrexford!" Hedley popped from behind a wheeled, rectangular wooden platform, which had a large rudder and tiller attached to one end. "A visit from you is always a pleasure." A smile. "You always ask such thought-provoking questions!"

"You are one of the few people who actually enjoys intellectual challenges," replied Wrexford dryly.

Hedley laughed. "Does that mean you have another devilishly difficult mechanical drawing to decipher?" Hedley had been a great help in solving one of Wrexford and Charlotte's earlier investigations.

"As a matter of fact . . ." He gestured to the three boys. "But first, may I introduce my wards and their friend Lord Lampson? They are aficionados of all things mechanical, and I am hoping you don't mind if they have a look around at some of your inventions, while the two of us confer."

"Not at all! I'm always delighted to encourage young people to take an interest in engineering!" exclaimed a beaming Hedley. "Come over here, lads, and let me show my prototype for a horseless carriage, powered by a miniature steam engine."

The engineer spent a few minutes explaining the workings, and then to the glee of the boys, he fired up the engine and said they could take turns riding it up and down the length of the main room.

"Milord," called Hedley, after assuring himself that Raven had the hang of steering the horseless carriage with the nautical-like tiller. "Let us go into my private office, where we can discuss your question in a modicum of peace and quiet."

Wrexford wasted no time in prolonged pleasantries once the door fell shut. "I must ask for your promise to keep what I show you in strict confidence. It's highly sensitive material, and . . ." Wrexford hesitated. "Let's just say that if the wrong people knew you had seen it, the repercussion could be . . . explosive."

Hedley blinked, then took a moment to remove his spectacles and wipe the misted lenses with a handkerchief. "Well, sir . . ." He perched them back on his nose, the lamplight catching the steely gleam of his eyes behind the glass. "I should hope that I've proved my mettle to you."

"I wouldn't be here if I doubted you. However, I felt beholden to make clear the seriousness of the situation, and the possibility of danger, as it involves a secret government project."

"Duly noted, milord." The inventor rubbed his calloused hands together in expectation. "Now that you've piqued my curiosity, please show me what you have."

The earl unfolded the drawing he had found inside Willis's instrument case. "Alas, I have only this sketch, not the complete technical plans." He watched Hedley's initial spasm of surprise quickly turn to a look of grave concern.

"So it's true," whispered the inventor.

"You knew of this development?"

"I've heard rumors," answered Hedley. Leaning closer to the sketch, he studied it for some moments before expelling a sigh. "After over a decade of bloody conflict raging throughout Europe and the New World, which resulted in horrific death and destruction, one would think that men of science could put their minds to inventing useful creations rather than a more efficient way of killing our fellow beings."

"I couldn't agree more," replied Wrexford. "But alas, technological advances in and of themselves hold no intrinsic morality. We must trust in human nature to do the right thing." His mouth curled in a humorless smile. "Call me a cynic, but I don't find that a very cheering thought."

Hedley made a face. "Nor do I."

"The technical plans have gone missing. The reason I'm here is to ask your opinion on whether you believe this firearm might actually work."

"Hmmph." Hedley's brow furrowed. "I've heard that an American engineer—a fellow by the name of Elisha Collier—has been experimenting with a revolving multichambered cylinder in both pistols and long guns. It's designed for firing six to eight bullets at a time before reloading. Theoretically, there is no reason to think it can't be done. But the mechanisms needed to synchronize the hammer, trigger, and revolving cylinder would be devilishly tricky to make."

The inventor looked up. "A weapon is of no practical use if it's not reliable under less-than-perfect conditions."

"Indeed," said the earl. "So you're saying that Collier's weapon doesn't work?"

"To my knowledge, it doesn't," said Hedley. "But that doesn't mean that *this* design isn't fully functional." After pondering his own words, he tapped a finger to Willis's sketch. "Might I ask if you know who created this, milord? That might help me to give you a more precise answer."

Wrexford didn't hesitate. "Jeremiah Willis."

"Damnation." Hedley blew out his breath. "I was afraid you were going to say that." For a moment, the only sounds in the private office were the hiss and thump of the steam engines in the main room. "If anyone could perfect such a complex design, it would have been Willis."

"I take it you've heard of his death."

"Yes. There's been talk of it among our fellow members here. One of them had a copy of A. J. Quill's latest print." Hedley gave a small shiver. "The artist hinted it was murder. Could that be true, milord?"

Wrexford didn't reply. Instead, he asked a question of his own. "You don't perchance know of anyone else who might be working on the design of a multishot weapon?"

"No, I've heard not a whisper." Hedley paused, his brows slowly drawing together. "But . . ."

"But what?" urged Wrexford, after the word trailed away into silence.

The inventor shook his head in consternation. "Sorry, it's just that I have a niggling feeling that something about the subject is hovering just beyond my memory's reach. Alas, I just can't seem to grab it."

"Perhaps it will come to you later." He refolded Willis's sketch and tucked it back into his pocket. "In the meantime, thank you for your thoughts."

Hedley made a face. "I don't feel I've been of much help."

"On the contrary," replied Wrexford. "It helps a great deal to know that only a genius is capable of making such a complex design functional."

They returned to the main workhouse, where the boys reluctantly relinquished the horseless carriage to its creator, but not before peppering him with a number of technical questions.

Smiling, Hedley patiently answered them, and then added, "You are welcome to come visit anytime, lads." He glanced at Wrexford. "It's a pleasure to be asked such intelligent questions."

"That's very kind of you." The earl acknowledged the generous invitation with a smile. "Come, lads, let us now leave Mr. Hedley to his work."

Their faces brightened as they realized that he would now be taking them to Angelo's Fencing Academy. After voicing their thanks to Hedley, they raced for the door.

Wrexford followed, but before stepping into the corridor, he turned for a last word. "If perchance you recall what it is you wanted to tell me about the subject we were discussing, please send a note to my townhouse."

"Good Lord!" As they crested the rise, McClellan stopped short, her brows rising in surprise at the sight in the meadow below.

Charlotte, too, found her eyes widening at the sight of the towering medieval-looking castle. She thought for a moment, trying to recall what she had read about the magnificent displays that were being constructed to astound both the foreign visitors and London's own population.

"I think," she said slowly, "that must be—"

"The Temple of Concord," said Sheffield as he crossed from one of the sidewalks to join them. "Or, rather, the temple is hidden inside the castle and won't be revealed until next month's gala celebration of the hundredth anniversary of King George the Third and his family—the House of Hanover—sitting on the throne."

He offered his arm to Charlotte. "I was hoping to find Wrex at the Royal Institution, but he had just left," added Sheffield. "However, as Riche had mentioned that you were coming to

Green Park, I thought I'd come join you and see if I might be of some help."

"Your company is always welcome," said Charlotte, deciding not to mention Belmont before she discussed her discovery with Wrexford. "I've no specific mission in mind. I simply wanted to stroll, and perhaps to encounter one of our possible suspects."

McClellan was still staring at the faux castle. "How is the temple going to be revealed?"

"Apparently, Lieutenant Colonel Sir William Congreve has designed a spectacular theatrical production. There will be a mock siege of the castle, complete with cavalry attacks and rockets fired by the Rocket Brigade," explained Sheffield. "As the climax of the show, the castle walls—which are fabricated out of canvas and wood—will tumble down, revealing the Temple of Concord inside as fireworks light up the sky."

"Extraordinary," murmured McClellan.

"Congreve designed rockets for our military use in battle," mused Charlotte. "Didn't the Rocket Brigade win accolades in the decisive victory over Bonaparte at the Battle of Leipzig last year?"

"Yes," answered Sheffield. "Rockets are far more mobile than artillery, which is very useful in the heat of battle. But Wellington doesn't like them. He thinks they scare the horses."

His brow suddenly furrowed in thought. "You know, Congreve was recently appointed the comptroller of the Royal Laboratory at Woolwich, which is part of the Royal Armory complex."

"That would mean . . ." Charlotte suddenly recalled that the Royal Laboratory was where government research was done on new weaponry and munitions. She looked around to make sure nobody was within earshot before going on. "I believe Willis did his work at the complex, so he would have been under the direction of Congreve."

"Wrexford mentioned that Pierson and his operatives have searched Willis's workplace and residence," pointed out Sheffield. "And I would imagine they did so quite thoroughly."

She nodded, but made a mental note to have a talk with Peregrine about his uncle. The boy had mentioned occasional visits to London. Perhaps knowing some of the details about his uncle's personal life would help her form a better picture of the man. And perhaps . . .

Perhaps there was a chance that he had made another set of drawings.

"Shall we go down and have a closer look at the castle?" suggested Charlotte. She noticed that there were a number of military displays—cannons, mortars, the metallic rockets invented by Congreve—arranged around the fanciful structure. She had read in the newspapers that the government had decided to delight the public and visitors to the city by permitting them to inspect the weaponry that had allowed the British and the Allies to defeat Bonaparte and the mighty French Army.

A pair of red-coated officers, all aglitter in gold braid and brass buttons, was stationed at each of the exhibits in order to chat with the visitors and explain how the weaponry worked. Already there were groups of interested spectators forming . . .

"Prinny is being very smart in promoting his own popularity," observed Sheffield. "The public loves things that go *bang!*"

McClellan choked back a snort of laughter. "He's not that clever. I'm sure the idea came from one of his advisors."

"Arthur Wellesley—the new Duke of Wellington—is our nation's hero of the hour," said Charlotte, who had done a drawing the previous month on the public's adulation of the general who had driven the French out of Portugal and Spain without losing a battle. "Whoever made the decision is wise to take advantage of that."

"Is there a reason you're heading to the display of rockets?" asked the maid as Charlotte veered off the main walkway. "You're not usually so bloodthirsty."

"I'm assuming the officers manning the exhibit are knowledgeable about the rockets," she replied. "And as Willis was working at the Royal Laboratory at Woolwich, it's possible that they were acquainted with him." A pause. "And whether he had any particular friends there."

"Ah." McClellan nodded in understanding.

"People are prone to revealing more than they think they are in a casual chat," murmured Charlotte.

"Especially to someone who is an expert at extracting information," replied Sheffield dryly.

She answered with a smile, then took his arm and quickened her steps toward the display of Congreve rockets, with McClellan trailing dutifully in their wake.

"I take it you want me to be frivolously charming," murmured Sheffield as they approached the weaponry.

"Charm is always perceived as unthreatening," Charlotte answered, her gaze locked on two officers standing slightly apart from the pair of soldiers who were explaining the rockets to a group of Austrian diplomats.

One of them was sporting fancy epaulettes and a chest full of medals . . .

"Why, that's Sir William himself," Sheffield whispered. "I met him at a soiree for mechanical engineers right after his appointment to the Royal Laboratory." Sheffield had been an early investor in Mr. Hedley's revolutionary "Puffing Billy," a steam-powered locomotive that traveled over iron tracks, and his interest in industrial innovations had led him to become a welcome member of the scientific community of inventors.

"Excellent," said Charlotte. "Let us go greet him."

"Ah, Sir William!" called Sheffield. "I hear you've designed quite an extraordinary spectacle to dazzle the crowd for the king's celebration."

"I do hope it will entertain the audience, Mr. Sheffield," replied Congreve, casting a critical squint at the castle. "There's still a great deal of work to do in order to ensure that all the logistics go smoothly."

"Oh, but I'm sure that the hero of the Battle of Leipzig will triumph over any tiny adversity that dares to rear its head," gushed Charlotte.

"Allow me to introduce Lady Wrexford," said Sheffield.

"I am a great admirer of yours, Sir William," she added. "My husband speaks very highly about your scientific expertise."

The praise brought a touch of color to his cheekbones. "How kind of you to say so, milady. Lord Wrexford is held in high esteem by Wellesley—that is, the Duke of Wellington—for his valor during the Peninsular War. And the Royal Armory is, of course, grateful for his help in refining a chemical compound for our mortar shells during the Spanish Campaign of '09."

"Wrexford is always happy to be of assistance to the Crown," replied Charlotte with a flutter of her lashes. "He's particularly fond of the Royal Laboratory and the work it does." A mournful sigh. "Which is why he was very saddened by the death of his dear friend Jeremiah Willis."

"Yes, a great loss to us and to science, milady," said Congreve. "I wasn't aware of Willis's connection to your husband. But then, Willis was a very modest man."

"They were kindred souls," she said, placing a hand over her heart. It wasn't exactly a lie—she was quite sure that the two of them would have been fast friends.

"Indeed, how fortuitous that we should meet today, sir!" Charlotte continued. "I know that Wrexford wishes to arrange a private memorial service for Mr. Willis. Might you know the names of his closest friends at the Royal Laboratory? I could then pass them on to my husband."

"Hmmm." Congreve rubbed meditatively at his chin. "Willis tended to keep to himself. Let me think. I'll send word to Wrexford if any names pop to mind."

"Thank you." Before Charlotte could go on, a loud hail from atop the castle drew Congreve's attention.

"I'm afraid I must ask you to excuse me, milady," he said, inclining a polite bow. "The men need to be shown how to position the block and tackles that will lower the castle walls during the gala celebration."

"But of course." She gave him a radiant smile. "I look forward to seeing your pyrotechnics, both here at the Temple of Concord, and at the Peace Celebrations in Hyde Park later this month."

His mouth twitched. "Be assured that the reenactment of the Battle of Trafalgar on the Serpentine will provide quite an explosive display of sparks and thunder. I trust you won't go away disappointed."

"Sir William!"

"Yes, yes, I'm coming!" Congreve started to turn away, and then hesitated. "I just remembered—if Lord Wrexford is looking for close friends of Mr. Willis, he ought to contact Randall Osborn."

"The Marquess of Auburndale's son?" asked Sheffield.

"Yes. I seem to recall my adjutant recently mentioning that Osborn and Willis had apparently become thick as thieves."

"Thank you again," replied Charlotte as she took Sheffield's arm. "Come, we mustn't keep Sir William from his work."

Once they had rounded one of the jogs of the castle walls, Sheffield let out a low chuckle. "You are frighteningly good at telling outrageous bouncers."

"The key to a good lie is having some grain of truth to it," she said. "I'm quite sure that Wrexford and Willis shared a passion for science, and thus would have felt a bond."

They were now at the back side of the castle, out of sight

from the swath of meadow where the weaponry exhibits were set up for the public to peruse. It was clearly the work area. Several large canvas tents were set up close by and Charlotte could hear the sounds of carpentry echoing within them.

A few makeshift doorways cut into the two corner towers gave entrance into the interior of the castle, and they paused for a moment to allow a pair of laborers carrying a stack of fresh-sawn boards to pass into the shadows of the nearest one.

"Shall we return to the main walkway and head down to the canal?" suggested Sheffield. "A Chinese bridge has been constructed, and it features a tall pagoda."

Charlotte nodded and started to turn . . .

Only to freeze in midstep as she saw a well-dressed man come around the corner of the far tower and head straight through the opening.

"You and Mac go loiter by one of the cannon displays," she said. "I'll rejoin you shortly."

Sheffield flashed a questioning frown, but didn't argue.

Charlotte hesitated for an instant, and then pulled off one of her earbobs and thrust it into her maid's hand. "Go!" she urged before darting into the gloom.

The scent of sawdust and paint hung heavy in the air. Here and there, flickers of lantern light pierced the shadows, punctuated by the sound of hammering. A makeshift passageway zigzagged between the outer walls of the castle and the half-finished Temple of Concord. After taking a moment to get her bearings, Charlotte began to pick her way toward the far tower, moving as fast as she dared through the piles of supplies stacked along the way.

Spotting a flutter of dark-on-dark movement up ahead, she crept a little closer and cocked an ear.

"What an apt metaphor for life—a grand castle that's merely an illusion." A note of cynicism shaded the man's voice. "Smoke and lies, and yet the crowds will be dazzled by the spectacle."

Charlotte smiled to herself. She had guessed right—it *was* Kurlansky, the private secretary to Prince Rubalov, the Russian military attaché. She had recognized his slender silhouette and the panther-like grace of his movements.

"An interesting philosophy." A well-modulated English voice, smooth and cultured. And she was fairly certain it was the mystery rider she had just heard at Rotten Row. "But then, you Russians tend to take a dark view of human nature."

That drew a sharp laugh. "And you English don't? Then pray tell, why are we talking?"

"It's purely pragmatic," replied the Englishman. He was only a dark silhouette as he shifted his stance. "I want information from you, and am willing to give something of equal value in return."

"I'm listening," replied Kurlansky.

To Charlotte's dismay, the Englishman lowered his voice, making his words impossible to hear.

But a glance around showed it was too risky to inch closer.

"I shall think about it," said the Russian. "My prince won't like it."

"And as I pointed out, you'll profit from that."

"So you say. But perhaps our objectives aren't the same."

The Englishman said nothing. Charlotte heard him turn and stride away, the staccato crunch of woodchips quickly swallowed by the hammering within the temple's skeleton.

Hoping to catch a glimpse of the Englishman, Charlotte gathered her skirts and retreated. She had almost reached the opening when a soft hail from just behind her nearly caused her to jump out of her skin.

"Have you an interest in architecture as well as art, Lady Wrexford?"

Damnation, aristocratic life was making her careless. She should have been paying more attention.

Composing herself, Charlotte turned and smiled at Kurlansky. "None at all, sir. However, my escort was all afire to see the bones of the temple before the silken panorama paintings are attached to the framing, so we just had a quick tour from one of Sir William's officers."

She touched her earlobe. "Alas, I seem to have lost one of my favorite garnet earbobs, so I decided to come back and search for it." A sigh. "But I realize that with all the debris, it's hopeless."

He came up alongside her. "Who knows? Lost items sometimes have a way of turning up."

"One would have to be very lucky," she said lightly. "And what brings you inside the structure, sir?"

"Curiosity," he replied with a hint of amusement.

"Well, enjoy your exploring. I really ought to return to my companions."

To her relief, Kurlansky made no move to follow her. Ruing the delay, she quickened her steps, once she exited the castle, but on seeing that the crowd had swelled, she knew there wasn't a prayer of identifying the Englishman. All she had to go on was his voice. And a bit of burgundy leather.

Spotting Sheffield and McClellan standing by a pair of field guns, Charlotte made her way over to join them. As she came near, she saw Sheffield was chatting with a gentleman whose back was turned to her. Nonetheless, from the tilt of his broad shoulders to the fashionable style of his high-top Hessian boots, he seemed to radiate an arrogant ennui.

Alerted by McClellan's brusque cough, Sheffield looked up. "Lady Wrexford! Are you acquainted with the Honorable Randall Osborn?"

"I've not yet had the pleasure of an introduction," she said.

As Osborn pivoted, a wine-dark flutter caught her eye as the decorative tassels on his boots brushed back and forth against the buffed leather. Charlotte felt her chest clench in recognition, but she managed to keep her expression unchanged.

"I'm delighted to meet you, milady." He gave her a long, appreciative look.

A little *too* appreciative.

"I've heard a great deal about you," he added.

"Indeed?" Charlotte flicked another look at his boots. She had an excellent eye for color and shapes—they were the same ones she had just seen in Hyde Park.

"Oh yes." His smile widened. "Polite Society is all abuzz over the fact that the tempestuous Earl of Wrexford has been brought to his knees."

"Wrexford on his knees?" She arched a brow. "Nonsense. His valet would never allow it—the fit of his pantaloons would be utterly ruined."

"Ha!" The smile turned into a laugh. "I shall be sure to correct the tabbies if I hear any further on-dits."

No doubt many people found Osborn's insouciance charming. However, in her opinion he was about as charming as a snake. Still, Charlotte was well aware that it behooved her to play along with his banter.

She looked up at him through her lashes. "Are people always inclined to do what you say?"

The question sparked a gleam in his eyes.

A predatory one?

"I've been told that I'm very persuasive," he replied.

"An excellent gift to have," said Charlotte. "Assuming that one uses it wisely."

Osborn's expression turned speculative. He was wondering, no doubt, whether she was flirting with him.

Two can play at cat and mouse, she thought.

After tipping her head up for a quick glance at the cloudless sky, she turned and touched Sheffield's sleeve. "The day is becoming too warm for further strolling. Shall we head to Piccadilly Street and find a hackney to take us back to Berkeley Square?"

Sheffield dutifully offered his arm.

"Good day, Lady Wrexford." Osborn touched a jaunty salute to the brim of his hat. "I sincerely hope our paths will cross again very soon."

Her reply was naught but a quicksilver smile.

Oh, you may count on it, Mr. Osborn.

CHAPTER 14

"Lord Wrexford!" The greeting rose above the *snick* of steel against steel. Henry Angelo—known as Harry to his friends—was London's most respected fencing master. He quickly finished off a dazzling flurry of slashes, which knocked the practice sword from his pupil's hand, and then cut a salute in the earl's direction. "It's been far too long since your last visit."

"Indeed, it has been," agreed Wrexford. "I've been rather busy lately."

"Ah, yes, settling into married life." Angelo smiled. "My sincere congratulations on your recent nuptials, milord." A mischievous twinkle came to his dark eyes. "I hope it hasn't slowed your step."

"As you see, I'm not dragging around a leg shackle," he replied dryly.

"I'm delighted to hear it. Have you come for a practice session?" asked Angelo. "It would be a good lesson for all my students to see a master swordsman in action."

"Regretfully, not today," answered Wrexford. "I simply wished to show the lads your establishment." He quickly introduced the three awestruck boys to the fencing master. "Raven and Hawk are my wards," he explained. "And Lord Lampson has been told that a portrait of his relative hangs on the wall. The Chevalier . . ."

"The Chevalier de St. Georges?" Angelo's gaze fixed on Peregrine. "You're related to the chevalier?"

"Yes, sir," replied the boy softly.

"Falcon is very skilled with a sword, too!" piped up Hawk.

Angelo smiled. "Is that so?' He gestured at a portrait hung high on the wall by the entrance to the academy. "That is indeed the chevalier, who was a dear friend and an extraordinary fencing master."

Peregrine stared up at the painted face, his eyes widening in wonder.

"And now, milord—that is, *young* milord—do take off your jacket," said Angelo as he moved with a graceful step to one of the wall racks and chose a slender foil. "Come step into the circle with me, and let me see what you know."

"Go on, lad. Don't be shy," urged Wrexford, seeing how Peregrine appeared frozen in place. "It's a great honor to have Mr. Angelo invite you to cross swords with him."

"You're really good," encouraged Raven.

Swallowing hard, Peregrine shuffled forward and accepted the sword.

Angelo assumed the ready position. "*En garde,* milord."

Within the academy, the fencing master was king of his domain, and was often sharp-tongued with his aristocratic clients. But Wrexford knew Angelo would be kind to the boy, no matter his level of prowess.

In truth, the earl didn't expect much. Granted, Raven and Hawk weren't easily impressed. Still . . .

Setting a hand on his hip, Wrexford watched Peregrine hesitantly raise his weapon.

But as soon as steel touched steel, it was as if an unseen current burned through the boy's nervousness. His body relaxed, his gaze sharpened.

Angelo moved slowly through a few basic feints, which Peregrine countered with ease. Quickening his tempo, the fencing master added a few more advanced maneuvers. Again the boy matched and parried them with ease.

"You've been taught well, lad," said Angelo, waggling a small salute.

"My uncle Willis learned swordplay from the chevalier, and he enjoyed passing his knowledge to me."

"Excellent. But now, let us pick up the tempo." With that, Angelo began to move with a catlike quickness, his blade dancing through the air.

Wrexford heard both Raven and Hawk gasp in delight as Peregrine still managed to hold his own.

"Bravo!" Angelo stepped back and inclined a small bow. "You have the makings of a very fine swordsman, milord."

Peregrine gave a shy smile. "Thank you, sir."

Wrexford felt a tug on his sleeve. "May we take fencing lessons, Wrex?" whispered Raven.

Hawk looked up, adding his own silent plea.

Hell's teeth. He hated to disappoint them, but . . . "You have to understand that Mr. Angelo is a very famous man here in London, and his services are in great demand. So I fear that—"

"Lessons for the lads? That's a splendid idea!" Angelo's hearing was clearly as sharp as his ripostes. "Have you any objections, Lord Wrexford?"

"Harry, I don't expect you—"

"It would give me great pleasure to teach your wards. And polish the skills of Lord Lampson."

Wrexford could almost feel the air being sucked out of the room as each boy held his breath. "You're sure, Harry?"

"Quite sure!" answered Angelo, with a grin. "In fact, why don't you leave them here with me now for their first lesson. I'll send them home in an hour or two."

The boys exchanged blissful grins.

"Don't say I didn't warn you," murmured Wrexford, but he, too, was smiling on seeing how excited the boys were.

"March into the side salon, you rascals!" ordered Angelo, much to the surprised chagrin of the baronet and viscount waiting for their scheduled lessons with the fencing master. As he came over to fetch two more foils from the rack, he winked at the earl.

"It's far more fun teaching young and willing pupils rather than lazy, overfed aristocrats," he confided.

"It's very generous of you, Harry."

"Oh, don't worry. You'll be paying me a hefty fee."

"As all five of us will be happy, I consider it worth every penny," replied Wrexford. "You know how I feel about blood and violence. But I'm also of the firm belief that a person ought to know how to defend himself."

"Oh, thank heaven you're home!" Charlotte shot from the armchair by the hearth, where she had been making some sketches from memory of the castle construction and weaponry displays in Green Park. "I was becoming concerned. The Weasels and Peregrine returned home several hours ago—with swords, I might add—"

"I'll explain about that in a moment," interrupted Wrexford. "After leaving the lads at Angelo's Fencing Academy, I wanted to make some inquiries about a gentleman whose name was given to them by an informant during their foray into the stews last night before returning here."

Charlotte sighed and looked at McClellan, who was sitting beside Sheffield at one of the work counters, where they had been passing the time by perusing the latest edition of *Ackermann's Repository*. "It seems you were right to suspect they were up to some unholy mischief."

To Wrexford, she added, "Mac happened to see that they had

allowed Peregrine to accompany them, and that mustn't happen again."

"I've already made that clear to them," he replied.

"Yes, but . . ." Charlotte frowned in thought. "While it was very kind of you to take the boys to play with steam engines and then swords, I confess to being perplexed as to why—"

"The fencing visit had to do with their foray into the stews," cut in Wrexford.

She stared at him in confusion. "But—"

"It turns out Peregrine is quite skilled in swordplay." To Sheffield, he quickly explained about their houseguest.

Charlotte sat down heavily, her own urgent news pushed aside for the moment as she contemplated his frightening revelation. "Dare I ask how you know that?"

"Don't worry, the fight in the stews was with sticks, not swords," answered Wrexford.

As if that was of any comfort, she thought.

"However, it led to a revelation about Peregrine's family tree, which led us to Angelo's." The earl told them about the Chevalier de St. Georges. "But I'm digressing. Far more importantly, the Weasels discovered an important clue through their inquiries down by the docklands." He quickly recounted what Raven had told him.

"Osborn!" she exclaimed.

"Yes, from what Raven's friend—the lad they call Smoke—overheard at one of the gaming hells near the East India wharves, it's possible that Osborn was involved in Willis's death. I've sent Tyler to make some inquiries, as we need to learn more about him."

"We already have," said Sheffield.

Wrexford suddenly frowned in consternation. "By the by, what are you doing here?"

"Waiting for you so we could have a council of war," replied Charlotte.

"You see, we, too, have been sleuthing," added Sheffield.

"And," interjected Charlotte, "we've discovered two of the key players involved in the theft of Willis's invention. And perhaps a third."

Wrexford let out a low whistle. "Indeed?"

"Yes." She shot an apologetic look at Sheffield. "My apologies, Kit, for not yet mentioning the other encounter that Mac and I had today. I thought it best to wait until Wrex was here so we could parse through all the pieces of the puzzle together."

Sheffield nodded in understanding. "However subtle, marriage adds a new layer to one's loyalties."

"But it doesn't alter the elemental bonds that tie friends together," she murmured, and then quickly resumed her explanation to Wrexford. "Mac and I were about to cross Rotten Row, when we happened to overhear a conversation . . ." She explained about the two riders.

"We then continued on to Green Park, where we met Kit—and then I had another interesting encounter. I spotted Kurlansky, Prince Rubalov's private secretary, slipping into the unfinished Temple of Concord. So I followed him and witnessed a clandestine meeting with an Englishman. Again I only heard the Englishman's voice, but . . ."

She drew in a quick breath. "But then I returned to Mac and Kit, and Kit was chatting with Osborn—who I'm now certain was both the rider with Belmont and the man trying to make a deal with Kurlansky."

Wrexford mulled over all he had heard for some moments before responding, "You are sure about the boot tassels?"

"Quite sure," answered Charlotte firmly. She had asked herself the same question, knowing that a mistake would send them off on a wild-goose chase. "Not only that, I'm equally sure he was the man trying to bribe Kurlansky."

She paused. "I've been thinking . . . it seems to me that Belmont is a henchman for the villain who originally stole Willis's invention and is running the auction. While Osborn somehow knows of the theft and is trying to get his hands on it before it's sold—"

"So that he can profit from the crime instead of the first thief," said Sheffield. "Sharks attract sharks. I've heard recent rumblings about Osborn. He's the youngest son of the Marquess of Auburndale, and word is, his behavior is becoming increasingly reckless. He's taken to playing in one of the seedier gambling hells in St. Giles, and is in debt to some very unsavory men."

"And Congreve mentioned that Osborn had been seen frequently around the Royal Armory and had come to be friends with Willis," exclaimed Charlotte.

"I wonder how Osborn learned about Willis and his invention?" mused Wrexford. "I assume Belmont heard of it through the family connection to Willis. But for such a closely-guarded secret to slip out—"

"As I keep pointing out," murmured Charlotte, "secrets have a way of slithering out of the darkest, deepest hideyhole." She thought for a moment. "Let us take heart from that. So far, the villain has been clever enough to keep his identity a secret, even from his own henchmen, but there will be a chink in his armor somewhere. We just have to find it."

"I can visit the gaming hells and see if I can uncover any more information on Osborn," offered Sheffield, "and whether he has any close cronies."

"Tyler ought to go down to Woolwich and visit some of the taverns around the armory," suggested Charlotte. "The men who work within the research laboratory—the blacksmiths, the gunpowder makers, the lathe operators—might very well know a lot about Willis's work habits and if he was collaborating with anyone else."

"Those are both excellent ideas," said the earl.

"What about . . ." Sheffield's brow creased in thought. "What about your houseguest—young Peregrine? Might he know something about his uncle's circle of friends and who might have stolen the invention?"

Charlotte felt her throat tighten. The Weasels and their new friend had already taken terrible risks in order to help protect her secret . . .

"No, it's far too dangerous to tell them about the theft of the invention," she said flatly. "It's bad enough that they know we're investigating Willis's death. The villain has already shown himself to be a murderer—and I don't doubt that Osborn would kill to get what he wants. If the boys go haring off . . ."

She looked at Wrexford.

"I have to agree," he said. "We will think about whether there is a way to coax some information out of Peregrine, but it would have to be done very carefully."

Very carefully, thought Charlotte. The Weasels were too clever by half.

"The races at Royal Ascot present our best opportunity to catch the conspirators at their own game," she mused aloud. "We know that the bank receipts will be collected from those who have bought into the bidding just before the Gold Cup race. So if we keep our eyes open, we should be able to spot yet another member of the villain's gang."

Sheffield huffed in frustration. "Who will likely be just another henchman."

"Yes, but the more pieces of the puzzle we have, the clearer the whole picture will become."

"Charlotte is right," said Wrexford. "Knowing about the plans for Royal Ascot gives us an unexpected advantage, and a chance to get closer to the truth."

"I've received an invitation to attend the races," said Sheffield, "So I'll be another pair of eyes to—"

A knock sounded on the door, and an instant later, Cordelia pushed it open. "Charlotte, I've just finished with Raven's lesson and—" She stopped abruptly, her smile quickly fading as she looked around.

"Forgive me." Her eyes lingered on Sheffield for a heartbeat before coming back to Charlotte. "I appear to be intruding on a private discussion."

"Not at all," replied Sheffield. "We were merely chatting about the upcoming festivities for the next few days."

Charlotte gave an inward wince. Cordelia had been a part of too many of their previous councils of war not to recognize an outrageous lie when she heard it.

Their friend's expression betrayed a flicker of hurt before hardening to a stony stare. "In that case, don't let me interrupt such a fascinating topic." She gave a cool nod to Charlotte. "I merely wanted to give you my greetings." She retreated a step. "Good day to you all."

The door closed with a tad more force than was necessary.

"Hell's bells," muttered Charlotte. After directing an exasperated huff at Sheffield, she gathered her skirts and hurried off in pursuit.

"Cordelia."

Up ahead, the angry tattoo of steps quickened.

"Please wait and hear me out!" Charlotte knew that the close-knit bonds of their group's friendships would be damaged—perhaps irreparably—if she let Cordelia leave without having a heart-to-heart talk.

Was it just her imagination, or did her friend's pace begin to slow?

Seizing her chance, Charlotte rushed around the corner and caught Cordelia's arm just before she reached the entrance foyer.

"In here," she ordered, drawing her friend into a side parlor and shutting the door behind them. "We need to have a talk."

Cordelia turned around to face her. Lifting her chin, she folded her arms against her chest. "What is there to say? Clearly,

I am persona non grata here." Her harsh tone, however, belied the glimmer of tears beading on her lashes.

Without a word, Charlotte stepped forward and enfolded her friend in a hug.

Choking back a sob, Cordelia didn't try to break away. They stood entwined in a shaky silence for several long moments, before Cordelia finally lifted her face from Charlotte's shoulder and gave a watery sniff.

"How embarrassing. I *never* cry."

"You have good reason to be upset," said Charlotte. "Would you like some tea?" A pause. "Or perhaps some brandy?"

"What I'd *really* like is to punch Kit in the nose," replied Cordelia. "He's being unfair—"

"Horribly unfair," agreed Charlotte.

"How *dare* he imply that I ought not be pleasant to Monsieur Rochambert! He has *no* right to bully me as to whom I may or may not choose as a friend."

"That goes without saying."

Charlotte's support seemed to dampen her friend's fire. Cordelia drew in a deep breath and then let it out in a harried sigh. "I don't understand—why is he treating me so badly? That I have the chance to discuss mathematics with such a luminary in the field is a special opportunity." The corners of her mouth trembled. "And yet he seems intent on making me feel as if I'm doing something egregiously wrong."

"Come, let us sit." Charlotte guided her friend to the sofa. "The simple answer to your questions," she continued, once they had settled in place among the pillows, "is that love makes us do stupid things."

"Love?" Cordelia gave a skeptical snort. "Ha!"

"But the real answers are far more complicated. Let me try to explain . . ." Charlotte took a moment to compose her thoughts. "For years, Kit has seen himself as naught but a superficial fribble. He has proven his true colors to all of us—he's smart and clever and loyal and kind—but it seems to me that he has yet to recognize his own true colors."

"B-But that's ridiculous!"

Charlotte waved Cordelia to silence. "It's clear as crystal that he's in love with you, but my sense is, he doesn't think he's worthy of your hand. He sees you as brilliant and brave and principled—in other words, a far more admirable person than he is . . ."

An inarticulate sound seemed to stick in Cordelia's throat.

"He thinks Rochambert's intellect and poise attract you. And that frightens him. And as he's too afraid to tell you his true feelings, he's . . ." Charlotte chuffed a sigh. "He's acting like an arse."

Cordelia blinked, tears once again welling up in her eyes. "That's because he *is* an arse." She looked away, as if searching for some way to steady her emotions. "Hell and damnation." Her voice dropped to a whisper. "How can he not know that I . . . that I admire and esteem him?"

Charlotte felt a stab of sympathy. She and Cordelia had both struggled against the strictures of aristocratic society. Women of their class were meant to be biddable. Independent thinking and intellectual curiosity were seen as unladylike. More than that, they were seen as dangerous. Charlotte had eloped to Italy to avoid living in a gilded cage. And Cordelia had been branded as an eccentric—a lady doomed to fade into pitiable spinsterhood, as no right-minded gentleman would want such an odd wife.

A large dowry could, of course, have altered that. But Cordelia's brother, the current Earl of Woodbridge, was still trying to replenish the family coffers after their father's profligate spending had left them close to ruin. And the fact that Cordelia herself was a partner in a thriving business was not something that could be revealed.

"I think neither of us finds it easy to speak about our feelings," said Charlotte gently. "The choices we made in how to live our lives made it imperative that we guard our hearts. Allowing the slightest crack in our defenses makes us vulnerable."

"B-But you and Wrexford . . ." Cordelia slowly turned back to meet Charlotte's gaze.

"Wrexford and I both struggled with admitting our feelings. Trust isn't easy."

Shadows rippled in the depths of Cordelia's eyes. Along with a glimmer of hope. "So, how did you manage . . ."

"By deciding that living behind impregnable walls, with only one's self for company, wasn't a very fulfilling life. And that taking a leap of faith was worth it."

Cordelia swallowed hard.

"Kit is feeling just as vulnerable as you are. And men tend to be more irrationally stubborn than we women are," counseled Charlotte. "Far be it for me to advise anyone on Life." She crooked a smile. "Heaven knows, I've made an ungodly number of mistakes. However, you might wish to think about giving him some . . . encouragement."

Cordelia reached out and found Charlotte's hand. Their fingers twined, warmth pulsing against warmth. "Thank you," she said softly. "For being a friend despite my flaws."

"None of us can sail a ship alone. We need friends aboard to help us steady the keel and keep a firm hand on the tiller when the weather turns rough."

A comfortable silence settled over them, the faint ticking of the mantel clock echoing the beating of their hearts.

"Speaking of friends and friendship," said Cordelia, after several minutes had passed, "I shall feel quite hurt if you don't include me in whatever investigation is afoot. Clearly, there is something very serious at stake, and I want to be part of it."

Her eyes narrowed. "Is there a murder involved? I noted that A. J. Quill raised some questions about the inventor who was found floating in the Serpentine."

"Yes," answered Charlotte. Cordelia had proven herself to be a loyal member of their inner circle, and had more than earned the right to be trusted without hesitation. "We have reason to believe Mr. Willis was murdered . . ."

Cordelia listened to the lengthy explanation of how the seemingly random accident had drawn Charlotte and Wrexford into a dangerous netherworld of international intrigue.

"Merciful heavens," whispered Cordelia, once Charlotte finished sketching out what had happened so far. "What can I do to help?"

"We know that an auction of Willis's invention is being arranged, though given the likely participants and the time constraints, it's got to be a highly sophisticated one."

"An auction?" Cordelia's expression turned oddly pensive. "How very strange."

"In what way?" inquired Charlotte.

Her friend hesitated. "It's just that at Lady Keating's soiree last night, Monsieur Rochambert was telling me and several other members of the London Society of Mathematics about some very advanced equations he was working on to . . ." Cordelia blew out a small breath. "I believe he said that they had something to do with auctions, but I confess, I didn't quite follow his reasoning. It was all awfully abstruse."

"I don't pretend to understand the mathematical mind, but exploring theories seems a common challenge," murmured Charlotte. "So perhaps it's merely coincidence." And yet she couldn't help recalling Alison's comment that there were many Frenchmen eager to see Bonaparte reseated on the throne of France.

"However," she added, "you might keep your ears and eyes open when you are around him."

As Cordelia nodded, another thought occurred to Charlotte. "Do you perchance know whether Rochambert is planning to attend tomorrow's races at Royal Ascot?"

"No, he and the other members of the French scientific delegation are leaving today for Oxford, where they have meetings scheduled with the English scholars before the pomp and rituals of the royal visit to the town," replied her friend. "As you know, there is a gala celebration taking place at the university in several days to honor Prinny, Tsar Alexander, and the King of Prussia. The visiting sovereigns and a host of Allied dignitaries will be receiving honorary degrees."

"Yes, we shall be journeying to Oxford as well for the festivities," said Charlotte, though she was not looking forward to formal dinners and tedious award ceremonies. "The tsar and his sister, the Grand Duchess of Oldenburg, are staying in Merton, which is Wrexford's college, so he has been asked to help play host to them."

"My brother attended Cambridge," said Cordelia with a wry smile. "So we are not beholden to make an appearance in Oxford. He's delighted, as it promises to be a very boring occasion."

Charlotte didn't disagree.

"But as it happens, Lady Thirkell doesn't wish to attend the festivities by herself, so she has asked me to accompany her to hear the lectures and attend the grand dinner at the Radcliffe Library. We shall be staying for two nights in the city," added Cordelia, and then pursed her mouth in thought. "Was there a reason you asked about the races at Royal Ascot?"

"Yes," answered Charlotte, and proceeded to recount the conversation she had heard in the park.

"So you're hoping to catch the villains in their perfidy—"

"We have no illusions that the leaders will be the ones collecting the information. But knowing the identity of yet another of their henchmen may help lead us to them."

"I see," said Cordelia. "I'm sorry that I can't be there at Royal Ascot to act as another pair of eyes and ears."

"As I said, you can still be very helpful by paying close attention while around Rochambert—especially during your

Oxford visit—and taking note if he speaks to anyone on the subject of auctions."

"And if I do see or hear something—"

"Don't do anything to draw attention to your interest," cautioned Charlotte. "Just wait until we arrive in Oxford and pass the information to us. We already know these men are ruthless. They have killed once. And I don't doubt that they will kill again if it suits their purposes."

CHAPTER 15

"Damn Beau Brummell," grumbled Wrexford, tugging in irritation at the intricate knot of his starched cravat. "Only an arse who does nothing but lounge in his club would decree that one must wear skintight black coats and formal white cravats to a horse race."

Charlotte looked around from her dressing table. "You look very handsome."

The earl responded with a very rude word.

"Be that as it may, if we wish to gain entrance to the Prince Regent's enclosure, we must follow the strict rules of dress," she pointed out.

More grumblings sounded in his throat as Wrexford shifted the top hat in his hands and drummed an impatient tattoo on the flat crown. His nerves were unaccountably on edge, and not simply because of the silly fashion requirement for being admitted into the exclusive enclosure for the royal guests.

"Be sure to put your pocket pistol in your reticule, even though it's not on any list of stylish accessories for ladies."

"I trust you are armed as well?" she said.

"Be assured that if trouble strikes, I am ready to strike back."

"Sheffield will be as well," she said. "And Tyler. He'll blend into the crowd of commoners, and keep an eye on the outer stables and paddocks."

"It goes without saying that I'll be armed as well, milord," murmured McClellan as she slid the last few hairpins into Charlotte's topknot. "I, too, will be among the commoners, watching for any havey-cavey activity."

Charlotte caught his eye in the reflection of the looking glass. "Are you upset that I confided in Cordelia? I thought it wrong to exclude her simply because Kit is behaving irrationally."

"No," he admitted. "As you say, there's no question that she's earned our unwavering trust. However, I confess that I do worry about whether her admiration for the Frenchman might color her judgment at a critical moment."

"Cordelia possesses one of the most brilliant and analytical minds I know," responded Charlotte. "She's built a thriving business by using steel-sharp logic to guide her decisions. Are you really saying that you think a handsome face and a flirtatious smile will turn her into a flighty female?"

Wrexford allowed a rueful smile. "I dare not answer that in the affirmative."

"A wise decision," she replied dryly. "In all seriousness, please put aside any reservations. Cordelia has proved her mettle. And will do so again if a situation calls for it."

A hail from Tyler announced that the carriage was ready to take them out of the city to Ascot Heath.

The trip, while tedious, was uneventful, and as the morning clouds blew off, the day had turned pleasantly warm by the time they arrived at the racetrack. The Gold Cup was to be the last race run, but they had come early enough to explore the grounds. Tyler and McClellan had taken the smaller, unmarked carriage and would join the throng of spectators gathering on the public side of the racetrack.

"I see Alison has come with Sir Robert," observed Wrexford, once they arrived at the royal enclosure. "I'll take you to join them, and then I'll stroll through the paddock area before joining the Austrian envoy's group." He felt Charlotte's arm stiffen. "We did agree that given the government's possible interest in your activities, you must appear to be a perfectly proper countess when we appear in public," he reminded her. "Which means you wouldn't dream of walking where manure might befoul your silken skirts."

She nodded grimly. "I was tempted to suggest that I attend the races as Magpie. My street urchin persona would have fit in well with the boisterous crowd of commoners." An unhappy sigh. "However, I decided that I had a better chance of spotting the exchange of information if I were in the royal enclosure." They had decided that when the time for the races arrived, each of them would contrive to join the social circle of the three main suspects—Wrexford with the Austrians, Sheffield with the Prussians, and Charlotte with the Russians—in order to watch for the villain's henchman.

"I don't expect any excitement outside the gathering of Prinny's guests," said Wrexford. "But my military experience has taught me that it's always wise to reconnoiter and know the lay of the land when the enemy is nearby."

"Charlotte!" called Alison with a jaunty wave as they passed through the guarded gate. The exclusive royal enclosure was starting to fill.

"Would you care for some champagne, Lady Wrexford?" asked Sir Robert.

"That would be delightful," she answered with a smile.

Much as Charlotte resented the restrictions of Polite Society, Wrexford knew she would abide by them. Her passions, however fiery, were always tempered by pragmatism.

"I see Kit over by the refreshment table. Remember, let us all stick to our assigned roles," he murmured.

*   *   *

The sparkling wine prickled like dagger points against her tongue, but Charlotte forced herself to swallow her irritation and concentrate on the task at hand. There were times when the persona of a grand lady was just as effective as that of a ragged street urchin.

Thankfully, either role fits me as comfortably as a second skin, she thought.

Spotting Prince Rubalov and his private secretary watching the horses being readied for the first race, Charlotte moved to join them.

"What a lovely pair of earbobs," murmured Kurlansky, a hint of humor quivered at the corners of his mouth. "With such a jostling crowd, do have a care that one doesn't come unfastened."

"Thank you for the warning," she replied. "I rarely make the same mistake twice."

"Do you enjoy horse racing, milady?" inquired the prince. His face was already flushed with drink.

"Racehorses are magnificent creatures and a beauty to watch in action," answered Charlotte. "But I can't say that I get as much of a thrill out of the head-to-head competition as most people do."

"But it's such an elemental metaphor for life," said Kurlansky. "There are a few lucky winners and there are losers."

"Is that true in every aspect of life?" she asked.

He considered the question. "I can't think of any exceptions."

She gave him a challenging smile. "I have heard that Russians have a pessimistic view of human nature. It appears to be true—"

"No, no, milady!" exclaimed Rubalov. "I assure you, we are really quite jolly fellows." He gave his secretary a jab with his elbow. "Isn't that so?"

"But of course," replied Kurlansky without batting an eye. "Shall I fetch you both another glass of champagne?"

After waving him away, the prince set out to prove his assertion by regaling her with stories of his sumptuous parties in St. Petersburg. Several other dignitaries quickly came over to join them—which played perfectly to Charlotte's objectives. A lady was not expected to comment, but merely to listen in rapt admiration. She needed only to give an occasional trilling laugh as Rubalov prosed on, while keeping a careful watch on the activities going on around them.

She wondered what Kurlansky's connection was to Osborn—

The *crack* of the starter's pistol drew her back to the moment. The first race, a preliminary contest, drew little attention from the crowd within the Prince Regent's enclosure. The royal guests had come to see the running of the prestigious Gold Cup—the interlude before was merely a time for enjoying the lavish array of food and drink, along with the titillating gossip.

Out of the corner of her eye, she saw that Wrexford had returned from his stroll. As planned, the earl had taken up a position close to the Austrian envoy, while Sheffield was close to the Prussian representative.

Charlotte flicked anther quick look around, and silently cursed the crowd. The villain had been clever. All the jostling and revelry would make it very difficult to spot any clandestine activity.

Fueled by the sparkling wine, the mood was turning more raucous. Many of the gentlemen were growing unsteady on their feet, their voices rising to be heard over the noises from the crowd of commoners on the other side of the track.

Charlotte suddenly felt a little disoriented. The cacophony of sounds—thundering hooves, popping corks, cheers, laughter, groans . . . The pungent scents of sweat and horse swirled with the sweetness of the fizzy champagne . . . The task of unraveling betrayals within betrayals . . .

Shaking off her momentary malaise, Charlotte made herself concentrate. This was no time for weakness. The stakes were too high.

A roar rose from the spectators as the leader of the current race galloped over the finish line. The excitement was now starting to build for the Gold Cup race. The entries—magnificent muscled stallions, their flanks glistening from the prerace warm-up—were led into the parade paddock. Tails swooshing, hooves flashing, they pranced with nervous energy, the silk-clad jockeys adjusting their reins and eyeing the competition . . .

She shifted slightly, keeping close to Rubalov as he and his coterie moved up to the fence. A gentleman—indistinguishable from the rest of the formally-dressed crowd, save for a discreet navy sash that marked him as one of the Prince Regent's staff—approached them.

Charlotte stepped closer, turning her gaze to the horses.

"My dear prince," she heard Navy Sash murmur, "might I ask you to do my bidding and step aside for a private word?"

Bidding. Charlotte guessed that the word was the coded signal for the invited participants to pass over their bank receipt to confirm their entry to the auction. Sure enough, Rubalov edged away to join Navy Sash, who leaned in to whisper a message to the prince.

Pretending not to notice what had just happened, she moved away to alert Wrexford. Catching his eye, she stopped and flicked a look back at the prince. He waited for a moment, and then came to join her.

"I think I've spotted the henchman," she whispered, and quickly told him what she had seen.

"Join Kit and pass on the information," he ordered. "And remember, the two of you are to stay here and do nothing to draw attention to yourselves." Without waiting for a reply, he moved off.

Much as she hated being out of the hunt, Wrexford was

right. It would be foolishly rash for her or Sheffield to chase after the henchman. While she was willing to risk her identity as A. J. Quill if need be, this was not the occasion to do so.

Fisting her skirts, she forced a ladylike smile and turned to join Sheffield.

Damn Beau Brummell, thought Wrexford once again as he sought to keep track of Navy Sash among the crowd of gentlemen dressed identically in black coats, white cravats, and pantaloons. To complicate matters, the dratted fellow had his top hat pulled low on his brow, making it impossible to see his face. Still, the earl managed to move stealthily through the spectators, keeping his quarry in view.

And he soon confirmed that Navy Sash was the messenger collecting the banking receipts that would allow the competing countries to enter the auction. *Russia, Austria, Prussia, and British Home Secretary . . .* they had guessed correctly on the major players, but Navy Sash also stopped to confer with a French diplomat and the representative of one of the larger German principalities.

Wrexford wondered if Pierson and Grentham knew about the added competitors. He wasn't so naïve as to imagine they had told him everything they knew about the game being played by the countries jockeying for power.

Navy Sash moved to the side gate and left the royal enclosure, quickening his steps as he headed toward the barns. The earl waited for several moments, and then took another footpath that his earlier reconnaissance had shown would reconnect to the main walkway.

A quick look around the corner of one of the hay sheds showed Navy Sash dart into the middle barn. Giving thanks for Tyler's skill with needle and thread, Wrexford drew his hidden pocket pistol from the inner pocket that had hastily been added to his snug-fitting coat. It was a pity that fashion prevented him from carrying his more accurate dueling pistol. But at close quarters, the difference was negligible.

The sharp smell of manure was cut by the sweetness of the hay as he slipped inside the barn and paused to allow his eyes to adjust to the murky light. The nickers and rustling of horses in their stalls made it impossible to hear the sound of footsteps or voices. He would have to proceed very carefully . . .

There were two flagged walkways running the length of the barn, each with stalls and storage areas on either side. Wrexford peered into the flitting shadows. *No luck.* He would trust his instincts. After folding over his lapels to cover the white of his cravat, he started down the left walkway.

The place appeared deserted. A quick check of one of the stalls showed the horses were work animals, not racing stock. He imagined the grooms were all busy in the other barns.

Which was likely why this one was chosen. From what Charlotte had overheard, Navy Sash was going to pass the collected notes on to Belmont, who would then meet with—

The sudden thud of hooves warned that someone was coming.

Wrexford ducked into an empty stall, just as a dark, amorphous shape—a horse and rider—materialized at the far end of the walkway. He heard the slap of leather, and the quickening of the horse's pace. Flattening himself against the half-open gate, he held very still, his gaze locked on the sliver of space affording a view of the walkway.

The horse and rider passed, and though they were shrouded in shadows, Wrexford was able to catch several details before they disappeared from view—the rider was wearing a hooded cloak despite the pleasant weather, and the horse had a brand on its flank.

Thank heavens that Charlotte has taught me to notice such visuals, he thought, taking a moment to commit the pattern to memory before edging out of his hiding place for a last look at the rider. For an instant, the cloaked figure was limned in the sunlight as the horse trotted through the open doorway and was spurred to a canter.

Not Navy Sash, decided Wrexford. The rider was taller and broader in the shoulders. *And not a groom.* Which begged the question . . .

He pushed aside such thoughts for later.

Hearing no other sounds of movement, he continued to make his way down the walkway. Finding no sign of his quarry, he cautiously crept across the stones and peered down the adjoining section of stalls.

"Oh, God . . . Oh, God . . ."

The strangled whisper was coming from the gentleman crouched down beside a body sprawled on the flagging. Then, pressing his hands to his mouth to stifle a horrified moan, the gentleman—it was Belmont—rose and rushed for the side door that led out to the paddock area.

The stones were already darkening with snakelike rivulets meandering out from beneath the body. Blood. And given the amount now spreading over the flagging, Wrexford guessed that the knife protruding from Navy Sash's chest had cut straight to the heart.

He hesitated. Belmont wasn't the killer—his hands had been lily-white. Which meant—

The faint slither of leather on the stones alerted Wrexford that someone was stealthily approaching. He held his breath and waited.

Sure enough, a gentleman dressed in the formal clothing required to enter the royal enclosure was creeping closer and closer to Navy Sash's corpse. *A foreign operative who had been spying on Belmont? Or the killer returning to retrieve the auction bids?*

The earl remained in hiding, watching as the man bent over and began searching through the dead man's coat pockets.

Catching the flicker of a pistol barrel as the gentleman shifted position, Wrexford started forward.

"Don't move," he said softly, coming up close behind the gentleman and cocking his trigger. "Toss aside your weapon."

The gentleman hesitated for a fraction, then did as ordered. It skidded across the stones and buried itself in a tangle of hay.

"Turn around—and do it slowly."

"But of course," came the unruffled answer, sounding as the gentleman shuffled his stance . . .

Wrexford saw the cobra-quick strike coming an instant too late. The fist hit his forearm, sending his own pistol flying into the gloom.

Hell's teeth—the indolent life of an aristocrat is making me slow and stupid.

He stepped back just in time to avoid the slash from the long knife that the gentleman had whipped out from inside his boot.

"The advantage appears to have changed hands," sneered the gentleman—or rather, the Honorable Randall Osborn. Wrexford recognized him as a fellow member of White's, the exclusive men's club on St. James's Street.

"Actually, it appears that we're now evenly matched," he replied, drawing his own blade from its hidden sheath.

"It doesn't surprise me that you've come prepared, Wrexford." Osborn's knife flashed again, driving him back another step. "Wellington speaks highly of your prowess. I daresay he'll be disappointed to hear you're a filthy traitor."

Wrexford laughed. "You may drop your pretense of patriotism. I know all about your sordid scheming. Your meeting with Belmont in the park did not go unheard."

Osborn's smugness wavered for a moment, and then the wolfish grin was back. "You're clever. But not quite clever enough." The two of them were circling each other, darting out cat-and-mouse feints to probe for a defensive weakness. "Tell me, for whom are you working?"

"I should think that's obvious," replied Wrexford. "Grentham's office. What about you? Who's the villain who arranged for Willis's invention to be stolen? And how did you learn about him and decide to steal it for yourself?"

Another flicker of uncertainty from Osborn. Wrexford seized the chance to attack and almost drew blood.

"That's enough, gentlemen." Pierson stepped out of the shadows. "Much as I'm curious to see who would come out the winner in a game of thrust and parry, I'm rather limited in my choice of operatives for this investigation and can't afford to lose either of you."

CHAPTER 16

"Damn your eyes," growled Wrexford, drawing back and dropping his guard. "It's not only dangerous, but also supremely foolish to send your troops into battle without knowing who is friend or foe."

"Surely you didn't think that you were the only one we had looking for Willis's invention," retorted Pierson with a cynical chuckle. "It seemed to me that the paths we had you two following wouldn't cross."

"I would have thought you too experienced in the vagaries of espionage to make such smug assumptions," he countered.

A shrug. "We were forced to cobble together our response to this crisis in a hurry."

Left unsaid, thought Wrexford, was the fact that if something went wrong, he would pay the price for bad planning and the government would simply find someone else to take his place.

"Who overheard me in Hyde Park?" demanded Osborn. "I was careful to check the surroundings and saw no one around."

"Never mind," snapped the earl. To Pierson, he added,

"Clearly, my network of eyes and ears is far more skilled than yours."

"As to that—" began Pierson, only to be interrupted by a sudden shout.

"Osborn?" A pause, then the shout came again, this time even louder. *"Osborn?"*

"Hell's teeth, that's Colonel Duxbury," muttered Osborn. "He must have seen me leave the royal enclosure."

Pierson reacted without hesitation. "Strip off the dead man's sash and pull out his pockets to make it look like a robbery . . . Tell him the two of you were having a smoke and saw a man fleeing the barn, so you decided to investigate." He withdrew into the shadows of an empty stall. "Osborn, take the colonel away with you to find a race official and discreetly arrange for a local magistrate to come deal with the crime."

To Wrexford, he added, "Stay here when they leave. I want a further word with you."

"I'm here, Colonel!" Osborn called in response to a third hail.

Wrexford had already crouched down and arranged the corpse as ordered. As he did so, he spotted a small silver watch fob partially hidden in the straw. Catching it in his fingers, he quickly pocketed it as he rose.

The echo of hurried footsteps shivered through the gloom, and a moment later, Duxbury appeared, his scarlet tunic bright as a candle flame in the glow of his lantern.

"What happened?" demanded the colonel without preamble.

"It appears to have been a robbery," replied Osborn. "Lord Wrexford and I were enjoying a smoke out of view of the ladies and saw a man fleeing the barn . . ." He gave a vague wave in the direction of the paddock area and the milling crowd of commoners on the far side of the racetrack. "So we decided to investigate."

To Wrexford, he said, "Allow me to introduce Colonel Sir Atticus Duxbury, my superior at Horse Guards."

"Milord," acknowledged Duxbury curtly, but his gaze quickly returned to the dead man. "Any idea who he is?"

"No, sir," replied Osborn. "But given the Prince Regent's presence, and the number of extremely important royal guests, it would be wise for us to handle the situation very . . . discreetly."

"Indeed." The colonel frowned in thought. He had a thin, ascetic face—sharply carved features without a grain of softness. Beneath his pale lashes, glimmered dark eyes that appeared not to miss much.

Wrexford watched him drop down on his haunches to examine the knife hilt protruding from the dead man's chest and the victim's disheveled clothing—though he showed a well-trained discipline in not touching anything. "It seems a clear-cut case of a random robbery. The poor fellow happened to be in the wrong place at the wrong time."

"You and I should go find a race official," suggested Osborn, "while Wrexford remains here to ensure that no one else stumbles onto the body. I'm sure the government doesn't wish for the crime to become public knowledge."

Duxbury appeared to hesitate.

"Your rank and uniform will ensure that the race officials won't question our orders on how to handle the situation, sir."

Before Duxbury could reply, another hail cut through the gloom. "Colonel!"

"Bloody hell," muttered Duxbury, "it's my aide-de-camp. He's like a faithful hound, always following after his master eager to earn a pat on the head." He rose and called, "I'm here, Major Waltham."

"Waltham is an able administrator," murmured Osborn.

"Yes, yes," said Duxbury. "And he deals well with all the tedious details of paperwork. But he hasn't the steel or the tactical imagination to be a good military officer. However, his father was a war hero from the last century, so . . ." His words trailed off as his aide-de-camp rushed to join them.

"Good Lord," Waltham pressed his lips together as he caught sight of the blood seeping out from beneath the corpse.

He was slender and of medium height, with sandy hair that was just beginning to show a bit of grey at the temples. His features were well sculpted, and Wrexford imagined that ladies found him attractive. However, there was a certain pinched tension to his mouth.

Wrexford guessed that the major was clever enough to know his superior didn't respect him or his talents.

"Don't stand there gawking—come with us, Major," snapped Duxbury, offering no explanation for the dead man at their feet. "Once we find the head race official and explain the need for absolute secrecy concerning this incident, I'll leave you to work with him on arranging for the body's removal."

He turned to the earl. "We'll return as quickly as we can, Wrexford. Don't let anyone approach."

Their eyes met.

"I assume you're capable of handling that?" His steely voice was clearly meant to intimidate a soft-as-butter aristocrat.

"Correct," responded Wrexford coolly.

Osborn cleared his throat. "Sir, we need to hurry . . ."

Duxbury turned on his heel and marched away without further comment, waving for Osborn and Waltham to follow.

The flickering lantern light disappeared as the three men reached the end of the walkway and turned the corner to exit.

"Osborn has a lot to learn about espionage," murmured Wrexford, hearing Pierson step out from his hiding place. "Which surprises me. Grentham and his operatives have a reputation for being ruthlessly competent."

"As I said, the situation required immediate action, and the need to move within the highest social and military circles limited our choice of operatives. So we've had to improvise," replied Pierson grudgingly. "Osborn's family is known to the top echelons of Horse Guards, so I was able to place him as a temporary private secretary to the two senior officers in charge of the Ordnance Office. He's not as experienced in skullduggery as I might have wished, but he's done several small tasks for us while at his regular position in the Foreign Office, so I believe he'll serve my purposes."

"Ah, yes, your purposes," he said. "A topic that I very much wish to discuss."

A smile tugged at Pierson's mouth. "What a pity that your wishes are not my command."

Wrexford hadn't really expected a full explanation. Still, the bloody intelligence operative owed him some basic information. "Given that you've placed Osborn at Horse Guards, I presume that Sir Atticus is a suspect."

Pierson drew in a measured breath as he considered the statement. "Actually, General Everett Malden, whose duties include overseeing all activities at the Royal Armory, is the one under surveillance."

"Malden is a highly decorated officer, who served with great distinction during the Peninsular campaigns," mused Wrexford. "And over the last year, he coordinated our efforts with the Allied armies on the eastern front—earning, I believe, the Order of St. George for his heroics at the Battle of Leipzig."

"You're very knowledgeable on military matters."

"Knowledge is very useful. It's a pity more people don't appreciate its value."

"Indeed," agreed Pierson. "So allow me to share yet another bit of knowledge about General Malden. For the past twelve months, he has served as an aide-de-camp to Prince Karl von Schwarzenberg, the Austrian field marshal and commander in chief of the Allied armies at the Battle of Leipzig. And he's become a great friend and confidante of the prince."

A pause. "From whom he's acquired a taste for the finer things in life. They carouse together, and in the course of the partying, Malden has acquired an Austrian mistress, who happens to be the prince's cousin."

The distant *crack* of the starter's pistol announced that the Gold Cup race was off and running.

"Unfortunately, Malden's grandfather squandered what wealth the family once had. So he's feeling pinched in the purse."

"Interesting," remarked Wrexford. "But so far, what you're implying is simply conjecture. Or do you have any real evidence of his perfidy?"

Pierson sidestepped the question with one of his own. "You seem to have excellent informants. Perhaps you'd like to pass their names on to me."

"They are not for sale."

"I'd pay them very well."

"Not as well as I do," said the earl. "And just so there's no room for misunderstanding, if you attempt to spy on me, I will walk away from this investigation in a heartbeat."

"And leave your country between a rock and a stone?" demanded Pierson.

"The choice is yours."

"I admire your sangfroid, milord," said Pierson softly. "Not many people dare to challenge me."

"And not many people choose to poke me with a sharp stick," retorted Wrexford.

Pierson's sphinxlike expression betrayed a hint of amusement. "Then let us sheath our weapons, verbal and otherwise. You have my word that I won't seek to interfere with you or your minions."

A pledge, thought Wrexford, that wasn't worth more than the spit and hot air with which it was formed. Pierson would honor it only if it suited his own objectives. However, he kept such assessments to himself.

"Is there anything else I should know about what you've discovered so far?" pressed Pierson.

Wrexford decided to say nothing about the watch fob or the rider he had seen and the mark that was branded on his horse's flank. Two could play at keeping secrets.

"Only that Prince Rubalov's private secretary seemed interested in talking to Osborn," he answered. "Any idea why?"

"We heard rumors that the Russians were sniffing around to see if Willis's invention might be acquired before it goes to auction," admitted Pierson. "I asked Osborn to get a sense of whether that was true."

"What about Belmont?" asked the earl. "How does he fit in?"

An unhappy sigh. "I would have preferred that you didn't stumble across his involvement. I'm aware that you have a family connection by marriage to him. However, you don't have a reputation for being a sentimental fellow, so—"

"Nonetheless, he *is* family," interjected the earl. "So I really must insist on knowing how he fits into the puzzle."

A weighty silence hung between them as Pierson considered the demand. Or perhaps he was taking the time to fabricate a plausible lie.

"Very well," he finally said. "I imagine it's no surprise that Belmont resented the—shall we say—dark side of his family. It rankled that the title and estate went to his older brother's mulatto son. And his unhappiness extended to his nephew's uncle. He couldn't bring himself to believe that Jeremiah Willis could be a brilliant inventor and engineer. The two men barely knew each other, but Belmont somehow learned of the revolving-pistol project, even though it was an extremely well-guarded secret. Even Congreve didn't know exactly what Willis was doing in his laboratory . . ."

Wrexford had an inkling of how Belmont had discovered the secret, but he wasn't about to say so.

"But no matter how he got the information, the point is, Belmont was careless with it. His lips tend to loosen when he drinks too much, and apparently he rattled on to the wrong people about how unfair it was that Willis would soon be famous for creating a new weapon that would revolutionize warfare."

"You're saying he didn't sell the information?"

"No, the bloody fool betrayed our government out of sheer stupidity," muttered Pierson. "He soon received a blackmail letter, demanding confidential information about security at the Royal Laboratory at Woolwich, or else his superiors at the Foreign Office would be told that he was planning to steal the invention himself."

"And he supplied the information to the blackmailer?"

"Yes," came the curt reply. "But when Willis was found dead in the Serpentine, he realized that to continue cooperating with the villains might very well put his own neck in a hangman's noose. So he came to us and proposed a deal. We would forgive his earlier transgression in return for him appearing to work with the villains, so he could try to learn their identity for us."

That explained the meeting with Osborn in Hyde Park, thought Wrexford. "However," he observed, "judging by what he relayed to Osborn, Belmont doesn't appear to be doing a very good job at uncovering anything helpful."

A shadow flitted over Pierson's face. "No. And if he doesn't stiffen his spine and get control of his nerves, he may give away the fact that he's a turncoat and put our plans of retrieving the stolen material in danger."

Though Wrexford didn't like Belmont, he felt a twinge of pity for him. The man had made a careless mistake. But then, in the exclusive clubs of London, the same scenario occurred nearly every night—a high-placed gentleman imbibed too much brandy and proceeded to murmur indiscretions. A few careless words and government negotiations were compromised . . . banking and trade policies upended . . . personal reputations ruined . . .

It appeared that Belmont wasn't evil to the core. He was merely unlucky in having chosen to vent his spleen in the wrong company.

"Perhaps if I talked with Belmont, I could learn more about his blackmailers." Seeing a flash of lantern light at the far end of the barn, Wrexford quickly moved to retrieve his pistol. "And help him devise a strategy to find what we need."

Pierson's gaze turned even more shuttered as he took a moment to flick a mote of dust from his cuff.

"Leave Belmont to us."

Wrexford didn't press the point. Time was limited, and there was a far more important issue to address while he had Pierson in front of him. "And what about the other obvious complication?" He gestured at the corpse. "Seeing as the villain's messenger has been murdered, we have to assume that someone else had reason to want to know who has bought into the auction. The question is, why? What good is the information if one doesn't have the technical plans and the prototype."

Pierson didn't answer.

"Damnation, don't send me chasing my tail! Did *you* have the fellow murdered in order to delay the auction?" A pause. "Or to see exactly who is entered in the competition."

Silence quivered between them. "I'd like to say I was that clever," muttered Pierson. "However, the answer to your question is that I'm as much in the dark as you are about what's going on." He cocked an ear as the sound of steps now warned that the others were returning. "I'm trusting that you—and your network of eyes and ears—will unravel the answer."

It was dark by the time they all reassembled at Berkeley Square. Charlotte watched as Wrexford kindled a fire to life in the hearth. Despite the summery evening, the chill in the workroom seemed to cut right to the bone.

He looked up for a moment and met her gaze. His expression was grim, his eyes dark with the brooding look that came over him when he was wrestling with a conundrum that was defying logic. During the carriage ride home, he had told her only of finding Navy Sash murdered before he then withdrew into a fraught silence.

She hadn't pressed him for details, knowing he would reveal them when he was ready. As he carefully arranged the chunks of coal and then reached for a taper, she thought about how comfortable she had become with his process of sorting through the pieces of a puzzle. It was very different from the way her mind worked . . .

But perhaps that is why we fit together so well. A smile touched her lips, despite the somber mood in the room. Mutual respect and admiration was a very good base on which to build a marriage.

"Would anyone care for tea?" said McClellan as she put a tray on the work counter. "And what few ginger biscuits escaped the Weasels and Peregrine."

"I'd prefer whisky," said Sheffield, who was already at the sideboard.

"So would I," confessed Tyler.

Sheffield wordlessly poured out five glasses and passed them around. He had come back from the Ascot Heath in his own carriage, and knew only the same basic fact as Charlotte and the others did. Impatience was plainly writ on his face, but he, too, knew Wrexford well enough to hold his tongue.

The earl rose and wiped his hands before taking up the glass Sheffield had placed on the mantel.

"The game has changed," he announced after taking a swallow. "Though exactly where the pieces now sit on the chessboard isn't at all clear."

Charlotte moved to take up a pencil and notebook from his desk. "Chess is a cerebral challenge. It requires patience and focus to analyze unexpected moves by an opponent. One needs to be vigilant in maintaining a strong defense, while looking for the opportunity to attack."

"I didn't realize you played," murmured Sheffield.

"I don't." Charlotte opened the notebook to a blank page. "But I've used the game as a metaphor in enough of my drawings to understand the theory." She looked to Wrexford. "Let us hear what happened, so we can begin sketching out who stands where on the checkered board."

The earl ran a hand through his hair. Which was, she noted, in dire need of a trimming. "As you know, I followed the man in the navy sash into the barn, only to find him with a knife through his heart. But let me start at the beginning and what I saw just before that . . ."

It took some time for him to explain about the cloaked rider, Belmont's panic, the appearance of Osborn and Pierson . . . and all the games within games that the revelations brought to light.

"Bloody hell," muttered Sheffield. "Perhaps you should tell Pierson to go to the devil and walk away when you can. It seems to me that you're being drawn into a dangerous web, one in which the spider—or spiders—are constantly weaving new patterns designed to trap—"

"To trap the unwary fly?" said Wrexford. He took another swallow of whisky. "I'm quite aware that Pierson is holding back information." A ghost of a smile. "But so am I."

"Hubris," warned Charlotte.

"Point taken," conceded the earl. "But hear me out. It's logical to assume that the cloaked rider was the killer—and I happened to see a mark branded on the flank of his horse."

Her fingers tightened on the pencil. "Describe it."

He came to stand by her. "A square, with three triangles inside it. Two at the bottom pointing up, with the third at the top, centered between them and pointing down."

She dutifully sketched what he had described. "Like that?"

Wrexford nodded. "Though it doesn't mean anything to me."

The others crowded around to have a look. McClellan and Tyler looked just as puzzled, but Sheffield suddenly snapped his fingers.

"By Jove—it's the mark of the Three Arrows," he exclaimed. Seeing the earl's blank look, he quickly added, "It's a rather ramshackle inn and livery stable on the outskirts of Oxford. Unlike you, my paltry allowance didn't allow me to keep a horse while at university, so I found that the Three Arrows was the cheapest place to procure one if I wanted to take a jaunt down to London or attend a party at Blenheim or Chatsworth."

"Well done, Kit," murmured the earl. He took a small object out of his pocket and placed it on the desktop. "I found this lying beside the dead man. Any chance that you know what it signifies?"

The small silver watch fob appeared to have an image on it. Charlotte leaned in for a closer look, but she couldn't make out what it was.

"I'll get a magnifying glass," said Tyler. He took a quick look and shrugged, then passed the glass to her.

"It seems to be . . ." Her eyes narrowed. "A stylized flower?" She studied it for a moment longer and then handed the magnifying glass to Sheffield.

The lamplight fluttered against the lens as he hunched over the fob. "It's a lily—the exact replica of the ones on the crest of Magdalen College." To Charlotte, he added, "Magdalen is one of the older colleges of Oxford University. And now that I think of it, they often use a single lily as a symbol of the college. It appears as the decoration on their dinner plates and glassware."

"How the devil did you recognize it?" asked Wrexford.

"As you know, I was too lazy to do my schoolwork. Instead, I amused myself by looking at all the crests and gargoyles of the various Oxford colleges, as well as getting myself invited to eat a free meal." A pause. "Though the food in Magdalen was terrible."

"We can't be sure that the fob belongs to the killer," observed Charlotte.

"I found it right by the dead man's right hand, when I was arranging his clothing to appear that he had been robbed," answered the earl. "And he wasn't wearing a watch or watch chain on his waistcoat." A pause. "Needless to say, I didn't mention my discovery to Pierson. If we are tracking yet a new set of villains, I'd rather pursue them without the government muddying the tracks."

"The fob could have been dropped at some other time," suggested Tyler.

"True," said the earl. "But few men other than the grooms enter the barns."

"And given the mark on the horse," mused Charlotte, "it does seem logical to think the two are connected."

"Well, we shall shortly have an opportunity to explore that," replied Wrexford.

They were scheduled to leave for Oxford on the day after tomorrow, reflected Charlotte. Which left her precious little time to parse over Wrexford's revelations and decide on the thrust of her next satirical drawing. There was a fine line between keeping the public's interest on Willis's death, and not provoking Pierson and Grentham to wonder how A. J. Quill had gotten wind of information known only to a handful of people.

Not to speak of dealing with the boys.

Her throat tightened. She and Wrexford had been wrestling with the previous day's discovery concerning Belmont, and what—if anything—they needed to do in terms of Peregrine. Things were now even more complicated . . .

"I can do some sleuthing around the Three Arrows," offered Tyler, "and see if I can learn who hired a horse for today."

The valet's response to the earl's reference to their Oxford trip drew her back from her brooding.

"And as for learning more about the fob and what it might signify, I happen to be acquainted with a very bright young chemist who was recently elected to a fellowship at Magdalen College," said Wrexford. "Daubeny owes me a rather large favor, so I imagine he'll be as helpful as he can."

"I, too, can do some asking around within the colleges," said Sheffield. "I happened to encounter a friend from Hoares Bank at the races—the fellow knows a thing or two about auctions—and I had an interesting exchange with him about the subject . . ."

Charlotte let her gaze drift away to the flames licking up from the coals. She hadn't told Sheffield about her conversation with Cordelia concerning the French mathematician—though she wasn't entirely sure why.

Choices, choices. The sudden tangling of complexities in her life—marriage, the boys growing out of childhood, the tensions tugging at their close circle of friends—had her feeling a little off balance.

Is it skewing my judgment? This was, perhaps, their most dangerous investigation. One small slip, and she could hurt all her loved ones. The thought of that responsibility caused a spurt of fear to rise in her gorge.

"Enough strategizing for now." Wrexford's voice drew her back to the moment. "I think we're all exhausted. We can reconvene tomorrow for any further planning, but for now I suggest we all get some sleep."

She saw Sheffield dart a look her way and then finish his whisky in one quick swallow. "Yes, a good suggestion."

Was her unsettled mood so obvious?

McClellan, too, seemed to be eyeing her with concern. But before she could say anything in response, a thump reverberated against the workroom door as their friend Basil Henning shouldered his way inside.

His eyes were bleary with lack of sleep, his jaw unshaved

and his snarled hair looked as if it hadn't encountered a comb in at least a week.

"You're looking well, Baz," said the earl dryly.

The quip drew a grimace from Henning. "Hmmph. Why is it that every time you stumble over a dead body you have it sent to me?"

CHAPTER 17

"Let me pour you some whisky," said McClellan.

The offer chased the scowl from Henning's face. His expression brightened even more when he spotted the untouched platter of ginger biscuits. "Sustenance would be welcome, too," he said, taking up two at once and wolfing them down. "The Weasels must not be around. Else there wouldn't be a crumb left."

"They are upstairs in their quarters with their new friend," replied Charlotte. "Assuming they haven't skewered each other with the fencing foils that Wrex purchased for them."

Wrexford thought he detected a note of trepidation in her voice. "A little blood never bothers boys."

"Swords?" Henning took a long swallow of his whisky and let out a blissful sigh. "It's a good thing you have a surgeon as a friend. I can stitch up most any wound." He ate another biscuit. "As long as they don't slice out a liver or a heart."

Charlotte closed her eyes for an instant.

"Speaking of blades," said Wrexford, "have you learned anything from the corpse that was delivered to your surgery?"

"Aside from the fact that if a knife severs the aorta, one hasn't a prayer of surviving?" retorted the surgeon.

"That goes without saying."

"Then I assume you're talking about the knife itself."

Wrexford allowed a small smile. "So you noticed it, too?"

Henning made a rude sound. "I haven't yet lost my wits or my eyesight."

"What?" whispered Charlotte.

"It's a very utilitarian steel weapon with a plain leather-wrapped hilt," replied the surgeon. "The flat, slender shape was designed to slide into a boot sheath."

"If it has no distinguishing marks, it sounds untraceable," observed Charlotte.

"Yes and no," said Wrexford. "I knew I'd seen ones like it during the Peninsular campaign, but I couldn't recall where or why I noticed them." He raised a brow at Henning. "That's why I had the body sent to you. I was hoping your memory might be sharper."

"It is, laddie." Henning glanced at the empty biscuit platter and released a mournful sigh.

"Answer His Lordship's question, and I might fetch some heartier sustenance for you," said McClellan.

"Some cold roast beef and cheddar would be most welcome," the surgeon replied with a grin. "As for the knife, there was a clever blacksmith attached to the First Division under Major General Sherbrooke around the time of"—Henning rubbed at his chin—"the Battle of Talavera. He made a knife of this design for one of the cavalry commanders, who wanted something simple, lightweight, and deadly, and it became a very popular weapon among the officers of the division."

McClellan rose. "I'll go fetch your food."

"Pour Baz another whisky," murmured Wrexford to Tyler. "By the by, I don't suppose you know whether General Malden served with the First Division?"

Henning shook his head. "Not that I know of. What makes you ask?"

"In light of this current murder, Grentham's dogsbody was compelled to confide more information about his side of the investigation than he wished. Malden is under suspicion because he's become good friends with Prince Schwarzenberg, the hard-partying Austrian field marshal, and has acquired a taste for the finer things in life, which his own purse can't afford."

"Bloody hell—you're working with Grentham and Pierson?" exclaimed Henning. "How could you be so daft as to let yourself get tangled up in a web woven by those two malicious spiders? They—"

"The fault is mine," said Charlotte.

Henning looked puzzled for an instant, and then a shadow of alarm seemed to ripple in his eyes.

Wrexford, too, felt a frisson of fear at Charlotte's oblique reminder that her secret might be known to some very ruthless men.

"Is there something I should know about?" said the surgeon softly.

"Yes—I was just about to tell you about the hellish conundrum we're facing," said the earl. He quickly explained about Pierson's cryptic comment, and the uncertainty of whether the government knew that Charlotte was A. J. Quill.

"Be damned to them," said Henning, after considering the earl's words. "Even if they know, they won't dare do a thing about it."

"What do you mean—" began Sheffield.

"The government will look like a gaggle of incompetent arses if they ever try to make a public furor over the truth," continued the surgeon. "To announce that a woman has played them for fools would make them the laughingstock of Britain—not to speak of the rest of the world."

"That might be true," said Charlotte, "but it doesn't mean

they can't employ subtle threats to my family and friends in private, in order to make me do what they wish."

"Pffft." Henning dismissed the suggestion with a snort and a very rude word. "When you think about it, exposure of the truth is actually *your* best weapon against them. You can counter any threat from them by saying you'll make the truth about A. J. Quill public, which would be an even worse humiliation for them." He grinned. "If anything, your true identity would probably make A. J. Quill even more popular."

Wrexford shook his head . . . and then started to laugh. "The devil take it—I think that Baz might be right."

"Perhaps," said Charlotte, her face still pale, despite the twitch of his lips. "But I would rather we didn't have to put that theory to the test."

"As would I," he agreed. So let us all agree to watch our steps very carefully. If, in fact, the government doesn't know about Charlotte's activities, I'd rather we didn't give them any reason to subject her to closer scrutiny."

"What can I do to help unmask the villains?" asked Henning, turning the attention back to practical matters.

"You're still connected with a number of our military comrades from the Peninsular campaign," replied Wrexford. "If you could make some discreet inquiries—"

Tyler cleared his throat with a cough, earning a reproachful look from the surgeon, who said, "I can, on occasion, temper my tongue."

The earl heaved an inward sigh. A council of war with their inner circle often became unruly. Everyone had strong opinions and didn't hesitate to voice them.

"As I was saying," he continued before any further digressions took place, "if you could find out if Malden served with the First Division, that would be a help."

Henning nodded as he reached for the generous repast that McClellan set on the table by his chair.

"That's assuming, of course, that what Pierson has told you is true," mused Sheffield.

Wrexford acknowledged the remark with a nod. "Trust me, I'm taking everything he tells me with a grain of salt. In this case, however, sending me on a wild-goose chase doesn't seem aligned with his interests."

He let out a breath and tapped his fingertips together. "There doesn't seem to be anything more for us to discuss tonight. Baz will deal with Malden, and as for the rest of us, we should all begin to marshal our thoughts for the next challenges." A pause. "Which will come when we visit Oxford."

Once they were alone, Charlotte waited in silence while Wrexford refilled his glass and took a seat by the fire next to her.

"You've been unnaturally quiet," he remarked as he rolled the glass between his palms.

"I suppose I have," she murmured. "I was thinking . . ."

"There is a great deal on which to ponder," he said when she didn't elaborate.

"Mmmm." Charlotte rubbed her palms together, finding the banked flames were doing little to dispel the chill in her bones.

"If you are worried about Pierson—"

"No, no, it's not that. I'm confident that we'll find a way to deal with the government if they wish to make trouble for us."

He waited patiently. One of the many things she appreciated about him was that he didn't feel the need to control a conversation. Perhaps it was his experience with science that had taught him not to rush things.

"It's the boys who concern me. We need to have a talk with them, especially with Peregrine here. They must be kept from being too reckless." A sigh. "To be honest, I am dreading it. Indeed, the thought terrifies me."

Wrexford smiled. "Nothing terrifies you. Least of all the Weasels."

"But they are growing up so fast! W-What if . . . what if they decide that they no longer want a self-appointed mother hen?" There—she had voiced her innermost fears. And strangely enough, just saying it aloud helped to loosen the knot inside her chest.

The earl rose, and after setting aside his whisky he came to crouch down in front of her chair. "If I didn't understand that your fears feel very real to you, I would laugh at the thought." He took her hands in his. "They adore you, not just as a mother hen, but also a beacon of Light and Truth, no matter how dark the world appears."

Charlotte blinked, surprised to find tears pearled on her lashes. "You exaggerate—"

"I don't," he said, and brushed a kiss to the back of her knuckles. "Change is always unsettling. And, yes, they are changing. No doubt we will find ourselves butting heads with them far more than is comfortable. But I daresay we'll all find a way to rub together without setting off too many sparks."

"Now you are making me feel like a peagoose for making a mountain out of a molehill." She expelled a sigh. "But we also need to consider how to protect Peregrine from the more sordid aspects of this investigation. Belmont is his legal guardian until the boy reaches his majority—"

"Come . . ." Wrexford pulled her up from her chair. "The best way to stop fretting about a problem is to face it head-on. Let us go have a chat with the boys without further delay."

It was, noted Charlotte, ominously quiet as they approached the schoolroom and adjoining bedchambers.

What if the swordplay has gotten out of hand?

She made herself stop being ridiculous. All three of them couldn't be lying mortally wounded . . .

Could they?

Wrexford pushed open the schoolroom door, and made a low sound deep in his throat.

"Shhhh!" chided Raven. "I'm thinking."

She edged up behind him and peered over his shoulder. Raven and Peregrine were lying belly down on the floor, a chessboard between them. Hawk was slouched on one of the desk chairs, observing the game, his face scrunched in a frown . . .

"Watching a game of chess is like watching paint dry," he muttered.

"Shhhh!" Raven studied the board a moment longer before moving his bishop. "Check!"

Peregrine took up his knight and nudged Raven's piece off the board. "Checkmate."

Raven cursed under his breath.

"You have to learn to see the game in patterns—the checkered tiles, and the rules that govern how the pieces move across them. It's like mathematics," counseled Peregrine. "You're getting much better at it."

Charlotte felt Wrexford's shoulder quiver in silent laughter. She, too, had to bite back a smile. It did Raven no harm to discover that he didn't know everything. And she was happy to see that he took the defeat with good grace.

"Oiy." Raven nodded. "I'm beginning to understand what you mean." He looked up at Charlotte. "I'm learning a lot from Falcon. It's challenging to try to see two or three moves ahead."

"Mental discipline is an excellent skill to have," said Wrexford. "And chess teaches you to think quickly and clearly about the consequences of each potential move. An ability that will prove very valuable in a great many situations."

He stepped into the room and perched a hip on one of the desks. "However, m'lady and I aren't here to talk about games."

Peregrine froze in fear, looking like a rabbit about to be pounced on by a fox. Charlotte felt a sudden surge of anger at Belmont and his wife. Whatever their resentment over the life choices made by the boy's father, it was despicable to make a child feel unwanted and unloved.

Ducking his head, Raven carefully began to place the chess figures back in their starting positions.

"We didn't mean to break the lamp in the Blue Parlor," said Hawk in a small voice. "But we confessed our crime to McClellan right away, as gentlemen should. And she said we were forgiven, as long as we understood there is to be no swordplay in the house, save for in the extra bedchamber, which she had cleared for us."

"I don't think Wrex and m'lady are here about the swords," cut in Raven.

"Correct, lad." Wrexford shifted. "We're here because there have been new developments in the investigations. We've discovered that our previous suspects are not, in fact, villains—"

"Which serves as yet another warning of what a tangled web of intrigue we are facing," interjected Charlotte. "And how careful we must be."

"Indeed," said the earl, his tone deadly serious. "There has been another murder." He looked at Peregrine. "We aren't yet sure how it ties in to your uncle's death, though we intend to find out."

"As you see, things have become even more dangerous," Charlotte hastened to add.

Raven darted a look at his brother before fixing the earl with a solemn stare. "So you're ordering us not to go into the stews."

Wrexford drew in a measured breath. "Actually, I'm not. I'm asking that from here on, the three of you think very carefully about your actions. Each of us must be aware that a small mistake or misstep could have grave consequences for everyone else."

Oh, well done, Wrex. Charlotte could see that the earl's answer surprised the boys. Not only that, it had cleverly outflanked any youthful rebellion.

Raven sat up straight and squared his shoulder. "I—I understand, sir."

"We must journey to Oxford for several days later this week, and both Tyler and McClellan will be accompanying us. The three of you will be holding the fort here, as it were, and any mischief would be a terrible distraction."

"I understand, sir," repeated Raven, with equal gravity.

"Oiy, you can count on us," chirped Hawk.

Charlotte knew the boys were adaptable and resilient, as they had a great deal of experience in dealing with the vagaries of life. But she worried about Peregrine, and how he would react to having such weighty—and likely confusing—responsibilities thrown at him. But then, she quickly reminded herself that he, too, was no stranger to adversity.

A sidelong glance showed the boy's expression was now pensive rather than fearful. "May I ask you a question, Lord Wrexford?"

"Of course, lad."

"Is Uncle Belmont evil?"

How to answer? Between black and white lay countless shades of grey.

Seeing Wrexford hesitate, she took it upon herself to respond. "Is there a reason you're asking?"

The boy looked down at the checkered board, with its opposing forces standing ready to play out yet another battle.

"You can confide in m'lady and Wrex," murmured Raven.

Peregrine swallowed hard. "The last time we were staying at our townhouse in London, I happened to hear Uncle Belmont conversing with a gentleman in the library. And he was talking about . . . government matters that he shouldn't have been sharing."

Charlotte saw Wrexford's expression sharpen. They already knew of Belmont's indiscretions. But knowing to whom he spoke might help in identifying the villains. "Do you mean to say that you've heard Uncle Belmont passing on confidential information?"

"I . . ." Peregrine's face betrayed the conflict warring inside him. "At Eton, the older boys all tell us there's nothing worse than a snitch."

"Granted, there is a certain code of honor regarding throwing a comrade to the wolves over some minor transgression," agreed Wrexford. "However, true honor demands that one doesn't protect a person who seeks to commit acts of violence or . . ."

Charlotte held her breath, hoping he wouldn't say the word 'treason.' Belmont was the boy's guardian, and the two of them had to live together. Better not to poison a relationship that was already fraught with tension.

"Or other wrongdoings," finished the earl.

The ensuing silence seemed to amplify the flutter of the ivy leaves outside the open window. She was just about to tell the boy that he didn't have to answer when he released a shuddering sigh and began to speak.

"There is a small alcove off the main sitting room of the library, which I find pleasant for reading, as it's always deserted. But on this particular evening, I heard Uncle Belmont and his visitor come in and pour themselves some brandy from the decanters on the sideboard. The gentleman asked Uncle Belmont some questions, and . . ."

Peregrine's voice faltered for a moment. "And he answered them, though I'm certain he wasn't supposed to be revealing the information."

"Did it concern your Uncle Jeremiah's experimentations?" asked Wrexford.

"Yes," said Peregrine, his voice barely louder than a whisper. "But I don't think I should say more. I promised Uncle Jeremiah never to talk about his work with anyone."

"You're quite right to guard such information," assured Charlotte. "Wrexford and I are merely wondering if you might know to whom Uncle Belmont was speaking."

The boy shook his head. "I was never permitted to meet any of the men who came to visit him."

"You didn't perchance catch a glimpse of the gentleman when you were in the library," asked the earl.

"I didn't dare take a look," admitted Peregrine. "I—I feared that I would be in grave trouble if Uncle Belmont knew I had overheard the conversation."

"You did the right thing," she said, seeing his stricken expression. "No good could have come out of a confrontation."

"D-Do you think Uncle Belmont might have played a part in Uncle Jeremiah's death?" asked Peregrine.

"Let us not jump to conclusions, lad. I've encountered no evidence to support that theory." Wrexford rose, a tacit signal to her that he thought that they had pressed the boys enough for now. "But be assured that Lady Wrexford and I will do our best to learn the truth."

"Don't stay up too late playing chess," said Charlotte as the earl turned for the door.

Raven rolled his eyes but didn't protest when she crouched down and planted a quick kiss on his cheek. Hawk grinned as she ruffled his curls and touched her lips to his brow . . .

Peregrine's eyes widened in shock as she enfolded him in a hug and kissed him, too. She heard his breath catch in his throat.

"Good night, fledglings," she murmured.

"Don't worry, m'lady," said Raven as she left the room. "We won't be flying from the eyrie."

Wrexford was waiting for her by the stairs.

"Thank you, Wrex," she murmured, catching his hand and giving it a squeeze. "You handled that far better than I could have on my own."

He smiled. "Does that mean I'm forgiven for allowing the Weasels to take up fencing?"

"That depends on whether any fingers or ears go missing over the next few weeks," she said.

"Harry's an excellent teacher. He won't put up with any mischief. And Peregrine is quite skilled. He'll set a good example for them."

She sighed. "I'm sorry he's aware of Belmont's indiscretions. It was good of you to quell his suspicions."

"A pity he didn't catch sight of Belmont's visitor."

"It's better that he kept himself safe," said Charlotte. "Though a fleeting glance might have proven helpful. Small details can be the key to unlocking a puzzle."

"Let us hope that is the case with the clues I discovered at Royal Ascot," he murmured. "For when we arrive in Oxford, I fear the intrigue surrounding the auction of Willis's invention will turn even more tangled."

The curl of the stairs brought them down to their personal quarters.

"And if the marks on the horse and the silver fob lead us nowhere, we'll be left to wander in the dark."

CHAPTER 18

"Good day, milord," greeted the head porter of Merton College as Wrexford and Charlotte stepped into the entrance archway of the Porter's Lodge. "And milady." He inclined a formal bow. "Welcome back, sir."

"I see things haven't changed appreciably," quipped the earl after a glance at the ancient stone buildings and cobbled courtyard of the Front Quadrangle. Merton College had been founded in 1264 by Walter de Merton, Lord Chancellor of England, and later appointed the Bishop of Rochester. It was one of the oldest and most prestigious of the self-governing colleges that made up Oxford University.

"*Change?*" The porter appeared shocked by the thought. "Good heavens, I should hope not, milord!" He blinked. "Over my dead body, sir."

"Nonsense, Jenkins—you're as eternal as the surrounding stones," replied Wrexford. He had no idea of the porter's age. At their very first meeting, the fellow had already looked as old as Methuselah. "By the by, have Tsar Alexander and his sister arrived yet?"

"They have, milord. They are quartered in the Queen's Room," replied the porter.

"And what about Mr. Sheffield?"

"Yes." The porter released a long-suffering sigh. "We've placed him in St. Alban's Quad." A sniff. "I do hope we won't experience any of the puerile pranks of his undergraduate days."

"He's become a paragon of propriety these days."

The porter's face betrayed a pinch of skepticism. "That is welcome news." He cleared his throat. "As for you, sir, your quarters are in the Hawkins Room in Fellows' Quad."

"I know the way," said Wrexford, gesturing for Jenkins to remain at his post. "Our baggage will arrive shortly, along with our personal attendants. If you would kindly escort them to the suite."

A formal bow. "But of course, milord."

"The Queen's Room?" said Charlotte as they started to cross the cobbled quad. "I'm surprised at the name. I thought all females are persona non grata within these hallowed walls."

"Oh, they most definitely are, save for ceremonial occasions like this," responded Wrexford, with a twitch of his lips. "However, the regal quarters in the archway between Front Quad and Fellows' Quad are so named because Queen Henrietta Maria, the wife of Charles the First, resided there during the time Merton's buildings were commandeered to serve as the royalist base at the start of the Civil War."

Charlotte eyed the imposing towers and spires, glowing mellow gold in the late-afternoon sun. "Remind me to do a series of social commentaries on the utter unfairness of prohibiting women from the opportunity of having a university education."

"Shhhh," warned the earl, with a mock grimace, even though he heartily agreed with her. "*I* will be persona non grata here if such a sacrilegious whisper reaches the ears of Reverend Mr. Peter Vaughan, our esteemed Warden of Merton.

"Hmmph, as if Cordelia couldn't think rings around most of the men here," commented Charlotte as they passed through the Fitzjames Gateway into Fellows' Quad. She stopped and drew in a deep breath as she took in the stately buildings. "I have to admit, it's magnificent. One can understand how such beauty and tranquility inspire the quiet contemplation of intellectual ideas and scholarly learning."

Wrexford made a rude sound. "Youth is wasted on the young. Free of parental control, most of the students are more interested in drinking and wenching."

Charlotte rolled her eyes. "*Men.*"

"We are, on the whole, a frivolous lot," he replied. "Speaking of which, shall we go find Kit, once Tyler and Mac arrive with our baggage?"

A short while later, leaving the unpacking in the capable hands of their retainers, they retraced their steps to Front Quad and turned right into St. Alban's Quad. Wrexford immediately spotted Sheffield, hands clasped behind his back, standing by the wrought iron gate of the Fellows' Garden and gazing out at Christ Church Meadow.

"Contemplating the sins from your schooldays?" he said as they walked over to join him.

Sheffield didn't reply to the jesting comment right away. His expression appeared pensive, with shadows pooled beneath his lashes as he gazed out at the broad expanse of meadow grasses and the glints of light flickering on the river beyond it.

"I did fritter away my days and nights in idle pursuits," he finally said, turning to face them.

"I think you've made up for lost time," murmured Charlotte.

That drew a faint smile. "As always, you're kinder than I deserve." Sheffield took another look at the meadow before shaking off his meditative mood. "I took a stroll earlier through Magdalen College and had a casual chat with the porter on duty. A silver fob engraved with a lily is given to the Fellows of the college."

They had arrived a day early in order to have plenty of time to do some investigating. The official celebration of the royal visit wouldn't begin until tomorrow evening, with a grand banquet at the Radcliffe Library for the Prince Regent and the visiting sovereigns.

"That's good to know," said Wrexford. "As I mentioned, my chemist friend resides at the college. I'm going to pay him a visit now and see if I can learn any further information that might help us identify the cloaked rider. Tyler is also making inquiries at the inn where the horse was hired."

"I fear that I would only be an impediment to your sleuthing in the colleges," said Charlotte. "So I'll leave you two and go see if I can rendezvous with Cordelia. She and Lady Thirkell are staying at the Lamb and Flag Inn, and I believe they're attending some of the symposiums arranged for the visiting foreign scholars."

Wrexford gave a surreptitious glance at Sheffield, but caught no change of expression. He hoped that emotions wouldn't flare up again and override reason during their time in Oxford. Each of them needed to keep a cool head if they were to make any progress in untangling the intrigue.

Charlotte, too, was looking at their friend with some concern. Whatever had been said during her private conversation with Cordelia back in London, she had chosen not to share it with him or Sheffield.

Wrexford trusted her judgment. But he also knew that Cordelia had a certain spark of recklessness . . .

"Do be careful," he murmured.

Charlotte merely nodded, but a glimmer in her eyes told him she understood his concern.

"My banker friend gave me the name of a tutor in Christ Church College who knows something about auctions," said

Sheffield. "While you head to Magdalen, I'll head over there and see if I can glean anything useful."

"Shall we meet up for a tankard of ale at the Bear in an hour to assess any new clues?" he suggested.

Sheffield readily agreed, but he had an air of abstraction that seemed to indicate his mind was elsewhere.

Romance did not make a good bedfellow with criminal investigation, thought Wrexford with an inward grimace. One was all about fire, and one was all about ice.

Charlotte watched the store clerk deftly wrap her purchases into a neat package tied with an azure-blue cord.

"I shall have it delivered to the Porter's Lodge at Merton without delay, milady," he said after making one small tweak to the bow. "And I'll see that your choices of art paper are packaged for travel and send them on tomorrow morning."

"You have a lovely selection of drawing materials," said Charlotte as she shook a handful of coins from her purse.

She hadn't been intending to shop, but Lady Thirkell, who had been resting in her quarters at the inn, had informed her that Cordelia had gone to explore a bookshop specializing in mathematical and scientific texts on a small side street just past Catte Street. Too restless to wait at the inn, Charlotte decided to join her friend at the bookshop in order to tell her the latest developments in the investigation. But she had allowed herself a small indulgence on discovering that the street was crammed with all manner of emporiums dedicated to book and manuscript making.

A selection of lovely colored inks in one of the display windows had caught her eye, and once inside, she had also found an interesting assortment of pens . . .

"At least I have accomplished something useful," Charlotte murmured to herself as she headed back out to the street. She couldn't help feeling a little frustrated at how being a countess had limited her opportunities to do her own investigating. In the past, she had had far more freedom to choose . . .

"Choices, choices," she whispered. Change was never without consequences. A smile touched her lips. However, she didn't regret for an instant the path she had chosen.

Even if the fancy silks and satins occasionally chafed against her skin.

Halfway down the crooked byway, Charlotte spotted the bookshop's age-dark sign, the gold lettering so faded that it was nearly illegible.

A brass bell tinkled as she entered the shop and was immediately enveloped in the scents of parchment, ink, and old leather. They brought back old memories—good memories—of the stately library of her childhood home. It had been one of the few places she could escape into her imagination. She took a moment to survey her surroundings. The floor-to-ceiling shelves were jammed with all shapes and sizes of books, and the narrow aisles leading into the side rooms were half-blocked with humble-jumble piles of yet more volumes.

A clerk approached, and in response to her query he pointed to the rear of the shop.

"Cordelia?" she called after squeezing through a low archway.

"Over here," came the reply from an alcove to her left.

Charlotte found her friend perusing the pages of what looked to be a very old codex.

"Fascinating," murmured Cordelia, before looking up. "I wish I could read Arabic. It looks to be a treatise on mathematics." She sighed. "A university town is so rich with knowledge, it feels as if it pervades the very air and one can simply inhale it with every breath."

"Perhaps one day in the not-too-distant future, women will be allowed to attend institutions of higher learning."

"And pigs may fly," muttered Cordelia. She put the codex back on the shelf and pulled out a more recent-looking book. "Hmmph," she murmured, pausing to read over a page before setting it aside with several other volumes she had selected for purchase.

Looking up, she added, "I'm sorry, but I've not yet had a chance to speak with Monsieur Rochambert about auctions. The French delegation was whisked away by the dons of Balliol College right after the symposium. No doubt to drink port and tell risqué jokes—"

Charlotte touched a finger to her lips to signal for silence, then looked around to make sure they were alone before edging a little closer. "The investigation has turned more deadly. There's been another murder . . ."

She quickly recounted the events that had taken place at Royal Ascot and how the clues Wrexford had discovered seemed to indicate an Oxford connection. "You must be extremely careful in broaching the subject with Rochambert."

"You . . ." Cordelia hesitated. "You think that he might be working with the villains?"

"I don't know," she admitted. "This investigation is horribly tangled in intrigue. We know that Russia, Austria, and Prussia are eager to possess the stolen invention. And Alison pointed out that it's possible Bonaparte also has designs on it, seeing the weapon as a way to regain the throne of France."

Charlotte's throat tightened. "Rochambert seems to admire Bonaparte—"

"But—" interjected Cordelia.

"But if he wished to help obtain the invention for Bonaparte, he wouldn't be interested in auctioning it to the highest bidder," finished Charlotte. "Yes, that lies at the heart of the question of who stole the invention. If a foreign power had the technical plans and prototype, it would have been spirited out of Britain long ago. So we have to assume that some unknown villain—one who is motivated purely by profit—chose to steal Willis's invention now, in order to take advantage of the fact that all the leading sovereigns of Europe are here in London and willing to pay a king's ransom to possess it."

She had explained to Cordelia the details about the sealed-bid auction. "You have to admit, it's fiendishly clever."

Cordelia looked shaken. "And you've no idea who is behind this nefarious plan?"

"Not yet." Charlotte released a sigh. "The task of rooting him out is complicated by the fact that we have to assume several of the foreign powers are also trying to find him, in order to get their hands on the weapon before it goes to auction."

"What a coil," whispered Cordelia.

"Indeed. We are tiptoeing atop a powder keg. One slip and all of Europe may explode into war again." Realizing what a grim picture she had painted, she quickly added, "But we've beaten diabolical villains in the past and we shall do so again. Not only for our country, but for Jeremiah Willis."

A martial gleam lit in Cordelia's eyes. "I take it you have a plan?"

Since leaving Wrexford and Sheffield, Charlotte had been thinking . . .

"The villain has accomplices—he can't be doing all this on his own. If we find whoever is creating the mechanics of the auction, it brings us one step closer to the dastard in charge," she explained. "The clues have led us here to Oxford, and Wrexford and Sheffield are pursuing leads within the colleges. So I do think you need to speak with Rochambert about auctions . . . but, as I said, very carefully. You must appear to have purely a mathematical interest in the subject."

"I understand." Cordelia allowed a faint smile. "Don't worry. I've learned a good deal about the art of sleuthing from observing you. If Monsieur Rochambert is up to no good, I shall coax it out of him at tomorrow night's gala banquet."

CHAPTER 19

Wrexford stared at his own scowling reflection in the looking glass as he smoothed at the folds of his cravat. "Damnation," he muttered, quickly averting his eyes.

So far, any progress on recovering Willis's invention had proven maddeningly elusive. His chemist friend in Magdalen College had confirmed that a silver lily watch fob was only given to a Fellow of the college, but further discreet questioning had not allowed him to narrow down who might have designed the auction for Willis's invention. There were at least a dozen Fellows whose knowledge in mathematics and economic expertise made them a possible suspect.

"I'm sorry, milord." Tyler brushed at an imaginary speck on the earl's formal evening jacket. "I've made a number of tries at identifying the man who hired the horse. But he's been deucedly clever at covering his tracks."

"My curse wasn't directed at you," said Wrexford. The valet had explained that nobody working around the inn could give more than a vague description of their suspect. "As of yet, neither Kit nor I have managed to uncover his trail. But however clever, nobody is perfect. He'll make a mistake. We just need to be close enough to see it."

He lapsed into a brooding silence. It had been a long and tiring afternoon of escorting the tsar and his sister around the university, including a visit to the Christ Church College Cathedral, the Chapel of New College, and finally a stop at the Bodleian Library, where the tsar was presented with a copy of the Oxford edition of Aristotle's *Poetics*.

As for the upcoming banquet, Charlotte had told him about Cordelia's planned interrogation of the French mathematician. It was, Wrexford conceded, a necessary move in their investigation. But he worried about her involvement . . .

"Ready?" Charlotte appeared in the doorway of his dressing room, and suddenly all thoughts of murder and mayhem were chased from his head. The gold-flecked light from the wall sconce dipped and darted over the slate-blue silk of her gown, mixing sparks with shadows. The changeable hue intrigued the eye. It was mysterious . . . which was a fitting metaphor for a lady of so many hidden facets.

"You look lovely," he said softly, his gaze meeting hers.

She smiled, and Wrexford felt his chest constrict. *If anything ever happens to her . . .*

Charlotte must have seen his expression tighten, for she quickly sought to lighten the mood. "I've heard that Tsar Alexander is a wolf in emperor's clothing. Perhaps you should warn him that I'll break his knuckles if he tries to put his hand up my skirts."

"No need for that," he drawled. "I'll break them first if his fingertips so much as graze your gown."

"I would rather the evening doesn't include any violence," she replied. "We're looking to extract information, but let us do so with charm rather than any more extreme measures."

On that note, Wrexford slipped on his coat and offered her his arm.

The way became more crowded as they approached the Radcliffe Library, whose striking neoclassical circular design made it one of the notable landmarks in the ancient town. Oxford's narrow streets were more suited to walking than carriage travel, so a great many of the two hundred invited guests were arriving on foot. The glow of early twilight accentuated the dazzling wink and sparkle of the myriad jewels and military medals adorning the royal retinues.

"You look like a stalking panther among a gaggle of peacocks," said Charlotte, eyeing his unadorned black-and-white evening clothes. After angling another look at the parade of pomp and privilege, she added, "What a pity I can't be loitering in an alleyway, dressed in my urchin garb, with pencil and sketchbook in hand."

"I'm sure the spectacle will be etched indelibly in your mind's eye," said Wrexford. "Speaking of spectacles . . ." He shifted so that Charlotte could see the colorful entourage approaching from the Bodleian Library courtyard.

"Is that—"

"Tsar Alexander," he confirmed as the tall, broad-shouldered Russian ruler lengthened his stride to stay several steps ahead of his followers. The tsar, often praised as a golden god of manly perfection in his youth, was still a handsome gentleman, though his crown of glorious blond curls was receding and his middle was thickening.

A titter of excitement ran through the crowd as the tsar was recognized, followed by cheers and applause. He acknowledged the greeting with a gracious nod and wave.

"He appears to have a certain magnetism," observed Charlotte, who was watching the scene with an unblinking gaze.

"He's a clever man, but mercurial," responded Wrexford. "The intellectuals of Europe had high hopes for him when he ascended the throne, thinking he would make a number of social reforms in Russia. However, he's disappointed them."

"The Russian bear is, I imagine, a very difficult beast to tame," murmured Charlotte.

"Perhaps because the Russian temperament seems prone to wild mood swings. There are whispers that Alexander's behavior is becoming a trifle erratic."

"You spent the day with him. What do you think?" she asked.

"I'll let you judge for yourself." The crowd—a number of spectators were being allowed into the upper gallery of the library in order to observe the banquet—was eager to follow the tsar into the building and started to jostle toward the entrance. "Shall we go in?"

It took some time to make their way up the circular staircase to rooms set up for the festivities. As they passed from floor to floor, Wrexford cast a longing look at the sections housing the book collections. The Radcliffe Library specialized in scientific works, and its current head librarian had recently acquired some very important rare editions.

"You can return another time for personal pleasure," said Charlotte. Gazing up, she narrowed her eyes. "I think I just saw Cordelia move past the receiving line."

"Ah, and there is Kit," said Wrexford, glancing behind them. They waited for him to reach them before continuing on.

"Any luck?" murmured the earl, impatient to know whether Sheffield's sleuthing had been more successful than his own.

"Perhaps," answered Sheffield, careful to keep his voice low. "My friend suggested a name—a brilliant but deeply unpleasant fellow—but there was no answer to my knock when I stopped by his quarters. I shall try again tomorrow morning."

They reached the top landing and were greeted by a welcoming contingent from the Foreign Office—Belmont wasn't one of them, noted Wrexford—before being waved on to the refreshment room. Tables were set with bowls of punch, while liveried footmen were circulating with trays of champagne. With the rumbles of laughter punctuating the clink of crystal and the babble of different languages, the noise was reaching a fevered pitch. It quieted for an instant as the Prince Regent made his entrance, and then rose again.

Wrexford noted a trio of red-coated military gentlemen bringing up the rear of the Prince Regent's entourage. "It appears that Colonel Duxbury and his aide-de-camp, Major Waltham, are part of the royal retinue." Judging by their companion's fancy uniform, the earl guessed that he might be General Malden, the other potential traitor mentioned by Pierson.

"Cordelia is conversing with Lady Thirkell and several members of the London Mathematical Society," observed Charlotte. "I'll go join them so you are free to maneuver."

Sheffield, he saw, had already melted away into the crowd. "A bit of reconnaissance may prove useful," he murmured, turning their steps toward the ladies and their group. "I have some unanswered questions . . ." Henning had not sent him any information concerning the knife used in the Royal Ascot murder. "And I think I know who might be able to answer them."

As luck would have it, the three Horse Guards officers had taken up a position by one of the arched windows. The lower casements were open, allowing a cooling breeze to waft in.

"Soldiers are skilled at assessing the terrain and choosing the best strategic position," said Wrexford as he approached them.

Colonel Duxbury allowed a perfunctory smile. "We're not on a battlefield, Lord Wrexford, so strategy is a moot point."

"Is it?" he responded. "With the Allied sovereigns all gathered here for the Peace Celebrations, I imagine there is a great deal of subtle skirmishing for power going on."

"An astute observation," said the officer next to Duxbury. His uniform indicated he was a general in the Royal Blues, the King's Household Cavalry, and his gold-braided tunic displayed an impressive array of medals, including the Order of St. George.

"Allow me to introduce General Malden," said Duxbury. To

Malden, he added, "This is Lord Wrexford . . ." A small pause. "Who dabbles in chemistry."

"I'm familiar with your reputation, sir," said Malden with a polite nod. "The earl also served for an interlude on Wellington's staff as a reconnaissance officer during the duke's early days on the Peninsula."

Duxbury's face betrayed a flicker of surprise, though he said nothing.

Neither of the two officers acknowledged the presence of their aide-de-camp, Major Waltham, who stood slightly behind them. Wrexford guessed that he was seen as a mere minion who handled all the myriad daily duties and made their department run like clockwork.

Irritated by the casual disrespect, the earl greeted the man with a courteous nod. "Major Waltham, I daresay it's no easy task to liaison with all the military contingents of our Allies and deal with their requests during their time here."

"Indeed, milord, it is challenging," replied Waltham, looking pleased to be consulted. "They're particularly interested in seeing our naval facilities and the sites for ballistics training." A smile. "And, of course, they hope to be invited to the gala soirees and balls."

"The Russians ought not be admitted," muttered Duxbury. "They're uncouth boors."

Ignoring the remark, Wrexford smiled at the major. "I'm sure you're handling everything with great diplomacy."

"Thank you, milord," said Waltham. "I do try . . ." He fell silent as one of the Duke of Wellington's adjutants approached.

"Excuse me, General Malden and Colonel Duxbury, but the duke would like you to join him in one of the side salons. Please follow me."

The two officers quickly marched off, leaving Wrexford and Waltham standing together.

The major took a sip of his champagne. "How was Wellington as a commanding officer, milord?" he ventured.

Wrexford welcomed the opening to chat about the Peninsular War. "He was Wellesley back then, not yet a duke. But his gift for bold strategy, which made him famous in India, was very evident . . ." He chatted for a bit about wartime experience, and then paused before making a query of his own. "Is my memory correct that both Malden and Duxbury fought on the Peninsula? I seem to recall that they served with the First Division under Major General Sherbrooke around the time of the Battle of Talavera?"

"Yes, General Malden was with the First Division, and then transferred to the eastern front to liaison with the Austrians," answered Waltham. "As for Duxbury . . ." He frowned in thought. "I'm fairly certain that he did serve in Portugal or Spain at the time of Talavera. My recollection is that he was recalled from active duty right after that to supervise a section of the Royal Laboratory at Woolwich. And then as Bonaparte's army moved east, he was sent along with Colonel Congreve and his rockets to reinforce Field Marshal von Schwarzenberg of Austria just before the Battle of Leipzig."

"So Colonel Duxbury fought with Malden at Leipzig?" mused Wrexford.

"Er . . . yes, it would seem so," agreed Waltham. "Though I can't say I've ever heard them discuss the battle."

"Duxbury appears rather . . . short-tempered." Wrexford took care to watch Waltham's expression. "One might even say resentful. As if he feels his own achievements haven't received due recognition."

The major shifted, discomfort writ plain on his face. "Forgive me, milord, but I feel honor bound to refrain from making any reply."

A loyal soldier. Perhaps Duxbury was right to say Waltham had little imagination or fire in his belly. But maybe there was nothing wrong with that. Not everyone dreamed of being a hero.

"It wasn't meant as a criticism, merely an observation," said the earl.

Waltham's expression relaxed. "Colonel Duxbury has very high standards, but he holds himself to them, as well as others."

"That speaks well for him as a good commanding officer," said Wrexford, taking more care with his probing. "He must also possess a technical knowledge about weaponry, given his assignment to the Royal Laboratory at Woolwich."

"Actually, I believe he was given the post because he's a strict disciplinarian. The government wished to speed up work on the various projects." The major took another sip of his wine and then allowed a small chuckle. "In fact, my impression is that the colonel prefers the simple, traditional weapons of yore. Like knives."

"Knives," repeated Wrexford, startled into full alert.

"Yes, he collects them. That's how I remembered that he had served in Spain and Portugal. He has a very impressive array of knives from our regiments and our Allied partisans, as well as a number from the French and Spanish forces."

"I must ask to see them sometime," replied the earl.

"I'm sure you wouldn't be disappointed." Waltham looked about to add something else, but an adjutant from Horse Guards approached and murmured a quick message.

"I'm afraid you'll have to excuse me, Lord Wrexford," apologized the major. "One of the Austrian military attachés is complaining that the banquet table for his delegation is not close enough to his emperor."

"But of course," responded Wrexford.

A flash of amusement seemed to spark for an instant beneath Waltham's lashes. "Perhaps I should seat them next to the delegation from the Kingdom of Saxony. They loathe each other, and a bout of fisticuffs might add a little excitement to a long—and likely boring—evening."

A smile twitched on Wrexford's lips. Waltham appeared to

have a sly sense of humor—which made him suspect that Duxbury and Malden underestimated their aide-de-camp's abilities.

"An entertaining thought," he replied. "As long as the evening ends with no blood being spilled."

On that note, a bell rang, summoning the guests to the grand banquet room.

Charlotte forced an appreciative laugh, reminding herself that Tsar Alexander's ham-handed flirtations were providing her with a unique opportunity to gather fodder for future drawings. The meal over, she had joined the Russians, who were quick to introduce her to their sovereign. She had to admit, the tsar radiated a certain degree of boyish charm. But up close, the signs of dissipation were beginning to show.

Granted, he still cut an impressive figure in his fancy uniform and glittering medals. However, he seemed far more interested in seduction than affairs of state.

She didn't like the lascivious look in his eyes as his gaze slid down to her bodice.

"You have a *very* interesting wife, Lord Wrexford," said the tsar as the earl came over to join them. "I like a lady with a clever tongue."

"Cross verbal swords with her at your own peril, Your Majesty," replied the earl.

"Ho-ho! Is that a challenge?" said Alexander.

"No, merely a warning," murmured Wrexford.

The tsar laughed again, but Charlotte noted that he stopped staring at her cleavage.

As the talk shifted to the upcoming Peace Conference that was to convene in Vienna come September, Charlotte turned her thoughts to the present moment, and her conversation with Cordelia just before the banquet had begun.

She darted a glance at Wrexford. There had been no chance

to tell him about it during the banquet—but she was sure that they were oh-so-close to confronting the villain. The new clues that Cordelia had uncovered included a name . . .

The earl caught her look and seemed to read her sense of urgency. Some of the guests were already beginning to rise and move on to the next gala spectacle of the night. The local officials had arranged for a special display of illuminations in the streets of the town center to serve as the entertainment for the public and the exalted visitors.

Earlier in the day, the tsar and his sister, the Grand Duchess of Oldenburg, announced their intention of taking a stroll to view the lights, and no doubt the streets would be packed with people hoping to catch a glimpse of the royal entourages.

"If you will excuse us, Your Majesty, my wife and I have made arrangements to meet with friends for the nighttime festivities."

The tsar gave an imperious wave. "You are dismissed, milord. But only if you and Lady Wrexford promise that I shall have the pleasure of your company again when we return to London."

"Your wish is our command," said Wrexford.

Charlotte doubted that Alexander recognized the earl's note of irony.

"You have that certain look in your eye that signifies some mischief is afoot," said Wrexford, once they reached a quiet spot by one of the side salons.

"We need to find Cordelia," replied Charlotte, darting a look around. "She'll explain . . . Ah, there she is." Taking the earl's arm, she headed for a group of guests near the grand arched windows.

On seeing their approach, Cordelia excused herself from the others and joined Charlotte and Wrexford in a recessed niche by the leaded glass. Turning their backs to the banquet room, they stared out at the view, pretending to admire the ghostly towers and turrets silhouetted against the dark, star-dotted sky.

"Tell Wrex what you've discovered," urged Charlotte.

"It was in one of the volumes I purchased at the bookshop yesterday," replied Cordelia. "It contained a series of essays on mathematics. And one of them was on the theory of auctions . . ." She hurriedly added a few arcane details. "But processes aren't what's important—the name of the author is! It's Mr. Robert Milson-Wilgrom."

"Who is—" began the earl.

"Who is a Fellow at Magdalen College," explained Cordelia. "Charlotte told me about the clues you found at Royal Ascot. And, well . . . it all seems to add up now."

"Let us not jump to conclusions—" counseled Wrexford.

"I haven't yet finished," interrupted Cordelia. "Just before the banquet started, I finally had a chance to speak privately with Monsieur Rochambert, and he confirmed—though rather reluctantly—that it was Milson-Wilgrom who asked his opinion on certain mathematical equations."

Her voice took on an edge of excitement. "It turns out Monsieur Rochambert offered some suggestions. But after showing his worksheets to Milson-Wilgrom at a private meeting, he was told very abruptly that his thinking wasn't relevant—and then he was warned not to speak of the project to anyone, as it was a confidential undertaking for . . ."

Cordelia frowned for a moment. "Rochambert was told it was for a higher authority. It made him quite unsettled."

Charlotte held herself still, waiting for Wrexford's reaction.

"I think," said the earl slowly, "that a visit to Mr. Milson-Wilgrom's rooms are in order."

"I very much doubt that he is there at this hour," she pointed out. "The whole town appears to be headed outside to enjoy the grand illuminations and spectacle of so many famous people promenading through the streets."

"All the better," he replied with a sinister smile. To Cordelia, he asked, "Do you perchance know where his quarters are at the college?"

"St. Swithun's Building," replied Cordelia. "The top of the entry nearest to St. John's Quadrangle."

"I'm coming with you," said Charlotte. "Nobody will suspect anything nefarious if we're strolling together. And two can search far more quickly than one."

He didn't argue.

Glancing around to make sure that no one had crept within earshot, she spotted Rochambert lingering in the shadows of the gallery stairwell, and couldn't help wondering whether he was as innocent as he appeared.

"By the by"—her eyes moved to Cordelia—"are you sure that you trust your French friend?"

A flush rose to Cordelia's cheeks. "Granted, I don't have your expertise in espionage, but to succeed in building my business, I had to learn to be a good judge of character. So, yes, I think his agitation over the incident is unfeigned."

Making a wry face, Cordelia added, "I've promised to promenade with him to see the illuminations. Lady Thirkell and I are staying at the same inn as he is, and he seemed nervous about walking the streets alone." She chuffed a small laugh. "It seems that the meeting with Milson-Wilgrom truly spooked him. He thinks he saw someone following him afterward."

"It's probably a good idea that you stay with him," said Charlotte, a suggestion that the earl confirmed with a nod. Neither of them added that the pairing would keep Rochambert from making any trouble on his own.

"You go ahead," added Wrexford. "We'll head down to the street on our own shortly so that we can head to Magdalen College without drawing attention to ourselves."

Cordelia nodded her understanding. "Good hunting," she murmured before moving off to join the Frenchman.

"I wonder where Kit is? I haven't seen him since our arrival," mused Charlotte as more people began to take their leave. "Though I suppose he kept his distance so as not to see

Cordelia and Rochambert seated at the same table and enjoying each other's company."

"I imagine he's with his banker friend," said Wrexford. "And will spend the rest of the night drowning his sorrows in a tavern."

"When this investigation is over—"

He turned away from the window. "The sooner we start following the latest clue, the sooner that will happen."

The evening had turned cool, with a hint of dampness to the air. As they stepped out onto the graveled square, a gusting breeze raised a pebbling of gooseflesh on Charlotte's bare arms. Repressing a shiver, she shifted her reticule, feeling the solid weight of her pocket pistol nestled within the dainty silk. An apt metaphor for all the contradictions of her own complicated life.

Ah, but contradictions and complications keep things interesting . . .

"Tyler and Mac are strolling the streets as well, and will keep an eye on the Russian, Austrian, and Prussian entourages," said Wrexford, following the curve of the circular wrought iron fence surrounding the library. "Let us head up Catte Street. From there, we'll make our way to High Street and follow it to Magdalen College."

CHAPTER 20

A myriad of candles had been placed on the exteriors of the buildings in the center of town, the undulating points of fire casting flickers of gold over the cobbled streets. The effect was magical. The ancient battlements and spires took on an other-worldly glow, much to the delight of the promenading crowds jostling through the narrow thoroughfares.

High mingled with low—the glittering jewel-bright finery of the visiting dignitaries punctuated the earth-toned homespun cotton and wool of the locals and dark sable-trimmed academic robes. Jugglers performed on street corners and hawkers trumpeted their wares, offering sweetmeats and mulled wine. Laughter echoed off the surrounding stone, giving the night a carnival feel. The tsar and his sister were among the revelers. They had announced that they would be strolling incognito, though their presence—along with Prince Metternich, General Blücher, and other European luminaries—quickly attracted cheers and a crush of followers.

"This way." As Wrexford guided Charlotte through the shadows and turned down one of the side lanes, the raucous noise from Broad Street receded. He thought he caught sight of Cordelia and her French friend up ahead, but the flutter of skirts was quickly swallowed in a tangle of drunken students spilling out from New College.

The lights weren't as bright in the narrow byways, the crenellated towers throwing jagged black shadows across the paving stones. The crowds were keeping to the main thoroughfares, and as they rounded the next bend, they found themselves alone.

His mind on the mission that lay ahead, Wrexford turned his thoughts to Magdalen College and where he might find a side gate whose lock could be picked—

Bang!

A pistol shot suddenly ripped through the cloak of quietude.

Whirling around, he grabbed Charlotte and ducked into a recessed doorway.

"I saw the flare of the sparks—it came from the side street just up ahead." She was already fumbling in her reticule for her weapon.

A lady's scream rent the night.

"Stay behind me," he commanded, knowing it pointless to order her to stay sheltered in the doorway. He drew his own pistol and moved to the corner. A quick look showed two men lay sprawled close together on the cobbles. One of them let out a groan, while the other lay still and silent.

A lady was crouched down between the bodies, and in the flickering light of the candles affixed above the doorways of the buildings, he could see blood on her skirt—

"Merciful heavens!" Charlotte shot past him, her dainty shoes slipping and sliding over the mist-damp stones. He was right on her heels, seizing her arm to keep her from a stumbling fall.

"Cordelia! Cordelia! Are you hurt?" cried Charlotte as she twisted free and dropped to her knees beside their friend.

Alert to any lingering danger, Wrexford checked the connecting alley as he cocked his pistol and moved closer. Cordelia's profile was as pale as death, her features frozen in shock.

"Cordelia." Charlotte's touch still roused no response. As if oblivious to all else, Cordelia leaned in closer to the unmoving man lying sprawled on the cobbles, her breath coming in ragged gasps as she touched him.

Wrexford shifted a step, and felt his chest clench as he spotted a pool of blood on the stones—just beneath a gleam of golden hair.

No. No. No.

"Don't you *dare* give up the ghost, Kit Sheffield," uttered Cordelia, her voice cracking as she stared down at her bloody fingers. "I . . . I . . . That is, life would be unbearable without you in it."

Charlotte had already hitched up her gown and was tearing strips of cloth from her underskirts. "We need to staunch the bleeding." She pushed closer, edging Cordelia aside. "Where is the wound?"

Wrexford whirled around as the thud of racing footsteps echoed through the narrow lane. "Thank God it's you two," he said, lowering his weapon as Tyler and McClellan materialized from the gloom. "Kit's been shot."

Tyler uttered an oath. "Who . . . How—"

"I've no idea what happened," snapped Wrexford. "Like you, we just heard the shot and came running."

"I can't find any sign of the bullet penetrating his chest," said Charlotte as McClellan rushed to join her. "Perhaps if we turn him very gently—"

"*Ouch!*"

An inarticulate sound—something between a laugh and a sob—slipped from Cordelia's lips. Brushing the tangled hair back from Sheffield's brow, she pressed a kiss to the purpling bruise. "You bloody fool! What on earth were you thinking to charge into the path of a bullet?"

"You know me—thinking isn't my strong suit." Sheffield winced as she gave him a fierce hug. "Much as I dislike your French friend, he didn't deserve to be assassinated."

Rochambert shifted and let out a groan, but then drifted back into unconsciousness. There had been only one shot, thought Wrexford, so the fellow must have hit his head on the paving stones as Sheffield knocked him out of the bullet's path.

"Hurry and tell us what you saw, Kit," demanded the earl after Charlotte's gentle shake didn't rouse the Frenchman. "Before Rochambert reawakens."

Sheffield gave a grunt as McClellan slid his coat down off his shoulders and began bandaging the wound.

"Thank God! The bullet went straight through the fleshy part of the arm without hitting any bones or tendons," said the maid. "Still, it's bleeding quite a bit and needs to be stitched."

Another exaggerated wince. "It hurts like the devil."

"You'll live," responded the earl sharply, though his heart stopped pounding against his rib cage. They had been extraordinarily lucky that the attack hadn't been lethal.

But it still begged the question of motive. The villain's actions didn't seem to be making sense.

And that worried him.

"Stubble the theatrics, Kit," he added as Cordelia took Sheffield's hand between hers and let out a soulful sigh. Emotions could wait for later. "I don't like it—these reckless attacks seem at odds with the intricate and ingenious planning of the theft and the auction."

Seeing Tyler about to speak, he added, "But we don't have time to speculate right now. We need to act quickly so as not to give away our involvement in these damnable intrigues within intrigues."

Rochambert started to groan again.

"Kit—did you see who fired the shot?"

"It all happened so quickly . . . I was following Cordelia and her friend because . . ." Sheffield drew in a sharp breath as Mc-

Clellan tightened the bandaging. "Because I didn't trust him, and wished to see whom he might contrive to meet during the outdoor festivities. But as I saw them pass the opening of the alleyway, a movement in the shadows caught my eye."

Sheffield squeezed his eyes shut for an instant. "I saw a glint of steel—as the assailant raised his pistol, it moved through a blade of the candlelight. I can't be sure, but I have an impression of catching a flash of red beneath the black cloak he was wearing. A sash, perhaps? Many of the diplomat guests were wearing one this evening."

He shook his head in frustration. "Sorry, that's all I can recall."

Wrexford put the information aside for later. "Tyler, escort Rochambert back to his room at the inn. Tell him to lock his door and wait for you to fetch him in the morning, when you'll arrange to have him transported back to London in safety. Then go fetch a surgeon—the innkeeper will know of one—and bring him back to Merton College."

Looking back to Sheffield, he asked, "With Cordelia and Mac's assistance, can you make it back to the Porter's Lodge? From there, have the night attendant help you to our quarters."

"I can get there on my own—"

"Don't be an arse," said Cordelia. "I'm not letting you go on your own."

Sheffield blinked, but bit back any protest.

"Go!" Wrexford commanded. "Before anyone stumbles upon us."

"What about you?" asked Tyler as he moved to lift the dazed Frenchman to his feet.

"Charlotte and I are going to pay a late-night visit to Magdalen College."

Mist was drifting in from the nearby River Chertwell, the silvery vapor muffling their movements along the high, ivy-covered outer walls of the college. Charlotte kept close to Wrexford. Given the state of her gown, it was a good thing that their foray into the college was meant to go unseen.

"There will be a tradesmen's entrance somewhere along here," whispered Wrexford, following a cart path that rounded one of the side towers. He stopped a moment later beside a portal of iron-banded oak and leaned down to inspect the padlock.

"This looks to have been here since the time of Henry the Eighth," he muttered.

"Is that a problem?" asked Charlotte.

"None whatsoever." A *snick* sounded. "We'll be in and out before anyone notices something is amiss."

Wrexford led the way into a small quadrangle and headed for one of the archways. Clouds had blown in to muddle the sky, obscuring the stars. The shadows seemed deeper and darker as they darted through the opening and crept past a series of imposing stone entryways.

He stopped abruptly. "This one," he whispered, indicating a set of steep stairs leading up to a wooden door that looked as if it had been standing sentinel since the Dark Ages. "We need to stay alert—the Porter's Lodge is close by."

The iron hinges gave a low groan as the door opened. It was black inside the stairwell, the silence like a weight, squeezing the air from the space. Taking her hand, Wrexford guided her through the circular turns to the top floor. He paused and then slowly crossed the landing and felt around for the door to Milson-Wilgrom's rooms.

The latch lifted with a tiny *click*.

"He's either careless in leaving his rooms unlocked . . ."

Charlotte felt his hand tighten as they slipped through the opening. She smelled it, too.

The coppery scent of blood . . . And the sweet-sick stench of death.

She quickly closed the door behind them, taking care not to

make a sound, while Wrexford found a candle. He drew the draperies before striking flint and steel to the wick.

A hiss sounded as a flame sparked to life.

Its undulating flicker danced over the crumpled body lying on the Oriental carpet. A garnet-red pool of viscous liquid had painted its own swirling patterns upon the faded weaving.

"It looks as if he's been dead for at least four or five hours," observed Wrexford as he gingerly lifted one of the corpse's arms. "Stiffness has already set in."

"Any idea if it's Milson-Wilgrom?"

"The victim is wearing the academic robes of Magdalen, so it seems a logical assumption." A pause. "Though logic isn't apparent in any of these recent developments."

He slipped a hand beneath the ermine-trimmed fabric and began a quick search of the man's pockets. "A purse, a pipe, and a pouch of tobacco." He pulled the purse out and gave it a shake. "Robbery doesn't appear to have been the motive. There's a goodly number of guineas in here."

Charlotte moved to the large mahogany desk. The papers and books were in disarray—but then, scholars were known to be an untidy lot. She checked the drawers, and saw no unusual signs of disturbance. "Nor does it appear that the killer was looking for something."

"Perhaps he knew exactly where it was," answered Wrexford, replacing the purse in the dead man's pocket and continuing his search. "Or perhaps the objective was murder. The villain, whoever he may be, has taken a violet turn of late."

"A falling-out among thieves?" suggested Charlotte as she examined some of the documents on the blotter. "If Milson-Wilgrom was hired to use his theoretical knowledge of auctions to devise a way to maximize profits from the sealed-bid format, he might have decided that his skills deserved more money, once he realized how much the stolen item might bring in."

"A reasonable conjecture," agreed Wrexford. "There's also the possibility that . . ."

The earl paused and Charlotte heard the crackle of paper. He pulled out a folded sheet from beneath the dead man's robes and opened it.

"What?" she demanded.

He rose and brought it over to the desk.

Equations—some crossed out, some only half finished—covered the surface.

"It looks like a rough worksheet, where he's trying out different formulas," said Charlotte. She did the same sort of rough sketching when finalizing a concept for her satirical drawings. "Does it tell you anything?"

"The mathematics means nothing to me. However, I recognize this." Wrexford tapped the small crest at the top of the sheet. "The notepaper came from Horse Guards."

"So Pierson may have been telling you the truth."

"About Malden?" The earl released a cynical snort. "I wouldn't wager on it. Though this does seem to narrow our choice of suspects." He refolded the evidence and tucked it away inside his coat. "However, it's Duxbury with whom I wish to chat. I learned earlier this evening that he oversaw the Royal Laboratory at Woolwich for an interlude last year."

Charlotte frowned in surprise.

"As we turned down High Street, I happened to catch a glance of him heading down Catte Street . . . and there's a foot passageway below the Radcliffe Library that connects to the lane where the attack on Rochambert took place."

A thought—not an edifying one—suddenly occurred to her. "I can't help but wonder . . ." She made herself go on. "My last drawing was on Congreve and his upcoming pyrotechnics displays for the Peace Celebrations, and in it, I made reference to his running of the Royal Laboratory at Woolwich and hinted at all the secret things done there." There was always a moral question about whether to try to stir an enemy into making a critical mistake, for there was the chance of doing unintentional harm.

"You fear that you may have spooked the villain into committing murder?" asked Wrexford.

"It's possible."

He didn't answer right away.

Charlotte felt her heart sink, but she was glad that he respected her enough not to try to sprinkle sugar on the unpalatable truth. "I never take the power of my pen lightly, and try to wield it with a respect for how fragile the balance is between doing good and doing evil." She felt her throat constrict. "It grieves me deeply when I make a mistake—"

"I don't think you have," cut in Wrexford. "It appears that the two murdered men—this fellow and the victim at Royal Ascot—both chose to involve themselves in a nefarious plan in hopes of profiting from their perfidy."

His mouth quirked. "As you well know, there's a Latin proverb for those who take such risks. *Si vivis gladio, gladio morieris.*"

"If you live by the sword, you shall die by the sword," she murmured, and suddenly made a face. "Ye heavens, don't remind me that you gave the Weasels swords."

"Fencing foils," he corrected. "It's not at all the same thing. They both have a moral compass that will always point true."

"I hope that is so. It is horribly easy to lose one's way—"

Wrexford leaned in and pressed a palm to her cheek. The sudden warmth dispelled the bone-deep chill that had taken hold of her. "They won't," he promised. "We won't."

Their eyes met and the candlelight seemed to brighten.

"Now, come—let us not linger. We need to take a quick look through the desk and other rooms to make sure there's no other clue—"

A rumble of thunder reverberated in the courtyard, followed by a flash of lightning that illuminated the draperies.

"And we had better hurry," he added as a few drops of rain pattered against the windowglass. "A storm looks to be blowing in."

*   *   *

Sheffield was lying on the sofa in the sitting room of Wrexford and Charlotte's quarters, propped up on the pillows and nursing a glass of whisky. A bandage bulged beneath his coat—he was now wearing one of the earl's—but the malt, noted Wrexford, had brought some color back to his face.

Tyler wordlessly moved to the sideboard and poured out two more drinks. "I'll fetch some towels," he murmured, eyeing Wrexford's and Charlotte's bedraggled clothing.

The passing storm's lashing rain and heavenly display of pyrotechnics had put a quick end to the town's gala illuminations. Though soaked to the bone, Wrexford conceded that the weather had helped cover their retreat from Magdalen College. Nobody would have noticed that half of Charlotte's underskirts were missing.

"Thank you," he replied after taking a long swallow of the warming spirits. It was only then that he noticed that Sheffield—aside from appearing far too comfortable under a down coverlet—was smiling.

"You're looking awfully cheerful for someone who's just been shot."

The smile stretched wider. "Cordelia said that she couldn't imagine life without me in it."

"Nonsense. You must have been delusional," retorted Wrexford. "Shock will do that."

"Stop it, Wrex," chided Charlotte, wrapping the blanket which Tyler had brought a little tighter around her shoulders. "Let us take some flicker of happiness from this devil-cursed night."

She expelled a harried sigh, but her expression softened as her gaze fixed on Sheffield. "I thought you needed a good knock on the head to recognize what was right in front of your nose. But apparently it took a bullet to make you both see reason."

"I thought reason had nothing to do with love," said Sheffield, the light in his eyes undimmed by the earl's needling.

"Apparently not," interjected Wrexford. "Or you wouldn't have been such a blockhead about admitting your feelings."

"That's akin to the pot calling the kettle black," shot back Sheffield.

"Enough," said Tyler, who had been watching Charlotte in concern. "I take it that you didn't find what you were looking for in Magdalen College?"

"Actually, we did," answered the earl. "Unfortunately, someone else visited Professor Milson-Wilgrom's rooms before we did."

"Milson-Wilgrom! Why, that's the fellow my banker friend suggested I speak with," exclaimed Sheffield. "However, when I stopped there earlier today, he didn't answer my knock."

"That's because he was already dead," said Wrexford.

Coals crackled in the hearth, echoing Sheffield's raspy intake of breath.

"Bloody hell, another conspirator dead," muttered Tyler. "Why?"

"A good question," said Wrexford.

"Two possibilities come to mind," offered Charlotte. He was glad to see that her earlier brooding seemed to have receded. "The conspirators are fighting among themselves. Or a foreign power is trying to get its hands on Willis's invention without having to pay a fortune for it."

"I wouldn't put it past our government to be doing the same thing," mused Wrexford. "They recruited me to use my wits to find the technical drawings and prototype, because they knew I wouldn't agree to cold-blooded murder, even if the victim is a traitor. But as Pierson pointed out, we'd be fools to think they aren't attacking the enemy with every weapon they possess."

"A dangerous strategy, as you and Osborn discovered," pointed out Tyler.

"And me," added Sheffield.

"It's still not too late to tell Pierson to go to the devil," murmured the valet.

"They don't give a fig about bringing Willis's murderer to justice," said Charlotte. "They simply want their monstrous weapon back."

Her hairpins had loosened, allowing a curl of still-wet hair to fall across her cheek. "We're the only ones who care about good and evil," she continued, "and right and wrong."

Wrexford reached out and took her hand. It was cold as stone. "I think you have your reply, Tyler. But in truth, I'd be happy if the two of you would—"

"No," said Sheffield flatly. "I now have—as it were—a stake in the game. So don't you dare suggest that I walk away." He grinned at Charlotte. "*E pluribus unum.* Our motley band of fools always comes together for one common goal, no matter how daunting."

"Right—so what's our next move, milord?" said the valet quickly.

"We all need to return to London at first light," he replied without hesitation. "I'll leave it to you to get Rochambert moved to a new hotel, where he'll be safe from further attack, while I mean to speak with some military friends about the workings at Horse Guards, and then arrange a private confrontation with Duxbury."

"And me?" asked Charlotte.

"We might not know who is responsible for poking a stick in the nest of vipers, but it's clear that they are starting to slither." His eyes narrowed. "I say that A. J. Quill sharpens her pen and makes them squirm even more."

CHAPTER 21

*S*quirm. It was the following evening before Charlotte was able to sit down at her desk and begin work on a new drawing. She studied the sinuous ink undulations she had sketched on her pad of paper, fanciful doodles that curled into serpent heads with forked tongues and bared fangs dripping teardrop beads of poison.

Her fingers tightened on the pen. Wrexford's suggestion of poking the tangle of villains and make them writhe out of their hiding place was all very well. But how to apply pressure without alarming the government to a point where they decided A. J. Quill needed to be silenced?

The line was razor-thin.

What if my passion for justice is putting my family and friends in danger?

To her horror, Charlotte saw her hand was shaking. Passions always had a price. Up until now, she had never questioned whether she was willing to pay them.

What if . . .

Charlotte turned to a blank page and stared at the pristine white paper. She could make a safe choice and do a colorful drawing on Congreve, his rockets, and the spectacular py-rotechnics he was designing for the Peace Celebrations. Most of her artwork was intended to make the public think. But on occasion, they simply needed an image to make them smile.

She began to sketch a dazzling explosion of sparks filling the sky, with the crowd and the dignities looking up in wonder . . .

And then, an idea suddenly took shape in her head. Perhaps she could do both.

Her pen flew across the paper, drawing a tangle of serpents in the ground just below the spectators. With the right caption . . . It was known that the Prince Regent was quarreling with the Tsar of Russia, and that other tensions had flared up between the visiting rulers. Perhaps merely asking the question of what hidden reason was provoking trouble rather than harmony was enough to prod the villains into making a wrong move.

Her hand steadied as she began to work out the details. Satisfied with the idea, Charlotte placed a large sheet of watercolor paper on her blotter and set to work creating the final drawing.

It was some time later when she finally dipped her brush in the fiery-red hue on her palette and painted in the last of the colorful fireworks in the sky. Leaning back, she studied the final version and nodded to herself.

Alea iacta est. As Caesar had said in crossing the Rubicon, *the die is cast.*

After rolling up the drawing and wrapping it for delivery, she flexed the tightness from her shoulders and went to stand by the window. Darkness had settled over the back garden, swallowing the last rose and gold glimmers of twilight. The earl had gone to a Prussian military reception in honor of Field Marshal von Blücher, hoping that Duxbury would be in attendance. She didn't expect him to return anytime soon.

A sigh fogged the glass. The rustle of ivy whispered through the mist.

Charlotte turned away, determined to shake off her worries.

She hurried into the corridor and up the stairs. The sound of laughter drifted out from the schoolroom, along with the *clack* and *whirr* of moving metal. Wrexford had taken the Weasels and Peregrine for an afternoon visit to Mr. Hedley's workshop, where the inventor had given the boys the parts to build a mechanical adding machine patterned after the "Pascaline," a seventeenth-century marvel designed by the French mathematician and philosopher Blaise Pascal.

She smiled, happy to hear them at play.

The sounds grew louder. Pausing in the doorway, Charlotte saw the three of them were sprawled on the carpet, a jumble of different-sized brass gears spread out among them.

Hawk had an odd construction by his side, and was turning a handle, making a set of numbered dials on steel rods go up and down, much to the delight of the others.

"M'lady!" he called, spotting her in the shadows. "We are making a machine that adds numbers, just like Professor Sudler's computing engine." Seeing his brother make a face, he quickly said, "That is, it's not quite as fancy as that machine, but it's quite clever."

"I can see that," answered Charlotte. She came and knelt down beside him, touching a caress to his tousled curls. "Tell me how it works."

The boys cheerfully explained about the levers, screws, and gears, though what mattered to Charlotte was hearing the unabashed exuberance in their voices. Peregrine, she noted, looked at ease here, in a way that he hadn't at his own home. His eyes had lost their wariness, and not only did he laugh at Raven's teasing—but gave it back in equal measure.

It did her heart good to see them having boyish fun.

"And how are your fencing lessons with Mr. Angelo progressing?" she asked, once they finished rattling off the details of the adding machine.

"I am learning to do a *passata sotto*!" announced Hawk.

"That's because he's small and it's easy for him to duck an attacker's sword," teased his brother.

"Mr. Angelo says it's a *very* useful skill for those who can master the technique," replied Hawk with great dignity. He rose, and after brandishing an imaginary sword, he spun through a series of lightning-fast moves that had Charlotte blinking in surprise.

Good heavens, she thought. Both brothers possessed a quicksilver agility, but Hawk had just performed a fencing maneuver that required speed and balance—and had done so with remarkable precision. "That was marvelous!" she exclaimed, clapping her hands together.

"Mr. Angelo says Hawk is slippery as an eel," remarked Peregrine with an admiring grin.

Raven snickered. "Mr. Angelo also said that being little makes him look innocent—and harmless. An adversary will underestimate him, which, in itself, will be a powerful weapon."

"Oiy." Hawk performed a lunge, and then cut a jaunty salute through the air with his imaginary sword. "And he'll very much regret his mistake."

Charlotte felt a lump rise in her throat. Make-believe duels with dastardly villains were all very well, but the idea of the boys crossing steel with a real-life miscreant made her blood run cold. "Let us hope you never have to wield a real weapon against a deadly foe."

"But sometimes," said Raven softly, "a pistol or a sword is the only way to save a loved one's life."

Charlotte knew he was thinking of their last investigation, and the horrible moment when it seemed that . . .

She closed her eyes for an instant, not wishing to picture the moonlight on the swirling river water and the raised oar ready to strike Wrexford. "Yes, that is true. But it is a great and terrible responsibility to possess a lethal weapon. One must never be seduced by its power and think it gives you the right to wield it for your own advantage."

"Uncle Jeremiah told me much the same thing. He . . ." Peregrine hesitated, his expression very grave. "He worked on designing weaponry. And he told me that he wrestled with his conscience about whether it was right to create a . . . a monster."

"He sounded like a very wise and very thoughtful man," said Charlotte carefully. "Moral questions like that one are very complicated and their ramifications are very far-reaching."

"What was your uncle designing?" asked Hawk.

Peregrine shook his head. "I—I promised him that I wouldn't tell anyone."

"Promises aren't to be taken lightly," she replied. "Though they, too, are complicated." Perhaps the boys were too young to understand, but still, she decided to go on. "There are circumstances in which one might have to decide whether breaking a promise is the lesser of two evils."

Raven frowned in thought, but didn't say anything.

As for Peregrine, he looked down at the jumble of gears and began to fit several of them together. "I think I comprehend what you are saying, milady."

Charlotte rose and shook out her skirts. She hadn't meant for things to take such a serious turn. "I look forward to seeing your adding machine when it is finished."

Hawk began to fiddle with the rods and levers. "There is still much to figure out."

She heaved a silent sigh. *Indeed there is—far more than you know.*

Then, recalling the finished drawing that needed delivering to Mr. Fores, she looked at Raven. "Might I ask you to come downstairs and help me with a small task?"

"Stop grumbling, Wrex," murmured Sheffield as he settled a little more comfortably into the padded leather armchair by the hearth, its leather softened by the pompous posteriors of countless club members. "You sound like a bear with a thorn in his arse."

The earl glanced impatiently at the tall case clock standing in the far corner of the reading room at White's. "They've been playing cards for hours."

"Which means that Duxbury's tongue will be well lubricated by brandy when you take him aside," replied his friend. "Speaking of lubrication, I think I deserve a nice Scottish malt for my heroics the other night." The bandage no longer bulged against his coat, so he rubbed at his shoulder to emphasize the point.

"Bah—there's nothing heroic about jumping in front of a bullet," retorted Wrexford, though he signaled to one of the club attendants to bring over some whisky. "However, I concede Cordelia was standing too close for comfort to the Frenchman, so you were forced to do something rash."

"Thank you. In that case, I shall deem myself deserving of the bottle, not just a wee dram." Sheffield stretched out his legs and propped his boots on the brass fender. A banked fire crackled softly, dispelling the chill of the rainy night. "What do you intend to say when—" He fell silent on hearing steps from behind him approaching their chairs.

"Wrexford. Sheffield." Osborn inclined a friendly nod as he came to stand by the fire and leaned in to warm his palms above the glowing coals. "A filthy night. I do hope the weather clears for the upcoming naval festivities on the Serpentine."

"Yes," said the earl with deliberate curtness. "It would be a pity to cancel the pyrotechnics."

"Oh, I daresay there will be more than enough fireworks to entertain the visiting sovereigns and dignitaries during their time in London," Osborn said with a knowing grin.

Wrexford didn't smile. Unlike Pierson, he had little faith in Osborn's temperament. The fellow was a little too sure of himself, which led to arrogance. Neither quality worked well within the shadowy realm of espionage.

"By the by, Sheff, I believe there was someone looking for you just now," said Osborn. "Perhaps you should check with the front porter. He would know who it was."

Sheffield arched a brow at the earl, but then slowly rose. "I might as well do so. I was planning on having a look at the card room to see if there's any interesting play going on."

"Oh, come, you know as well as I do that the members here play like old women. If you want serious stakes, you know where to go." Osborn lowered his voice. "Some of the Prussian military men have been frequenting the Bloody Lizard and their daredevil drinking and wagering would make your hair stand on end."

"Whatever amusements I wish to partake in," said Sheffield, "I know where to find them."

"And yet, from what I've heard," said Osborn, once Sheffield was out of earshot, "Sheff has become rather tame of late."

"Don't believe everything you hear," replied Wrexford. "Is there a reason you wish to have a private talk with me?"

Osborn perched a hip on the arm of the earl's chair. "I thought it would be a good idea for us to share what information we gathered in Oxford."

"Alas, aside from the fact that the tsar's sister is a difficult, demanding lady who dislikes music, I have nothing of interest to pass on."

"Indeed?" Osborn regarded him with a searching stare. "I confess that surprises me. Certain people have mentioned your involvement in previous investigations of interest to the government, and your prodigious skills at unraveling some very tangled knots."

"As I said before, don't believe everything you hear. Facts often get muddled as they pass from mouth to mouth."

"I shall keep that in mind, milord. But . . ." Frowning, Osborn tugged at his cuff. "Surely, you're not unaware of the fact that a Fellow of Magdalen College, by the name of Milson-Wilgrom, was found murdered on the morning after the Radcliffe Library gala banquet?"

"Yes, I've learned of that now," said the earl. He had no intention of revealing what he knew about the crime or the dead man's possible connection to the auction of Willis's stolen invention. "As it happens, my wife and I departed from Oxford at first light that morning, as family matters required our attention." A pause. "Is there any reason to think it has anything to do with our concern?"

Osborn's frown deepened. "I was hoping that you could tell me."

"And why is that?" replied Wrexford.

"Because my inquiries have turned up the fact that you paid a visit to a Fellow of Magdalen College—a Professor Daubeny—on the afternoon of the murder." His voice held a note of triumph. "Are you saying it was merely a coincidence?"

"Do you know anything about Professor Daubeny?" responded the earl.

Osborn's smugness wavered for an instant. "I don't see why that's important—"

"Daubeny is a chemist of rising fame," interjected Wrexford. "Which is my field of expertise as well. We met to talk about science, not stolen secrets."

It was clearly not the answer Osborn had expected. "I—I thought . . ."

"You would do well to think longer and harder before jumping to conclusions."

Osborn gave a wry grimace. "It's clear that you don't think me a very good operative."

"What I think is that you act on impulse. That can cause you to be careless and prone to making mistakes," answered the earl. "Which is dangerous because mistakes put your fellow agents and the mission in peril."

A ripple of emotion stirred in Osborn's gaze. "I stand chastised, milord." He rose. "I shall take that as a challenge and endeavor to prove to you that I'm not quite so bumble-brained as you think."

"You can begin by following Pierson's orders," said Wrexford. "It's my understanding that in order to keep us from any further tripping over each other's feet, he's assigned you to handle sleuthing around the Royal Armory and to deal with Belmont. Confining your activities to those objectives will help avoid any more misunderstandings."

"And what has Pierson asked you to—"

"Wrex." Sheffield appeared in the doorway, interrupting Osborn's question. "May I have a word with you?" He shifted. "In private."

Wrexford's gaze remained on Osborn. "Of course."

"Of course," echoed Osborn. After inclining a polite nod, he turned and left the room.

CHAPTER 22

Sheffield waited for the footsteps to die away. "Something about him puts my hackles up," he muttered.

"Osborn is brash and cocky, and wishes to impress his superiors. Which in my experience makes him no different than most of the junior officers and administrators serving our government," observed Wrexford. "He'll either learn quickly, or find himself in trouble." A tiny flame flared to life in the banked coals, then died away just as quickly.

"But forget Osborn for now. What about Duxbury—"

"That's what I came to tell you. The game is about to break up," said Sheffield. "The head porter just told me that Duxbury usually exits the club and heads down St. James's Street toward the palace."

"Tonight he shall have company on his walk," replied Wrexford. His flash of teeth was clearly not meant to be a smile. "And the opportunity for convivial conversation."

The earl hurried out into the night and turned left, where he took up a position in the shadows outside of Lock's Hatters. The rain had blown off, leaving a clear sky and it wasn't long before the sound of bootsteps announced that someone was approaching. The scent of cheroot smoke floated through the air a moment before the gleam of gold epaulettes winked in the starlight.

"A pleasant night for a leisurely stroll, is it not?" said Wrexford as he fell in step beside the colonel.

Duxbury blew out a plume of ghostly vapor. "Actually, I'm rather in a hurry, milord. I have some work to finish at Horse Guards before my duties are done for the evening."

"Be assured that I won't slow you down," the earl replied. "I simply have a few questions to ask about the unfortunate incident at Royal Ascot." Was it his imagination or did Duxbury's spine stiffen?

"I don't know what you think I can tell you," came the curt response. "You and Osborn were the ones who found the victim."

"Yes, but you appear to be a careful observer. I was wondering whether you noticed anything unusual about the knife stuck in the man's chest when you crouched down to have a closer look."

"No." Duxbury quickened his pace. "It appeared to be a very ordinary weapon, with no distinguishing marks or embellishments."

"And yet . . ." Wrexford let the words hang in the breeze before continuing. "And yet, another military man has said that the weapon isn't ordinary at all. It was made by a blacksmith attached to the First Division under Major General Sherbrooke during the Peninsular War."

Duxbury stumbled as his boot caught on one of the cobbles.

"Apparently, the style became quite fashionable with the regimental cavalry officers of the First Division because it was lightweight, perfectly balanced and lethally effective," he continued. "And if I recall correctly, you served in the First Division."

"Only for a short time, before being recalled to take up a position at Horse Guards."

Wrexford noted that he omitted any mention of running the Royal Laboratory at Woolwich.

"And besides, I don't pay attention to fashion." The colonel's face looked unnaturally pale as they passed through a dappling of moonlight. "I have my own preferences for weapons. I wasn't interested in what the junior officers thought was au courant."

"Ah, I see." They walked on for several strides in silence. "But you do collect military knives?"

Duxbury came to a sudden halt, his hands fisting at his sides. "What are you implying, milord?" he demanded.

"I'm merely trying to gather all the facts and put them together in logical order."

"F-For what reason?"

"Curiosity," replied Wrexford. "My scientific mind likes to make sense out of things."

"I've more important things to do than play intellectual games, milord," snapped Duxbury, and resumed walking.

"Murder isn't a game, Colonel." Wrexford calmly kept pace. "By the by, I happened to see you in the streets near Magdalen College the night of the banquet at the Radcliffe Library. As I'm sure you've heard, one of the Fellows was found murdered in his rooms. You didn't perchance spot anything unusual, did you?"

"No," answered Duxbury curtly. "In fact, I was nowhere near Magdalen College."

In fact, thought Wrexford, *you are lying through your teeth.*

The footpath rounded a hedge and ended at Horse Guards Road.

"And now," added the colonel, "if you'll excuse me, I have work to do." Without waiting for a response, he crossed the street to the parade ground and hurried toward the stately white stone building that housed Britain's military headquarters.

"What sort of work?" murmured Wrexford, watching the colonel's uniform tunic fade from scarlet to black as his silhouette grew smaller and smaller. "Spinning new strands in your web of treason?"

"What a marvelous machine!" exclaimed Charlotte, after the Weasels and Peregrine had given a demonstration of their finished construction to her and Tyler in the earl's workroom.

"Indeed," agreed Tyler. "Well done, lads."

"Falcon made some improvements to the gearing arrangement," said Raven. "It performs even faster now."

"He's really clever with bits and bobs of metal," chimed in Hawk.

Peregrine shrugged off the compliments, but Charlotte could see that they meant a lot to him. The boy was clearly starved for friendship, and she was pleased to see the three of them forming such close-knit bonds.

"Wrex should take you to show this to Mr. Hedley," said Tyler. "I'm sure he would be delighted to see what modifications you've made—"

The door clicked open. "I stopped by to see if Wrex had returned from White's yet, and Riche said you were all back here," announced Sheffield. He eyed the mechanical adding machine on the earl's desk. "Ho—what mischief is afoot?"

"We have been performing scientific research," said Raven solemnly, "which is serious work, not mischief."

Tyler stifled a chuckle.

"Do come in, Kit," said Charlotte, "and have a seat by the fire. You should be resting and recuperating. A bullet wound is nothing with which to trifle."

"Yes, it would be a great pity to stick your spoon in the

wall," said Tyler as he moved to the sideboard to pour a medicinal brandy, "just when your love life might finally be taking a turn for the better."

Hawk's eyes widened. "Are you in *love*, Mr. Sheffield?"

All three boys pivoted and fixed him with unblinking owlish stares.

"I . . . That is, it's . . . um . . ."

"Yes," said Charlotte. "He is. And should be allowed to deal with the complexities of the heart without his friends making a mockery of it."

Sheffield flashed her a grateful look.

"Kit usually deserves all the mockery he gets." Wrexford walked in and tossed his hat onto the work counter. "However, in this case, we will hold our tongues until he has regained full strength."

Sheffield merely smiled and savored a sip of his brandy.

"Love makes one impervious to life's slings and arrows," murmured Tyler. "Or so they say."

"Enough about the vagaries of love," chided the earl. "We have a damnably difficult mystery to solve."

"Did you learn anything useful from Duxbury?" demanded Sheffield.

"Yes. The fact that he felt compelled to lie about recognizing the knife used in the murder at Royal Ascot, as well as his whereabouts at the time you were shot, certainly tells us that he's hiding something. As to what . . ."

Wrexford shrugged off his coat and loosened his cravat. "Tyler, you need to do some more sleuthing in Woolwich and see what you can learn about Duxbury and his time as supervisor of the Royal Armory and Royal Laboratory. Try to find out if he has any close cronies still working there who might have helped him steal—"

"Wrexford," warned Charlotte. She didn't wish for Peregrine to know that the theft of the revolutionary new weapon had been the reason behind his beloved uncle's murder. The boy might wonder whether he had inadvertently given something away to Belmont.

Tyler quickly dispelled the awkward moment. "I'll begin my inquiries tomorrow." He gestured to the tray of decanters. "Would you care for brandy or whisky, milord?"

"What a daft question!" Henning's rough-cut voice rumbled through the half-open door. "Of course he prefers a good Scottish malt." His words were followed an instant later by the surgeon himself, looking even more disreputable than usual. His greying hair was standing in spikey tufts, his jaw was unshaven, and his coat . . .

"Good heavens, Baz, what is that noxious slime smeared around your pockets?" inquired Charlotte.

Raven and Hawk looked at each other and began chortling.

A bad sign. The more disgusting a substance, the more it amused the Weasels.

"On second thought," she added, "we probably don't want to know."

Henning stared down in bemusement at the stains and rubbed meditatively at his chin. "I think it must be whatever I had for breakfast."

Charlotte repressed a shudder. "I'll ring for Mac and have her bring some nourishing sustenance."

"As the word *whisky* derives from the Gaelic *uisge beatha*, which means *water of life*, it's all the sustenance a man needs," responded the surgeon. He nodded a thanks to Tyler, who handed him a full glass. "However, a bit of bread and beef to put down the gullet wouldn't go amiss."

McClellan appeared a moment later, and after a brief exchange with Henning—in Gaelic—which made him laugh, she departed for the kitchen, promising to return with refreshments for everyone.

Hawk cleared his throat. "I hope she won't be too upset that all the ginger biscuits seem to have vanished without trace."

The comment reminded Charlotte that the boys were still in the room. Raven, she noted, had cleverly drawn his companions back into the shadows of the earl's massive desk, no doubt hoping to have their presence forgotten.

"Well, then, since your stomachs are full, I suggest the three of you take your adding machine up to your rooms and retire for the night."

"But—" began Raven.

However, a stern look from Wrexford silenced whatever protest was on his lips.

"Good night," she murmured as they reluctantly trooped out into the corridor.

Wrexford watched them disappear around the corner before clicking the heavy oak door shut. "Now that there are no innocent ears to sully—"

Henning huffed a rude snort.

"To sully with talk of sordid intrigue," continued the earl, "we need to parse over what we know, and see if we're any closer to identifying the villain." He cracked his knuckles. "I confess, I still haven't put my finger on the thread that ties all of these crimes together."

Charlotte reached for a pencil and a notebook.

"Ah, Charlotte is about to begin one of her famous lists," said Sheffield with a fond smile. "We shall have this solved in a trice."

"I'm a visual person—I see things more clearly when I write everything down," she replied. "So let us start with the suspects." The book fluttered open. "Duxbury and Medford are the most obvious right now, but let us use our imagination and see if we can see connections that might point to someone else."

"Congreve," said Sheffield suddenly. "What about Sir William Congreve? He used to run the Royal Laboratory, and he's an expert at innovating weaponry. He, of all people, would have recognized the monetary value of Willis's invention."

"An interesting thought," responded Charlotte, her pencil poised over the paper.

"However, I shall nip it in the bud," interjected Wrexford. "I've worked with Sir William in the past, and am of the opinion that there isn't a malicious—or treasonous—bone in his body. Wellington, who is not easily impressed, also admires his courage and character."

"Then we shall leave him off . . . for now."

McClellan returned with a platter of food, which she quietly placed on the work counter, and then took up a position next to Tyler. "What list are we creating?"

"Possible villains," he answered.

"We're trying to look beyond the obvious," added Sheffield.

"Belmont," said the maid without hesitation. "I think we can all agree that the villain is an exceedingly clever man. What if Belmont is merely playing the hapless fool to confuse the scent and send the government hounds chasing after the wrong fox?"

Wrexford took his time in considering the question. "Put Belmont on the list," he said. "Pierson may have a reputation for not making mistakes. But nobody's judgment is perfect."

In the ensuing silence, the whisper of Charlotte's pencil moving over the paper sounded unnaturally loud.

"Any other suggestions?" asked Tyler.

Nobody spoke up.

"Then I suggest we all get some sleep. Tyler, come tomorrow, you have your assignment." He thought for a moment. "Baz, perhaps you could ask around among the veteran soldiers you know to see what more you can learn about both Duxbury and Malden."

The surgeon mumbled an assent through a mouthful of roast beef and fresh-baked bread.

"And despite Pierson's warning to leave Belmont to him, I

think I shall have a talk with Peregrine's guardian," added the earl.

"What about me?" queried Sheffield.

"For now, you have time to convince Cordelia that the other night was not an aberration, and that you actually do possess some redeeming qualities," drawled Wrexford.

And me? wondered Charlotte as the others filed out of the workroom, leaving her and the earl alone. An idea came to mind. But she was fairly certain Wrexford wouldn't like it.

"I was thinking . . ." she began.

He picked up a bit of bread from the platter and crumbled it between his fingers. "Should I be worried?"

"For my next drawing, I'm planning another poke of my pen into the tangle of vipers, and the government may well feel that A. J. Quill is touching a very sensitive spot. I would guess that they don't want the public to begin questioning whether there's something rotten within the highest ranks of our military."

"If I didn't know you better," said Wrexford softly, "I would be tempted to think that you're deliberately trying to provoke Grentham and Pierson in order to know for sure whether they're aware of your secret."

"I confess, the idea appeals to my conscience—"

"It shouldn't," he muttered.

"Oh, come Wrex. You're just as determined as I am not to let fear color our actions," replied Charlotte.

"Yes, but I'm supposed to be the voice of reason in this family."

She smiled. "Much as it might surprise you, I do on occasion listen to you. What I was just about to add is that as much as I won't back down from any confrontation with Grentham and his minions, I won't ever do it out of sheer hubris."

Charlotte turned to a fresh page in the notebook. "In this case, I believe the new drawing I have in mind will force the villain to move more quickly than he wishes. And that's when mistakes happen."

As her pencil began moving over the paper, the quick lines and shadings forming a rough sketch, she suddenly stopped. "Actually, I think I see a way to do it without drawing blood from the government . . ." Charlotte described what she was thinking.

"Clever," he conceded.

"Then I shall get to work." A glance at the mantel clock showed that if she hurried, there was still time for the engravers to have the finished print in Mr. Fores's shop by morning.

"No rest for the wicked . . ." A discreet cough caused Wrexford to turn around.

"Pardon me, milord and milady," said the butler, his craggy face illuminated by the light of his candle lantern. "But this missive just arrived." Another cough. "And I assumed you might wish to see it right away."

"Thank you, Riche." He glanced at the handwriting as the butler quietly withdrew. "Hmmph."

Charlotte couldn't read from his face whether the sound indicated good news or bad news.

Wrexford cracked the wax wafer and unfolded the paper. Another "hmmph" as he read it, and then he looked up. "It's from Hedley. The other day when I visited his laboratory with the boys and showed him Willis's sketch of the pistol, it triggered something in his memory concerning the development of multishot weapons. However, he couldn't quite recall what it was."

"But he has now?" she asked.

"Yes, but it's only the suggestion that I should have a talk with Durs Egg about the subject."

Charlotte knew that Durs Egg was considered one of the premier gunsmiths in all of Britain. "Egg makes pistols for the Prince Regent," she mused.

"As well as for a great many other influential gentlemen in the highest circles of Society and the military," replied Wrexford.

"Was he familiar with Willis's work?"

"That is one of the questions I shall ask him when I visit his workshop tomorrow." Wrexford looked down at the note again. "And yet, I have a feeling that Hedley is referring to something in the past." Charlotte saw a frown slowly dig a furrow between his brows.

"But damned if I know what it is."

CHAPTER 23

Dawn's rosy hue was just tingeing the sky, the pale light stirring the birds in the back garden of the townhouse to greet the new day with a chorus of early-morning songs.

A flicker of sunlight touched the windowglass, teasing Peregrine awake. Hearing a mechanical *clack-clack* cut through the avian twitters, he rose and eased open the door to the adjoining bedchamber.

Raven and Hawk were hunched over the adding machine, watching the gears spin.

"Do you think that if we add a bit more oil to the levers, we might increase the calculating speed?" asked Raven without looking up.

Peregrine shook his head. "One must keep a light hand with lubricants. Too much of it defeats the purpose." He sat down cross-legged beside them. "Why are you up so early?"

"Couldn't sleep," replied Raven.

"We've been trying to put together the puzzle of what Wrex and m'lady are looking for," explained Hawk. "We know they're trying to identify the dastard who murdered your uncle. But . . ."

"But there's something else," said Raven darkly.

"You think there's something they're not telling us?" asked Peregrine.

"I *know* there's something they're not telling us." A scowl. "I just haven't yet figured out what it is."

"What can . . ."

Clack-clack. The gears slowed and came to a halt with a whispery sigh.

"What can we do—" began Peregrine.

"Nuffink," cut in Hawk, darting a nervous look at his brother.

"Unless . . ." muttered Raven.

"Unless what?" asked Hawk warily.

"Unless we break the rules."

"I don't think that's a wery good idea."

"*Exitus acta probat,*" retorted Raven.

"What—"

"The outcome justifies the deed," Peregrine translated without hesitation. Seeing Hawk's surprise, he added, "They make us study Latin ad nauseam at Eton."

"And before you tell me that dressing up a bad idea in Latin doesn't make it any prettier, allow me to point out that both Wrex and m'lady occasionally act on the same maxim," said Raven. He fixed his brother with a solemn stare. "Remember what we overheard—this investigation may threaten a family secret. We need to know what's going on so that we can do our best to help."

Hawk's opposition crumpled in a heartbeat. "What rule do we need to break?"

"You two stay here," answered Raven. "There's less chance of getting caught if I do it myself."

"You're up early, milord." McClellan looked up from mincing a pile of peeled ginger as the earl's shadow spilled over the kitchen worktable. "Shall I bring a plate of shirred eggs and gammon to the breakfast room?"

"I'll just have a cup of coffee in here," he replied, taking a seat on one of the stools. "Tyler and I will be having our breakfast at a tavern near the docks before he heads on to Woolwich."

"The food won't be nearly as good as it is here," she commented.

"Alas, our breadboxes must make sacrifices as we pursue every possible clue."

She handed him a mug and Wrexford took a sip, then let out an appreciative sigh. "Black as sin and hot as Hades—nobody makes such good coffee as you do, Mac."

"Do pour another mug," called Tyler as he joined them at the table.

"Keep your voice down," counseled McClellan. "Cook tends to turn moody when Upstairs invades her bailiwick."

"Heaven forfend that we upset Cook," said the earl dryly.

Tyler made a shushing sound. "That's *not* a jesting matter, milord. The household will be up in arms if she starts burning the ginger biscuits."

McClellan wordlessly refilled their mugs.

"Tyler, while you head off to make more inquiries about Duxbury and his time at the Royal Armory and Royal Laboratory, I'm going to pay a visit to the workshop of Durs Egg." He explained about Hedley's note. "It may be a waste of time, but Egg is an expert gunsmith, and perhaps he'll offer some information that helps us see things in a new light." He didn't really hold much hope of that. But with time ticking down, they couldn't afford to dismiss any chance, however faint, of tracking down the elusive villain.

Tyler blew out his cheeks. "Damnation, it all comes down to the stolen plans and prototype of Willis's weapon. If we find those before the villain can auction them off, the threat to our country is over, and we'll have him on the run." He cracked his knuckles. "Then we shall see how he likes being the hunted rather than the hunter."

If. For a tiny word, its resonance carried a terrible ring.

Setting down his mug, Wrexford rose abruptly. "Let's be off. We don't want you to miss the boat that ferries the workers down to Woolwich."

Charlotte made herself sit still as McClellan threaded a ribbon through her topknot. She longed to shuck off her fancy silks and do some real sleuthing in the backstreets and alleyways. Dressed as Magpie—her unfettered urchin persona—she felt that she could be far more useful than the Countess of Wrexford . . .

Hell's bells. It was a damnable nuisance to be corseted in all the myriad rules that governed an aristocratic lady's behavior.

As if reading her thoughts, McClellan put down the hairbrush and put a hand on her hip.

Their eyes met in the looking glass.

"To every thing there is a season, and a time to every purpose under the heaven," murmured the maid.

Charlotte couldn't help but allow a wry smile. "It's a good thing Wrexford isn't present to hear you quote the Scriptures. He would likely say something exceedingly sarcastic."

"Be that as it may, the point is that however frustrating it may feel to be laced up in rules, this investigation will be solved within the highest circles of Society, not in byways of the stews," replied McClellan.

Charlotte knew in her heart there was no reasonable retort to that.

The maid handed her a pair of butter-soft kidskin gloves. "The dowager's carriage will be arriving at any moment."

Through her connections with the leading hostesses in London, Alison had arranged a morning promenade in Green Park with several members of the American diplomatic delegation.

Including Captain Tobias Hockett.

Ever since meeting the naval officer at the Prince Regent's reception at Carlton House, Charlotte couldn't shake off the feeling that there was more to his presence here in London than met the eye.

A prickle of anticipation teased at her flesh as she smoothed the leather over her forearms.

"Then let us hurry downstairs and not keep her waiting."

"Why are you dusted in flour?" inquired Peregrine as Raven crept into the schoolroom. "That is, assuming I'm allowed to ask a question."

Raven shook himself vigorously like a dog, sending up a powdery white cloud.

Harper, who was sleeping on the rug, raised his shaggy head and gave an indignant sneeze.

"Shhhh," warned Hawk.

"Don't worry, they've all left. However—"

"You've got oatmeal in your ears," observed Peregrine.

Raven gave another shake and dislodged the flakes, earning a canine grin from Harper. "However, I had to stay hidden in the grain cupboard until Cook and the scullery maid finished with their morning tasks."

"You were eavesdropping on Wrex and m'lady," guessed Hawk.

"Yes, and on Tyler and Mac, too," replied Raven. "And it's a damnably good thing I did so. Because I now know why they are so worried."

He turned his gaze on Peregrine. "Some evil dastard has stolen the plans and prototype to your uncle's new weapon.

And we need to find them and get them back before they're sold to the highest bidder."

Peregrine turned paler than the flour dust. "A-Are you sure?"

It was Raven's turn to sound uncertain. "S-Sure of what?"

"If Wrex and m'lady say they've been stolen," whispered Hawk, "you may be sure it's true."

"It's just that I . . ." Peregrine fisted his hands. "I find it hard to believe that someone managed to find them."

"Why?" pressed Raven.

The question seemed to hang in the air, dark and heavy as a storm cloud, thrumming with the threat of thunder and lightning.

Raven reached over and clasped Peregrine's hand. "Remember, the three of us are bound by blood. Perhaps not in the traditional way, but our trust and loyalty is no less true."

Peregrine stared down at their twined fingers, a sigh sending the quicksilver shadows skittering over their light and dark skin. His grip tightened, his eyes pooling with unshed tears. "You're the only real family I've got now, if you'll have me," he said. "My blood relatives wish me to the devil."

"It goes without saying that you're one of us," replied Raven. "Birds of unconventional feathers should fly together."

Peregrine looked up through his lashes. "The answer to your question is that Uncle Jeremiah was growing very unsettled by certain incidents within the Royal Laboratory. A gentleman— he didn't say who—was asking questions about his project." A pause. "Questions that the gentleman shouldn't have known enough to ask about."

Another sigh. "So Uncle Jeremiah decided to keep only a rough sketch of his current experiments in his laboratory. The complete plans and prototype he hid in a very secret place."

"Do you know where this secret place is?" asked Raven.

"Oiy," answered Peregrine softly.

"Will you take—" began Hawk.

"Will I take you to it?" finished Peregrine. A look of steely resolve lit in his eyes. "I was hoping you would ask me that. "

Quickening his steps, Wrexford turned the corner onto the Strand and made his way to No. 132. The simple wooden door, a dark burled walnut that echoed the close-grained wood of a gunstock, was flanked by two bow windows filled with a variety of firearms. The morning sun glinted off the polished metal, sparks of brass and gold darting through the pale flickers of silver and steel.

There was, reflected Wrexford, a certain lethal beauty to the implements of death. That they could wreak both good and evil was perhaps a mirror of mankind's own essential dual nature.

He stood for a moment admiring the exquisite craftsmanship of the weapons before he opened the door and stepped inside.

The shop's main display room was deserted—it was still unfashionably early for any customers to be arriving—and as the jingle of the brass bell over the door stirred no sign of life, he reached up and gave the cord another shake.

The sound of shuffling stirred in one of the interior workrooms. A short, slender man, his silvery hair tied back in an old-fashioned queue, appeared from the shadows. Everything about him was rather nondescript—his homely face, his shapeless nut-brown coat, his old-fashioned breeches . . .

Save for his hands. He was wiping them with an oily rag, and Wrexford immediately noted the graceful movement of his long, tapered fingers.

"May I help you, sir?"

"I am looking for Mr. Egg," replied Wrexford.

"Which one?" A wry smile. "I am Ursus Christian Egg, the proprietor of this establishment—though everyone calls me Durs." He inclined a small bow. "Joseph Egg, my nephew, is also part of the business."

"It is you, sir, with whom I wish to speak," answered the earl.

"Dare I hope you wish to try one of my pistols, Lord Wrexford?" A twinkle flashed in Egg's eye. "I'm aware that you are a loyal customer of Joseph Manton—and with good reason. Joe makes very fine weapons. But as a superb marksman, you might also find that some of the nuances of my creations are to your liking."

Wrexford immediately liked the gunmaker's puckish sense of humor. "As I'm also a man of science, I know that experimentation brings interesting discoveries. So you are right to chide me about being a creature of habit."

He glanced at the display cases lining the walls. "I shall have you recommend something for me. But first, I wonder if I might have a few moments of your time to ask a few very specific technical questions on firearms."

"Be careful what you wish for, milord," came the reply. "I can talk for days on the subject." Egg smiled. "Fire away."

"If you don't mind, might we go somewhere private?"

Egg's face betrayed a flicker of surprise, but he nodded politely and led the way through a back corridor to a tiny office squeezed in behind the workshops and the storage rooms. The scent of wood shavings, whale oil, and beeswax hung heavy in the air.

"Please forgive the spartan furnishings," apologized Egg, gesturing to a pair of straight-back chairs set facing his work desk. "I'm a man of simple tastes, and I choose to put my resources into embellishing my weaponry, rather than my own creature comforts."

"And your clients applaud you for it," replied Wrexford. "Your weapons are recognized as works of art, as well as precision instruments."

The gunmaker colored at the compliment. "Thank you,

milord. But clearly you didn't come here merely to exchange pleasantries. How can I help you?"

Wrexford placed Willis's folded sketch on the desk. "Before I go on, I need your word of honor that this conversation will remain completely confidential," he said. "It concerns a matter of grave importance to the country. And as you are a gunmaker to the Prince Regent, I assume I can count on your loyalty and discretion."

"You can, milord," answered Egg, without batting an eye.

The paper unfolded with a whispery sigh. "Please have a careful look at this," said Wrexford. "And tell me whether, in your professional opinion, the design can work."

Egg took a pair of spectacles out of his desk drawer and perched them on his nose. Drawing the sketch closer, he smoothed out the wrinkles and leaned in closer.

The muffled *tap-tap* of hammers and the rasp of a saw floated in from the adjoining workshop. Outside in the corridor, an apprentice whistled the tune of a popular ballad as he carried a crate of wood into one of the storerooms.

"This is Willis's work, isn't it?"

"You're aware of his experimentation?" asked Wrexford. "I was under the impression that his work on weaponry was a closely-guarded secret."

"It was—and I assume it still is, despite his unfortunate accident. But like you, he trusted in my integrity." A sad smile. "You see, there was a connection between our two families."

Wrexford's brows rose in surprise. "How so?"

"During the war with our American colonies, Willis's father escaped enslavement by slipping away and offering his services to the British forces. He became manservant to one of our officers, and came to England with him in '78, when the Experimental Rifle Corps was disbanded—"

"Experimental rifles?" queried the earl.

"Are you not familiar with the Ferguson rifle?" asked Egg.

Wrexford frowned in thought. "I think that I may have heard it mentioned during my time on the Peninsula . . ."

"Then allow me to digress, milord. You'll understand why in a moment," said Egg. "Major Patrick Ferguson was a Scottish officer in our army and began his career during the early part of the last century. He served for a time in the West Indies, then returned to Britain to help train the army's light infantry. It's there that he came to the attention of General Howe, for he had a genius for creating mechanical devices. You see, he had designed a breech-loading flintlock weapon that promised to revolutionize warfare."

"Ye gods," uttered Wrexford.

"I had just established my shop in 1772, and the government came to me, along with three other prominent gunmakers, and asked us to make a small batch of the rifles," continued Egg. "Trouble was brewing in America, and they were anxious to test its mettle in actual combat."

"Did it work?" asked the earl.

"Actually, it worked quite well. The design was ingenious—Ferguson based it on an earlier design by Isaac de la Chaumette, but made significant improvements. In his model, a twist of the trigger guard lowered a breech plug just enough for a round bullet to be dropped into the chamber, which was then screwed back in place. Compared to traditional muzzle-loading weapons, the rate of fire for his new weapon was astounding. A well-trained rifleman could fire anywhere from six to ten shots a minute."

Wrexford let out a low-pitched whistle. The math was staggering when one considered two armies facing each other. "While a skilled foot soldier can get off three, maybe four, with a traditional musket."

"Precisely," murmured Egg.

"So what went wrong?"

"Between myself and the three other gunmakers, about one

hundred of the new rifles were made, and after war broke out in the colonies, Ferguson was asked to create a special experimental rifle brigade drawn from General Howe's light-infantry regiments. They had some successes, but after the Battle of Brandywine, where, by the by, Ferguson was gravely injured, it ended up being disbanded, as it turned out that the weapon simply wasn't reliable under combat conditions."

Egg sighed. "First of all, each of the rifles was made by hand, so every piece was unique and not interchangeable. If something broke, there was no replacement part, so the rifle was useless. The basic design of breech screw also put a great deal of pressure on the wooden stock. They simply broke down under heavy use."

"So you're saying there's nothing wrong with the concept, it's just that we don't yet have the engineering skills to make it work."

"In a word, yes. Methods and materials are constantly evolving, milord," explained the gunmaker. "Things that were impossible only a decade ago are now becoming commonplace."

Wrexford nodded in understanding. "But what of your connection with Willis's family?"

"Ah, yes. I was just getting to that. It so happens that Willis's father worked for one of the officers in the Experimental Rifle Corps—the fellow in charge of keeping the weapons in working order—and so he did some tinkering with the rifle mechanisms. The officer sent Willis's father to see me when they arrived back in England, knowing that I had made some of the original rifles. I was impressed with the fellow's mechanical skills and suggested that I and his benefactor write him a letter of recommendation for employment at Watt and Boulton's steam engine factory."

"And from there, he went on to become a very successful inventor himself," mused Wrexford.

"Yes, he was a very gifted fellow," responded Egg. "It pleased me greatly to see him triumph over all the adversities in his life."

An admirable sentiment, thought Wrexford. Which made him like the gunmaker even more.

Egg sat back in his chair and took a meditative moment before going on. "Willis the younger—that is, Jeremiah—introduced himself to me when he arrived in London. We became friends, though not very close ones. He was a very reserved man and tended to keep people at arm's length. It was understandable, of course, given his circumstances. There is always some degree of professional jealousy when one is an innovator, and there were those who turned ugly because of his race and tried to discredit his accomplishments."

"Which meant, I imagine, that he had to be twice as good at what he did," observed Wrexford.

"And he was," said Egg. "It grieves me deeply that his life was cut short. I can't help but wonder . . ." The gunmaker tapped his fingertips together. "Could there be any truth to the recent drawing by A. J. Quill? It hints at foul play, and heaven knows, the artist seems to have a way of ferreting out every secret and scandal in London."

"Alas, I don't know the truth," answered Wrexford.

"And yet you are here, with a sketch for a revolutionary firearm," replied Egg shrewdly. "Which says something."

"Getting back to Willis's sketch," said Wrexford, deliberately deflecting any further discussion on the inventor's demise. "What I came to ask is whether you think this design works."

A grim smile played on Egg's lips. "As you just heard, milord, the question is really far more complicated than that." His gaze dropped to the sketch. "I firmly believe that a revolving-cylinder design for a multishot weapon will work. It's simply a question of when. Willis was a brilliant engineer, and while I'd need to see the finished technical plans to say for sure, my guess is that he worked out a functional design."

Wrexford was still puzzled. Surely, the concept was the hard part. Making it merely required a glorified blacksmith.

However, when he said as much, Egg rolled his eyes. "On the contrary, milord. The challenge of making precision parts for a complicated mechanical devices is what's holding back a number of grand technological innovations. The truth is, we need to fabricate sophisticated machines to *make* machines. Lathes, drills, tiny screw-making devices—the list is daunting. But unless Willis had discovered a way to make the types of complicated pieces needed to bring his weapon to life . . ."

Egg let his words trail off.

Unless, thought the earl. "But it's possible that he did."

"If anyone could, it was Willis," came the reply. "So, yes, of course it's possible."

Wrexford contemplated the sketch, willing the faint pencil lines to give up their secret.

"In fact," added Egg as he sat up a little straighter, "a man visited the shop last week, and as we were talking about gunmaking, he mentioned there was a fellow in America experimenting with the same revolving-cylinder concept as Willis."

"What was the man's name?" asked the earl.

"I was afraid you were going to ask that." Egg blew out his breath. "I'm sorry, but he didn't say."

Bloody hell. Every damnable clue seemed intent on dancing just out of reach.

"Thank you for your time, sir," Wrexford said, pocketing the sketch.

"And yet, I fear I've been of little help," apologized Egg.

"On the contrary, you've given me a number of things to mull over." Wrexford rose. Perhaps one of them would spark—

"Just one last question," he said as a sudden thought came to mind. "Do you remember the name of the British officer who brought Willis's father back to England with him?"

"Aye, that I do, sir." Egg looked happy to have a definitive answer. "It was Waltham. Captain Reginald Waltham." His smile became more pronounced. "His son is also a military man, and serves at Horse Guards."

Waltham.

Wrexford uttered another thanks—along with a promise to return and purchase a pistol—and hurried out of the shop.

The investigation had led them into a bewildering tangle of intrigue and innuendo . . .

But has the key piece of the puzzle finally fallen into place?

CHAPTER 24

"Have you been enjoying your stay in London, Captain Hockett?" asked Charlotte. She and the American naval officer were strolling together along the canal in St. James's Park, while Alison had commandeered the other three members of the American delegation to take her for a closer look at the new Chinese bridge—topped by a magnificent seven-story pagoda—which now spanned the water.

"Very much so," he answered. "So far, I have seen the popular sights, including the British Museum, the Tower and its menagerie, and Hampton Court. And tomorrow I'm being taken to see the Royal Observatory and the Naval College at Greenwich."

Sunlight flickered over the still water. The afternoon was pleasantly warm, with naught but a gentle breeze ruffling through the trees.

"Have you any other suggestions for a first-time visitor to the city?" asked Hockett.

"That would depend on your interests, sir," she answered, seizing the chance to probe a little about why he was here. "If politics are a passion, you might ask for a tour of Parliament."

Hockett laughed. "Politics are far too devious for me. As a military man, I prefer to know who my enemy is, and fight him face-to-face."

An interesting answer. Charlotte wondered whether it was true.

"Politics does seem to be a wolf-eat-wolf world," she replied. "With each country looking to snatch some small advantage in its jaws that will give it an edge over the rest of the pack."

He turned his head, a glint of curiosity rippled through his gaze. "In my experience, ladies aren't usually so cynical."

"Perhaps that's because most ladies aren't usually encouraged to speak their minds."

"Touché," he murmured. "Daggett did warn me that you were . . . different."

"Oh?" said Charlotte, masking her misgivings with a coy smile. Daggett had been part of their previous murder investigation. He had promised to keep their clandestine activities a secret . . . but perhaps he had let something slip.

"Dare I ask what else he said about me?"

"Nothing that should give you any cause for worry," replied Hockett lightly.

Charlotte said nothing in response, and they walked on in silence to the footpath leading up to Piccadilly Street, where they stopped to wait for Alison and others before continuing on to Hyde Park.

"Lady Wrexford." She looked around to see Kurlansky detach himself from Prince Rubalov's retinue and walk over to join them.

"The parks are crowded today," he observed. "Excitement seems to be growing for the gala reenactment of the Battle of Trafalgar on the Serpentine tomorrow evening."

"I hear that for the battle's climax, Lieutenant-Colonel Congreve has promised a spectacular display of fireworks to light up the night sky," said Charlotte. She began to introduce Hockett, but Kurlansky waved her off.

"The captain and I met the other night at a diplomatic reception and enjoyed a very stimulating conversation on the state of the world," explained the Russian.

"As for the state of the world, I think we can all breathe a sigh of relief that peace now reigns over Europe—and will soon do so between Britain and America," said Hockett.

A mischievous—or was it malicious—gleam fluttered beneath his dark lashes as Kurlansky looked at Charlotte. "As your husband is one of the most eminent men of science in your country, I'm sure he's familiar with the theory of *horror vacui*—the scientific principle first espoused by Aristotle that nature abhors a vacuum. Napoleon is gone, but that leaves a rather large void."

"And you think that the powers that be will be battling to fill it." Charlotte allowed a deliberate pause. "No matter the cost?"

Kurlansky shrugged. "The men who seek power rarely pay for the miseries that their wars for power cause."

A summons from Prince Rubalov cut short the exchange.

"Forgive me, but I must be off." The Russian touched a salute to the brim of his hat. "Enjoy the coming festivities. Tomorrow's nighttime pyrotechnics promises to be quite a spectacle."

As Kurlansky sauntered off, Hockett shifted his stance, edging a little closer to Charlotte, but the approach of Alison and the other American envoys forestalled any private conversation concerning the Russian's remarks.

"The Chinese pagoda is quite marvelous," announced the dowager with a jaunty wave of her cane. "Now on to Hyde Park. I've heard the model sailing ships designed for the naval battle reenactment are equally impressive."

With Alison setting a brisk pace, they made their way up the gently-sloping meadow to Piccadilly Street and crossed over into Hyde Park.

"Our military attaché is accompanying Tsar Alexander and a group of the Allied generals on a visit to Woolwich this afternoon," mentioned Mr. Schuyler, the leader of the American delegation. "They are to be given a tour of the armory and the laboratories, whose innovations are said to have played a great part in the defeat of Napoleon."

"I'm surprised you didn't wish to be part of the tour, Captain Hockett," said Charlotte.

"I spend enough of my time surrounded by weaponry," he responded. "I much prefer to explore the cultural offerings of London."

"I heartily agree with you," said Schuyler. "We Americans have so much to do in developing the potential of our new country. I, for one, prefer not to squander our resources in making war. I fervently hope the diplomatic negotiations that will soon begin between my country and Britain will quickly bring an end to the hostilities."

All laudable sentiments, thought Charlotte. Assuming they were heartfelt.

"Ladies have always known that talking out differences with an adversary is far more effective than punching him in the nose," said Alison dryly.

"Then perhaps Britain ought to appoint a lady as prime minister," said Schuyler. "Ha, ha, ha!"

"Perhaps that day will come," said the dowager, once the male chortling had subsided. "Indeed, the last time Britain was ruled by a female, the country didn't do too badly."

Hockett cleared his throat with a cough.

On that note, they strolled through the final turn of the walkway and saw the glimmering waters of the Serpentine just ahead. A crowd was lined along the near bank, admiring the flotilla of small warships designed for the mock battle. As Alison was hailed by a group of British diplomats from the Foreign Office, Hockett offered his arm to Charlotte.

"While the others socialize, would you care to have a closer look at the ships?" he asked.

Charlotte sensed it was not mere chivalry that provoked the offer. She readily agreed, as she had her own reasons for wanting another tête-à-tête with him.

They found a spot close to the water's edge, and Hockett began to explain how the battle would be reenacted. "The model ships are exact scale model replicas of a British naval frigate—"

"Why are there two sizes?" she asked. There was a flotilla of close to one hundred ships that were six feet long clustered near them. And a short distance away, moored to the Serpentine Bridge, were two larger frigates that were fifteen feet long. From the masts and rigging to the hulls and gunports, the detailing was exquisite in both sizes.

"These smaller ships are the actual warships, and are specially designed for the evening's entertainment. They'll be divided into two fleets—the British force and the combined French and Spanish force."

He pointed out a ship with a large cockpit set in the deck just behind its mainmast. "Half of them have been constructed with a bomb well."

"A bomb well?" said Charlotte.

"Before commencing the reenactment of the battle, each of the ships representing the French and Spanish fleet will have a keg of gunpowder placed in the well, and a timed fuse will be lit," explained Hockett.

Seeing her puzzled look, he added, "Fuses are made from cording impregnated with specially-formulated chemicals. They burn at a set rate, and so by cutting them to specific lengths, one can control the timing of the explosion fairly accurately."

"You mean half of these ships are going to be blown to smithereens?" exclaimed Charlotte.

Hockett smiled. "The public will find it vastly entertaining. Most people enjoy seeing things that go *boom*!"

"Much as I would like to deny it, I fear you are right," she replied. "But with no one to sail them, how are all these warships going to get into position?"

"The plan is to use the larger frigates as guide boats. Each of them will be manned by a pair of British sailors—one man will row, and one man will use a large pole to push all the small ships into place." He gestured toward the bridge where the two larger frigates were rocking gently at their moorings. "The sailors have been practicing the maneuvers this week. The timing is important—for the actual event, they will need to row like the devil to get out of danger. For the actual battle, the Navy will be bringing up an additional four guide boats from the workshops at the Royal Armory at Woolwich."

"Fascinating," she murmured.

"Would you care to have a closer look at them?" he asked.

The footpath leading to the bridge was deserted. Charlotte glanced around and saw Alison and the Americans were engaged in an animated conversation with the British diplomats.

"Yes, I should like that very much." She waited until they were some distance from the crowd before asking, "So, alluring as the frigates may be, what is it that you wish to discuss away from prying ears, Captain?"

He slowed to a halt and lifted a hand to shade his eyes as he regarded the ships ahead. "Actually, it's more of a friendly warning than a discussion," he replied. "Daggett mentioned that your husband occasionally serves as, shall we say, an advisor to your government. I have some information that might interest him, so I thought I would pass it on."

Timeo Danaos et dona ferentes. The lines from Virgil's *Aeneid* popped to mind. *Beware of Greeks bearing gifts.*

"Why?" asked Charlotte. The deadly intrigue within intrigue of this current investigation had her wary.

"Why tell you?" He turned his head. "Because Daggett considers both of you to be trustworthy friends."

"I'm listening."

Hockett drew them into the shadows of the leafy trees shading the graveled walkway. "Kurlansky took me aside for a private conversation last night. He asked whether America is participating in a secret auction for an invention that might shift the balance of world power to the country who possesses it."

"And *is* America going to offer a bid?" asked Charlotte.

He regarded her thoughtfully. "You don't seem surprised by my shocking revelation."

Charlotte responded with a cool stare.

"I see that Daggett didn't exaggerate. You *do* possess nerves of steel."

She still said nothing. In her experience, most people were uncomfortable with silence. It made them say more than they should to fill the void.

Hockett smoothed a crease from his sleeve. "As it happens, America is not bidding. Unlike the leading European powers, our sovereign—that is, our president—is not here in London and able to make such a momentous decision at a moment's notice."

"I see." Charlotte carefully considered his words. "But you think Russia is going to participate in the bidding?" Was that the message he was trying to convey to her and Wrexford? "If this invention is as valuable as you say, I would imagine Prussia and Austria would also be in the thick of the bidding."

"No doubt you are right, and, yes, I think the Russians want very much to possess the item." He paused. "But . . ."

She waited, sensing that he was finally getting to the point.

Hockett pursed his lips. "The Russians have made an art out of intrigue." He drew in a measured breath. "If I were Britain, I would keep a very close eye on them."

The breeze tugged at her bonnet strings.

"And on your own military officials at Horse Guards," he added, his voice dropping to barely a whisper.

"Malden or Duxbury?" she asked quickly.

"I merely overheard a snatch of conversation when I stepped out into the garden during last night's festivities to smoke a cheroot. So I didn't see who was with Kurlansky. However, their words seemed to indicate that their plans didn't include bidding at an auction."

Biting back a huff of frustration, Charlotte quickly murmured her thanks. The information at least corroborated that they were coming closer and closer to identifying the villain. "Perhaps now it's best that we rejoin the others."

"But of course." Hockett turned and they began to retrace their steps. "A final word of advice, Lady Wrexford. Do be careful as you move forward. My sense is that the path leads to a tangle of very dangerous vipers."

"Bloody hell," said Raven as he slipped back into the schoolroom.

"M'lady doesn't like it when we swear," said Hawk. "She says it isn't gentlemanly."

"To the devil with being a gentleman," he retorted. His expression tightened. "Mac just left the house, and Riche isn't certain as to where she has gone. Which means that with Wrex and m'lady out, as well as Tyler, we have—"

"We have no one to tell about our plans," finished Hawk. "Which means we're caught between a rock and a stone."

"I—I don't understand," said Peregrine.

"House rules," muttered Raven. "And while some can, on occasion, be broken, this one can't."

"Oiy," agreed Hawk. "We all made a solemn promise that none of us would hare off and do anything dangerous without letting one of the others know where we were going—and why."

"Then I suppose . . ." Peregrine's shoulders slumped. "I suppose we just have to be patient and wait."

Rather than sprawl down beside the others on the rug, Raven moved to the window and stared out at the back garden.

Hawk fingered one of the pawns on the chessboard and slid it forward. "To be good at chess," he murmured, "you have to be patient."

Peregrine moved his knight.

"You also have to be aware of strategy," said Raven, without turning around. "And be willing to improvise when the game takes an unexpected turn."

His brother waited expectantly.

"Your move," murmured Peregrine.

"Shhhh. He's thinking," whispered Hawk.

Outside, the notes of sparrow's song floated in the breeze, twining with the faint hum of the buzzing bees.

"Improvise." Raven suddenly turned, a smile blossoming on his face. "I have an idea."

Hawk and Peregrine scrambled to their feet.

"Change into shabby but respectable clothing. We'll pack our most disgusting jackets and hats in a sack to take with us."

"I thought we had to stay here," said Peregrine.

"Not if we head straight to the docklands and the office of Nereid and Neptune," replied Raven. "Mr. Sheffield and Lady Cordelia count as family. And they'll likely have a wherry tied up at their dock that can sail us down to Woolwich faster than a carriage can navigate the streets."

"Oiy," agreed Hawk, after a moment's hesitation. "Even a high stickler would have to agree that's keeping our word."

"Hurry and change," urged Raven. "I'll be back in a moment."

After a flurry of thumping drawers, Hawk and Peregrine reappeared from their bedchambers clad in well-worn garments. Hawk had a canvas sack held at arm's length.

"*Fawwgh.*" Peregrine crinkled his nose and grinned as Hawk set it down on the rug. "That's truly disgusting."

Raven returned and darted into the adjoining room to change. He was back in a flash. "Ready?"

MURDER AT THE SERPENTINE BRIDGE 291

"What's that?" asked Hawk, eyeing the length of dark wood that his brother was about to shove into the sack.

A hesitation, and then a sigh. Raven held it out for closer inspection. It was an unadorned ebony walking stick topped with a modest brass cap. There was nothing about it that would catch the eye . . .

Snick. However, a touch to a button on the side of the cap released a hidden lever. Raven rotated the brass and drew out a sliver of sharpened steel.

"A sword cane!" exclaimed Peregrine, his eyes widening in interest.

"Wrex won't like that," said Hawk. "We're not supposed to touch his weapons."

"This isn't precisely a weapon," reasoned Raven. "After all, Tyler stores it with the other walking sticks." He resheathed the steel. "Regardless of the consequences, I don't think we should go unarmed. Wrex and m'lady are of the opinion that the villain is devilishly dangerous."

Hawk didn't argue.

After sliding the stick into the sack, Raven tugged the drawstrings tight and slung it over his shoulder. "Let's be off."

He led the way down the curved staircase, adding a caution to do so quietly, so as not to alert Riche to the fact that they were leaving. The three of them were about to cross into the foyer when the sound of a parlor maid approaching from a side corridor stirred the stately silence.

Raven drew back into the shadows, signaling the others to join him. "I think it's best that we go out through the music room to the side terrace and circle around to the street."

They tiptoed back the way they had come and slipped outside without being spotted. On reaching the gate that opened onto Berkeley Square, Raven checked up and down the cobbled street before leading the way into the large center garden.

"It will take us some time to get to the docklands on foot," said Hawk as they picked up their pace and headed for Piccadilly Street. "Maybe we should—"

"Peregrine!"

A sharp hail sounded from behind them.

Peregrine froze in his tracks, and slowly turned around.

"It's a good thing I spotted you." Belmont was striding toward them, an agitated expression on his flushed face. He stabbed a finger through the air. "Come with me, boy. Now."

"Why—" began Peregrine.

Belmont halted, his mouth quivering in fury. "How dare you question my command!" He speared a look at Raven and Hawk. "Inform Lord Wrexford that my ward's stay with you has ended. He's returning home with me."

"But my things," protested Peregrine.

"We'll send for them later," snapped Belmont.

"You better go with him," whispered Raven as he shuffled his feet and shifted his sack. "We'll follow along and wait in the alleyway behind your townhouse. Climb down to the back garden when you get the chance . . ." Peregrine had told them that it was even easier to escape from Lampson House than it was from Wrexford's residence. "We'll improvise from there."

"Peregrine!" roared his uncle. "Come this instant or you'll feel a birch rod on your backside."

The boy hurried to join him.

Raven watched as Belmont seized Peregrine's arm and the two of them disappeared around the corner of Bolton Row. He gave them a moment or two, then nudged his brother. "I think we should shadow them and keep an eye on Falcon. Wrex doesn't trust that muckworm Belmont." His eyes narrowed. "And neither should we."

CHAPTER 25

"I like the Americans," announced Alison as she and Charlotte started down the footpath to Stanhope Gate, where the dowager's carriage was waiting. "They are not so corseted in rules and etiquette, which makes them far more interesting than European diplomats. They're not afraid to speak their minds."

"There is much to be said for democracy, which allows talent rather than birth to determine one's possibilities in life," said Charlotte. She thought of the Weasels, and how their extraordinary gifts would have flickered out and died within the darkness of the slums, if not for a miracle. With all the changes swirling through the world, perhaps . . .

The dowager's voice pulled her back to the present moment. "And how did you fare with your American?" Alison had played her part in making sure that Charlotte had private time with Hockett. "Did you learn anything helpful?"

"Perhaps," she answered. "He warned that the Russians may be conniving with someone within our government to outwit the villain who came up with the nefarious plan to steal Willis's invention and get their hands on it before the auction."

"Good heavens." Alison made a face. "It seems that deception and duplicity are tangling into an even tighter knot."

"Yes, and if we don't manage to unravel it quickly . . ." Charlotte steadied Alison's small stumble. "I'm so sorry that the outing was so rigorous."

"Nonsense," replied the dowager with a wave of her cane. "Fresh air and exercise is an excellent tonic for my old bones."

Charlotte surreptitiously slowed her steps.

"As is the chance to participate in the sleuthing."

Despite her fretting over Hockett's information, Charlotte couldn't hold back a smile. "It's rather frightening how good you are at it."

The two spots of color on the dowager's cheeks grew brighter. "Am I?"

"Absolutely."

They walked on in companionable silence as the path wound through a glade of trees.

"Ye gods." Alison came to a sudden halt.

Charlotte tightened her hold on the dowager's arm. "What—"

"Russians," muttered Alison.

Hell's bells. Had overexertion momentarily disoriented the dowager's mind? "Lean on me," she said. "The carriage is not far off—"

"My wits aren't wandering," assured Alison. "On the contrary, I've just recalled an interesting connection." Her cane thumped against the gravel. "You've mentioned that fellow Osborn on several occasions."

"Yes," interjected Charlotte. "He's one of Pierson's operatives."

"He's also part Russian."

Charlotte glanced up at the sun, inwardly cursing the cloudless sky. "I fear you're mistaken. Osborn is the youngest son of the Marquess of Auburndale, whose august lineage traces back to the time of William the Conqueror—"

"Yes, yes, as I said, my wits aren't wandering!" interrupted Alison with a huff of impatience. "And the marquess's two older sons have impeccable English lineage as well. But the youngest Osborn's mother was Auburndale's *second* wife, and she is half-Russian—the daughter of a diplomat from St. Petersburg to the court of George the Second, who married one of the queen's ladies-in-waiting."

Charlotte didn't bother asking her great-aunt if she was sure. Alison knew the family trees listed in *Debrett's Peerage* better than John Debrett himself.

"Ye gods," she said, echoing the dowager's earlier exclamation. "We must hurry back to Grosvenor Square and let Wrexford know."

Raven sidled to the opening of the alley running behind the back garden of the family's townhouse and darted a quick glance out at the street. "That's odd—Belmont didn't come by carriage. They're going by foot." A shrug. "But Lampson House is on Curzon Street, so it's not a long walk."

"Oiy," agreed Hawk. "And Falcon said his uncle is clutch-fisted with his purse, so perhaps he sent their coachman and carriage back to the estate."

"C'mon, let's keep them in sight." Raven adjusted the sack on his shoulder. "With luck, Falcon will be able to slip out and join up with us soon."

The two of them fell in step with the other pedestrians, weaving in and out to keep an eye on their quarry. Belmont, however, surprised them by turning right onto John Street, rather than left.

"Where's he going?" muttered Hawk as Belmont suddenly veered toward a gap between the buildings, which opened into a warren of winding alleyways that ran up toward the old burying ground.

"Nowhere good." Raven reached around and drew the

sword cane from the sack as Belmont disappeared into one of the gloomy passageways. "Let's get closer so we don't lose them."

They both moved with practiced ease over the ruts and filth, their steps stealthy and silent. While up ahead, Belmont's curses echoed off the sooty brick as he squelched through the muck.

"Where are you taking me?" Peregrine's voice rose in question.

"Quiet, brat. You'll find out soon enough."

"No! Not until you explain yourself, sir."

Hearing Belmont's steps come to a halt, Raven stopped abruptly and cocked an ear. Hawk was right behind him, both of them holding still as statues.

"Explain myself?" A mocking laugh. "I'm your legal guardian. You may be the bloody baron in name, but until you reach your majority, it is I who hold the power."

A quick peek around the corner showed that Belmont had grabbed the boy's arm in a viselike grip.

"So listen well, Peregrine," warned his uncle. "I've just searched through your letters, so I know that Willis shared his secrets with you—"

"Y-You opened my private correspondence!" cried Peregrine. "Uncle Jeremiah was right to be suspicious of you. You're a blackguard and a—"

A hard slap cut short the rest of his words. "How dare you speak to me like that!" said Belmont in a shaky voice. "I've done my duty to my late brother, no matter that his choices stained the family name."

"It's *you* who have stained the family name," replied Peregrine, his chin lifting in defiance despite the ugly welt on his cheek. "You've betrayed my father's trust," he challenged. "I can't help but wonder what else you've betrayed."

Belmont went white as a ghost.

"Uncle Jeremiah—" continued the boy

"Your uncle's secretiveness is to blame for the unholy trouble that now grips the government," said Belmont. "We are going to meet with an operative of state security and, by God, you are going to tell him exactly where the prototype and plans of your uncle's invention are hidden. His letter mentioned a place in the Royal Armory."

He gave Peregrine another hard shake. "Our lives depend on it."

"I will tell Lord Wrexford, and no one else," replied the boy.

Belmont raised a threatening fist. "You'll do as I say or—"

The rest of his words were swallowed in a sudden thunderous bang. Sparks exploded in the murky gloom, hellfire-gold against the plume of smoke that curled through the air for an instant before dissolving into the spray of blood.

His head half blown apart, Belmont was spun around by the force of the bullet, his lifeless body toppling to the ground as Peregrine stumbled back with a strangled scream.

"Run, Falcon!" cried Raven, stepping out from his hiding place and frantically waving his arms. "Run!"

Peregrine reacted in a flash. He steadied his footing just as a masked man rushed out from the adjoining passageway and grabbed for the tail of his jacket. Wrenching free, the boy ducked away and scrambled over a broken crate. As his boots hit the ground, he broke into a dead run.

The assailant set off in pursuit, but a pelting of well-aimed rocks thrown by Hawk knocked him to his knees.

"This way!" shouted Raven, shoving Peregrine into one of the narrow passageways. With Hawk leading the way, all three of them flew into the shadows.

"I'm sorry, milord, but the major is not here at headquarters today," replied a junior adjutant in response to the earl's request to see Waltham. "He's supervising the tsar's visit to the Royal Arsenal at Woolwich."

Wrexford kept a rein on his frustration. "Then take me to Mr. Osborn."

"I'm afraid Mr. Osborn is also absent. I believe he's attending to some duties at the Royal Laboratory and will be gone for the rest of the day."

Damnation. He turned to take his leave, and then changed his mind. Perhaps it was time to go on the attack.

"What about Colonel Duxbury?"

"Yes, sir. He's in his office—"

The earl shouldered past him. "I'll announce myself." He was familiar with the Horse Guards building and knew where to find his quarry.

"B-But, m-milord . . ."

Ignoring the stuttered protest, Wrexford marched to one of the spacious rooms overlooking the parade ground and pushed through the closed portal.

A startled Duxbury looked up from the pile of papers on his blotter.

"Colonel," called the ashen-faced adjutant. "I tried to—"

"Never mind, Phillips. You may leave us."

Wrexford nudged the door closed with his boot heel, and after a glance at the array of military knives in the display case, he approached the desk.

Duxbury had recovered from his initial surprise. "To what do I owe the pleasure of a visit, milord?"

"I doubt there will be a mote of pleasure involved for either of us," he replied.

"Would you care to elaborate?" Despite the show of sangfroid, a blade of sunlight from the leaded window showed sweat was beginning to bead on the colonel's forehead.

"I have some further questions to ask you about the murder at Royal Ascot, as well as your movements in Oxford on the evening of the gala banquet," said Wrexford.

"I have no idea as to what you're implying. And furthermore, by what authority do you storm into my private office and seek to ask insolent questions?" Duxbury rose, his spine steeling to ramrod straight. "I suggest you leave immediately, or, by God, I'll have you thrown out."

"You can either answer me here," responded Wrexford. "Or we can go to Whitehall and conduct an official interrogation in Lord Grentham's office."

At the mention of Grentham's name, Duxbury's eyes betrayed a flutter of panic.

"The choice is yours."

The fight seemed to drain out of the colonel. His shoulders sagged, and his breathing turned ragged. "I—I can explain . . ." He braced a hand on his desk. "What would you like to ask?"

Two quick strides brought Wrexford to the display case. He tapped a finger to the glass. "Was the murder weapon one of the knives from your collection?"

"Yes."

"Did you kill the man?" The victim's identity was still unknown.

Duxbury slowly moved back to his chair and sat down heavily. "No, I did not."

"And yet," pressed Wrexford, "you appeared so quickly on the scene."

The colonel wet his lips.

"That, coupled with your proximity in Oxford to another violent incident, does raise some very serious suspicions."

"I . . ." A breath in and out. "I concede that my actions might trigger questions. Which I shall now endeavor to answer to your satisfaction."

Wrexford came closer and perched a hip on a corner of the desk. During his walk from Egg's workshop to Horse Guards, he had been moving the pieces of the puzzle around in his head. A picture had begun to form, but he was curious as to whether Duxbury's confessions would confirm it. "Go on."

"The reason I entered the barn at Royal Ascot was because I had been watching Waltham, and I wished to see what had drawn him away from the group of important guests."

"Why?" murmured the earl. "Why watch him?"

"Because . . ." Another harried inhale and exhale. "Call it intuition, but I've had the niggling sense for some time that he's up to something havey-cavey. And before you ask, I can't prove anything. But I've found him riffling through restricted military files—always with a plausible administrative explanation—and have spotted him inside my office and that of General Malden's when the daily schedule indicates we are otherwise engaged."

"As you say, all may have innocent explanations."

"And I'm quite sure he took my knife," said Duxbury. "The case is locked. There are some very valuable jeweled ceremonial daggers from the King of Spain's captured baggage train on display. Waltham is the only other man who knows where the key is. I didn't think about it at the time, but he saw me open and close the case once to add a knife that Wellington gave me on his triumphant return from the Peninsula. So he saw where I hid the key."

"Yes, but that only works in his favor. Surely he would know that your suspicion would fall on him."

"Perhaps," said Duxbury. "But a very clever man might assume that the chance of a very ordinary weapon being traced back to my collection was virtually nil. And that even if such a thing happened, I would be loath to admit to owning a knife used in a murder."

"A fair point," conceded Wrexford. "What about Oxford?"

"Again I was following him in hope of spotting some proof that he is up to no good." He stared down at his hands, which were fisted on the blotter. "I heard a shot, but because of the twisting alleyways, I only caught sight of two men sprawled on the stones, with a lady screaming bloody murder."

That explained the flash of red that Sheffield had seen. A soldier's tunic. But the question remained as to whether Duxbury was telling the truth.

"So, what motive would Waltham have for murder?"

The colonel drew in a quick breath, his nostril flaring in frustration. Or perhaps fear. "That's the devil of it, milord. I don't know!"

Wrexford was growing more and more sure that his suspicions were correct. "How much involvement does Waltham have with the Royal Laboratory?"

"He handles supply logistics and personnel . . ." Duxbury's eyes suddenly narrowed. "You think—"

"Where's Osborn?" asked the earl abruptly.

The colonel considered the question, his brows drawing together as he frowned. "I'm not sure. I assumed Malden has sent him on a task." A pause. "Should I be concerned?"

"No," said Wrexford. Waltham's journey to Woolwich appeared to be part of his official duties. And yet, knowing what he did now, it stirred a frisson of alarm. "Never mind Osborn," he added as he rose from the desk.

"Is there anything I can do to help?" asked Duxbury.

"For now, you must hold the fort, as it were," he answered. "I need to confirm a few more things, so it's important for you to act as if nothing is amiss."

"Faster! Faster," urged Raven, the thudding echo of pursuit creeping closer.

The alley twisted and the way turned darker as it ran through a cluster of warehouses. Quickening his pace, Raven darted forward and took the lead from Hawk. He knew a place down one of the snaking side footpaths where he hoped to lose Belmont's killer.

"Follow me!" Slipping, sliding, he skidded down a sharp incline and chose the left-hand fork. The stench of decay filled the air as they sprinted deeper into the maze.

His breath coming in gasps, Raven checked over his shoulder that Hawk and Peregrine were right behind him. It wasn't far now . . .

Looming up from the shadows, he spotted what he was looking for—two stone warehouses connected by a raised brick passageway that crossed over the path. There was perhaps two or three feet of space beneath it, and though a planked base had been built to block the footpath, the wood was old and Raven knew there was an opening just big enough for a wiry boy to slip through . . .

"Shite." He stumbled to a stop, seeing a fresh board had been nailed over the opening.

"What?" wheezed Hawk.

Peregrine cocked an ear. "He's coming."

The sword cane was already out of Raven's sack. Twisting the blade free, he stabbed at the wood, exposing the nails and working to pry them out. Hawk dropped to his knees and grabbed the plank, pulling, pulling . . .

With a splintery groan, it popped free.

Raven hacked away the dangling shards and wiggled through the exposed opening.

"Give me your hand," he barked at his brother, and then quickly yanked him through.

"Falcon!"

Peregrine had been slow to follow, and just as he started to slither to safety, the killer came barreling around the turn.

Raven seized Peregrine's collar and gave a mighty heave, dragging him halfway through.

A vicious oath rent the air, followed by the sound of ripping fabric as the killer shoved a hand through the opening and caught hold of Peregrine's breeches. The boy tried to kick free, but his legs were trapped. He started to slide back . . .

And then, a piercing howl spiraled through the shadows as the sword cane's blade stabbed through flesh and sinew.

Raven wrenched the weapon free as the killer's hand spasmed, releasing its grip. Hawk yanked with all his might, and though bloody fingers tried to snatch a new hold, Peregrine slipped free.

The wood planking shuddered as the killer smashed his shoulder against the wood, trying to enlarge the opening enough for him to crawl through. The boys, however, were already on their feet and flying like bats fleeing the fires of hell. Raven took the lead, weaving a trail through one turn after another before finally darting up an alleyway that led out to a quiet side street bordering the old burial grounds and Audley Chapel.

Lungs burning, the three of them stumbled out into the sunlight.

"Oiy," gasped Hawk, bending double and bracing his forearms on his knees. "That was cutting things awfully close to the bone."

Peregrine fingered the tear in his breeches. "Oiy." His gaze then lingered on the bloodstains spattered over his jacket sleeve. "I—"

Raven gave him a shake. "You can't think about it now. We need to keep your uncle Jeremiah's invention from falling into the wrong hands."

"What should we do?" asked Hawk. "Wrex—"

"We don't know when Wrex or m'lady will be returning home," cut in Raven. "And the dastard likely heard that what he's seeking is in the Royal Armory at Woolwich." He thought for a moment. "Hawk, you follow our original plan and go tell Mr. Sheffield and Lady Cordelia what's afoot. They can send word to Berkeley Square and then come by boat to Woolwich."

He looked at Peregrine. "The hiding place—where is it? We must tell the others where to rendezvous with us."

"There's a statue of Hephaestus, the Greek god of fire, in the center of one of the small quadrangles within the Grand Stores complex by the laboratories," answered Peregrine. "It's easy to find—there is a stone tower rising up at the water's edge. The quadrangle is just behind it."

Raven took a purse from his pocket and shook out some coins. "Run to the river and hire a wherry to take you to Nereid and Neptune's dock," he said, handing the money to Hawk.

"How are you going to get to Woolwich?" asked his brother.

"By hackney," answered Raven. "From here, it's the quickest way."

Hawk's face pinched into a dubious frown. "A jarvey isn't usually inclined to convey young people."

Raven shook his purse. "He'll be more than happy to do so when he sees the color of my blunt." Hearing no further argument, he turned for Oxford Street. "Now let us go knock the killer's plan arse over teakettle."

CHAPTER 26

"Wrexford!" On hearing steps in the entrance hall, Charlotte stopped pacing circles around the parlor and hurried to the doorway. "You must hear what Alison and I have learned!"

"I, too, have much to share." He looked grim, she noted, worry deepening the lines of fatigue bracketing his mouth.

"Would you care for tea?" asked the dowager from her spot on the sofa. "Or perhaps something stronger?"

"Thank you, but no. I need to keep a clear head."

Deciding the dowager's revelation was more of a tantalizing possibility rather than a confirmed piece of the puzzle, Charlotte quickly said, "Our news can wait. I take it that Mr. Egg proved helpful?"

"Very." Wrexford took a seat in the armchair facing Alison. "Actually, tea would be welcome."

"Shall I ring for a cold collation from the kitchen?" asked Charlotte. "McClellan has not yet returned from her errands, else I would ask her to join us."

Taking the cup from Alison, he cradled it between his palms, the plume of vapor curling up to cloud his gaze. "Durs Egg proved extremely knowledgeable about breech-loading, multi-shot weapons. Indeed, he was involved in making an experimental rifle for our troops during the war with the American colonies . . ." He went on to explain about Ferguson and his special brigade, as well as the technical reasons why the new weapons were deemed unfit for military use.

Charlotte frowned. "Are you saying that Egg thinks Willis's weapon won't work?"

"He's not sure." Wrexford sighed, dispelling the steam. "Even if it works on paper, he thinks the current state of technology might not be quite advanced enough to produce such a sophisticated weapon."

"Thank heaven," murmured the dowager.

"I don't disagree," said the earl. "But that wasn't the key discovery." He finished his tea in two long swallows and stood up. "I think I now know the identity of the master villain." He quickly recounted Egg's revelation about the connection between Willis the elder and Major Waltham's father.

Charlotte pondered the new information. "But it sounds as if the two men had a cordial relationship, with Waltham's father being supportive of Willis the elder's ambitions."

"Yes, I've been thinking about that," replied Wrexford. "And I have a theory, though it's naught but conjecture."

Alison edged forward on the sofa.

"As Charlotte knows, I've been growing more and more convinced that Colonel Duxbury is the villain in this. He was present at both the Royal Ascot murder and the assassination attempt on Rochambert."

"And he lied about recognizing the knife used in the murder," murmured Charlotte.

"Yes," agreed the earl. "But after what Egg told me, I began to think more about Major Waltham and began to see some disturbing connections. Waltham's duties included overseeing ordnance projects at the Royal Laboratory, so it stands to reason that he learned about Willis and his work."

Charlotte sensed what he was thinking. "And you believe that Waltham might have become . . ." She hesitated. "Resentful? Perhaps he thought Willis the elder had somehow learned of gunmaking innovations from his own father, and came to believe that Willis's son was unfairly receiving the accolades and acclaim as a brilliant inventor."

Wrexford nodded. "As I said, it's merely a theory, but the family connections seem too strong to be mere coincidence. Jealousy may have festered—"

"Enflamed by race," pointed out Charlotte. "There are all-too-many people who feel that those of African descent are inferior simply by virtue of their skin color. To concede them any possibility of intellectual brilliance throws into question their assumption of superiority."

"Major Waltham has done little to distinguish himself in his military career," said Wrexford. "Influence matters in moving up the ranks. And according to Egg, Waltham's father was a respected officer, but had little ambition. After returning from the war, he enjoyed serving as an instructor for young officers here in England."

"Lack of influence may have also rubbed his pride raw," mused Charlotte.

"But"—Alison shifted on the sofa—"you said that Duxbury lied about the knife, so he must have something to hide."

"You're right." Wrexford smiled. "Which is why, when I found that Waltham was not at Horse Guards earlier, I decided to have a private tête-à-tête with Duxbury." He went on to recount what the colonel had told him.

"Though I confess, for a moment the thought occurred to me that the two of them might be working together. Given the complexity of the theft and the plan for the auction, it makes sense that there's more than one villain at work." He made a wry face. "However, I'm convinced that Duxbury is telling the truth."

Charlotte glanced at the dowager and then let out a pent-up

breath. "You may not be wrong about suspecting there are two villains. You haven't yet heard what we stumbled upon."

Wrexford listened in pensive silence as she recounted her exchange with Hockett.

"We have to consider that the American may simply wish to foment confusion and ill will between Britain and its Allies by passing on such supposed friendly confidences," he said carefully. "Hockett's country wishes to become a player on the world stage, so it's to America's advantage to weaken those relationships."

"Yes, but you haven't yet heard Alison's information," replied Charlotte.

Wrexford crossed his arms and raised a questioning brow.

"Osborn," announced the dowager, "is part Russian."

Charlotte saw the earl's skepticism disappear in a flash. "Bloody hell." A pause. "You're sure of this?"

A martial gleam winked off the lens of Alison's quizzing glass as she fixed the earl with an imperious stare. "Of course I'm sure."

"And we checked *Debrett's Peerage* while we were waiting for you," added Charlotte.

"Damnation. How the devil did Pierson and Grentham miss that important detail?" he wondered aloud.

"Men think it beneath them to pay attention to family connections, believing it's naught but frivolous feminine gossip," said Alison. "They make a mistake to ignore what it can tell them."

"It's an easy thing to miss," pointed out Charlotte. "Osborn is the marquess's youngest son, and was born of a second wife."

Wrexford started to pace.

"I've been thinking back on my encounters with Osborn, and seeing him as part of the nefarious plot sheds a new light on certain things," Charlotte continued. "His pressing Belmont as to the identity of the villain could have been to assure that he and Waltham were safe from suspicion. What better way to keep an eye on what the government knows than to be the fox in the henhouse."

Wrexford moved to the window and seemed to lose himself in watching the soft fluttering of the ivy leaves against the glass.

The more she thought about it, the more Charlotte was convinced that the pieces of the puzzle were finally fitting together into a clear picture of the diabolical plot. "Osborn's attack on you in the stable at Royal Ascot could have a darker explanation than mere misunderstanding. He might have learned that Pierson had asked for your help, and feared your skills at uncovering the truth."

His lips thinned to a grim line but he held his tongue.

"As for his clandestine meeting with Kurlansky, perhaps Osborn and Waltham have decided that the auction plan has become too risky, and are making a deal with Kurlansky to sell it directly to the Russians."

The earl turned abruptly. "Waltham is in charge of escorting the tsar and his retinue on today's tour of the armory and the laboratories. And as Osborn was away from Horse Guards, he may also be part of the group." His jaw tightened for a moment. "God only knows what dark mischief is taking place beneath the cloak of friendship."

Before he could go on, McClellan appeared in the doorway, several large parcels clasped in her arms. After a glance at their faces, the smile died on her lips. "What's wrong?"

"We may have discovered the identity of the villain—or rather the villains," answered Charlotte. "And are hoping that it's not too late to stop their nefarious plan."

The maid dropped the parcels on a side table and dusted her hands. "What can I do to help?"

"Let us not all go running off half-cocked," said Wrexford. "I sent Tyler to Woolwich this morning to do some sleuthing. We need to wait until he returns to decide our next move. Even if Osborn is there with Waltham, they will have left by now, as there is a ceremonial banquet tonight at the Guildhall for various dignitaries, including the Prince Regent and Tsar Alexander."

"Then perhaps I should fetch another pot of tea and a platter of ginger biscuits." McClellan suddenly looked around. "Speaking of which, where are the Weasels and Peregrine? They aren't upstairs."

"I . . ." Charlotte blinked. "They have no lessons today with Mr. Lynsley, so I assumed they were tinkering with their adding machine." But even as she said it, she knew that it was odd that they hadn't come down to listen in on the discussion.

"They may well have gone to Angelo's Fencing Academy for a lesson with Harry," said Wrexford. "Or to the Royal Institution. Hedley made it clear they are welcome to visit his workshop anytime."

"Yes, of course." The momentary tightness in her chest relaxed. "And I'm glad that they are beginning to feel at home in their new environs." After all, it wasn't as if they could get into trouble within the elegant environs of Mayfair.

"Well, you may tell them that I would have taken them to Gunter's for sweets if they had been here." Alison rose and patted back a yawn. "I think I shall toddle off to my carriage and return home. A nap may be in order before supper."

"Indeed, solving heinous crimes single-handedly is rather tiring," said Wrexford, managing a flash of humor to lighten the weight of the challenges that still lay before them.

Feeling a twinge of guilt, Charlotte rose as well. "I shall see you out."

By the time she returned, McClellan had refreshments arranged on the table.

"What a day," murmured Charlotte, gratefully accepting a fresh cup of tea. Closing her eyes for an instant, she savored the spicy scent before darting a reluctant glance at the escritoire by the window. "I will fetch paper and pencil in a moment so we can begin to draw up a plan—"

A sudden rush of steps in the corridor caused her to fall silent.

Riche appeared in the doorway, his normally stoic face betraying a spasm of alarm. "Mr. Griffin is here, and says it's most urgent."

"Hell's bells." Wrexford shot to his feet and waved for the Runner to enter.

"M'lord, m'lady," gasped an out-of-breath Griffin. "Mr. Belmont's body has just been discovered in an alley near here. He's been shot dead."

The cup slipped from Charlotte's fingers, slopping tea over her gown.

Wrexford spun around. His wife's face was so white that he feared she might faint. Panic flared in her eyes as her gaze met his. He knew she was thinking of the boys, but didn't dare say so in front of Griffin.

McClellan quickly took charge, crouching down beside Charlotte and blotting the spill with one of the pillows.

"F-Forgive me," stammered the Runner. "I should have tempered my—"

"No need to apologize, Mr. Griffin," said Charlotte. "It was an unexpected shock—he is family by marriage—but I am fully recovered."

"Do go on, Griffin," urged Wrexford. "What can you tell us about the crime?"

"Very little, I'm afraid," replied the Runner. "A grocer's boy taking a shortcut back from a delivery stumbled upon the body. Belmont was shot in the head from close range. The body wasn't searched, so it doesn't appear to be a random robbery."

His brow creased in a frown. "There is a welter of footprints around the scene, but it is impossible to tell whether they have any relevance. The maze of passageways is used for a number of activities." A cough. "Not all of them on the right side of the law."

The earl nodded and thought for a moment. "Please keep me

informed of any further developments. In the meantime, I will ponder on what this might mean to the particular matter we are investigating."

"Very good, milord." Griffin dabbed a sleeve to his forehead, betraying how unsettled he was. "Send word to Bow Street if you need me."

Wrexford waited for the door to close and the sounds of the Runner's steps to recede before moving to gather Charlotte into his arms. "The Weasels will be fine," he assured her, despite the fear lingering deep in his own heart. "They are exceedingly clever." *Ye gods—as abandoned children, they had managed to stay alive in the brutal London slums.* "And they are exceedingly skilled in survival."

"Y-Yes, but . . ." Her voice wavered. "But they are not immortal." A sudden sob shuddered through her. She hugged him, her fingers clenching his coat as if seeking to hold on to some vestige of self-control. And then she began to weep.

He held her close, stroking her hair as Charlotte's unspoken fears spilled out. His heart ached for her, and how impossibly hard she was on herself.

"I—I should have demanded that we walk away from this cursed investigation," she mumbled. "Instead, I let hubris make me think I could challenge a tangle of vipers and escape without any consequences."

Wrexford gave her a gentle shake. "What is true hubris is to think that *you* are to blame for the evil that is coiled around the highest circles of the government. On the contrary, you are a force of good, of justice. Your conscience—"

"My conscience?" She raised her tearstained face. "Oh, Wrex, how can I ever live with my conscience if anything has happened to the boys?"

"We don't know that they are in danger," he reasoned. "And if they are . . ." He pressed a kiss to her brow. "Then God help Lucifer, because I will descend to the deepest pit in hell and rip his heart out if he dares to harm so much as a hair on their heads."

"I don't think Lucifer has a heart," murmured McClellan.

"Then I shall slice off his ugly head and put it on a pikestaff," he replied.

The maid nodded. "Aye, that will do very nicely, milord."

As Wrexford had hoped, the exchange brought a touch of color back to Charlotte's face. "Now that we've put the devil out of his misery," she said, "let us turn our attention to tracking down the miscreants."

"Waltham and Osborn should both be at the Guildhall," observed the earl. But before he could go on, the echo of voices in the corridor caught his ear.

The others heard it at the same time. Charlotte rushed to the door and flung it open.

"Hawk!" she cried, falling to her knees and seizing the boy in a crushing hug. "Thank God . . . Oh, thank God you're safe." Leaning back, she took his smudged face between her palms just as Cordelia followed the boy into the parlor.

Tears pearled her lashes. Wrexford couldn't tell whether she was laughing or crying.

"But where are your brother and Peregrine?"

A bank of sullen grey clouds had blown in from the east, bringing with it a fitful wind that was raising whitecaps on the river and rattling the rigging of the ships tied up at the Royal Dockyard.

Hugging close to the deepening shadows, Raven and Peregrine crept through the orderly rows of storage buildings, angling their steps toward the perimeter wall of the Royal Arsenal complex.

Raven paused by the corner of a warehouse to peer out at the surroundings. Spotting a group of soldiers trundling a cart of cannonballs toward the armory, he hissed a warning to Peregrine and flattened himself against the brick until they had passed.

"Which way?" he whispered.

"Cross the street and we'll find a footpath that leads around the perimeter of the laboratories," answered Peregrine. "There is a small archway in the wall by the tower that gives access to the Grand Stores complex. It's usually unguarded."

The clouds had thickened, hastening the muted shades of twilight. "If it's not, we'll figure out a diversion," said Raven. After another quick check around, he gave the signal and the two of them scampered across the cobbles.

"Follow me." Peregrine took the lead and darted into a narrow opening between the outer buildings and a line of loading platforms flanking the docks. A gust rocked the boats moored to the stanchions, the masts groaning as the swirling waters pushed them against the pilings.

With wraithlike stealth, they crept forward, but a sudden flurry of grunts and curses forced them to stop and take shelter within a cluster of barrels. Huffing and heaving, a half-dozen soldiers came out of the gloom carrying the hull of a small sailing ship—though only around fifteen feet in length, it looked to be a scale model of a British war frigate—and marched it down to a large river barge tied to the wharf, where they added it to three other identical hulls that were lashed to the deck.

"Be sure to secure the bloody things carefully—use plenty of rope and blankets," warned the officer in charge. "They're the guide ships to be used in orchestrating the mock naval battle that will take place on the Serpentine tomorrow evening. And there will be hell to pay if anything happens to them."

More thumps and scuffling.

"That's the last of them. And now our job is done and we're all entitled to an extra round of ale for the night duty," announced the officer, once he had inspected the cargo. "A detachment of sailors from the naval yard at Greenwich will arrive later to sail the barge up the river to the Palace Yard Stairs, once the tide has turned. From there, they'll be unloaded and carted to the Serpentine in Hyde Park."

Raven and Peregrine waited for the sound of boots to fade away. After a quick check that the docks were deserted, Raven signaled that it was safe to continue.

The path followed the bend of the river, bringing them to the archway giving entrance to the Royal Armory complex. It was unguarded, and a moment later, the boys were standing beside a tall bronze statue of a muscled blacksmith holding a giant hammer, poised to strike a resounding blow against the anvil by his side.

"See his features?" murmured Peregrine. "It made Uncle Jeremiah smile to see that the artist used a Black man as his model for the god of fire." His mouth quivered in sorrow for an instant, and then he crouched down by the massive stone base and felt around for the brass plaque with the artist's name.

"One, two, three . . ." he counted softly from left to right. "Here." He tapped one of the stones set in mortar. "We need to slide this one out."

Raven unlocked the sword cane and pulled out the blade— they had changed into their urchin clothes and had abandoned the sack before entering the Royal Armory complex.

"There's only a small amount of mortar disguising the fact that the stone is loose," said Peregrine. "But we need to work quietly. There are guards constantly making the rounds of the area."

"I'll start. You keep watch."

Steel scraped against the hardened limestone-and-clay mixture. They took turns with the sword, slowly chipping away the mortar. A guard passed close by, his steps echoing over the river sounds, but he didn't enter the quadrangle.

The stone was soon free, and Raven used the blade to help them wiggle it out from the base. Inhaling a steadying breath,

Peregrine slid his hand into the opening and withdrew a rectangular package wrapped tightly in oilskin and tied with manila cording. A long loop in the rope allowed him to slip it over his head and wear it securely against his side.

"Should we—" he began, but Raven suddenly shushed him to silence.

The scuff of leather over the cobbles was light but unmistakable. And the steps were coming closer.

Keeping the sword cane's blade bared, Raven rose and signaled Peregrine to join him. They inched around the statue's base, positioning themselves for a sprint to the archway, if need be.

A probing lantern beam cut into the quadrangle from the adjoining square. *Probing, probing, probing . . .*

The light disappeared for a moment—and then suddenly it was back.

Peregrine hitched in a breath as the beam flickered over the crumbs of mortar. It moved on, only to dart back and hover, giving the pale bits of limestone a luminous glow.

"Guards, guards! I've found the intruders!"

Raven grabbed Peregrine's arm. "To the docks—we'll lose them there," he said, and then bolted for the opening.

"Hurry!" bellowed the man with the lantern, the blade of light bouncing wildly as he set off in pursuit. "After them—they mustn't escape!"

The boys hopped a low wall and jumped down to the cobbled wagonway running along the waterfront. A myriad of storage areas and sheds spread out in either direction from the main dockyard square. Raven hesitated for an instant and turned left, heading back the way they had come.

"We need to keep moving," he rasped to Peregrine as he ducked into a mazelike jumble of crates. With the alarm raised, the number of soldiers searching for them would soon threaten any chance of escape. They needed to find a clever hiding place.

And quickly.

More shouts. Boots clattered over the paving stones.

Raven cut sideways and raced down one of the narrow aisles between the stacks of raw lumber waiting to be turned into gun carriages. From there, he abruptly reversed directions.

"What are you doing?" wheezed Peregrine as they paused for an instant to catch their breath. "You're heading straight back into the teeth of the pursuit."

Raven looked around. The crisscrossing lantern beams were drawing a noose of light around them. "I have an idea. But we have to hurry."

Hunching low, he took off at a run—still headed back in the direction from which they had come.

Fog was drifting in from the water, silvery swirls undulating like serpents as they coiled around the pilings. The two of them reached a section of the wharves where a number of piers stuck out into the eddying river. Raven cut closer to the water's edge, weaving in and out of the carts and barrows. Barely a stone's throw away, a group of soldiers thundered past them, muskets in hand.

From behind them, a shot rang out.

"Hold your fire!" ordered the man leading the pursuit. "They must be taken alive!"

Raven skidded to a sudden stop. Their pursuers couldn't see them yet, but in another heartbeat . . .

"In there." He grabbed Peregrine and spun him around to face the river barge loaded with the model frigates. "Hide in one of the hulls—the soldiers have just loaded them and won't think to search there."

The clatter was growing louder.

"Just keep silent and stay hidden. Don't trust anyone. The frigate—and you—will be brought to the Serpentine for the reenactment. We'll find you there."

Peregrine hesitated. "W-What about you?"

"*Go!* We can't let your uncle's plans fall into the villain's hands. I'm going to draw them away." Raven thrust the sword cane into Peregrine's hands and gave him a push. "Don't worry, they haven't a chance of catching me."

As a beam of light cut over the stack of cargo just behind them, Peregrine darted across the wharf and dove into the shadows.

Raven whirled, and in the same instant, the man with the lantern rounded a cluster of crates and broke into a run. But Raven was already just a quicksilver blur flying through the vaporous night.

CHAPTER 27

"My love, he can't answer when you're smothering him with kisses," murmured Wrexford.

He crouched down beside them, and threaded his fingers through Hawk's tangled curls. The boy looked so small and impossibly fragile.

It took a moment to swallow the lump in his throat before he could find his voice and turn his gaze to Hawk's companion. "Perhaps Cordelia can explain what's going on."

"Belmont has been murdered," began their friend. She had brought Hawk back to Berkeley Square from the docklands in her carriage.

"We know that—Griffin has just been here," piped up McClellan. "But he had no idea as to the why."

"Belmont found a letter from Mr. Willis, which revealed that Falcon knew where the plans and prototype weapon were hidden," said Hawk. "So he snatched Falcon and was going to turn him over to someone in the government—he didn't say who—to save his own skin."

"How do you know that?" demanded Wrexford.

"Because Raven and I followed them into the alleyways near Audley Chapel," answered Hawk. "We overheard them arguing—and then a shot rang out and Belmont's skull was blown to flinders!"

Charlotte let out a horrified gasp.

"The killer tried to grab Falcon, but we shouted for him to run." His tongue nearly tripping over itself, Hawk hurriedly explained about the chase and how Raven's quick-thinking stab had allowed them to escape.

"I'm sorry we took the sword cane without permission, sir—"

"We'll discuss that later," cut in Wrexford. "Where are Raven and Peregrine?"

"They knew that none of you were home, so they went to retrieve the plans and prototype at the Royal Armory complex," said Cordelia—fatigue looked to be taking hold of the boy—"while Hawk came to alert Kit and me. We decided it was best for Kit to head straight to Woolwich, and for me and Hawk to come here and inform you."

Wrexford was already at the side cabinet by his desk, checking the flints on his dueling pistols. "Please fetch my riding cloak from the storeroom," he called to McClellan.

"Shall I have the carriage readied?" she asked.

"No, it will be quicker to go by horseback."

Charlotte rose. "I'm coming—"

"No." He said it softly but firmly. "I will quite likely need to wield my lordly influence with the officers in charge at the armory." He donned the cloak and shoved the pistols into its deep pockets. "Even if you dress as an urchin, a companion would harm my chances of avoiding trouble."

Anguish was writ plain on her face. "Wrex . . ."

"You know I'm right." He tucked a small pocket pistol into the waistband of his breeches, then pulled her into a fierce hug. "I will move heaven and earth to keep them safe."

* * *

Raven squeezed through the tiny gap between the storage buildings, then dropped belly-down to the ground and crawled across the quadrangle, using the line of stacked crates as cover. Just as he reached the shadows of the far wall, a pair of soldiers ran by, muskets and cartridge boxes rattling as a harried shout from the Shot Yard called for reinforcements.

He waited, flattening himself to the ground and holding very still until the sounds receded. The main search had moved to the Gun Yard, but a series of barked orders from the carriage-building complex seemed to indicate a sweep of the storage areas was being organized. After a quick glance around, Raven rose and shimmied up a drainpipe to reach the sloped roof of a Georgian brick pavilion. The slates were slippery, but he crested the ridge and slid down to the other side of the building, where a portico jutted out into the quadrangle, its flat roof affording a perfect vantage point to keep watch on the statue of Hephaestus.

Turning up his coat collar, he settled in to wait . . .

After riding to the docklands, Wrexford had hired a ferryman to bring him and his horse to the south bank of the river. From there, a hard gallop skirting along the marshes had now brought him to the Royal Arsenal complex. Rising out of the swirls of fog, the octagonal tower by Gun Wharf stood silhouetted against the night sky, a silent sentinel standing guard over the country's weapons of war.

Reining his horse off the path by the water's edge, the earl spurred toward the west gatehouse. The clatter of the stallion's iron-shod hooves on the cobbles brought a hail from the guards on duty.

"Halt!" Two soldiers appeared, their muskets gripped in readiness. One of them raised a lantern. "Who goes there?"

He slowed to a halt in front of them, his spine ramrod-straight as he looked down his nose at them. "The Earl of Wrexford, here on urgent government business," he announced in his most imperious voice. "I need to speak with your commanding officer now."

The lantern light flickered slowly over his impeccably tailored clothing and magnificent horse.

"Y-Yes, milord," replied the soldier nervously, lowering the beam. "But there may be a delay. Things have been at sixes and sevens here tonight."

Not a good sign. Wrexford's hand fisted on the saddle's pommel. He wondered where the boys were, and whether Sheffield had arrived yet.

"How so?" he demanded after the soldier with the lantern sent his comrade off in search of their superior.

"Intruders, milord."

"Have they been apprehended?"

"I . . ." The soldier shifted from foot to foot. "I don't think so, sir."

From the nearby wharf came the sound of voices, followed by the splash of oars dipping through the water. Wrexford turned to see a longboat rowed by a half-dozen sailors towing a cargo barge out into the middle of the river.

His stallion snorted and shifted.

"I need to cool down my horse. I've ridden him hard." He dismounted, taking the reins in one hand. "If I recall correctly, there's a quadrangle with a statue of Hephaestus—"

"Effy-what, sir?"

"A blacksmith," he said.

"Oh, aye." The soldier bobbed a nod.

"Direct me to it."

"It's just around the outer wall and through the first archway, sir. Make a right, and then a left into the next quadrangle." A hesitation. "Would you like me to lead you there?"

"And leave your guard post when trouble is afoot?" snapped the earl. "I think not."

The soldier cringed as Wrexford turned abruptly and walked away without further comment. A flurry of shouts echoed from somewhere inside the arsenal's walls. Shoving his free hand into his cloak pocket, he gripped his pistol and quickened his steps.

After passing through the archway, he headed to the right. The clatter of footfalls ahead alerted him to the search party just an instant before they broke free from the gloom.

"Halt and identify yourself!" ordered the leader. Unlike the four soldiers behind him, he wasn't in uniform.

The earl took another step forward, bringing himself into the lantern light.

"Wrexford." Osborn's voice betrayed a note of surprise. "W-What are you doing here at this hour?"

"I might ask you the same," he replied.

"I was here with the delegation overseeing the tsar's visit earlier today, and stayed behind to discuss certain security matters," answered Osborn. He waved at his men to continue on. "Go rendezvous with Talley's party. I shall join you shortly."

Wrexford remained silent. Osborn seemed on edge. And an edgy man tended to make mistakes.

"Did Grentham send you?" demanded Osborn as soon as they were alone.

"Actually, it was Duxbury who suggested I could find you here."

Is that a flicker of fear? wondered the earl.

If so, it quickly gave way to bravado. "Well, don't look to be claiming credit for my triumph when I recover Willis's plans and prototype," said Osborn. "The gutter rats who know where they're hidden are now trapped inside the arsenal walls." He gestured at the buildings. "I'm arranging a sweep of the area that will drive them like quail toward our waiting muskets."

"Clever." Wrexford whipped out his pistol and took aim at the other man's chest. "But not quite clever enough."

"Good God, have you gone *mad*?" blustered Osborn.

"Tell me, how did you injure your hand?" The earl indicated the bandage wrapped around Osborn's right palm.

"I . . . I dropped a brandy bottle and cut it badly on the broken glass."

"Let's try again, shall we? I think that if we remove the wrapping, we'll find that the wound was made by the blade of a sword cane." He paused. "One that belongs to me, in fact."

Osborn stared at him in mute shock, which quickly sharpened to speculative edge. "So that's it. Belmont mentioned his brat had come to be friends with your two wards."

"Never mind the boys. The game is up," said the earl. "I know of your Russian family connection, and your murder of Belmont. And while I haven't yet finished piecing together exactly how you and Waltham came to be partners, I have no doubt that I will do so—"

"Wrex!"

The earl looked away for an instant at the sound of Sheffield's shout.

Osborn seized his chance and hurled his lantern.

It struck Wrexford's weapon a glancing blow, then shattered on the stones, sending up a whoosh of flames from the spilled oil. With a spooked whinny, Wrexford's stallion reared, its hooves slashing at the smoky air. Sheffield broke into a run, but in the few seconds it took for him and Wrexford to calm the horse, Osborn had disappeared into the night.

The commotion drew another rush of military men, this group led by a colonel with auburn side-whiskers who approached with pistol drawn. An ominous *snick* sounded as he cocked the hammer—and then came to an abrupt halt.

"Is that you, Wrexford?"

The earl recognized the man as a fellow member of White's.

"What the devil is going on?" asked the colonel.

"You've a traitor running loose here, Milton," Wrexford replied. "Marshal your men and send them after Osborn."

"But . . ." The colonel shook his head in confusion. "But Osborn is from Horse Guards."

"Yes, a bloody fox in the henhouse," replied the earl.

A shocked frown. "W-Why should I believe you?"

"Because Grentham sent me," said Wrexford. "You may choose to doubt it, but if Osborn gets away, mark my words, you'll answer to the minister."

Grentham's name had the desired effect. Uncertainty flickered, and then died in the blink of an eye. Pivoting on his heel, the colonel barked out a series of orders that sent his troops running to spread the alert.

"I need to return to my headquarters to coordinate the hunt," added Milton. The sword hanging at his side jangled in the mist-swirled breeze. "I trust you're not making a fool of me."

"I'm not."

A gruff nod, and then the colonel was gone.

"Wrex," whispered Sheffield, "you need to come with me."

His heart hammering against his ribs, Wrexford followed in silence, hardly daring to hope . . .

A shiver in the shadows caught his eye as they turned into yet another small quadrangle.

"Weasel!" The word wrenched free from his throat as Raven slipped down from the statue of Hephaestus and came running. Flinging the reins to Sheffield, he crouched down and seized the boy in a bear hug.

"Thank God," he whispered, once he had assured himself that there was no blood or broken bones.

"We have it, Wrex! We have the missing invention," Raven said in a rush. "But—"

"But where is Peregrine?" demanded the earl.

"Somewhere on the river, sir." Raven hesitated. "That is, I'm fairly certain that he's heading upstream."

"What the devil . . ." Wrexford glanced at Sheffield, who lifted his shoulders in equal puzzlement. "Hawk and Cordelia arrived at Berkeley Square," he went on, "so I know about Belmont's death, and your escape from the killer—"

"And then we rushed here." Raven sucked in a breath and quickly explained all that had happened.

"We can head to the naval docks at Greenwich and organize a ship and detachment of marines to go fetch the boy from the barge," suggested Sheffield.

A reasonable idea, and yet Wrexford felt himself waver. Two officials within the highest ranks of army headquarters were involved in treason and murder. How far had the rot spread?

"Wrex," said Raven softly, "there's one other thing. It was all happening so quickly and we didn't have time to think . . . The pursuit was closing in, and we had to react in a flash. I pushed Peregrine to the barge and told him to hide in one of the frigates—all that mattered at the moment was keeping him out of enemy hands. But . . ." His voice faltered.

"But what, lad?"

"I think Belmont's killer was the man leading the chase. I–I recognized his voice. And while I'm not sure, he was close enough that he might . . . Well, he might have seen Peregrine sneak onto the barge."

"You were right to tell me." He ruffled Raven's hair. "You lads were exceedingly brave and resourceful. I couldn't be prouder of you."

Still, it begged the question of what to do now? With Osborn on the loose, the situation was fraught with consequences. Frowning, Wrexford considered his choices. First and foremost, he decided that no one save for their small circle could be trusted . . .

"Kit, take my horse and ride back to Berkeley Square with Raven," he said. "I'm going to stay here and see that Milton gets messages out alerting the right people as to what's happening."

"What should I tell Charlotte?" asked Sheffield.

"Tell her that I'm going after Osborn." A pause. "And that

I'm pleading with her not to try any heroics of her own until she hears from me."

"Let us hope she's not tempted to shoot the messenger," said Sheffield wryly as he swung Raven up into the saddle. "What about Peregrine and the barge?"

He thought for a moment. "I don't think we should attempt to get the boy off the barge just now. I'd like for you and Tyler to take one of your company's wherries and shadow its progress up the river. Don't interfere unless Osborn shows up. In the meantime, I'll . . . I'll improvise."

Dawn was still just a hazy half-light as Charlotte crept into the schoolroom and ventured a peek into the adjoining bed-chamber.

The sight of Raven and Hawk sleeping in blissful oblivion, their bony limbs tangled helter-pelter in the blankets, drew a silent prayer of thanks—and then a rush of guilt for savoring an instant of joy when Peregrine was still missing. Drawing her wrapper more tightly around her shoulders, Charlotte tiptoed back to the corridor and headed for the kitchen to fix a pot of coffee.

"You should be sleeping," came a chiding voice from behind the coal-dark silhouette of the stove.

"So should you," she replied, nearly weeping in gratitude as the ambrosial scent of fresh-ground beans brewing on the hob filled her nostrils. "But thank heaven you're not."

"Sit." McClellan appeared from the pantry carrying a pitcher of cream. "Sheffield and Tyler should be on the river by now, shadowing Peregrine's progress."

Charlotte nodded absently, still searching her mind for some way to be useful. She hated feeling so helpless.

"Drink that." McClellan thumped a mug and the cream down on the worktable. "And may it drown that alarming spark in your eye before it turns to flame."

She ducked her head. "You must be imagining things."

A snort.

"Be that as it may, I'm not going to do anything reckless." Charlotte took a drink of coffee, willing it to warm the chill from her bones. "I just wish there were a way I could help, rather than simply sit here and fret."

"Wrexford will have the pursuit of both Osborn and Waltham well in hand," pointed out the maid. "Sheffield and Tyler are keeping watch on the barge. And as for the Royal Navy, we have no reason to believe that their hearts aren't carved out of straight and true oak. So I don't see that there's anything else to do."

Charlotte swirled her coffee.

McClellan was right. If all went well, the stowaway and his model frigate would end their voyage on the placid Long Water of the Serpentine and the danger would be over.

If all went well . . . But what if it doesn't? What if they had to improvise?

She set down her mug. "I have an idea."

"Thank you for coming, Captain Hockett," said Charlotte as she and McClellan moved out of the shade of the plane trees by the Serpentine Bridge. It was well past noon and the afternoon sun had the dark water dancing with diamond-bright sparkles.

"I'm always happy to be of service to a lady." He eyed the small package in her hands. "You mentioned in your note that you have something for me to take to Captain Daggett in America?"

"Yes, it's just a trifling gift." On her way to the park, Charlotte had made a hasty stop on Bond Street and purchased a pair of York tan gloves. The leather was of excellent quality, but Daggett would no doubt be puzzled as to why she had sent them. "However, I should be grateful if you would deliver it to him."

"Consider it done." Hockett tucked the package in his pocket. "Our delegation sails for home tomorrow."

He shaded his eyes to watch the procession of horse-drawn carts, each filled to the gills with identical crates, which were arriving on the opposite side of the lake. "It seems the preparations for the mock naval battle are already beginning."

He pointed to the last carts in the line, which were loaded with barrels of gunpowder. "As I told you, they will be packing the cockpits of half the small ships with explosives, so that the climax of the battle will have the enemy fleet blown to kingdom come while fireworks light up the sky."

Charlotte forced a smile. "I'm sure it will be a memorable evening."

"Would you care to take a stroll over the bridge and have a closer look at the proceedings?"

"Actually . . ." She gestured to the pair of guide boats that were still tied to the landing beside the bridge. "I'm more interested in these frigates. You mentioned that they are maneuvered with oars, but I don't see any oarlocks."

Hockett fixed her with a sphinxlike stare. "What prompts you to ask?"

"I'm simply curious," replied Charlotte.

His expression turned even more unreadable, but then gave way to an enigmatic smile. "That's because it's a special design . . ."

He led her down the shallow steps and then stepped into the cockpit with practiced ease. "Each frigate is equipped with a set of custom oars, which are shorter and have wider spoons than normal ones." Hockett indicated the brass sockets set in the ship's railing. "There are oarlocks in the storage box, and the oars are lashed to the inside of the hull."

Charlotte had craned her neck to follow his explanations. "I see. That sounds rather straightforward."

Hockett stepped back up to the landing, setting off a soft *swish* of the Serpentine's water as the hull rocked gently to and fro. "Most things aren't as complicated as they seem, once you understand how they work."

"Perhaps that's why men rarely explain things to women," she replied. "They're afraid we'll realize that we're just as smart as they are."

He laughed. "I daresay you might be right." A pause. "Though no one would ever question your sharpness, Lady Wrexford."

"I shall take that as a compliment." Charlotte smiled. "Even if it wasn't meant to be."

"Be assured that it was."

As they returned to the footpath and began walking to where McClellan was waiting, she turned her gaze to the flurry of naval activity on the opposite shore. "Just one last question. Will the sailors running the naval reenactment be using these two model frigates to maneuver the two fleets of small battleships?"

"No. My liaison officer mentioned that these are merely the practice boats. They've constructed four frigates equipped with special weighted keels for stability, as the crewmen will have the devilishly tricky job of handling long poles to push all the small ships into position for the grand finale. They're being brought upriver by barge from the Royal Armory."

"I see," she murmured.

A glint of amusement sparked beneath his lashes. "Your warships gave our American fleet a thrashing during our recent conflict." A pause. "So I must admit that I wouldn't be unhappy if anything happened to make a few waves in the Royal Navy's plans for this evening."

CHAPTER 28

"Bloody hell." Wrexford smacked a fist to his palm in frustration. "How the devil did you and your men miss apprehending him?"

Duxbury looked equally unhappy. "I assure you, milord, I headed to Waltham's residence as soon as I received your note. I positioned my men around the building to prevent his escape, and then sent in a search party. However, he must have gotten wind of trouble and left earlier."

"Any idea of where we might look now?" muttered the earl.

"Alas, no. I've ordered checkpoints to be set up on all the main roads leading out of London . . ." The colonel gave a weary shrug. "But I can't say I have much hope in that. He's too clever."

The earl knew it was unfair to vent his spleen on Duxbury. "Well, keep thinking of where you might search, Colonel. In the meantime . . ."

Wrexford glanced at the clock. *How is it that the minutes seem to be taking hours to tick by?* "I need to make some further inquiries into Osborn's whereabouts. Send word to my townhouse if you have any news."

He hurried out of Horse Guards and started to cross the parade ground at the back of the building. It was still too early to head to the Serpentine. By Sheffield's calculation, the barge wouldn't arrive at the Palace Yard Stairs, the closest landing place on the river to Hyde Park, for another two hours.

His steps slowed to a halt and he closed his eyes for an instant, aware that his lids felt heavy as lead. Hunger and fatigue squeezed at his innards . . . He knew the warning signs well enough to sense that his judgment was beginning to fray around the edges.

And that was dangerous. Too many people were depending on him.

Nourishment and a catnap would work wonders, decided Wrexford.

As would Charlotte.

He had always dismissed Love as a mere word. A vague abstraction. It had been both frightening and exhilarating when he realized that she had woven herself into the very fiber of his being. Now he couldn't imagine his life without her smile, her counsel, her steady heartbeat as she put her arms around him and drew him close . . .

Without a second thought, he turned for Berkeley Square.

"Wrex!" Charlotte shot out of the drawing room as he came down the corridor and caught him in a hug.

"Sorry, I've no good news to report on the villains—" he began.

"Hush," she ordered, sliding her hands up the slope of his shoulders and then framing his face. Their eyes met. And then their lips.

Fatigue and fear gave way to . . . something he couldn't begin to describe in words. He stood unmoving, taking strength from her embrace, and then finally forced himself to pull back. "I need to—"

"Hush," she repeated. "We'll talk about all that once you're seated and have put some food and drink down your gullet."

He allowed himself to be led to one of the armchairs by the hearth and let out a deep sigh as she forced him down into blissfully soft cushions. An instant later, a glass of brandy was in his hands.

"Drink," she ordered.

Its potent heat helped to revive his flagging spirits. "Thank you," he murmured after a second swallow.

"Mac will be here in a moment with some roast beef and bread." She took his hand and gave it a squeeze before pulling over a hassock and lifting his legs up to rest on it.

"The Weasels—"

"Are safe upstairs," answered Charlotte.

He heard the underlying tension in her voice and knew it was for Peregrine.

"We'll bring Falcon home safely," said Wrexford, though they both knew such a promise was no less fragile than a flicker of sunlight. "Osborn and Waltham are still on the loose," he continued. "Duxbury is coordinating a search, and I've sent word to Pierson through Griffin about the situation."

His jaw clenched for an instant. "Perhaps Grentham's department can finally do something right."

Charlotte touched her palm to his cheek. "Did you tell them about Peregrine and the barge?"

Wrexford heard the same flicker of doubt in her voice that gripped his own heart. "No," he answered. "I don't trust them not to use the boy as some sort of sacrificial pawn if it suits their objectives. Indeed, I don't trust *anyone* but us with Peregrine's life."

"Thank heavens," she whispered. "What about Osborn? Or Waltham?"

"With their scheme blown to flinders, I imagine their foremost concern is saving their own necks."

Charlotte started to say something, but the clatter of cutlery announced McClellan's arrival with a tray from the kitchen.

"Bless you, Mac." He accepted a plate from Charlotte. It

wasn't until he had gobbled down the slice of beef that he noticed the maid had taken a seat on the sofa . . . and had taken up a needle and thread to work on a filthy bundle of cloth.

"Why is Mac sewing another hidden pocket into one of your urchin's jackets?"

"I know you must have a plan for rescuing Peregrine," she replied. "But plans have a way of going amiss. So it's always wise to have an alternative."

"But—"

"Before you object," she cut in, "finish your meal while I explain what I have in mind . . ."

Wrexford listened in grim silence. She was right—he needed to eat.

"I don't like it," he said as soon as she finished. "Too many things can go wrong."

"As if that can't be said about our previous investigations," she challenged. "And yet, it never stopped either of us."

He conceded the point with a harried sigh.

"As the Earl of Wrexford, you have great clout, and can convince officials to do as you ask. But if I go to the celebration tonight as the Countess of Wrexford, I'm helpless—I'm corseted into too many confounded rules! In my urchin guise, I have freedom to improvise." A pause. "And you yourself just said, we can't trust anyone but ourselves and our small band of friends. Raven and I won't do anything rash. We'll simply be there in case we're needed."

Much as he disliked it, Wrexford knew she was right.

"Very well," he said grudgingly. "Though I can't imagine that you will need to launch any heroics."

"Better to be safe than sorry," she murmured.

Charlotte glanced up through the overhanging leaves, willing the summer twilight to deepen into dusk. Shadows would cover a multitude of sins. If the beau monde, resplendent in their fancy finery, had any notion that the tattered urchin lurking near their exclusive enclosure for watching the upcoming spectacle was, in fact . . .

She forced the thought from her head.

"Stay still," she hissed at Raven. They were crouched within a cluster of trees just behind the Serpentine Bridge. Hawk had been sent to the Palace Yard Stairs to await Sheffield and Tyler, who would be arriving at the same time as the barge. Sheffield was to join Wrexford at the Serpentine, while Tyler and Hawk would continue to follow the wagons transporting the frigates to the naval staging area.

"I think we should move down into one of the frigates now," replied Raven. "That way, we'll be ready to react quickly if need be."

Charlotte ventured a look around. He had a point. She knew from past experience that when trouble struck, every second could be precious. And this part of the Serpentine was deserted. The great crush of spectators was milling around the center stretch of the Long Water, which afforded the best view of the upcoming battle and pyrotechnics.

"I could set up the oarlocks," added Raven.

Another glance up at the sky, where a thin line of clouds had blown in to haze the fading pinks and golds of sunset. The wagon bringing the models and the hidden stowaway should be arriving on the opposite bank at any moment.

"I'll go first," she whispered. "Wait for my signal to follow."

The frigate rocked beneath her weight, sending ripples over the dark water as she slipped aboard and took cover within the cockpit. All was exactly as Hockett had left it . . .

Save for a dark shape pushed up against the bow locker.

Scooting closer, she saw two neatly-folded Royal Navy tunics and matching caps.

Repressing a smile, Charlotte waved a quick signal for Raven.

He appeared in a flash, his quicksilver movements stirring not a whisper of water.

"Put this on over your jacket." After handing him a tunic, she donned hers and then passed him a cap.

"Is impersonating a midshipman a crime?"

"It's probably a lesser offense than stealing one of His Majesty's naval vessels," she replied. "So let us not get caught."

Raven sniggered. "As if a bunch of flat-footed sailors could ever catch up with us."

"Don't spit in Neptune's eye," she chided.

He wiped the smile from his face and peered over the gunwale at the flickering of lantern lights in the staging area. "Now what?"

"Now we wait."

Wrexford entered Hyde Park through the Stanhope Gate and cut over to the footpath leading to the Serpentine. All around him, shadows danced through the breeze-ruffled trees, and the first faint dappling of moonlight scudded over the grasses, reminding him of a previous evening just a short while ago . . .

And the chance walk in the dark that had set all of this in motion.

In the distance, he could hear the buzz of the crowd, thrumming in anticipation of a gala entertainment. Little could they know that beneath the show of peace and harmony, a ruthless game of wolf-eat-wolf was playing out amid the sumptuous banquets and elaborate pageantry.

One in which his loved ones might find themselves eaten alive.

"Over my dead body," muttered Wrexford. It wasn't just pragmatism. To his surprise, Charlotte's passion for justice had rubbed off on him. Though she claimed that beneath his snaps and snarls, his heart had always been in the right place. He wasn't sure that he agreed . . .

The footpath curled down to the carriageway, which led

straight to the naval staging area on the north side of the Serpentine. Supply wagons surrounded the swath of lawn on three sides, to keep out unauthorized visitors. Its fourth side was open to the water, where a large crew of sailors was busy lining up the fleets of small battleships along the edge of the water.

"Wrex."

He turned to see Sheffield loitering among the trees, smoking a cheroot as if he were merely a carter taking a break from his duties.

"The barge was unloaded without incident, and the two wagons just arrived ten minutes ago. All four model frigates are here, though I've had no chance to ascertain which one is Peregrine's hiding place."

"My thanks, Kit. Well done," said the earl. "From here, I should have no problem extracting the lad."

"Shall I come with you?"

Wrexford shook his head. "No, let us stick to the plan that Hawk explained to you and Tyler." The boy had told them about Charlotte and Raven waiting in one of the frigates moored at the Serpentine Bridge, just in case of an emergency.

Sheffield made a wry face. "So I may need to use my nautical skills for a second time today."

"Heaven forfend," uttered Wrexford. "Where's Hawk?"

"I told him to head back to the other side of the water and inform Charlotte that the frigates have arrived."

"You should cross the bridge now, too. I intend to get Peregrine out of danger quickly and quietly."

Wrexford waited for Sheffield to disappear into the trees before approaching the entrance to the restricted area. As he stepped onto the grass, the two sentries—they were soldiers, not sailors, he noted—snapped to attention and stepped together to block the opening.

The taller of the two took command. "I'm sorry, sir, but this part of the Serpentine is off-limits."

"I'm the Earl of Wrexford, and I'm here on important government business," said Wrexford in his most officious voice. "Step aside."

The soldier in charge hesitated. "W-We have strict orders. No one is permitted to go in or out."

A carriage rattled by on the road, sending up a spray of gravel as it rounded the bend and then slowed to a halt among the ordnance carts still being unloaded.

"Summon the officer in charge," ordered the earl. A flutter of movement in the darkness beneath the nearest wagon of the perimeter wall caught his eye. It was gone in an instant, and he hoped that he was mistaken in thinking it might have been Hawk.

"The major is on his way here, but has not yet arrived."

The answer stirred a frisson of—

"But I'm here now." Waltham's voice no longer sounded like that of a mild-mannered subordinate. His tone now carried a steely edge of command. "Arrest this man," he snapped to the quartet of soldiers following behind him.

Damnation—I misjudged the depth of Waltham's obsession. Wrexford hadn't thought the man mad enough to make yet another try to get his hands on Willis's invention.

"On what bloody charge?" he demanded.

The moonlight silvered the curl of Waltham's mouth. "Treason."

Wrexford glanced around, gauging his chances of making a run for it. But the sentries already had their muskets aimed at his chest. "How dare you arrest a peer of the realm!" he shouted at the top of his lungs. With luck, Sheffield was still within earshot. "I demand that you summon your superiors!"

Waltham had drawn his pistol, and for an instant the wild look in his eye had the earl about to fling himself forward. However, the major regained control of his emotions, and seemed to realize that bloodshed would ruin his plans. "Lock him away in the guardhouse." Another smug smile as the major gestured to a stone building behind the naval staging area. "We wouldn't want to ruin the government's gala Peace Celebrations."

As the sentries grabbed hold of the earl, Waltham turned and ran toward the water's edge.

"What the devil is going on?" Charlotte frowned, watching the sudden flurry of moving lights on the lawn across the water. Harried shouts rose from within the military enclave. Wrexford should be there by now . . .

"Looks like trouble," said Raven as he began untying the lines mooring the frigate to the landing stanchions.

Already the other side of the Serpentine was glittering with the tiny lights lit aboard the hundred small warships floating in the water. Half of them had faint plumes of smoke rising from the lit fuses in the gunpowder bombs.

"Holy hell." Raven squinted in alarm as he saw one of the four large guide-boat frigates waiting to be launched suddenly start to slide toward the water.

A *boom* sounded from the other end of the Long Water. Charlotte knew it was the signal for the battle reenactment to begin.

"Launch the fleet!" The order echoed through the air as the small warships were shoved off, their sails catching in the night breeze, and fanned out over the water. A roar of delight rose from the crowd.

The clatter of footsteps racing over the stone bridge caused Charlotte to whip around and draw her pocket pistol.

"Waltham is here," cried a breathless Sheffield as he stumbled down the landing stairs. "He's arrested Wrex."

"What about Peregrine?" demanded Charlotte, after swallowing the acid-hot spurt of terror that rose in her throat. She would not—she could not—give in to fear.

"I saw two imps—I assume they were Hawk and Peregrine—pushing one of the guide-boat frigates into the water," answered Sheffield. He climbed into their frigate and took a seat on the center bench. "I'll handle the rowing." Raven helped him slot the oars into the brass oarlocks.

"Hurry," said Charlotte. "The other frigates have just been launched."

As if punctuating her warning, the roar of cannon fire exploded, lighting up the darkness with showers of golden sparks.

Charlotte flinched, and then remembered that mortars had been set along both banks of the Long Water and were firing blank shells to add drama to the battle reenactment.

The crowd cheered in delight as another round of explosions filled the night.

Spotting a small figure silhouetted in the bow of the guide-boat frigate to her left, she tightened her grip on the tiller and changed course.

"Row, Kit! Row!" she cried, seeing that one of the other guide-boat frigates was chasing Peregrine's ship.

"Hawk must be handling the oars," called Raven, who had crawled out to the bowsprit of their vessel. "Peregrine looks to be clearing a way through the small warships by pushing them aside with the sword cane."

Charlotte realized she had no idea as to how long the mock battle was supposed to last. Wrenching her gaze from the fire-lit flotilla, she sought to find Peregrine and Hawk's pursuer.

Oars churning through the water, the pursuing guide-boat frigate was nearly abreast of the boys.

"On guard, lads!" she cried, praying they could hear her over the din of the cannons and the raucous crowd. And then, her heart leaped into her throat.

Silhouetted by the sparks and smoke, a military man—it must be Waltham, she realized—rose from the rowing seat of the pursuing frigate and jumped onto Peregrine's ship. To her horror, he grabbed a handhold in the rigging and pulled a pistol—

Hawk raised an oar and knocked it from his grasp.

His face sheened in sweat, Sheffield summoned the strength to row harder.

Waltham turned and lashed out a vicious kick, which caught Hawk off balance and sent him tumbling into the water. He then drew the sword hanging from his dress uniform and scrambled up to the bow of the ship.

"Give me the bag, boy, or I'll carve you into fish bait!" he bellowed at Peregrine.

Charlotte heard the threat just before another volley of mortar fire boomed in her ears. Sheffield was narrowing the distance between the two frigates but the gap still looked agonizingly large.

Peregrine danced back, and despite the shorter length of his blade, he skillfully parried Waltham's lunge. Their swords crossed in a series of quicksilver flashes of steel, and the sheer force of Waltham's attack forced his much smaller opponent to retreat. With his back foot on the base of the bowsprit, Peregrine was trapped.

The mortars boomed again.

All of a sudden, Peregrine unslung the bag from his shoulder and held it out over the water.

"*No!*" screamed Waltham, and made a snatch at it.

Peregrine coolly cut a slash across the major's arm, and as Waltham flinched and hopped back, the boy slipped free to the other side of the deck.

A number of the little warships were hitting up against the guide-boat frigate's hull and spinning in its choppy wake. Cursing and swinging his sword in a menacing arc, Waltham regained his footing and came after the boy.

Charlotte felt for her pistol, thinking she would have to dare a shot. Despite his prowess, Peregrine couldn't fend off the muscular major for much longer—

"Jump, Falcon! Jump!" shouted Raven as he heaved a rope

to Hawk, who was bobbing in the water not far away. "We'll pull you in!"

Peregrine hesitated—and then lobbed the bag into one of the small smoke-shrouded warships that contained the explosives. "You want my uncle's invention? Go get it!"

Charlotte saw one of the other bomb-filled warships at the far edge of the fleet explode in a ball of fire.

The fuses were all set for the same time—the boy had only seconds to get out of danger.

"Jump!" she cried, just as Peregrine ducked under Waltham's blade and dove into the water.

Two more warships exploded in flames. The crowd erupted in wild cheers as the sky overhead came alive in a blaze of fireworks.

Tossing aside his sword, the major grabbed up an oar and began paddling frantically toward the smoking warship that held Willis's invention.

Sheffield helped Raven haul the two soaking boys into the cockpit. "Swing the tiller around!" he yelled to Charlotte as he returned to his seat and began a frenzied pull for safety.

A moment passed, and then another. Charlotte lost all sense of time in the cacophony of thundering guns, roaring crowd, and crackling fire. She saw Sheffield's jaw drop and turned just in time to see the small warship hit up against the stern of Waltham's frigate and explode, blasting a hellfire hail of burning splinters and flaming sail canvas high up into the night.

"Merciful heavens," she uttered, throwing up an arm to shield her eyes from the glare. Smoke billowed up from the sinking frigate, and as it swirled in a ghostly vortex, a dark shape suddenly cut through the vapor.

"Halloo!"

At the sight of Wrexford standing by the mast of one of the other guide-boat frigates, Charlotte nearly swooned in relief. *ThankGodthankGodthankGod.*

But emotions must be shoved aside until later. As the vessel came abreast of theirs, she ducked to hide her face from the crew. The earl hopped aboard and ordered the sailor who was manning the oars to return to the opposite shore.

Sheffield blew out his breath and slumped over the oars. "Ye gods, it's about time you showed up."

"My apologies. I was detained for a bit."

"How—" began Charlotte, after grabbing his hand and brushing a quick kiss to his knuckles.

"Never mind that now. I'll explain once we're back at Berkeley Square." After eyeing the exhausted Sheffield, the earl ordered him off the bench and took up the oars. His swift, sure strokes quickly had them back at the stone landing.

"Is everyone unhurt?" he asked as they all clambered back onto dry land.

"Oiy!" said Hawk. "Guess what—I learned how to swim!"

Raven made a rude noise. "You were paddling like a puppy." Charlotte saw that despite the teasing, he was holding his brother close. "But you stayed afloat."

"Weasels, please give Kit a hand in climbing up to the footpath," she said, after stripping off her naval clothing and ordering Raven to do the same. A bit of blood was seeping through Sheffield's shirt around his recent bullet wound.

Peregrine hung back. "I—I'm sorry if I did wrong," he stammered, fixing her and Wrexford with a worried look. "But I threw my uncle's invention into one of the bomb-filled warships to make sure that the villain didn't get his hands on it." He hesitated. "In truth, I think Uncle Jeremiah was having second thoughts about his work and . . ."

"What's gone is gone." Wrexford gave a wry smile. "And perhaps that's not a bad thing."

He ruffled the boy's still-wet curls. "You've shown great courage in every way. Your uncle Jeremiah would be very proud of you."

"Actually, his work isn't entirely gone, sir." Peregrine pulled a slim oilskin packet from inside his shirt. "I saved the plans. I . . . I trust you to take them and decide what should be done."

"It is a responsibility that I won't take lightly, lad." Wrexford gingerly took the wrapped papers. "Like your uncle, I will need to think very carefully about whether any country—even ours—ought to possess such a monstrous weapon."

The boy bobbed a shy nod and hurried off to join the others.

Releasing a pent-up breath, Charlotte slowly turned and touched a palm to Wrexford's cheek. Gunpowder grit was streaked over his skin, a bruise was purpling on his chin, and his lower lip was cut . . .

"Ouch," he murmured as she kissed him, and then pulled her close.

"I love you," she murmured, clutching his coat and never wanting to let go. "I don't say that nearly enough."

"Such endearments don't always come easily to us," he whispered. "Perhaps because they echo so strongly within our hearts."

"Still, let us try to do better at it." She chuffed a small laugh against his shoulder. "Especially if we can't stop embroiling ourselves in murder and mayhem."

He smiled. "It ensures that life is never boring."

"True." Charlotte fingered a tear in his coat. "But it wreaks havoc on our clothing."

"Speaking of which . . ." Wrexford touched his lips to her brow. "Shall we take our raggle-taggle family home?"

CHAPTER 29

The following day seemed to pass in a whirlwind blur. Wrexford had spent much of the morning closeted with Pierson and Griffin, assessing the plot and its rippling effect on the government, as well as deciding on how to present the death of two high-ranking officials to the public.

As for her own responsibilities . . .

Charlotte brushed an errant lock of hair from her cheek, leaving a faint smudge of scarlet paint. She had been wrestling with how to depict last night's spectacular extravaganza. Her finished drawing of the mock naval battle and fireworks was certainly dramatic . . . and she had woven in just enough subtle hints in both the visuals and the caption to make the public wonder what dark mischief had been afoot beneath the glittery lights.

"To hell with it if I ruffle Grentham's feathers," she whispered. "That's what I'm here for."

After rolling up the artwork and setting it aside, Charlotte went down to the earl's workroom and curled up in one of the armchairs while he finished the letter he was writing.

"At last, some peace and quiet . . ." she began, only to sigh at the sudden clatter of steps in the corridor.

"I've taken the liberty of telling Riche to send up a selection of your most expensive brandies and Scottish malts," announced Sheffield as he opened the door for Cordelia and the dowager and gestured for them to enter. "I think we all *richly* deserve it—ha, ha, ha!"

Wrexford winced at the pun. "I haven't yet decided whether you've made up for your recent idiotic behavior with Lady Cordelia. So you may be confined to swilling cheap claret."

Harper pricked up his ears and gave a sympathetic *whuffle* before resuming his slumber by the hearth.

"Surely blood and sweat—not to speak of a bullet—buys redemption," retorted Sheffield. "As well as a decent drink."

"You may bring me a brandy, Tyler," said Alison as one of the footmen marched in with half-a-dozen elegant bottles cradled in his arms and handed them over for the valet to arrange on the sideboard.

"I thought Alison and Cordelia should be here to, er, celebrate with us," explained Sheffield.

He had an oddly evasive look in his eye, but Charlotte decided not to question him. "Do sit down, everyone, and Tyler will serve the libations," said Charlotte. "We do indeed have much to celebrate."

She and the earl had paid a long visit to Belmont's widow and his oldest son, who was now head of the family. The conversation had been a difficult one. Charlotte and Wrexford had decided that the family deserved to know the truth of how Belmont had, however unwittingly at first, allowed himself to be sucked into a sordid scheme.

His widow and heir had been stunned. But they had been extremely grateful that the government had agreed to announce that Belmont had died a hero's death while defending his portfolio of important papers from a foreign operative. And so they had readily agreed to Charlotte's suggestion for a new arrangement regarding Peregrine's upbringing. Indeed, she sensed they were greatly relieved to have reduced responsibilities.

The boy would officially remain the ward of the new head of the Belmont family, and would continue to attend Eton and pay occasional visits to the estate being held in trust for him. But his real home would be at Berkeley Square . . .

Among an exceedingly eccentric household, Charlotte thought with a wry smile. *But one in which he will have love, laughter, and companionship.*

A chortling from the three boys drew her back from her musing. They were sprawled in front of the banked fire, sneaking bits of ham from the platter of refreshments to feed to Harper.

"That's quite enough," growled Wrexford. "The hound is getting fat as a Strasbourg goose."

"He wouldn't get fat if he got more exercise," piped up Hawk. "Peregrine is taller than Raven—surely he's big enough to take Harper for a walk in the park, especially if Raven and I accompany them."

"I shall think about it." Wrexford tried to look stern, but the corners of his mouth betrayed a telltale twitch. "In the meantime, it's time for the three of you to take the beast and run along to the schoolroom. Your elders have some private matters to discuss."

"Can we take the ham with us?" asked Hawk.

McClellan placed a fist on her hip. "I suppose the next thing you'll want is ginger biscuits."

Raven and Peregrine both fixed her with a hungry look.

"Ye heavens, one would think you were fed naught but bread and water around here," she grumbled as she piled two plates with the remaining meat and sweets. "Now off you go. But if I catch you back down here eavesdropping, your diet will consist of cod-liver oil for the next fortnight."

Raven emitted a gagging sound and raced for the door, the other two following right on his heels. Harper rose and gave a sybaritic stretch before padding after them.

"Damnation, did I just see the Weasels carry off the last of the ham?" groused Henning as he entered the room.

"There's more in the kitchen," assured McClellan. "Heaven forfend that we let you starve."

"At least I know I'm never in danger of dying of thirst in this house." The surgeon poured himself a tumbler full of whisky and took a noisy gulp. "Speaking of dying, I hear there's another dead body to add to the count after last night."

"If you live by the sword . . ." murmured Wrexford.

"I heard the dastard was blown to smithereens." Another gulp of whisky. "Serves him bloody right."

Charlotte gripped her glass, trying not to picture the wild eruption of fire and smoke. "Thank heavens the violence has ended and the threat is over."

"Speaking of threats . . ." Tyler refilled Henning's glass before asking, "What about Pierson?"

"There was absolutely no mention of Charlotte or A. J. Quill as we knotted up all the loose ends," said Wrexford.

"Does that frighten you?" asked McClellan.

The earl pursed his lips in thought. "Actually, no. The fact that he and Grentham made a mistake about Osborn is rather comforting. They're ruthlessly good at what they do, but they're not perfect."

"I agree," said Charlotte. "I intend to go about my work without constantly looking over my shoulder. If a challenge comes in the future, I shall meet it."

"*We* will meet it," corrected Wrexford. "Here's to knocking their teeth down their gullet if they try to bully you," he added, cocking a salute with his glass. But before he could go on, there was a discreet *tap-tap* on the closed door.

"Forgive me for interrupting, milord, but there is a gentleman asking to see you." Riche's voice was muffled by the thickness of the varnished oak. "He's rather insistent."

Charlotte looked at the earl, who raised a questioning brow.

Expelling a sigh, she pinched at the bridge of her nose. "I suppose you had better say yes. Otherwise, whoever it is, he'll likely just come back tomorrow."

To her great surprise, it was Kurlansky who strolled into the room.

"My apologies," he said, looking around and then bringing his gaze to rest on Charlotte. "I appear to be interrupting a private party."

"You are welcome to join us," she said coolly. "Though I confess, I'm not sure what you think you might gain from it."

"Touché, milady." The Russian curled a sardonic smile. "Allow me to add that politics is not personal. There are grander strategies at play."

She remained silent. Whatever his game, she would let him make the first move.

"However," Kurlansky continued, "in this case, I find myself inclined to make an exception." He paused again, allowing for a reaction. When none came, a flash of amusement lit in his eyes and he continued to speak. "I have great respect—and admiration—for both your intellect and your sangfroid, Lady Wrexford. So I feel you deserve an explanation of the events that have just played out."

"We have pieced together most of the puzzle," murmured the earl. "Though I hardly need to tell you that, as you'll be departing England empty-handed."

Kurlansky gave an appreciative chuckle. "Indeed, I'll be leaving tomorrow. And by the by, Osborn has already left these shores, so you need not waste your efforts trying to find him."

His gaze came back to Charlotte. "How did you figure out his connection to me, milady?"

It was Charlotte's turn to flash a smile. "You gentlemen tend to assess ladies by your own measures of strength and weakness. But you discount feminine knowledge at your own peril. You see, Lady Peake has been part of Polite Society for—"

"For too many years to count," interjected Alison. She regarded Kurlansky with an imperious stare. "By now, I know every branch and twig of the beau monde's family trees."

"And unlike you, Wrexford understands the value of a lady's insights." Charlotte was careful to phrase her next revelation so as not to give too much away. "The earl sought our advice when trying to narrow down the list of possible suspects in the matter of Mr. Willis's death and the disappearance of his secret project for the government."

"And when I heard that Osborn was on the list," said Alison, "I remembered that his mother was half-Russian."

"Ah." Kurlansky quirked a rueful grimace. "I have learned a valuable lesson about underestimating the fairer sex."

"Ignore it at your own peril," drawled Sheffield.

Henning added a rough-cut laugh.

Charlotte held her tongue. She had no need to impress Kurlansky with her cleverness. In fact, she would rather he didn't speculate about how intimately she was involved in the earl's investigations. Instead, she flicked a sidelong glance at Wrexford, who nodded a private signal that he would take over the cat-and-mouse conversation with the Russian.

"Now that we've answered your question," said the earl, "I assume you're going to tell us what motivated Osborn to form his sordid scheme."

"Two of the elemental evils of human nature—the lust for money and power," shot back Kurlansky. "Though born into a life of privilege, Osborn thought he deserved more than a younger son is given. So he decided to find a way to grab more. He's smart and ambitious, so he had no trouble getting a position in the Foreign Office, where he was able to learn little secrets about powerful men that assured his own advancement."

"A clever young man, rising fast through the ranks," mused Wrexford. "No wonder he caught the eye of Grentham's department when they got wind of a possible plot to steal Willis's invention."

Kurlansky nodded. "As you say, Osborn's clever. When he heard that Grentham's minion . . . I believe his name is Pierson . . ."

He shrugged when no one answered. "Believe me, we all know a great deal about each other's clandestine operations."

"Go on," urged the earl.

"When Osborn heard through his own sources that Pierson needed to plant an operative at Horse Guards, he had his superior suggest him for the job."

"And once there, he managed to figure out what Waltham was up to," guessed Charlotte. "And demanded to be part of it."

"Waltham had a devious mind, and he also had a grudge against the government, though I'm not sure what it was," answered the Russian.

Wrexford didn't offer an explanation.

"But then, Osborn was growing reckless in his own personal habits. He enjoyed the hedonistic life of an aristocrat, and began to play for serious stakes in some of the more notorious gaming hells of the city."

"And came to owe money to some very dangerous people," offered Sheffield. "Which I imagine made Waltham's scheme appear to be a godsend."

"Indeed," agreed Kurlansky. "However, when Waltham decided to run an auction among the leading powers of Europe—including Russia—Osborn suddenly saw an opportunity to double-cross his partner in crime."

"He came to you and offered you the invention for a set price," guessed Wrexford. "The amount was a king's ransom, I wager, but far less than you would have paid in bidding against Austria and Prussia."

"Correct," confirmed the Russian. "It was an excellent plan."

A pause. "However, the trouble for both Waltham and Osborn was that in order to get the money, they had to show the prospective buyer the actual invention—and prove that it worked." A pause. "They attempted to get the invention from Willis, but as you know, an unfortunate accident disrupted their plans—"

"So Osborn began pressing Belmont," interjected the earl, "thinking Belmont knew where it was because of his family connection to Willis."

"Correct again. And Belmont claimed that his ward, the young Lord Lampson, was the one with that knowledge."

"But the boy slipped through Osborn's grasp."

Kurlansky raised his brows in question. "I'm curious—did he know the hiding place?"

The earl laughed. "You don't really expect me to answer that, do you?"

A shrug. "It was worth a try."

"There are just a few loose threads dangling," replied Wrexford. "Or rather, bodies. Why was the lackey who collected the bank receipts for the auction at Royal Ascot murdered?"

"Osborn wanted to get his hands on the receipts in order not to underprice himself. The murdered fellow—William Vickrey—was Professor Milson-Wilgrom's valet and was supposed to turn them over to Belmont, who, in turn, would give them to the professor."

Ah, thought Wrexford. *So Osborn had stolen the bank receipts. Which meant that the mysterious man on horseback leaving the stable had been Professor Milson-Wilgrom,*

"I imagine Osborn was going to share the information with you," interjected Charlotte. "And the two of you would come up with a price—adding, of course, a hefty payment to you for advising Prince Rubalov to recommend the shady deal to Tsar Alexander."

"Of course." Kurlansky didn't bat an eye. "Treachery and bribery is part of our country's history. However, you're wrong on one thing. I didn't need Rubalov's approval. He takes his orders from me."

"And Milson-Wilgrom's murder?" asked the earl.

"That was Waltham. After the murder at Royal Ascot—he didn't know that Osborn-was the killer—he became convinced that Milson-Wilgrom was planning some nefarious deception of his own, so he decided to eliminate him."

"My guess is Waltham was going to do that anyway as the professor knew too much," speculated Wrexford.

"I agree," responded the Russian. "Just as he was probably planning on getting rid of Osborn." A smile. "I know Osborn wasn't going to leave Waltham alive once the deal was done."

"One key point that I have been wondering is how Waltham knew that young Lord Lampson was hiding in the model frigate?" asked Wrexford.

"Osborn needed money for his flight, so he stopped by Waltham's residence and offered to sell him the information."

Kurlansky smoothed a wrinkle from his cuff. "I assume it was Waltham who perished last night in the tragic mishap during the naval reenactment on the Serpentine."

"I've heard no official confirmation of what happened," said Wrexford. "Perhaps we'll never know exactly what took place."

"What a pity. I can't help but wonder whether Waltham took Willis's secret with him to the grave."

The earl lifted his shoulders. "Speaking of secrets, you aren't concerned that I will immediately pass all your revelations on to Grentham. And that he might retaliate for your part in the plot?"

A chuckle rumbled in Kurlansky's throat. "As I said, politics isn't personal. It's expected that we all look for opportunities to gain an advantage over one another. He would have done the same in my position. As for holding grudges . . ."

He moved to the sideboard and poured himself a small measure of Scottish malt. "I'm heading to the Peace Conference in Vienna, where our countries will be negotiating the future of Europe. Grentham may need me as an ally as we all jockey behind the scenes to ensure the best results for our own self-interests. And so, the game starts anew."

Candlelight winked off his glass as he raised it in salute. "To a group of very worthy adversaries—though I also hope that we think of each other in more kindly terms."

After a tiny hesitation, Wrexford lifted his glass as well. Charlotte and the others quickly did the same.

"Perhaps," murmured Kurlansky, "we'll match wits again."

"Be careful what you wish for," said the earl softly.

"We Russians have aphorisms, too," replied Kurlansky. "One that immediately comes to mind is 'The still waters are often inhabited by devils.'" He drank his whisky in one quick swallow and put down the glass. "And now, let me not delay your celebration any longer." A courtly bow. *"Dasvidaniya."*

"What in the name of Lucifer did he mean by that?" grumbled Sheffield, once the Russian was gone.

"I believe it was a friendly reminder that however cordial and conciliatory he appeared just now, he could be a very dangerous man under other circumstances," said Charlotte.

"Ha! He would be a fool to challenge us," replied Sheffield. "He may be a master of intrigue and deception, but we have a far more powerful force on our side." He shifted on the sofa, his thigh brushing up against Cordelia. "Friendship." A tiny hesitation. "And love."

Alison raised her quizzing glass and fixed him with an owlish stare.

The scrutiny caused a touch of pink to bloom on Sheffield's cheeks, but still, he continued. "Light will always overpower darkness."

Charlotte felt a sudden prickle of tears as she looked around the room. *Friendship and love.* Her gaze lingered on Sheffield, and her breath caught in her lungs as she recalled that terrible instant of the gunshot . . .

She blinked, emotion welling up in her throat. It felt impossible to summon words to express . . .

"Ye gods, Kit's wound must have brought on a fever," drawled the earl.

Leave it to Wrexford and his sarcasm to keep things from turning too maudlin.

"Just because *you* haven't got a smidgeon of poetry in your soul," retorted Sheffield.

Wrexford made a rude sound. "Oh? You're a poet now?"

"No, I think he's merely a man who has finally come to his senses and admitted he's in love," said the dowager.

Charlotte couldn't hold back a smile as the room went awfully quiet . . .

"Halloo?" came a tentative hail from the corridor.

"Good heavens, Wrexford," exclaimed Alison. "Your townhouse has more traffic than Piccadilly Street this evening."

The door pushed open, admitting Cordelia's brother, Lord Woodbridge.

"Jamie!" Cordelia's eyes widened in surprise. "W-What are you doing here?"

"Kit asked me to stop by." Woodbridge made a puzzled face. "Why is Riche standing outside the door with a serving trolley filled with champagne?"

Sheffield rose rather abruptly. "Never mind that now. I'll explain shortly." He cleared his throat and offered a hand to Cordelia. "It suddenly does feel awfully warm in here. Would you, umm, mind accompanying me to the garden for a short walk."

Cordelia stared up at him, her face going through a series of odd little contortions.

"I'm feeling a little unsteady," murmured Sheffield. "And wouldn't want to fall flat on my arse."

"Well, since you put it so delicately . . ." Cordelia put her palm on his, and Charlotte felt her heart swell as their fingers twined together.

"We'll be back shortly," said Sheffield. As he passed Charlotte, he added softly, "Please call the Weasels and Peregrine down from the schoolroom. But *don't* let them bring the hound—he'll drink all the champagne."

Everyone remained tactfully silent until the footsteps receded.

"Hmmph." The candle flame lighting a gleam in her eyes, the dowager took a moment to polish the lens of her quizzing glass. She smiled. "It appears we will have another wedding to plan."

"Lord, what fools these mortals be," said Henning with a grin, which earned him a scowl and a swat from Alison's cane.

"Just a little jest," he added, rubbing at his shin.

"Happiness is rare enough in this world," said Charlotte. "Let us not make light of it." She looked at Wrexford. "We must cherish it and keep it close to our hearts."

His mouth slowly curled up at the corners as he held her gaze. "To love." He lifted his glass, the whisky glowing like liquid gold in the lamplight.

A ripple of murmurs, followed by the soft rustle of fabric as everyone joined in the toast.

"Aside from the hustle and bustle of planning a wedding, let us also appeal to the heavens for peace and quiet for the remainder of the summer," suggested the dowager. "I don't think my old bones can take any more excitement for the moment."

"Peace and quiet? With *this* group?" Henning couldn't hold back a skeptical snort. "Ha! And pigs may fly."

AUTHOR'S NOTE

There are times when an author gets extraordinarily lucky and history provides a setting for a mystery more perfect than any writer would dare to imagine! The actual Peace Celebrations held in London during June 1814, which play a leading role in this book's plot, did indeed bring the major sovereigns of Europe, along with a host of leading political figures and military brass, to the city for a nonstop whirl of sumptuous parties and entertainments, state dinners and gala fireworks. The events I describe in the story—the naval battle on the Serpentine, the visit to Oxford with the candlelit streets and the banquet at the Radcliffe Library, the horse races at Royal Ascot, and the reception at Carlton House—all took place. I have made every effort to describe the settings accurately.

I have also taken pains to use some smaller historical details to add color to the story. The Prince Regent and the Tsar of Russia really did have a personal feud going . . . the tsar and his sister really did stay in the Queen's Room in Merton College at Oxford and attend a gala banquet at the Radcliffe Library (for those who might wonder whether I have gotten the famous building's name wrong, it wasn't named the Radcliffe Camera until the 1860s) . . . Sir William Congreve, inventor of the Congreve rocket, really did design the fireworks displays for the gala spectacles staged in Hyde Park for the dignitaries and public. I've posted a number of colored engravings showing the naval battle on the Serpentine, along with some of the other grand entertainments built for the Peace Celebrations, on my website. Just go to the DIVERSIONS tab and scroll down to *The London Peace Celebrations.*

Jeremiah Willis, the brilliant inventor whose prototype for a multishot pistol lies at the heart of the mystery, is fictional. But he is based on Elisha Collier, a Boston inventor who did create a design for a flintlock revolver in 1814. Collier came to England in 1818, and his invention was patented that year. (It's said that his design inspired a young Samuel Colt.) Furthermore, the British Army actually had an experimental rifle brigade. Armed with multishot Ferguson rifles, the Experimental Rifle Corps fought against America in our Revolutionary War. Durs Egg, the real-life gunmaker who makes a cameo appearance in the story, was one of the men who created the prototypes based on the design of Major Patrick Ferguson, which was patented in 1776. As recounted in the book, the rifles did work, but weren't reliable under battle conditions because the technology wasn't yet available to construct them properly.

One of the things I love about history is that it is not etched in stone. Our view of the past is constantly evolving. More and more stories are coming to light of extraordinary people whose important achievements in so many fields of endeavor have been marginalized or left out of the traditional narratives because of prejudice—race, gender, ethnicity, sexual orientation . . . Their deeds enrich our understanding of history and give us a truer picture of the past—and offer inspiration for the future.

Though my inventor, Jeremiah Willis, is, as mentioned, purely fictional, I created him in homage to the many amazing individuals whose accomplishments have been hidden in the shadows. He was inspired by men like Joseph Bologne, Chevalier de St. Georges, a man of mixed race who composed classical music that was much admired by Mozart, was a champion fencer (his portrait did hang in the famous Regency fencing academy run by his friend Harry Angelo) and a respected military commander who led a regiment while fighting for the French Republic during the 1790s. (I've taken the artistic liberty of making the chevalier a relative of Jeremiah Willis.)

The actual plot of my book—the theft of an innovative multishot pistol by dastardly villains (none of the villains are real people) and a cunning plan to auction it off while the leading sovereigns of Europe are gathered in London—is purely fictional. Though given all the jockeying for power that was going on after Napoleon had been exiled to Elba, and the innovation being worked on by Collier, it seems a plausible scenario . . .

As for the auction, the format used by the villains in this story—where the highest bidder wins, but is required to pay only the price of the second-highest bid—is in actuality known as a Vickrey Auction. The purpose of this structure, exactly as Sheffield and Wrexford reasoned out, is to cause each participant to make a sealed bid that reflects their own maximum estimate of the property's true value, rather than trying to assess what the other participants may bid in an attempt to avoid the possibility of offering more than is necessary.

This form of auction is named after William Vickrey, the economist who first described the dynamics of this type of process and other related matters of economic theory. He used "game theory"—which is a mathematical method of modeling how rational decision makers reach various strategic decisions—to analyze how parties would logically respond to rules and incentives in such situations. Vickrey won the 1996 Nobel Prize in Economics for his work.

Now, it might seem that introducing a Vickrey Auction into

a story set in the Regency Era is a clear anachronism. But not so! As with virtually all breakthrough ideas, twentieth-century game theory has antecedents in much earlier times. In 1838, Antoine Augustin Cournot published a mathematical solution for what came to be called "Nash equilibrium," a key advancement in game theory (more than a century later described generally by John Forbes Nash and made famous by the book and movie *A Beautiful Mind*). Even earlier, Charles Waldegrave wrote an analysis in 1713 of a then-popular card game called le Her and outlined what is called in game theory "a minimax mixed strategy" (a description of which I will spare you). So relevant aspects of game theory were not unknown at the time my story is set.

Even more relevant to the timing of the plot here is the recollection by both Charlotte and Wrexford of a similar approach to structuring an auction so as to maximize the price bid for a property that was used in the 1790s by Johann Wolfgang von Goethe, perhaps the greatest figure in the history of German literature. This is entirely based in fact. However, to avoid having the Author's Note run on too long, I have posted a full history of Goethe's auction process on my website under the DIVERSIONS tab. Suffice it to say here that Goethe has been credited as having run the first known Vickrey Auction. So it's entirely possible that an ingenious criminal might have conceived of the auction process described in Pierson's note.

As for Professor Milson-Wilgrom, the brilliant but evil creator of this book's auction, I plead guilty to having a little fun with his name (if one can view the study of economics, which Thomas Carlyle did, after all, deem "the dismal science," as fun). The winners of the 2020 Nobel Prize in Economics were Paul Milgrom and Robert B. Wilson, who were honored for "improvements in auction theory and inventions of new auction formats." So I couldn't resist a little syllable switch to craft a hyphenated handle for my fictional villain. (And I also named his servant Vickrey!) Thus endeth, I promise, the discourse on economic theory!

I hope you've enjoyed these brief backstories to what inspired this latest Wrexford & Sloane mystery. As always, I'll end by recommending *The Birth of the Modern* by Paul Johnson, a magisterial overview of the world during the early nineteenth century for those wishing to learn more about the Regency Era.

—Andrea Penrose

Don't miss the next in Andrea Penrose's
enthralling Wrexford & Sloane mystery series

MURDER AT THE MERTON LIBRARY

A perplexing murder in a renowned library at Oxford
University and a suspicious fire in the London research laboratory of a famous inventor set Wrexford and Charlotte
on two separate investigations which put each of them in
harm's way in this Regency-era mystery . . .

Responding to an urgent plea from a troubled family friend, the
Earl of Wrexford journeys to Oxford only to find the reclusive
university librarian has been murdered and a rare manuscript
has gone missing. The only clue is that someone overheard an
argument in which Wrexford's name was mentioned.

At the same time, Charlotte—working under her pen name,
A. J. Quill—must determine whether a laboratory fire was
arson and if it's connected to the race between competing con-
sortiums to build a new type of ship—one that can cross the
ocean powered by steam rather than sails—with the potential to
revolutionize military power and world commerce. That the
race involves new innovations in finance and entrepreneurship
only adds to the high stakes—especially as their good friend Kit
Sheffield may be an investor in one of the competitors.

As they delve deeper into the baffling clues, Wrexford and
Charlotte begin to realize that things are not what they seem.
An evil conspiracy is lurking in the shadows and threatens all
they hold dear—unless they can tie the loose threads together
before it's too late . . .

Read on for a preview . . .

PROLOGUE

Dust motes danced in the air, flickering like tiny sparks of fire as a blade of sunlight cut through the grisaille glass of the medieval window. The head librarian flinched, his eyes involuntarily squeezing shut as the harmless little flashes ignited the crackle of gunfire inside his head.

Smoke, screams, the glint of steel, the stench of blood . . .

Bile rose in his throat. Panting for breath, he shook his head, trying to clear his mind of the visceral horrors.

And then, mercifully, the episode passed, and the hammering of his heart softened to a steadier pulse. He raised a hand and traced his fingers along a row of books on the age-dark oak shelves of the study alcove in which he stood, the smooth calfskin and corded spines a calming caress against his flesh.

"It's peaceful here," whispered the librarian as he inhaled the parchment and leather scent of the Merton College Library. *An oasis of tranquility within Oxford University, a world away from the brutalities of the battlefields.* The wars were over, he reminded himself. Napoleon had been exiled to the island of Elba, and the ravaging armies no longer fomented death and destruction.

And yet . . .

And yet the horrors refused to retreat from his head. The army surgeons had told him it was a temporary trauma brought on by his body's struggle to recover from his grievous war wounds. They had said that the shock would soon fade.

But it hadn't.

Things had improved since he had arrived here and taken up the position of head librarian. However, over the last fortnight, one memory—a quieter one, but no less disturbing—had been coming back with increasing frequency.

He feared that it had been sparked by his recent conversations with a visiting researcher from the Continent—an erudite scholar who served as personal librarian to King Frederick of Württemberg.

Damn the fellow for wanting to discuss the Peninsular War.

Though he had not meant any harm, of course. Indeed, the two of them had formed a pleasant friendship over the past month. But the scholar's talk of military strategy and the disastrous British retreat that led to the Battle of Corunna had stirred old demons.

And now, the whisper of hazy words and a flickering image were becoming sharper, and more insistent. . . .

The sound of approaching steps drew the librarian back to the present.

"Mr. Greeley?" His assistant, a tall, gangly fellow with unruly chestnut hair, spoke softly. An observant young man, he had noticed that the librarian did not like loud noises. "The next batch of scientific books have arrived for us to sort through and catalogue for Mr. Williams."

Under the aegis of its head librarian, George Williams, the Radcliffe Library at Oxford had been reorganized into the university's main repository for scientific books and manuscripts. But the herculean task of collecting the requisite material from all the self-governing colleges that made up Oxford University—Merton was one of the oldest and most prestigious of them—was not finished, and Greeley had offered to help with cataloguing the collections.

"I've looked through them," added Greeley's assistant, shifting the small crate cradled in his arms. "It's a small consignment of rare old manuscripts from the library of Balliol College. I would be happy to stay late and finish it."

"Thank you, Mr. Quincy, but you've done more than your fair share today." The library was due to close in an hour, but Greeley welcomed the excuse to stay late, hoping that the task would help calm his unsettled mind. "I enjoy looking at old manuscripts. Give them to me."

Greeley took the crate from Quincy and headed to his private office, a small space crammed into the far corner of the West Wing. His desk, as usual, was in a state of cheerful disarray. It drew a rare smile as he took a seat and placed the crate on his blotter. *Scholarly ideas*—they were far more comfortable companions than people.

Wads of balled-up paper had been wedged around the manuscripts to keep them from shifting and damaging the fragile covers. He pulled them out and tossed them into a scrap pail— only to pause on recalling what he had discovered the previous week among the crumpled paper of another consignment.

Greeley glanced at the pile of documents on his desk, then reluctantly pulled a colorful print out from among them and unfolded it.

It was a commentary from several months ago by the infamous A. J. Quill, London's most popular satirical artist. Greeley paid little attention to current events, preferring to keep himself cloistered within the ivory tower of academia, but he was aware of the man's work and appreciated his clever drawings and scathing humor.

Everyone knew that the moniker was only a pen name, and speculation as to A. J. Quill's real identity was a parlor game throughout the beau monde. *Senior government official, high-ranking military officer, a titan of the Bank of England or the East India Company*—given all the intimate information that A. J. Quill knew, the assumption was that he had to be someone within the highest echelons of power.

A man who knew how to ferret out every secret in London, no matter how well hidden.

Greeley studied the print for a moment longer, then made himself push it away, feeling a little foolish for letting it upset him. It meant nothing. The earlier recurrence of the disturbing memory had put him on edge, that was all.

Opening the ledger that came with the crate, Greeley drew in a calming breath and began the meticulous task of cataloguing the manuscripts.

He worked in peaceful contemplation as the familiar sounds of the library quieted after the closing hour. But then, without warning, the bedeviling memory once again exploded inside his head. And all of a sudden, a long-ago moment—two men huddled together, their whispers teasing through the night breeze—flickered free of the muddled haze. The words were no longer just an amorphous buzz. They sharpened to a startling clarity.

Oh, surely not.

And yet, as he shot a glance at the print he had put aside, a chill ran through him, as if cold steel had kissed up against his spine.

What if the scene that I am remembering is true?

He sat for a moment longer, the question bedeviling him, and then rose abruptly.

Several hours later, after studying the recent newspapers in the reading room and doing some research in the West Wing's archives, he had uncovered enough unsettling information to send him rushing back to his office to dash off a letter. A glance at his pocket watch showed that there was still time to hand it off to the late-night Royal Mail coach heading to London.

After returning to the library, he resumed his work. Shadows flitted over the books and papers on his desk. A breeze tickled against the ancient leaded window. Looking up, he released a sigh. "Perhaps I have let my imagination run wild." At the moment, evil seemed very far away.

Still, as Greeley put down his pen and shuffled through the hastily scribbled notes he had made concerning his suspicions, he was glad he had sent the letter. *Truth—I must know the truth.* And if anyone was capable of discerning truth from lies, it was the man to whom he had sent the letter.

He paused and once again picked up the print by A. J. Quill, the candlelight flickering over the colors as he re-read the captions. *Damnation.* He folded it up and shoved it back into the jumbled pile of papers on his desk, willing himself to put the matter aside for now.

But on suddenly recalling another book in the West Wing that might help confirm his hunches, he got to his feet. The challenge of fitting the pieces of a puzzle together—especially this one—had his blood thrumming. Taking up the glass-globed candle on his desk, he went to fetch it.

As he retraced his steps, a flutter of light caught his eye. It was coming from his office.

Moving quietly, Greeley crossed the corridor and slipped into the room. A man was riffling through the crate of rare manuscripts. A grunt of satisfaction sounded as he grabbed one of them—

"Stop!" commanded Greeley.

The intruder whirled around.

No—this cannot be. Greeley blinked. And then blinked again. "Y-You!"

"Yes, me." A smile. "How nice to see you, Neville. It's been what . . . six years?"

Greeley didn't reply. He had forgotten how the man's slate-dark eyes always seemed to hold a touch of malice.

"What are you doing here?" he demanded. "And why are you stealing—"

"Oh, my dear Neville, you completely misunderstand my intentions," interjected Slate Eyes. "I learned earlier today that this manuscript had been delivered to you, and I am merely borrowing it for a bit." He sighed. "I would have asked, of course, but I have heard that you are so easily distressed these days."

A smile, sheened with an oily gleam in the flickering candle-light, touched his lips as he held up the manuscript. "Be assured it will be used for the Higher Good—and I know how much you value such altruistic ideals."

Dropping his voice, Slate Eyes added, "But a caveat—for now it's best to be hush-hush about your loan of it to me. It needs to remain a secret for reasons too complex to explain. But as I said, it's all for the good." A pause. "And of course, I will pay you handsomely for your discretion."

"How dare you suggest such a thing!" retorted Greeley. "My silence—and my honor—isn't for sale."

"Honor? Oh, yes—one of your precious principles." Slate Eyes gave a mocking smile. "Only look where they have gotten you."

That sneer. It was then, in a flash of recognition, that Greeley knew for sure his suspicions were correct. And he suddenly realized how Slate Eyes was the key to how the pieces of a horribly perfidious puzzle from the past fit together.

"Go to the devil! Whatever you have planned, I am sure it is nothing good." He grabbed the manuscript from Slate Eyes and put it back on his desk. "Evil," he whispered. "You reek of evil."

"Good heavens, I—" Slate Eyes assumed a look of injured innocence. "I have no idea what you mean by that."

"No?" Greeley then said a name.

Slate-Eyes contrived to look even more baffled. "I'm afraid

you're not making sense." A pause, and then he made a sympathetic *tsk-tsk* sound. "But then, I've heard that you are troubled
by demons."

"I remember now . . . I smelled a rat back then," said Greeley slowly. "And the odor is growing even more foul as we
speak."

"What are you insinuating?" Slate Eyes shifted. "If I'm being
accused of some scurrilous deed, it seems only fair that I have a
chance to defend myself."

"How dare you speak of fairness?" Greeley clenched his
jaw, the other man's look of amusement sparking an unholy
rush of anger. "You wish to have it spelled out? Very well—
here's exactly what I think . . ."

It all came out in a rush. The past, and how it connected with
the present.

A moment of silence hovered between them once Greeley
finished his lengthy exposition. And then came a mournful
sigh.

"My dear Neville, I fear your terrible wartime experiences
have confused your wits." Slate Eyes closed his hand around
Greeley's arm with surprising force. "Come now, sit down and
calm yourself."

The unexpected move threw Greeley off balance. A shove
forced him to fall back into his chair. He looked up—the slate
eyes were now a reptilian black—and realized that he had made
a terrible mistake.

Steel flashed, but he was an instant too late in seeing the
deadly strike coming.

The knife cut through wool and linen, angling upward to
slice between two ribs and lodge its point deep in Greeley's
heart.

A whoosh of breath, a spurt of blood . . .

And then a sepulchral silence.

"A pity you made me do that. But I couldn't risk having you

repeat what you just said to anyone else." After calmly cleaning his blade, Slate Eyes picked up the manuscript and tucked it inside his coat.

Two quick breaths blew out the candle flame as well as his own lantern. Slate Eyes watched the plumes of smoke curl upward, ghostly pale against the ancient oak ceiling, before turning and slipping away into the darkness.

Visit our website at
KensingtonBooks.com
to sign up for our newsletters, read
more from your favorite authors, see
books by series, view reading group
guides, and more!

Become a Part of Our
Between the Chapters Book Club
Community and Join the Conversation

Betweenthechapters.net

Submit your book review for a chance to win exclusive
Between the Chapters swag you can't get anywhere else!
https://www.kensingtonbooks.com/pages/review/